SKEWED

SKEWED

ANNE McANENY

THOMAS & MERCER

Published by Thomas & Mercer, Seattle
www.apub.com

Amazon, the Amazon logo, and Thomas & Mercer are trademarks of Amazon.com, Inc., or its affiliates.

ISBN-13: 9781477827994
ISBN-10: 1477827994

Cover design by David Drummond

Library of Congress Control Number: 2014953212

Printed in the United States of America

For MJM

Political language . . . is designed to make lies
sound truthful and murder respectable,
and to give an appearance of solidity to pure wind.

—George Orwell

Skewed: inclined or twisted to one side; distorted in a way that is regarded as inaccurate, unfair, or misleading; crooked.

CHAPTER 1

Bridget Perkins, 30 Years, 0 Minutes Ago

Grady McLemore didn't get caught off guard, so what the hell just happened? His knees crashed to the floor, the pain evaporating in the face of his gritty resolve. His left hip went next, collapsing beneath him like a rusty joint. Still, he had time. Grady McLemore fell to no one, and he wasn't about to risk the future of the one person he cared most about in the world. His eyes found Bridget. He'd never admit to anyone the countless hours he spent imagining their future, where he would finally allow himself to trek the long road to the political pinnacle before an adoring, demanding public.

But now this. Had he tempted fate? Had it been gluttony to envision a picture-perfect life with Bridget while fulfilling his own needs?

Screw that. Fate may have played its strongest hand in the form of this intruder behind him, but it couldn't hold a candle to Grady's resolve. It should have known better.

Grady blinked, eyelids grating against corneas. There was someone in the room, wasn't there?

A shot of agony bolted through his arm as his elbow slammed down. The chemicals riding shotgun in his bloodstream showed no intention of slowing, not while his heart still pounded. They might shut him down, cell by cell, limb by limb, but he would not leave Bridget alone here. Risking unconsciousness with her survival in question was not an option. For God's sake, what if the creep hid her away somewhere? Would Grady receive insane threats and ultimatums in the mail?

Through hazy eyes, he gazed at Bridget, the perfect complement to all he lacked. The magnetic qualities that drew people to her rushed through his fading mind: her down-to-earth spirit, her compassion for the less fortunate, her unbridled allure, and a laugh that could tease a smile from the dead. If only he'd put an end to her impulsive bravado, that dodgy habit of hers that never failed to spark a glint in her eye. It might now be the very trait that extinguished her singular light.

Grady spotted the other man in a shadowy fog. Enough of this. Grady raised his gun, his arm cement, the gun a cannon. Freighted with a sense of foreboding, he fought to retain the laser-like focus that had taken him this far.

Was he moving as fast as he thought?

He aimed. Fired.

And never saw it coming. The kick from the assailant jolted his arm just as the bullet soared through the chamber.

Bridget leapt for cover, desperate to protect the twins inside her.

Mere milliseconds made the difference as the lead messenger of death followed its altered trajectory.

Bridget Perkins landed with an unexpectedly light thump, given her twenty-five extra pounds and the force of the bullet destroying her balance. Her eyes remained open despite the blood seeping from her head.

CHAPTER 2

Click. Click.

"Hey, Jane Doe," said Detective Chase Nicholls, the best-looking slob on the Kingsley police force. "Make sure you get that brain gunk on the wall. Lab guys love that stuff."

I aimed my DSLR camera at my favorite detective and twirled the focus ring, the tactile sensation of the slim ridges providing a jolt of satisfaction. I brought Nicholls's spiked-up, glistening hair into focus and caught him in three-quarter face to highlight cheekbones that looked like they worked out.

Nicholls claimed to be part Cherokee, a lineage I credited for his blazing dark eyes, the aforementioned bench-pressing zygoma, and the coffee-tinted skin that stayed pristine despite the mounds of grease he shoved down his gullet. A unique presence here in Central Virginia, Nicholls grew up in the suburbs of DC, was raised by parents from Brooklyn, and then moved here as a teen. He tended to strut rather than walk and emitted a New Yorker vibe so tough, it practically buzzed. Sugarcoating was as foreign a concept to the guy as manners.

Just as my shutter snapped, he shoved his pinky nail in his mouth. I'd have a tough time explaining in court why that shot was relevant if this case went to trial. Lawyers made us turn in every photo now—even the blurry ones.

"I'll give you two quarters, Nicholls, if you let me get one good shot of you for the hongray, hongray ladies out there." He'd recently joined three Internet dating sites.

"Never gets old, eh, Janie? With the quarters-nickels thing?"

"It'll get old when you retire Jane Doe and come up with *anything* original."

"How 'bout Haiku Twin?"

I sneered. "Even less original." The public had deemed my brother and me the Haiku Twins at birth for reasons I tried to repress on a daily basis.

Nicholls's perfect teeth finally loosened whatever lurked beneath his nail. He spit it with a light thunk into an empty corner.

"Real sterile," I said. "Could you show some respect for Dizzy?"

Nicholls stepped over the exploded head of Dizzy the Drug Lord and checked out some receipts near the body. I went to my kit and switched the filters on my camera to get clearer shots of the torso and neck. Poor Dizzy. Despite his status as a high-achieving leader in Kingsley's competitive underworld, no onlookers had assembled outside to mourn his sudden passing. Crowds usually offered an opportunity for unstructured shots upon my arrival, but I'd yet to capture a criminal partaking in the notorious *return to the scene*. Usually, I'd overlap crowd photos with my exterior four-corners shots to determine who was scoping out what and which gory details piqued their interest, but the crowd sizes had lately become inversely proportional to the crime rate. Corpses piled up weekly; murder had become mundane. In Kingsley, it'd be like gathering every time a bird flew by. Why bother?

"How's Barton?" Nicholls said, bored with Dizzy's purchases.

"Still in the hospital, but stable. They're watching to make sure it doesn't turn into pneumonia."

"Gonna take more than pneumonia to bring your grandfather down. Lemme know when he's ready for visitors. I'll send in some hookers."

"Can't imagine why the ladies aren't lining up at your quarters, Nicholls," I said to his departing ass.

He turned and shot a finger-gun at me, then went to address the scant reporters while I captured an image of Dizzy's brain matter and blood on the lilac wall. The body fluids had formed the profile of an ancient kung fu master who'd taken a pop to the eye, his long, drippy beard cascading to the floor. I leaned in and got a nice, clean shot of some scratches running parallel to Kung Fu's facial hair. There'd be traces of lilac paint under either the victim's nails or the perp's—although in this case, the victim had been a perp more often than not. His nickname, Dizzy, fit him well. He'd spent a lifetime spinning, looking both ways for either trouble or fortune while checking behind him in case the inevitable happened. Which it had, sometime between two a.m. and four a.m., according to the medical examiner, who'd left a couple minutes ago.

Alone in the room, I felt the familiar stirring in my gut and realized my opportunity. I glanced around for the right prop to stoke my habit—the one that could cost me my job and reputation, maybe even land me in jail. I spotted statuettes, dried flowers, do-it-yourself magazines that taught Dizzy how to customize hollow-point bullets, and a chipped candy dish with a discarded wrapper—all tedious. And then I saw it—a chewed tennis ball, its skin split along a seam, long discarded by the German shepherd outside, the one wondering what had become of its master's head.

I grabbed the ball from the fireplace mantel. Grimy with remnants of dog saliva and crawling with bacteria, the fuzzy green orb would help me create my best photo in months. I placed it near

Dizzy's cupped, nondominant hand—didn't want to disturb any gunshot residue on his shooting hand.

I snapped away with my personal camera. Much better. Now Dizzy was a guy who expended his final breaths playing fetch with his favorite pooch. I picked up the ball and tossed it in the air as a flash from the open window caught me off guard.

"Hey!" I protested, shoving the ball into my loose jacket pocket. Behind the offending flash stood a ruddy-faced photographer who looked like he ate beans straight from the can and followed them up with fries. No way could he be comfortable out there in the tight alleyway. Wheezing and coughing, he aimed his lens down and snapped several photos of Dizzy. The window screen would leave a hazy residue on his photos, but the cheaper rags liked that effect. It gave the picture an air of authenticity, as if sneaked without permission, which this one was.

I backed away from his flash, my relationship with cameras contradictory at best, schizophrenic at worst.

As the odor of stale cigarettes and wet perspiration crawled from the photog's clothes to my nose, I cringed. I didn't care if he took photos—wasn't my job to manage the crowd—but this guy was overstaying his welcome and coating my insides with a stench worse than the corpse's.

"You mind?" I said.

"Hey, ain't you the Haiku Twin?" he shouted through the screen. "The one with the brother?"

As if there were multiple sets of Haiku Twins. I flipped him off as his flash blinded me again. Great. My brother would love that one on the campaign trail. The smelly paparazzo wannabe took off.

"You about finished in here, Janie?"

I turned around to see Detective Alex Wexler, Nicholls's partner of a few months, fresh off the rough-and-tumble homicide detail of central Wyoming. I asked him once if he'd ever hosted

Wile E. Coyote in central Wyoming's single jail cell and he'd almost smiled. Surely he questioned his decision to move to Kingsley, Virginia, where gang murders didn't even make the front page.

"Almost done, Wexler. A few more." He remained rooted, looking uncomfortable. As I filled my frame with snaps of Dizzy's head, I became hotly aware of Wexler's presence. He was a few years older than me, and his aloof attitude made him difficult to decipher. I had a gift for siphoning information from corpses, but the living gave me a harder time. Now Dizzy here, he was easy. Never allowed anything to fester beneath his nails or in his conscience. Smelled fresh, looked clean—at least the parts that weren't covered in blood—always thought he was the best-looking guy in the room. Kept his dirt hidden, along with his secrets. The gel in his hair didn't allow for flyaways, even under the force of a bullet traveling a thousand feet per second, and he exerted that same control over his peeps. The accounting software on his desk signaled a guy who kept a balance of criminals and cops on the payroll, and the pressed pants and funky belt suggested leadership with a hint of derring-do.

But Detective Alex Wexler? A tougher hide to penetrate. Kept himself distant and never betrayed his emotions with careless expression. Everything tightly controlled, with a personality as neat and tailored as his clothes. The guy could be a museum display, with those onyx eyes that anchored his square, serious face. Untouchable. Unknowable. Sacrosanct. That was Wexler. And I did hate leaving precious things untouched, especially the sacrosanct— or situations deemed permanent by the finality of a photo.

The tension in the room built to a crescendo and I couldn't take it anymore. I hit Wexler with my upturned green eyes, the ones that closed deals with guys when I wanted them closed. *Yes, Wexler? Something you want to say?*

He shuffled just an inch, then held out an envelope. "This came for you at the station."

I glanced at him for an explanation, because 8-by-10 envelopes came for me all the time, filled with photos and evidence files.

"Wasn't sure you'd get it," he explained. "The mail guy almost sent it back."

I took it, our fingers as close as they'd ever been, and read the address.

Miss Janie

Twin

Kingsley, Virginia

No last name. No street or zip. And yet, despite Kingsley's phone book boasting a plethora of Janies, this envelope had found me. Of course it had. Thirty years of this stuff, I should be used to it. Sometimes months would pass where I could be *Janie Perkins, Plain Citizen*. But the infamous recognition always returned, washing over me like a wave of revulsion tinged by empty indifference. I hadn't asked to be born famous, to a dead mother no less, but tragic endings rarely led to bright beginnings.

With a sigh, I tucked the envelope under my arm, unable to muster up a "Thanks."

Wexler swallowed away his discomfort. "Guess that's one of the benefits of working in a smaller city."

I would have felt grateful for his attempt to lighten the situation, but I was too busy wallowing in reflexive self-pity. "Yeah, Wexler, that's it. This found me because Kingsley has a mere two hundred thousand people. Now I see why you're the whiz kid on the force."

He retreated without reacting, neither hurt nor embarrassed. It crossed my mind that he might suffer from Asperger's syndrome and be unable to process sarcasm, but I decided against it. I'd seen him give as good as he got. Nicholls had once asked him if blood washed out more easily from a pricey, tailored jacket than from one off the rack. "As a matter of fact, it does," he'd answered, "but only because I don't trust my wardrobe to a Tide to Go pen."

He'd suffered flak for weeks over the word *wardrobe*, but he'd taken it in stride.

"Thanks!" I shouted as he disappeared.

I stepped into Dizzy's bathroom to open the envelope in private. Might as well get it over with. One more weirdo to decipher, one more psycho to expel from my nightmares. As I closed the door, the incoming medics made a racket.

"I'm in here," I shouted. Let them assume I was capturing vital photos of Dizzy's Irish Spring and Turkish towels.

Catching a glimpse of myself in the toothpaste-speckled mirror, I cursed my forgotten lipstick. Its absence made my small face look downright undersized. Didn't matter how many push-ups I did to bulk up my narrow shoulders, or how much I fluffed my hair, I always looked small. At 5'3" and 104 pounds, I was tiny, but I felt all of my twenty-nine years and deserved to look thirty-nine. Meanwhile, it was typical of my brother, Jack, at 6'1" and 190 pounds of muscle and confidence, to have hogged all the nutrients in the womb. He'd been gentlemanly enough to let me enter the world first, yet to this day, he sucked the life out of the peaceful, anonymous existence I craved.

I sat myself on Dizzy's fuzzy, zebra-striped toilet seat and examined the envelope. Although the writer had tried to be precise, a tremor showed through in the labored cursive. The postmark read Ridge, West Virginia, and had been mailed a couple days ago. I loosened the barely sealed flap to reveal two blown-up photographs, and I handled them by their edges—fingerprints might come in handy if the contents were the work of some nut job who intended to follow through this time.

The first photo made me gasp.

This psycho had been in my house.

The second photo made my heart stop.

CHAPTER 3

My brother, Deputy Attorney General John B. Perkins, checked his Rolex for the fourth time, but I doubted he knew or cared what time it was. He just wanted out of this chat with me, his favorite twin. Using a pencil eraser, he slid the first photo across his ridiculous mahogany desk toward my propped-up foot. He let it come to rest next to some phallic statue that declared him an Outstanding Community Servant.

"What'd you do to earn this?" I said, nudging the penile substitute with my boot. "Pick up people's trash?"

"The people can take out their own trash."

"It's just *people*, Jack. No *the*."

"I do put away the human trash, though. For good."

The last two words made him sound like a high-paid announcer for an overproduced Mr. Clean ad.

"Relax, bro. No reporters here."

He jotted the line down anyway with a self-satisfied grin on his handsome face and I knew I'd hear it as a sound bite after his next campaign stop. My brother was vying to be the youngest attorney general in Virginia history. He'd graduated law school at twenty-two, so he was a bit ahead of the game at twenty-nine, and he'd turn thirty just in time to serve. Through either good fortune or careful planning, the cases he'd worked on the past couple years had garnered him positive press and public recognition around the state—conditions that, unlike me, he considered advantageous. '

The photo he'd just dismissed was the more innocuous of the two that had arrived in the mail. It showed our childhood living room, the one my grandfather had found appropriate as a playroom for his grandchildren despite its previous incarnation as a crime scene. The photo was taken from the edge of the room, near the kitchen, where Jack used to play with his Tonka trucks and I would get in his way. Our grand floor-to-ceiling stone fireplace dominated the image. In front of the fireplace's bluestone hearth, to the left, sat the green sofa with the huge, maroon rose appliqués. Across from the sofa stood the rectangular marble table with the iron base, its top laden with family photographs. I knew the table well, the scar on my ankle a souvenir from when I skidded into it during an epic fight with Jack. He'd never been violent with me, but our wrestling matches as seven-year-olds had taken definite turns toward the dark side.

Two small bumps were visible across the bottom of the photo, though I doubted Jack had noticed. When I'd spotted them in Dizzy's bathroom, they'd stood out like neon lights shining brightly in a foggy brain. I figured they were the photographer's fingers on the lens, or possibly the shoulder and knee of someone on the floor. Despite my uncertainty, I knew one thing—they'd eat at me if I didn't determine their source.

The second photo had provided the answer. The smudges had indeed been parts of someone lying on the floor. I just hadn't expected them to belong to my mother.

The prenatal loss of a mother redefined the parent-child relationship. There could be no flaws, no bad memories. As surely as Jack and I were the perfect children-to-be in my mother's eyes, Bridget Perkins would always remain inhuman, and therefore beyond human, in my eyes, because I'd never known her as a flesh-and-blood entity. I could assign her no faults and, obviously, no one was eager to share them with me postmortem. Our relationship was absent the conflicts of the teenage years, the outbursts ignited by emerging hormones, and the arguments over boys, drinking, and grades. The walls of my emerald-green room had become my sounding board—and the absorber of my moods—because when rages flared with no one to rise to their venting, I sulked within them. Left to my own devices, I crafted a mother much like the impossibly thin, gown-laden princesses I had drawn—sometimes dozens a day—with their flowing manes of hair and floor-length hoop skirts balanced by exquisite jewels and crowns. I never acknowledged, even to myself, that the figures were my mother, but I named them all Bridgina, Bridgetta, or Bella Brigitte. Hardly a coincidence. Hardly requiring a PhD to decipher. Lacking a relationship marred by reality, the entity of *mom* became the product of a lonely girl's imagination, inspired by aged photos and stories from which Grandpa had smoothed the rough edges, polishing the bright spots to a brilliant shine. In his eyes, and mine, she became a goddess, an inspiration, and the heroine of every tragic fairy tale.

Jack stared clinically at the second photo. When I'd seen it, I'd gaped disbelieving, unable to accept the shattering of my carefully constructed image.

Jack grimaced, but only slightly. Really? That was the whole of his reaction?

The image showed the prettiest girl in the county, maybe even the state, in her diner uniform, her apron stained and crooked. She lay on a cold, hardwood floor, her face tilted toward the camera, a frozen stream of viscous blood oozing down her otherwise gorgeous face. Her knees pointed the opposite direction from her face, as if she'd been in the midst of a skyward pirouette when the gods struck her down, jealous of her beauty and grace.

The photo had to be someone's twisted rendition of a still life. Still life, but barely.

I'd been lucky, inheriting many of my mother's better features—full lips, dark lashes, rectangular jawline, and those slightly exotic green eyes that hinted at Swedish ancestry—but I'd missed out on her luminescence. Even in a dying state, Bridget Perkins had possessed an unspeakable glow. As I had in Dizzy's bathroom, I fought the impulse to grab a pencil from Jack's desk and erase the blood distorting her face, to make her perfect . . . to revive her. If there was one crime scene I wanted to alter, this was it.

Jack glanced a final time at the photo before putting it down. "About these," he said, pointing to the images with a detachment normally reserved for smelly vagrants, "I have no idea. You know how many nuts I deal with on a daily basis?"

"As usual, Jack, this isn't about you, but thanks for your consistency."

I pursed my lips into a pissed-off pucker and plopped my other foot on his desk.

"You mind?" he said, stacking the flecks of dried clay from my boots next to a marble paperweight that abutted the award on his desk. They formed some sort of ancient barrier wall, maybe to keep *the people* away from the mighty Jack Perkins. I watched him with disdain as he fussed with his useless bric-a-brac. Was his office particularly windy, with heavy papers flying about, in need of an Outstanding Community Servant to tame them?

"Jack, Jack, over here." I snapped my fingers so he'd look at me. "Is it possible these photos are some publicity stunt related to your book?"

"What? No! I wouldn't do that."

"You would if it would help you get elected. So, did you?"

Jack sighed in the strange way he had since we were kids, with a little glitch at the end. Sort of a *ha-hmp*. I'd never heard anyone else do it. "No," he said, "I didn't send them. I've never seen them before, although they're similar to stuff in my book." His face took a turn for the upbeat. "By the way, an autographed copy is on its way to you."

I feigned delight with a jazz wave of my hands. The promise of more pictures of my dying mother failed to elicit my enthusiasm for Jack's debut as an author. "Thanks. You're sure these particular photos aren't in your book?"

He shrugged. "I don't know. You think I actually wrote the thing?"

"It's a sappy retrospective on your mother's murder and your life. Forgive me for thinking you were involved."

"It's called a ghostwriter, Janie. Not exactly a new concept. Half the morons in public service can't put together a coherent sentence without a teleprompter. You think they write their own stuff?"

I pulled my feet from his desk, hoping to scratch it, and grabbed my photos back. Unlike my emotionally stunted twin, I couldn't stop staring at the last moment the Haiku Twins had a mom who wasn't yet brain-dead. In the split second of life captured by this image, my mom's last thoughts must have been racing through her head. Were they of shock and disbelief? Of the twins in her womb? Had she experienced flashbacks in reverse, where our imagined futures rushed through her brain like a convoluted film teaser—a film she wouldn't live to see? Or was she just thinking *Shit*.

From what I'd heard about her, most likely the latter.

Suddenly, my stomach turned sour as something in the second photo jumped out at me. I should have seen it earlier.

"Hey, did you take a good look at this picture? Notice anything disturbing?"

"Let's see, Janie. I guess our dying mother on the floor was enough for me. But with your job, it probably takes a little more to get your hackles up." He leaned forward. "Tell me, Sis, what did it for you?"

I leaned forward, putting our similar faces as close together as they'd been for some time. "Mom's eyes are still open in this photo. Her head is still tilted and there's no shirt near her head."

"Brilliant. Maybe you can get a promotion for that detective work."

I slammed my finger down on my mother's body, no longer worried about damaging the photo, because these were copies. I'd left the originals with a friend in the lab, who promised to verify their authenticity and check for fingerprints. "This picture had to be taken within moments of Grady McLemore shooting her."

"Oh? You've come around to saying his name now? Surprised your tongue didn't disintegrate."

I ignored him. "This isn't a police photo, Jack. This was taken *before* Grandpa Barton arrived at the scene, before the police arrived—and they got there fast."

Jack took a second look and furrowed his forehead, distorting his trimmed and plucked brows. "That's impossible. Grandpa Barton got there right after she was shot. Grady was still passed out on the floor, for God's sake."

"Yes, and Grandpa always said he rushed over and Mom's eyes were already closed. When he cupped her head and tilted it upward to face him, that's when she opened her eyes. Then he ripped his shirt off to rest her head on it and help stop the bleeding."

"Jesus, Janie, what'd you do, record him?"

"I made him tell the story a lot."

"Ever hopeful," Jack mumbled.

I scowled at him. "In this photo, no one's touched Mom yet. There's no smeared blood. Everything's pristine."

15

"So?"

"So it proves Grady McLemore was lying. According to him, he shot her just as he was passing out. Wouldn't have left him much time to set up this touching photo op. But if he didn't pass out right away, or if his self-injected drugs hadn't kicked in yet, then he was busy taking this photo."

Jack's handsome, camera-ready face glistened with a gotcha expression, making me feel like a hunter who'd stepped into her own trap, with a limb-crushing snap. Jack could barely speak through his wide grin. "Janie, you may have just guaranteed my book will be a bestseller. This is going to catapult me in the polls."

"What? Why?"

"Because if you're right, this photo is evidence of the mysterious third party."

"Bull. Effing. Shit," I said. "No way."

"You said it yourself. It was taken before anyone else got there."

"Yeah, by Grady McLemore."

"No." Jack leaned forward even farther, making his smile blur into a smear of glowing white. "By the third party that Grady swore was there."

"Oh come on!" I said. "The Haiku Killer? The guy who materialized out of thin air, who the police found no evidence of?"

"And now they have it. If Grady was passed out, which the police report supports, and the cops hadn't arrived yet, then someone else took this photo. Besides, if Grady had taken the photo, they would have found a camera near his body, not to mention the alleged needle that he injected himself with." He sneered like a rat conquering a stubborn piece of gristle as he delivered his closing line. "They found neither."

"He could have had an accomplice."

"So now *you're* introducing a mysterious third party. That's rich." He tapped the photo and leaned back in the deluxe leather chair that loomed eight inches over his head. "This has fascinating possibilities."

I wanted to kick myself—and my brother. I show him a picture of my mother with a fresh bullet in her skull and he views it as an opportunity.

"You know what else is a possibility?" I said. "That these are the Photoshopped work of some psycho geek toiling away in his parents' basement, hiding from the government and messing with us on *the anniversary of the Haiku Twins' birth*."

I put the last part in finger quotes. Our mutual birthday had always been labeled that way. Some source material that reporters kept referencing must have phrased it like that on our first birthday and it had stuck like a hated nickname. Every year, our birthday elicited new crazies, and this thirtieth *anniversary*, coming up soon, was bound to unleash a few more. The case had riveted the public's attention for the better part of a year. By the time Jack and I were born, a month after our mother was put into an induced coma, people had virtually adopted us as their own. Gifts had poured in. My mother's beauty and Grady's popularity, along with the drama of the trial and the mention of the infamous Haiku Killer, had kept the story alive far longer than my mother. And who didn't like a matched set of unlikely heroes? Jack and I were two adorable innocents who forged through dire circumstances to an improbable victory. The people of Virginia, so emotionally invested in our early welfare, had never let go of their Haiku Twins.

Jack shrugged away my idea. Reality didn't matter to him as long as he got a sound bite out of it. "You ever read the letters he sends you?"

I squeezed my face into something that probably resembled a rotted peach pit. "Was it you who gave him my email address?"

"Your own father can't email you?"

"Grady McLemore is not my father."

Jack started to protest, but I nearly lunged across the desk. "Don't you dare," I said, giving each word its own breath. "You've broken a lot of promises over the years, Jackie Boy, but do not break this one."

Years ago, Jack had undergone a DNA test to determine if Grady McLemore really was our father. I swore that if he ever told me the results, I'd make sure his DNA ended up in a police lab, labeled *victim.*

Jack lowered his head in a facsimile of shame. "All right." His voice came out in a chastened tone that would not play well to a voting public. He undoubtedly made a mental note to eliminate it from his stash of public personae. "Sit down," he said.

I let the anger go quickly, a skill I'd mastered early in life, when I'd flare up at the slightest mention of how my alleged father was in jail for *killing my whore of a mother*—that from so-called friends who'd internalized the dark whispers of judgmental parents. Even at a young age, I knew my mother was a saint and that I had no father, incarcerated or otherwise. The fact that my brother now worshipped that phony murderer-cum-jail hero was the sharpest edge of the wedge driven between us. It hadn't always been this way, but at age nineteen, my brother had adopted the spineless, lying Grady McLemore as a surrogate father figure and created a wide, dark chasm between us, one I wasn't sure we could ever bridge. All our lives, we'd been like two opposing magnets forced to exist in a tight, confined space. Left alone, we clashed, but when defending our mutual territory against enemies, we became an unbeatable duo. Back to back, we'd spin on our shared axis, peering out into the world, protecting each other and thinking as one. We'd progressed through the natural stages, from high-strung toddlers to overactive youngsters to moody teens, but nothing had broken our bond. To this day, our conduit remained tenuous but intact.

"He asks about you," Jack said. "All the time. He can't get over how much you look like Mom."

"His victim?"

"The love of his life."

"Loves of lives acknowledge each other in public, Jack. They don't sneak around to fancy hotels under assumed names."

"It was Mom who wanted to keep their relationship secret until after the election."

"According to the guy who benefitted from her keeping it quiet."

Jack shook his head at my apparent naïveté. "Mom was savvy. She knew it wouldn't play well with the voting public if Grady had knocked up a lowly waitress out of wedlock."

That did it. I whipped my hand across his pretentious desk and took out his Community Servant award. As it crashed to the floor, a piece broke off and nicked a nice chunk of wood from his floor, giving me a warped satisfaction I knew I'd regret later.

Jack sat open-mouthed, disgusted, and perhaps a little afraid. He used to be the coolest big brother, but now he wallowed in that quagmire of narcissism that eventually consumed all political types.

I shoved the photos back in their envelope and turned to go. "I trust you won't refer to our mother as a lowly waitress again. She was a beloved art teacher and sculptor-in-training."

"You need help, Janie," he said, growing bored with me and rediscovering his balls. "You get so defensive over this woman who was barely more than a fairy tale to us. You treat her like some princess in a kids' story we were forced to hear way too many times."

"If she was the princess, Jack, where was her prince? Oh, that's right. Rotting in an eight-by-ten jail cell, *pining away* for the woman he hid from the world."

"Rapunzel got hidden away," Jack said, seeming to regret the lame retort the moment it exited his mouth. We always did bring out the eight-year-olds in each other. I strode toward the door, but Jack's final words found my back.

"Love you, Sis," he said.

I sighed, sans glitch. "Love you, too."

As I exited the building, I smiled at the thought of the mighty Jack Perkins crawling around his floor, gathering the broken pieces of his precious award, like Humpty Dumpty trying to put the pieces together again. Then something tapped at my brain. What if he had put the pieces together better than me?

I needed to find Sophie Andricola.

CHAPTER 4

"All's I remember is she was hot," Nicholls said from the front seat of his car. "Think she's still single?"

I raised a skeptical brow. "You and Sophie Andricola don't even orbit the same sun."

"I'm more interested in our space junk colliding than our horoscopes matching up."

"Give it up, Nicholls," I said.

"Maybe Wexler here has a shot. He goes for those intellectual types."

Wexler was seated next to Nicholls while I rode like a prisoner in the back. They were giving me a lift to Sophie's because she lived on a remote trail in a neighboring town where the GPS didn't know the roads.

Wexler settled his silver to-go cup in the drink holder. Steam rose from it and the scent of hazelnut fought it out with Nicholls's discarded bag of garlic chips. "What are you drinking there, Wexler?" I said, craving a cup myself.

"It's a custom blend from that tea shop on Broad."

Nicholls guffawed. "The one where they charge like a hundred bucks for chopped leaf crap from a compost pile?"

"That's the one," said Wexler. "Minus the crap."

With zero embarrassment, Wexler took a bite of his muffin and cleaned his hands with a moist-wipe. Seriously, how did this guy expect to make it in hardscrabble Kingsley, where he and his coworkers avoided nightly bullets like unwitting players in a game of Whack-a-Cop? They were out battling a skyrocketing murder rate and here he was traipsing around with designer tea and a healthy snack—and looking cool doing it.

"What does this Sophie Andricola do?" Wexler asked between sips.

"She's some Canadian chick," Nicholls said, running his tongue along his teeth, probably in place of brushing them. "She does loopy stuff with photos, computer forensics, and random clues. Like an idiot savant or something."

"Minus the idiot part," I added. "Think of her as a crime consultant."

"Like Sherlock Holmes?"

"Exactly," I said. "Plus, she's an amazing artist. A Mensa type."

"We had this murder case a few years back," Nicholls explained. "In the distant background of one of Janie's photos, there was this unexpected shot of yellow in a field behind the victim's house."

"We tried what we could with digital enhancement," I added, "but deciphering that tiny speck of color required the rare combination of computer geekery, keen observation, and an artist's eye."

"Anyway," Nicholls continued, "there was nothing there when we went back to search, but this Sophie chick somehow figures out it's a shoe. A lemon-pucker slingback, she called it, like a hundred yards away. Ended up solving the case for us."

"How?" Wexler asked.

"The wife had hired a sniper to kill her husband from a low spot in that field, but she'd failed to realize the sniper had the hots for her. She was a helluva looker."

"Says the objective detective."

"So the sniper breaks into the house *before* the shooting and takes one of the wife's shoes to rest his elbow on 'cause the field was muddy."

"And according to his later testimony," I said, "he sniffed it and stroked it while he waited. Had a serious foot fetish."

Wexler chuckled and I saw the left corner of his mouth tilt up. "Who thought to bring the yellow spot to Miss Andricola's attention?"

"I did," I said. "I knew something was off. If there'd been a yellow flower in season or a colorful bird in the area, or even an old piece of crime tape floating around, I'd have noticed. But there wasn't."

"And that's *your* gift," Wexler said.

"What do you mean?" I said, caught off guard by the sudden focus on me.

"Any detective worth his salt can learn to be observant. But you, Janie, you know when something's off. That's what makes you a strong photographer."

When he added my name to the sentence, I got an unexpected rush. It was a sensation I welcomed and wouldn't mind feeling again.

Nicholls chortled, as he always did when someone paid me a compliment. He turned to Wexler. "Uh, want me to pull over so you can climb in the backseat with Janie there? I promise not to look."

With no mortification, Wexler turned to his less refined partner. "Definitely not."

"Why not?" Nicholls said.

"Because you always peek."

Wexler turned and winked at me, leaving me at a loss for a reaction, but not wanting him to look away.

The car veered onto a dirt road and hit a huge bump, ending the conversation and sending the flurries in my stomach into a whirlwind.

Wexler started a new topic. "Janie, why do you need to see this Sophie person?"

Nicholls and I exchanged a glance in the rearview mirror. He shrugged and I agreed. We decided to let Wexler in, even though every telling of the story chipped away at my core. I took a deep breath. "You know I'm one of the Haiku Twins, right?"

"I know the general story, although I'd love to hear it from the horse's mouth."

"Let me tell it! Please?" Nicholls sprayed spit onto the windshield in his excitement.

"Wexler," I said, "do you mind hearing it from the horse's best friend's crumb-filled mouth?"

"Not at all, but feel free to whinny or stomp if he gets something wrong."

"Go ahead, Nicholls," I said, happy to share the burden.

"All right, lemme set the scene. So Bridget Perkins was Janie's superhot mom—even won some beauty contests as a teen. Born and raised in the humble hamlet of Caulfield, about twenty minutes away, where our darling Janie grew up. You probably haven't been out there much, Wexler, but let's just say fifteen miles in any direction from Kingsley and you'll start droppin' *g*'s, tippin' cows, and shovelin' grits down your throat—"

"Drowned in cheese and butter, of course," I added.

Wexler turned a serious face to Nicholls. "Janie doesn't drop her *g*'s." It was as if the veracity of Nicholls's entire story would be undermined if he got such a basic, early fact wrong.

I came to Nicholls's rescue. "My brother went all Henry Higgins on me in high school. You know, from *My Fair Lady*?"

Wexler turned back to me. "Well, now you've got to do it."

I grinned and recited, "The rain in Spain falls—"

"Hello! Thought I was tellin' a story here."

Wexler and I exchanged an amused glance, like benevolent parents agreeing to humor their temperamental teen.

Nicholls continued. "So, even today, you'll see the occasional Confederate flag flying from a barn in Caulfield, along with Southern plantations and small farms. Lotta subdivisions goin' in now, but used to be, every few houses, you'd see rusty pickups mounted on cement blocks—"

"And that'd be the front yard," I said with a proud smile.

"Anyway, Janie's mom, Bridget, went and got herself knocked up by slick, rich Grady McLemore in the middle of his campaign for senate. They were both single, so no big deal, but they knew enough to feed that morsel to the public *after* the election. At the same time—Christ, thirty years ago now—a serial killer was lurking, scaring the bejeezus out of the whole state and leaving freaky notes with his victims. The notes were always written in haiku. You know what that is?"

"Five-seven-five," Wexler said. "Fourth-grade English. But is it syllables or words?"

"Syllables," Nicholls said. "Five syllables in the first and third lines, seven in the middle. Like if I said, 'Wexler is a wuss. He wears a *wardrobe*, that puss. No plain clothes for him.' You get it?"

"Got it."

"But haikus don't have to rhyme," I added, "and they're usually about nature, not impeccable wardrobes."

"Anyway," Nicholls said, "Grady McLemore claims he went over to Bridget's house that night to save her from—are you ready?—the Haiku Killer. Had this whole story about how Bridget found a real haiku and the killer was after her. I mean, it was perfect on McLemore's part, right? Inserting this infamous serial killer into the mix when it was the hottest topic in the state. Put everybody on edge, right?"

"I suppose," Wexler said. "But why would Janie's mom have thought she had a note from the real Haiku Killer? Seems like people would have been writing them left and right, like it would have been the in thing to do."

"It was," I said. "If it happened today, it'd be trending on Twitter."

"That's true," Nicholls said. "Reporters used 'em as headlines and everything. The guy was like our own Son of Sam. And for reasons no one'll ever know, Janie's mom was convinced she had the real thing." Nicholls twirled his finger near his temple to indicate *crazy*.

I kicked the back of his seat. "Remember," I said, "our only source on this is Grady McLemore, egotistical liar and murderer. My mom probably never mentioned the Haiku Killer."

Wexler rubbed his chin. "Who were the Haiku Killer's other victims?"

"A priest, a philosophy professor, and a doctor," I said.

"Religion, philosophy, and medicine," Wexler said. "Renaissance killer."

"Wow," I said. "Not many people come up with an angle I haven't heard before, Wexler. Nice job."

"But if that were true," Nicholls said, reaching over and grabbing a chunk of Wexler's muffin, "why go after a waitress?"

"To represent the commoners, the serfs, or the bourgeoisie," Wexler explained. "But if Janie's mom did find an actual haiku, she wasn't an intended victim. She self-selected by finding it."

"Or there never was a haiku," I reminded them loudly. "And Grady was just desperate to avoid the chair."

"Whatever," Nicholls said. "Lemme finish. So that night, Grady rushes over to Bridget's house to save his damsel in distress. Of course, he's never been there, 'cause the relationship was hush-hush and all that, and he doesn't know the layout of the place. He storms in with guns a-blazing and shazam! He gets a syringe full of the good stuff—"

"Allegedly," I added.

"—and he gets one errant shot off before collapsing to the floor."

Wexler tapped his to-go cup, lost in thought. Unlike most people, he didn't pepper Nicholls with questions. He didn't gasp or shake his head or start spouting off theories. His silence threw me because, from the scores of times I'd told the story, I knew where the newbies jumped in: *Well, who was the Haiku Killer? Did your mom know the guy? Did Grady McLemore describe him? Did they ever catch the guy? How'd she get the haiku? What did it say?*

I could barely contain myself when Wexler stayed mum, as if the steam from his beverage had spelled out all the answers. Where was his outrage over Grady McLemore's cojones in trying to cover up the murder of his alleged lover by invoking the serial killer of the day? Where was his boiling hatred of a man so cowardly and selfish that he shot a pregnant woman in the head?

I leaned forward, ready to spew the usual words that summed up Grady—*vermin, narcissist, womanizer*—all the ones that explained what an insane liar he was—but I found no taker in Wexler.

"Got it" was all he said.

"That's it?" Nicholls said. "No questions? No ideas?"

"Nope."

"Well, you're either a freakin' genius or you've got the emotional range of a mushroom."

Wexler turned and caught my eye again. "I'm no mushroom."

The indirect answer with the hint of humor sent a rivulet of sensation through my midsection. I didn't like what it meant for my no-dating-cops rule.

"It's pretty straightforward," Wexler said. "McLemore's in jail, meaning no verification of a third person. He fabricated the story to cover up an affair gone wrong. Not sure how he thought he'd get away with it in the first place. Apparently, he didn't."

"Or maybe," Nicholls said, "McLemore found out one of his twins was gonna be a whiny pain in the ass."

I kicked Nicholls's seat, much harder this time.

"The prosecution's theory," I said, "was that my mom threatened to spill the beans about their relationship. And when Grady failed to convince her to keep their affair a secret, he shot her in a rage and tried to cover his involvement by injecting himself with tranquilizer and delivering that cockamamie story about the Haiku Killer. The rest, as they say, is history."

"That's the version that won over the jury," Nicholls explained to Wexler. "A lot of people still doubt the conviction, though, choosing to believe the real Haiku Killer was in Janie's living room that night. McLemore's got a huge fan base, especially with the ladies."

"Hybristophilia," Wexler said, finishing his muffin. "A certain segment of women fall in love with guys who commit horrendous crimes. They think they can change them, or they enjoy finally being in control of a relationship. Ted Bundy got thousands of love letters and proposals—even had women showing up at his trial decked out to look like his victims."

"Pale and lifeless?" Nicholls said.

"No," Wexler said. "Long, brown hair, parted in the middle, attractive, young."

"Grady has Grady's Ladies," Nicholls said. "It got heavy press here in Virginia way back when. One of his fans was this TV actress who produced a movie loosely based on the case. Cast herself as Janie's mom."

I shot Nicholls a look of disgust. "Please tell me you never watched that schlock, Nicholls."

He shrugged. "I mighta checked it out on Netflix after I met you."

"Why does that make *me* feel dirty?" I said.

"'Cause I'm a pig," he said, then glanced at Wexler. "McLemore's still got this hybristo thing workin' for him. When he got quoted in an article about Janie's brother running for attorney general, the poll numbers went berserk, especially with the ladies."

"We're like the Kennedys," I said. "Scandal increases our popularity."

Wexler waited a thoughtful moment. "I still don't know what this has to do with Sophie Andricola."

Nicholls turned onto Sophie's road. I stared at the envelope on my lap. If Sophie could do even half of what I thought she was capable of, she might hold the power to silence the doubters once and for all. I just wasn't sure which doubters.

CHAPTER 5

Bridget Perkins, 30 Years, 11 Hours Ago

Bridget Perkins rubbed her naked stomach. At seven months pregnant with twins, she was small compared to women five months along. She'd been lucky so far—no stretch marks and minimal morning sickness. Her biggest complaint was ever-present exhaustion and people's unmasked disapproval of her so-called *fatherless* pregnancy. Sex education in Caulfield, Virginia, wasn't so backward and bashful that people believed in immaculate conceptions of diner waitresses, but that didn't stop them from stating the plainly stupid: *So there's no father? . . . No father, eh? . . . Well, let's hope it's a girl, because a boy needs a father.* As if a daughter didn't.

It hadn't helped that Bridget had inadvertently saddled herself with a loose-girl reputation. When one gossipy lady in town heard that Bridget wouldn't say who the father was, she'd started a rumor that Bridget didn't *know* who the father was. The surprising part was how readily people had gobbled up the rumors, like they'd known all along that Bridget Perkins was a hussy, despite two-plus decades of proper manners, a lifetime of near-abstinence, and a stellar reputation as a private art teacher for six promising high-schoolers who came to the house to work with her. In Caulfield, no accumulation of good works could stand up to the bold proclamation of a full uterus. She stroked that proclamation now and one of the babies kicked, making her smile.

The water pipes in the bathroom squealed as the water heated up. Grady must have turned the spigot on full force. She reflected on the sensuous, warm night they'd spent together, awed that such an evening could become the routine of her life.

Bridget McLemore . . . she liked the sound of it, even if the implications of being a senator's wife intimidated the heck out of her at times. But Grady was going places, and he seemed determined to take her along for the ride. If that ride had gotten off to a bit of a bumpy start, well, they'd make the best of it and cross the finish line together.

She rolled to her side on the silky sheets that cost more than she made in a month. The Aberdeen Hotel skimped on nothing. The old-fashioned clock ticked its way into her brain and her eyes went wide when she saw the time: 12:05 p.m. She and Grady hadn't fallen asleep until after three, and it'd been years since she'd risen this late. With a sigh, she remembered she had to be at work in less than three hours.

The sound of Grady's razor on his morning scruff scraped lightly against her ear. In the shower door's reflection, she spied his naked backside while he shaved. As the steam settled and her eyes adjusted, she made out the image of his rectangular face, echoed in the mirror's image against the glass shower door. A reflection of a reflection, kind of like their relationship. Despite her confidence that it would all work out in the end, how would they ever transition their coupling into something acceptable under the glare of the political spotlight? Reporters were relentless—the public even more so.

"Hey, Grady," she said in her high, smooth voice, the one that had shined in the church choir until Pastor Gibson had suggested she take leave *due to concerns over her balance on the risers.* The floor, where Bridget had cast her eyes after the request, wasn't considered an option, so she did the right thing and rejoined the congregation. Odd that the same concern hadn't been shown for Melinda Blake when she'd been pregnant, but Melinda had come complete with a husband to catch her if she fell.

"Yes, sweetie?" came Grady's strong voice, the one that sent tingles down the spines of the women at his campaign stops, and probably accounted for eighty percent of his volunteers being female. Combined with his long, lean frame, confident stance, and ability to connect with folks in any walk of life, it was amazing he wasn't already president. The few people who might think him phony were converted upon meeting him in person. He knew this, of course, and it was one of the reasons he made endless personal appearances, including the one at Field Diner a year and a half ago, where he'd ordered scrambled eggs and fruit.

"Have you or we or anyone figured out how it's all going to work?" Bridget said, her Southern accent as pronounced as her dimples. "This whole you-get-elected-and-then-introduce-the-world-to-the-woman-who-just-had-your-twins thing?"

"Well, there's a couple ways to finagle it. Sam and I discussed it yesterday, as a matter of fact."

Bridget cringed. She didn't like Sam Kowalczyk, and she sure didn't like being another tool in his substantial bag of tricks when it came to getting candidates *positioned*—Sam's favorite word. *We've got to position Grady better with the middle class. Let's see if we can't improve Grady's position with the old folks; they vote, you know.*

"And just how does Sam intend to position me?" Bridget said. "Hopefully nowhere near him."

Grady poked his head out of the bathroom, a thick layer of shaving cream smeared across his jutting jaw, the razor small in his strong hands. At least Grady didn't deceive the agriculture community; he really had spent summers on a farm and had sweated hard for every one of those taut muscles. Bridget enjoyed the fleeting thought that she'd never get tired of looking at that body, and if she did, she might as well roll over and die.

"I don't know everything he's got up his sleeve," Grady said as he broke into a smile at the sight of her wrapped in the sheets. "But I've got a few ideas about positioning you right now."

She pulled the sheets up and grinned, her pageant-winning lips curling upward. "Stop that. I've got to get to work, and you need to get me back to town with enough time to change into my uniform. You know how you like a girl in uniform."

Grady ducked back into the bathroom but reappeared a moment later with his shaving cream wiped off. In a few long strides he was back in bed, cuddled up next to her, smelling of spice and wholesomeness. He wrapped one arm behind her neck and slipped the other beneath her back, then lowered his face to within inches of hers. She knew she'd succumb to whatever he wanted next—and that it'd be pure pleasure. His kisses were an unfathomable combination of soft but intense, gentle yet lustful, and they were only the start. Any additional activity between the two of them would make her late for her shift; still, she made no effort to escape his embrace, his lips, his unspoken demands.

"I hate that you're still working," he said, pulling back to see her face. "I don't like you being on your feet all day. Let's tell everyone about the babies—about us—today. Right now." He brushed his lips against hers. "We'll start with the bellhop."

Bridget, smiling yet resolute, pulled at the ample dark hairs on his chest. "Much as I like the adorable hat on that hop, the word is mum."

"Why?"

"It's the one thing you promised—to keep our secret—and Grady McLemore does not go back on his word."

"I don't, but I want the world to know how much I love you and how excited I am about the twins."

"Well, I refuse to live the rest of my days being the person responsible for you losing an election. We just need to smooth out the rough parts, like transitioning to a relationship after you're sworn in."

"Sam thinks we should make it look like I adopted them after falling in love with the stunning, single mom struggling to make ends meet. 'She charmed the socks off this lonely, hardworking man,' I'd say."

"Just the socks, eh? You think that would work?"

He opened his mouth slightly and leaned down to kiss her full lips. "I can make anything work. You know that."

"I'd have to think about it. I mean, I want the kids to know you're their real daddy."

"Then I'll make that work." He scooped up her leg until it was slung across his hip. Bridget could feel him wanting more. She wondered if she'd be able to convince her horrid manager that she'd gotten a flat on the way to work.

Lying back, sometime later, Bridget felt fulfilled beyond expectations. A perfect ending to a stolen night—and morning.

"Question for you," Grady said. "How should I pronounce *Caulfield* when I'm in town? The locals seem picky about it and now that I've opened a campaign office there, I want to get it right."

"I'll tell you my system."

"I knew you'd have one," he said, tickling her.

"It depends on the depth of your roots. If both sets of grandparents dropped out of high school there, married as teens, and never traveled more than fifty miles in any direction, then it's *Cough-eld*, emphasis on the first syllable, kind of like *scaffold* but with a *cough*. If you're the first generation born and bred there, and you never lived more than a stone's throw from your birthplace, it's

Caw-field. But if you're passing through, or worse yet, seeking us out because we were mentioned as a quaint town in a glossy magazine, then it's *Call-field*, and we'll just point you in the direction of the giant twine ball attraction so you can snap a whimsical photo."

Grady tried out the options. "What about a guy seeking votes, born a hundred miles away, but who plans to raise a family there with a beautiful woman?"

The image made Bridget's dimples pucker. "Go with *Caw-field*. Folks'll give you some leeway."

"You mind if Sam drives you back to *Caw-field*, then?" Grady said as he sprang out of bed.

Frown lines cut into Bridget's forehead. "Matter of fact, I do. Why can't you take me? I was looking forward to the ride together."

"He's got me scheduled with a 4-H club and a hunting group. Didn't know about it until yesterday, but I'll try to come by the diner tonight." He enveloped her with his dark eyes. "Maybe you can serve me."

Bridget's mood had shifted and there would be no winning her back. "You should have told me. I don't like being alone in a car with a man who has the charm of a wolverine and the beady eyes to match."

Grady chuckled. "Sam adores you. He just has trouble showing it. Why don't you flirt with him in the car, tell him what a nice snout he has?"

Bridget swung her legs out of the bed. As Grady returned to the bathroom, she threw on the thick white robe provided by the Aberdeen Hotel. She'd never worn anything so heavy yet so soft. With her finger, she traced the outline of the robe's golden *A* monogram above her right breast. But even this little perk couldn't squelch her ire over having to spend time alone with Sam Kowalczyk. And then she spotted the engraved, brass key chain for the suite. It was worth more than her daddy made in an entire insurance commission. She'd show Grady for not driving her home. He could answer for the missing key and pay out of his own pocket—and she could savor a bit of twisted delight in his not even knowing he'd been had. It wasn't her usual style, but she dropped the key chain, complete with key, into her robe pocket, then opened and drank an expensive Perrier while Grady finished up in the bathroom.

When he came out, Bridget approached him and stroked his face. He'd done a perfect job of shaving. Smooth as ever. She let a single finger traverse down his face all the way to his naked stomach, just to tease him before disappearing into the shower. And when he pulled her close and kissed her, as she knew he would, her free hand slipped into her robe pocket, slid out the key chain, and dropped it into her makeup kit. Goodness, she deserved a memento.

CHAPTER 6

The dark, fragrant wood that comprised Sophie Andricola's log cabin had to be a hundred years old and, like the enormous red oaks framing it, gave off a living, breathing vibe. The sixty-foot-tall sentries seemed to be judging my worthiness to intrude upon their master, but before they could render a verdict, the garishly dressed Sophie Andricola opened the front door and stared at her uninvited guest with neither judgment nor question.

The garnet gemstone piercing her brow was new, as was the tattooed snake slithering up her neck and vanishing behind her left ear. Should I assume it was feasting upon her brain? I forced my eyes away, but they drifted back, lured by the spell the serpent had cast.

"Hi, Ms. Andricola, I tried to call in advance, but no answer and no voice mail."

"Janie Perkins," Sophie said in a warm voice with a Canadian lilt. "Welcome."

Sophie had relocated to the Kingsley suburbs after a controversial case in which she had discerned the guilt of a Royal Canadian

Mounted Police officer through his computer history and the symbolic meaning of demonic sculptures in his home. Before she could be called as a witness, though, the officer's computer had disappeared from the evidence room and her car had been found blown to sharp, hot bits in a deep gulley. After a barrage of negative media coverage and a cold shoulder from her employer, she'd moved to Virginia to start a private consulting business in her strange trifecta of specialties. Clearly, the Canadian officer had been connected and the truth was a little-valued commodity by his superiors.

"You took the photo with the lemon-pucker shoe," Sophie said.

"And you solved a murder," I replied.

She smiled, accepting the praise, and I wondered what had happened in this woman's life that made her hide such stark beauty behind piercings and tattoos while remaining a near recluse in a stand-alone cabin.

"Won't you come in?"

I expected incense, dim lights, and a black cat or two, but instead entered an open, modern home, naturally bright and crowned by a hand-painted ceiling fan showing pastel sunsets. The stone fireplace hogging the entire east wall of the living room boasted intricate etchings on one-third of the stones, while framed photos of cheery people covered a mantelpiece and hung on the walls. Not so different from the home where I was raised.

"What a lovely place," I said, failing to hide my surprise. "You've made it so . . . welcoming."

"Had to. Dark and woeful when I bought it."

Given the first impression most people had of Sophie, I grinned, and then felt myself drawn to the fireplace to examine the etchings more closely. The random scratches of the first one gave it a rough-hewn, primitive quality, but upon closer inspection, they proved to be hundreds of tiny, deliberate scores. As my eyes and brain finally coalesced, I pulled back. The etching was a simply drawn man lunging a spear into a prone woman on the ground.

"Everybody goes to that one first," Sophie said.

My eyes widened, but not so she could see. I inspected the next etching. Same style, different death. It showed an enormous vulture careening toward an infant wrapped in a loincloth. Tears spurted from the infant's eyes, but the extended talons of the predator suggested the tears would soon turn to blood. As my eyes adjusted, I could decipher the etchings more quickly—with no small degree of horror: a woman being burned at the stake; a man hanging upside down from a tree branch while a forked-tongued snake eased down his leg; a pile of dead pigs, eyes open, with a grimacing farmer lording over them.

I whipped around to my hostess, hoping to catch her raw reaction to a stranger's appreciation of the art, but I got very little. She stared blankly at the etching in the upper-right corner, that of a toddler reaching up to hold its mother's hand. No death, no violence. Until I strained my neck and saw a bullet exiting the mother's chest, a distant look on her face as if she'd already moved to the next dimension, leaving the toddler to fend for itself.

"They come to me," she said. "I filter them through simplification and light. Imagine not letting them out." She grinned unexpectedly. "Can I get you some water? Or tea? I'm afraid I gave up coffee. Too much stimulation."

"No, thanks. I'm sorry to bother you like this."

"Please." Sophie gestured toward a sofa with throw pillows sporting bright wildlife scenes. "Make yourself comfortable."

I wondered if I could, given the gruesome death scenes lingering nearby. But then I remembered my own job and how I could debate the merits of competing taco trucks while hovering over bodies shredded by rivalry and hatred. I sank into the couch. Sophie made herself comfortable with one leg up on a cushion in order to face me more fully.

"I'm hoping you can help me with a photo enhancement," I said.

"Of course. In relation to an ongoing case?"

"A rather dated case."

I explained the situation and showed her the more revealing photo of my mother's body, hoping it wouldn't end up on her fireplace stones.

She glanced at the image for only a moment, then jerked her head to the window across the room as if a confused bird had slammed into it and riveted her attention. As a glassy look coated her face, I knew there was no bird and I instinctively stayed quiet. Sophie was processing her first impression, allowing her divergent brain quadrants to merge.

She whipped her head back to the image, her eyes narrowing, her lips parted enough to reveal a tiny blue star on her tongue. I didn't want to believe it was a tattoo, but I knew it was.

Sophie raised her eyes and found mine in such a direct manner that I felt accused. "I'll need the day with both photos."

"What are you thinking?"

"I'm not. It gets in the way. How can I reach you?"

With that, we exchanged contact information and Sophie escorted me from the cabin just as my cell phone rang. My brother's number.

"Yes, Jack, what is it?"

"It's Grandpa Barton. Things have taken a turn for the worse. I'm on my way to the hospital."

My heart flipped. Grandpa Barton was my rock, my courage, my everything. "I'll meet you there."

"Uh, you, well, I should probably tell you . . ."

"Yes, Jack?"

"I was at an event when I got the call about Grandpa. Some reporters may have gotten wind."

May have gotten wind? If I knew anything about my brother, it was his penchant for exploiting situations to his political advantage, no doubt inherited from his alleged father. Wouldn't surprise me if Jack staged dramatic personal calls at every public appearance so he could look like a sought-after superhero. All he needed was the cape and tights, which, if I remembered correctly, he'd worn for Halloween when we were ten. No doubt he'd gotten a call from the doctor, feigned a mirror-perfected expression of shock and dismay, then turned to his handler while leaning into a live mic. *My dear grandfather is in the hospital! The man who raised me after my mom was killed in that Haiku Killer fiasco. Must go!*

Yes, how in the world would those reporters have *gotten wind*?

I shoved my phone into my back pocket, as much to hang up on my brother as to force myself not to see *Haiku Twins' grandfather* trending on Twitter. Without another conscious thought, I waved down Nicholls and Wexler, who were parked at the end of the road. They pulled up and I hopped in.

"Can you get me back to the station so I can pick up my car? Grandpa Barton's not doing well."

Nicholls and Wexler both sensed my need for silence. During the drive, we held our own quiet vigil for the only family member I both loved and liked at the moment.

CHAPTER 7

Bridget Perkins, 30 Years, 10 Hours Ago

Bridget Perkins's eyes shifted from the side mirror to the road ahead. She didn't want anyone to see Sam Kowalczyk dropping her off at home. Despite Sam's fondness for the shadows, he had appeared alongside Grady in recent newspaper photos; locals might remember him as Grady's driver. At one campaign stop near DC, a sultry woman had been so desperate to get at Grady, she'd tried to bribe her way into the car by offering Sam a menu of sexual favors. To his credit, Sam hadn't ordered, but he was becoming better known as a conduit to the candidate, and Bridget didn't need anyone making the connection between her and Grady. Not yet, anyway.

"Maybe just drop me off here," she said when they were a mile from her house.

"This is too far," Sam said. "Let me get closer."

The thought of Sam getting closer in any respect sent shivers through her body. She tried to give him a fair shot, but everything about him repulsed her, from his personality on out. Despite a strong conviction that beauty began and ended on the inside, she found that belief hard to apply to Sam. His ugliness grew like a sunburst from within, bright and blinding by the time it reached his ruddy skin, snub nose, and close-set eyes that formed a horizontal slit of bad intentions beneath too-dark brows. She didn't appreciate his awkward Polish jokes, either. He told them with no flair and delivered them preemptively to prevent others from doing so first. Bridget felt sure he'd been bullied as a child, and she tried to rustle up some sympathy by concentrating on that aspect of his past.

"I'm fine here, thanks," she said.

"Well, I'll watch you walk home, then."

The way he said it made her squirm. Given the extra sway in her backside with the new weight up front, Sam was undoubtedly smiling like a letch on the inside, more than eager to watch. "Maybe you're right. Why don't you drop me off after the next bend?"

"Yes, ma'am." He cleared his throat, then bucked up the courage to say something. "No need to worry about the license plates, Miss Perkins, if you were concerned about anyone associating this car with Mr. McLemore."

"What? No. I never even thought of that."

"Because the plates are clean. Can't be traced to my name or Grady's."

"Great, but doesn't Grady own this car?"

"No, ma'am. It's mine, but if the cops do run the plates, let's just say they won't get the whole story."

Fantastic. She could be driving with a murderer, for all she knew. "You didn't steal the plates, did you, Sam?"

He chuckled. "No, ma'am. But I've got connections. Being on the inside comes with its advantages. You play your cards right, you can use your time to your best advantage. Even learned some chess in there, and I'll tell you, if ever there was a game that teaches you to play all the angles, that's it. You play?"

"No, not really my cup of tea." She forced a smile. "My mind is too scattered, I suppose. Never able to muster the concentration needed for something like that."

Grady's platform included prison reform and prisoner rehabilitation, and unfortunately for Bridget, he didn't just talk the talk; he walked the walk—he'd hired the ex-con next to her as the main handler for the campaign. Granted, Sam was excellent at his job, had a good head on his shoulders, and showed a natural instinct for reading people, polls, and crowds, but none of that diminished the yuck factor Bridget felt around him.

Sam slowed for a curve in the road just as Abner Abel's meat truck reared its rickety grille. Great—what a trip this was turning out to be. The last person Bridget wanted to see was her critical neighbor, he of faithful church attendance and endless judgment. She dreaded the slow passing of Sam's pretentious Mercedes and Abner Abel's wobbly ham-hauler. The narrow road barely fit two cars as it was.

Anticipating the inevitable wave when the opposing windows lined up, Bridget lowered her hat, pushed her sunglasses up her nose, and crossed her arms over her protruding belly before lowering the visor.

"Uh, someone you don't want to see?" Sam said in his nasally voice, with a hint of sarcasm.

"You could say that again." She feared he might, just to be funny.

Mr. Abel's truck slowed to a crawl. Good Lord, Bridget could have gotten out and pushed the old jalopy faster than he was driving it. Was he moving like a drugged sloth for safety reasons, or because he wanted a good gander at the people in the unfamiliar car? Perhaps he hoped it would be someone he could recruit to next Sunday's service. *Without proselytizing, there'd be more hospitalizin'—of the soul, that is.* He'd actually said that years ago when he knocked on the door of a house where she was visiting a friend. She'd had no idea that was how he spent his Friday nights and had wondered what else she didn't know about the man. Did he sin? Did he covet? Was he trying too hard?

Bridget peered out from beneath her woven hat brim. Mr. Abel was staring straight at her through his windshield, his eyes in that permanent half-closed state. But she knew that behind the numb expression lay a fierce determination to bring the sheep—and ignorant sheep they all were in his eyes—closer to the Lord.

As the vehicles crept within scraping distance of one another, Bridget shuddered. She caught a glimpse of her neighbor's skeletal face. A decade ago, when he'd dropped her off after babysitting, he'd reached out a bony hand to remove a beetle skin from her hair; she'd have sworn death oozed over her like a gooey, cracked egg.

"Could this guy go any slower?" Sam said. "He's like a Polack goin' at a second-grade math problem."

"Just drive," Bridget whispered without moving her lips. She crouched down so far that her bottom hung off the edge of the seat.

Abner Abel cranked his head sideways, getting an eyeful of Sam's mottled skin while trying to look past him at the passenger. He waved through the open window like he was pawing through quicksand. "Afternoon, sir," he said.

Sam gave a perfunctory nod and peeled away after clearing the back of the truck.

"That was torturous," Bridget said, rising from her slumped position.

"Ma'am, it's not my place to say, but you're never going to please everyone. A bare majority'll do the trick, sometimes even a plurality. But you'll go nuts if you take every perception personally."

Bridget shot him a reproachful glare. "Been dealing with that man's perceptions my whole life. I grew up next to the Abels, and they think they walk on hallowed ground. And Lord have mercy, not a one of 'em would ever find themselves in the position I'm in."

"You'd be surprised about people, Miss Perkins. Mighty surprised."

"You don't know this family."

"No, ma'am, but I can get information on 'em if you want."

Bridget looked askance at her driver. "No, thank you."

"I know a thing or two about secrets. Not that I'd ever tell, mind you. That's one reason Mr. McLemore keeps me around. But you shouldn't elevate people just because they have religion. That might be their bailiwick, but it shouldn't make you feel inferior."

"Who said I feel inferior?" Bridget felt frustration welling up inside her because Sam had hit the nail on the head. "Besides, I didn't say I don't have religion. As a matter of fact, I do."

"That's all well and good, ma'am, but there are those who let it warp them. Tell you the truth, I feel removed from organized religion myself. If we're all made in God's image, some people might consider themselves right up there with Him, wouldn't you say?"

Bridget pulled back to look at Sam in full. "No one should consider himself equal to the Lord, Sam."

"Now, that's funny coming from you, Miss Perkins."

"What's that supposed to mean?"

"Nothing, really. Just figuring things out. It can be hard to know right from wrong and good from evil. Living a moral life is not for the lazy, that's for sure. But what's a person to do when they come upon a situation after they've already sworn their loyalty?"

Bridget removed her hat and faced him full on. "Come out with it, Sam. You disapprove of this pregnancy but you're forced to accept it because you swore loyalty to Mr. McLemore. Is that what you're trying to say in your roundabout way?"

"Now, ma'am, I've said too much."

"Seems like you're passing judgment that should be reserved for the Lord, Sam, but then again, you might be right up there with Him."

Sam shook his head and snorted, clearing either his thoughts or his sinuses. "Now I've gone and confused the whole issue. Believe me, I wasn't judging you or those babies." He glanced at the latter, making Bridget fear he might reach out and pat her stomach. "Truth is, I admire you an awful lot, and those babies might make a world of difference."

"Just out of curiosity, Sam, what were you in jail for?"

"Manslaughter," he said, pulling his lips back and showing tiny teeth in some sort of shameful grimace. "As you know, accidents happen."

Bridget froze and found herself wordless, her hands reflexively covering the babies. Was he equating her pregnancy with his criminal past? *Accidents happen.* She'd have to talk to Grady about parting ways with Sam once and for all, as soon as the election was over.

A rusty Plymouth swerved around the bend, going fast enough to put a visible tilt in the vehicle holding two bleary-eyed workmen. Sam veered just in time to avoid a collision, and they both breathed a sigh of relief. "Like I said," Sam muttered, "accidents happen."

An unbidden image of Sam *manslaughtering* her flashed through her head. "Well, Sam, I think I'd like to get out now. We're pretty close."

He pulled off to the side, where a deteriorating fence had given way to mud and corrosion. "I'm sorry if I upset you at all, ma'am. I'm better at helping others communicate than I am at doing it myself."

Bridget tried to smile but it came up short.

"You sure you'll be okay here?" he said.

"Yes, fine. Thanks for the ride." She grabbed her overnight bag and got out, hoping no other locals would pass by. At least she wasn't barefoot and sticking her thumb out. That would really have completed the picture for some folks. Honestly, it would have been easier for them if she'd been growing two heads instead of two babies. Sometimes they acted like they were wearing dog cones while averting their eyes from her waist.

A minute later she reached the top of her driveway, barely able to see the 150-year-old house from all the century-old trees hiding it from prying eyes. Of course, few prying eyes cared about a random house with a middle-aged man and his daughter, but she knew everything would change once Grady claimed her as his own. Oh, Lord, if they didn't play it right, what a scandal it would be.

The noise reached Bridget first and she turned around to see her father rounding the bend in his blue pickup truck. Everyone in town knew Barton Perkins's Ford, as much for its loud transmission and grimy exhaust as for the big horns on top that advertised his company: Ram Insurance.

She hopped in on the passenger side, explaining that her friend had dropped her at the top of the driveway. Despite Barton's pride in his new white pebble driveway, the ride felt to Bridget like a series of ruts held together by the occasional patch of dirt. She experienced every thud and thump in triplicate and held fast to her expanding midsection.

"Your message didn't say which friend you stayed with last night," Barton said. "Or should I not ask, considering?" Barton had grown more comfortable teasing Bridget about the pregnancy lately, having accepted early on that she must have had good reasons for keeping the father a secret.

"I was with Lucinda," she lied, "the waitress I work with. She's havin' a tough time with that nasty boyfriend, and she thought if I was there he might not smack her around."

"Using a pregnant woman as a shield. Nice. But you tell Lucinda

I'll show that boyfriend what a real bruisin' is. She just needs to say the word."

Bridget smiled. Her dad had always been her hero, and his status was well earned. But his chivalrous offer made her feel guilty about using Lucinda as a cover story. Of course, she'd feel a whole lot worse if Lucinda showed up at the diner with another black eye today. "I'll tell her, Daddy. She's a sweet lady."

"That's what they used to say about you." He reached over and put a hand on her shoulder. "You know I don't believe all the stories, right?"

Bridget laid her hand on his. She wanted to tell him the truth, but how could she? Her dad had a habit of talking a blue streak after a few drinks. Ironically, he kept a picture in the living room of her and Grady, commemorating Grady's first visit to Field Diner. On the day of the photo, Grady had posed with all the employees and customers. He'd kissed the drooling babies, let his hand linger in the palms of the drooling moms, and made a speech that soared so gracefully from platitude to platitude that everyone felt they'd been treated to a choreographed ballet. All the while, he'd rested his rust-brown eyes on Bridget's green ones. Before leaving, he'd sent Sam back in to get her number under the pretense of using her for a campaign poster. She'd resisted, but when Grady had lowered his car window and smiled, she'd jotted the number down and crossed her fingers.

Two days later, the phone had rung and Bridget's life had changed forever.

"Don't worry, Daddy. It'll all sort itself out."

"I have an inkling you're protecting someone, and I sort of admire you for it. I just hope you know what you're doing."

Her conscience clenched as she swallowed a mouthful of familiar dust. "You know I love you, right, Daddy?"

"Sure do, kiddo."

The truck lurched to a stop, and Bridget got out and hurried up the porch steps.

Barton called after her. "Hey, Bridge, I'll be home late tonight. Closing a deal with some good ol' boys over a couple o' drinks."

She waved, only half absorbing what he said. Barton Perkins lived and breathed insurance commissions, but had she known it would be the last time they'd speak, save for five incriminating syllables, she might have paid more attention.

CHAPTER 8

Few places yanked one into the here and now like the cold, commanding exterior of a hospital emergency room. But when I pulled up, I was whisked to the past. Flashes pierced my eyes, and shouts of "It's his sister! The Haiku Twin!" and "Jack Perkins's sister!" assaulted my ears. As I raised an arm to ward off the intrusion, I imagined what the crowd must have looked like the day Jack and I had come home from the hospital in the arms of Grandpa Barton. So many pictures had been snapped of us, it was a wonder any piece of our souls remained. Those leeches had sucked every coo, wince, and tear from the tragic Haiku Twins and splashed the images across their full-color rags for at least a month. But who could blame them? We were big news and they had papers to sell. It wasn't every day that healthy twins were born to a brain-dead mother who'd been shot weeks earlier by the man rumored to be the father.

As I strode up the long entryway, I cursed my brother, who sought this kind of attention regularly. While our disrupted debut into the world had caused me to spend my life hiding behind a lens, stealing only the souls of the dead, Jack had reveled in becoming one with the flash. In his eyes, a moment without attention was a moment unfulfilled by its potential. Even this—a visit to an old man lying in a hospital—was fair game for political exploitation.

The double doors of the hospital opened, but not before reflecting another twenty flashes getting a shot of this Haiku Twin's backside. At least I'd worn my flattering jeans.

On the elevator to the intensive care unit, a bulky nurse kept sneaking glances at me in the shiny bronzed doors. I let her look to her heart's content and almost escaped without comment, but as the doors parted to release me from the temporary viewing box, her restraint failed. "I met him once, you know."

Okay, that was a new one. My interest was piqued, and for a split second I thought she'd mistaken me for someone else.

"Who?" I said.

"Your father. Grady McLemore."

I sneered at the cherry-cheeked caretaker, but it went unnoticed because she was gazing into space with a look of distant wonder, as if Elvis himself had descended through the elevator shaft.

"So handsome and sincere," she said. "I do believe he personally related to each and every person he met. Looked me right in the eye, he did, and said he wanted to help. Not just me, of course, but everyone, you know what I mean?"

"Gosh," I said, putting on my best expression of mindless awe, "how'd that work out for you?"

The nurse returned to earth and shot me a reproving glance. "You look like your mother," she said, turning haughty. "But your brother, he definitely favors the senator."

"Senatorial *candidate*," I said, stepping into the hallway. "And you know who else looks like him? The son of the waitress the next county over and the one over from that. Seems there's a whole bunch of baby McLemores straggling through life without their baby-daddy."

The nurse shook her head in disgust, her chins following along as the elevator doors closed.

I turned around to see my brother glaring at me.

"Why do you do that?" he said.

"What?"

"Piss off the voting public."

"Are people ever just people to you, Jack?"

"Seriously, Janie, why would you say something like that?"

"I don't like them putting the man who murdered our mother on a pedestal. Let them think he was out sticking it to every waitress in the state, for all I care."

"Hanging out with cops is doing wonders for your language, Sis."

"For Christ's sake, it's been thirty years, and that nurse is still getting off on a handshake with the guy."

"Whatever. I don't understand you."

"And yet I totally get you. Shallowness must be easier to decode."

Jack turned and marched down the hall. I followed his strides that dwarfed mine.

"How is he?"

"Not good," Jack said, fiddling with his phone. "Try not to upset him."

I scowled at my brother's back, but as we entered the room, my expression softened. There was Grandpa Barton, looking small next to the loud, dinging machines monitoring his every shallow breath. Dr. Kyle, a longtime family friend, stood over him, then turned to us. "Hi, Janie. I'm sorry to tell you, but Barton's condition has progressed to full pneumonia. We need to put him in a medically induced coma to get him through this rough patch."

My heart both filled and hollowed, some dichotomous combination of sympathy for Grandpa Barton and resentment for the bitter irony of the situation. Thirty years ago at this same hospital, Grandpa had consented to keeping my mother in a coma in order to save his grandchildren. And now, look at him—as hopeless and helpless as his daughter had been. I sighed at the transparency of his skin. When had his face gotten so gaunt? His perpetual tan usually compensated for his lack of fat, coating the gray pallor of grief that seethed beneath his constant smile. But pneumonia had finally defeated the sun's mask, exposing life's tolls as well as Grandpa's true age. While the rest of the world used the base ten system of numbers to figure their age, Grandpa Barton had always used base death: *Let's see, Bridget was twenty-five when she died and that's been thirty years, so that makes me seventy-seven.*

"What's the prognosis?" I asked.

"Hard to say. He'll have to be pretty strong to fight this one off." The words hung heavy in the air, because Dr. Kyle knew as well as anyone that Barton Perkins was a man who raced tractors for fun and could single-handedly push trucks out of the mud.

"We need him around a while longer, Dr. Kyle. You do whatever you have to."

"Absolutely," Jack said, looking up from his phone. "As long as the end result isn't twins."

Both Dr. Kyle and I supplied looks to let Jack know how inappropriate his comment was. The smile disappeared. Guess that one wouldn't be going into the quip bank of his mental teleprompter.

Dr. Kyle stopped once more on his way out of the room and took in the sight of my brother and me. "Jackie and Janie," he said wistfully. "Good to see you two together. As dark as those days were when you kids were born, there was so much hope here at the hospital, so much goodwill." He gestured to Grandpa. "Barton was a big part of that. And to tell you the truth, if it weren't for you two coming into the world the day Bridget left us, I don't think he would have survived. You gave him a reason to continue. Maybe you can do the same for him now."

Dr. Kyle sniffed back tears, as did I.

Filling the vacated space next to the bed, I took Grandpa's rough hand in mine. He didn't stir, but my memories did. Not memories I actually possessed, but ones I'd formed by making him tell me the same stories year after year. On that long-ago day when Jack and I entered the world, he'd been forced to name us. He'd never much cared about things like that, but when compelled by the fretful staff to come up with something, he couldn't see the point in changing our names from what the nurses had been calling us: Fetus Jane and Fetus John. And thus we became Jane and John, which morphed into Janie and Jackie as soon as Grandpa's sister got her hands on us. Of course, we'd been given our mother's last name— Perkins. My brother had once toyed with taking the name of his alleged father, but when he found his car keyed the next morning, he'd abandoned the idea—and I'd paid for a new paint job.

Grandpa Barton opened his eyes. "Janie," he said, his voice as soft and fleeting as butterfly wings.

"Yes, Grandpa? I'm here. So is Jack. How are you feeling?"

He squeezed my hand, though the force was negligible.

"The words," he whispered. "Not sure I got them right."

The rapid blinking of his eyes disconcerted me. He didn't seem like himself.

"What words, Grandpa?"

"Bridget's words. Last words."

"You got them right, Grandpa. They were *Find Grady*. And you did."

Hadn't been real hard to *Find Grady*, as he'd been lying twelve feet away, the proverbial smoking gun in hand.

"Mighta been . . ." Grandpa drew a labored breath. ". . . *find Grady hater*."

I pulled back so I could see the frail, cracked lips of this fragile man. Was he delirious? Drugged? For three decades, he'd sworn my

mother's last words were *Find Grady*. She'd been accusing her murderer, just like in the movies. I turned to an orderly who'd entered.
His protuberant incisors and blank eyes gave the impression of a
dull, hungry shark and did not fill me with confidence, but I had
no one else to ask.

"How medicated is he? Does he know what he's saying?"

The orderly shrugged. "I dunno. They all talk crazy. The pneumonia stuff alone makes 'em sputter nonsense half the time."

Pneumonia *stuff*? I slayed him with my eyes and clutched
Grandpa's hand more tightly.

"Grandpa, what do you mean? Why would she say *Find Grady
hater*?"

He closed his eyes and his hand went limp. I cursed myself for
wasting time with the orderly. After a few attempts to stir Grandpa,
I gave up and rested his hand back on the narrow stretcher before
the orderly wheeled away the one person who had actually stayed
around for Jack and me our whole lives.

A nagging thought kept knocking around my head: If Grandpa
slipped quietly into death from the coma, would his last words
prove to be the same as his daughter's? And if he was right, mightn't
those words change the narrative of my whole life?

CHAPTER 9

Bridget Perkins, 30 Years, 9 Hours Ago

Bridget threw her overnight bag on her twin bed. The pilfered hotel key slipped out onto the pink quilt she'd had since she was fifteen. Her mom had helped her choose it a few weeks before being diagnosed with ovarian cancer, and Bridget knew she would keep it forever. *What if I don't like it when it's in my room?* Bridget had asked as she and her mother had stood in line. *Why don't you live with it for a while and see what you think,* her mother had said. *If it's not right, you can add your own touches to make it perfect.* Bridget had smiled, already excited to customize the purchase. She'd spent hours laboring over it with small, cross-stitched roses along the edges. *But remember one thing, dear,* her mother had added with a wink, *it's not the same with a man. Once you bring him home, there's no changing him, so make sure he's going to be just right for your home.*

Bridget scooped up the key, smiling at the memory. She laid it on the tall table next to her recent clay project. It was darker in theme than most of her pieces, but it was turning out well, and she sensed it would be one of her favorites, perhaps even her most haunting.

She pulled out her uniform and changed quickly, then retrieved her newest journal from its hiding spot. She hoped one day to share her journals with her future daughter, but at the same time she was woefully ashamed of how the twins had been conceived. The journals might have to remain a secret.

Grabbing the jet-black pen she favored, she wrote twelve words, then taped the key chain to the page with a romantic finality, remembering her mom's perfectly pressed roses. Daddy had framed and matted Mom's best work in the dining room, and when the extended Perkins clan celebrated Thanksgiving in there, he always raised a toast to his late beloved and said, "Elizabeth, you pressed your love upon my heart as surely as you pressed those roses." It always made Bridget well up.

Looking now at the ostentatious key chain and its fancy *A*, she slammed the journal shut, unsure if the mother would be proud of the daughter's pressed work.

With the journal back in place, Bridget left for work, unaware of what a difference her final entry would make decades later.

CHAPTER 10

"I don't know what he meant, Jack," I said with controlled annoyance. My brother and I were alone in a private area while awaiting word on Grandpa Barton. The thought of a life without him left me feeling like the vague outline of a person. "It sounded like he wasn't sure about Mom's final words. Probably carried that with him all these years, tossing them around in his head. For God's sake, does it ever end?"

Jack looked at me like I was the slow kid in the back of the class. "Uh, it's not like there's ever been any doubt about who shot Mom. Grady admitted it. Besides, we have your photos to back up Grady's story now. What'd you do with them, by the way?"

"None of your business." I couldn't bring myself to admit that I'd taken his words to heart and brought them to Sophie for analysis.

"Well, just so you recall, there was plenty of circumstantial evidence to back up the presence of a third person in the living room that night."

"Same evidence could have proved that any person had entered through the back door anytime the day before. Leaves on the floor? A mud stain on the rug? Please."

"Grady's getting out soon, either way."

"Great. Planning to take him on the campaign trail with you like some kind of warped surrogate father?"

"It's not like I thumbed through the books of available father figures and blindly chose. I took what I got, whether you accept it or not." Jack somehow managed to slurp down coffee, argue, and text all at the same time.

Suddenly I couldn't stand being around him, and the nausea that had threatened since they took Grandpa away came on full force. "I've got to get out of here," I said, rising. "Call me as soon as there's word."

Before he could protest, I took off. Let him deal with it for now. As I rode the elevator down, a text came in about a crime scene three miles away. When the elevator opened, I considered my exit routes. Even though the reporters had surely grown bored and departed, I sneaked out the more discreet back door.

Three spots down from my Explorer, an old man in a wheelchair was struggling to lower himself over a curb because the concrete ramp was blocked off for repairs. I checked the time and figured the smelly body on Halter Street would stay dead another ten minutes while I lent a hand.

"Help you, sir?"

The small man looked up. He reminded me of Truman Capote if he'd been a few degrees closer to normal. Round eyes on a puffy face, a permanently puckered mouth topping a stodgy body, and a curious look that seemed a combination of polite and bashful.

"Oh, my," he said, a bit taken aback and quick to avert his eyes, "I would be much obliged, but I couldn't accept your help without confessing that I know who you are."

"Please tell me you're not a reporter," I said as I grabbed the handles of his chair and leaned him back to ease him over the curb. It was tough, but I'd done too many push-ups in early morning hours to let a wheelchair defeat me.

"Oh, no, no," he said. "But I am the uncle of a reporter, and she mentioned to me that your grandfather was here. How is he doing?"

"Are we off the record?"

"Oh, quite, quite," he said, amused by my formality.

"I'm sure word will get out anyway. They've put him in a coma to help him through the pneumonia. I just hope it's not disorienting for him." I struggled with the final inches of curb and brought the chair to rest in the parking lot.

"I'm so sorry," he said.

"Me, too. But he's a strong guy." I blinked away a tear before the man could turn his head. "Where's your niece? Is she the one picking you up?"

"Yes, I finished up early and she was running some errands. She'll be here soon. Told her I'd wait there in the shade." He pointed to the far corner of the lot.

"I'll help you," I said.

"Normally, I wouldn't dream of asking a young lady, but a push would be lovely. I hurt my shoulder last month and I'm not sure I can negotiate this terrain." He shook his head and guffawed. "Never thought I'd look at flat pavement and worry about negotiating it!" He had himself quite a laugh at his own expense. "I was in the war and everything."

I felt bad, but I didn't have time for a long conversation, so I ignored the questions he was hoping for, the ones that would take him on a stroll down memory lane to first loves, horrid battles, and grand victories. "Happy to give you a lift," I said.

"Don't you have places you need to be?"

"Yes, but it's nice to spend a minute among the living first."

He peeked back. "You spend time amongst the dead, dear?"

"I'm a crime scene photographer."

He clapped his hands and let out a bellow of excitement. "Ha! I was the battalion photographer in my unit way back when. Could I trouble you with a question?"

"Sure," I said, breathing harder as the parking lot seemed to suck up the edges of his wheels with every spin.

"I'd like to take some of my old war photos and make them digital or what-have-you. You know, put them on a doodad of some sort."

"You need a scanner and a flash drive."

"Mmm," he said. "Okay."

"Do you know what a scanner is?"

"Is it something I could get at a thrift store?"

"I doubt it."

"I'm hoping to surprise my grandnephews. For Veterans Day."

"Can't your niece do it? She must have a scanner at her office."

His head fell toward his chest. "She tries her best and has good intentions, but you know how it is. Life gets in the way."

I let his lamentations wash over me and wondered if Grandpa Barton had felt that way about me. I promised him last month that I'd get some branches trimmed from the big hickory at the top of the driveway so he wouldn't climb up and kill himself. Until this moment, it had completely slipped my mind. I swallowed my guilt. "I'll tell you what. You live around here?"

"I'm staying at the Aberdeen Hotel while I get some back treatments. My niece invited me to stay, but her house is three stories with no bedroom on the main floor. It was easier for everyone if I stayed at the Aberdeen. Lovely place, very quaint."

"You have your photos with you?"

"They're at the hotel. About twenty-five of them I felt were worthy for the kids. Don't want to bore them to death, after all."

Grandpa Barton had often worried he was doing the same when he told family stories, but I'd never been bored. Suddenly, a rush of goodwill washed over me.

"I'll come by the Aberdeen tomorrow and scan your photos. Won't take me long. Will that work?"

"My dear, it would be a miracle. But let me bring the photos to you and save you a trip."

"It's no problem. I'm in the car all the time, anyway."

"You are such a saint."

"You can thank Grandpa Barton. I'll do it in his honor."

"In my prayers tonight, I shall give you and your Grandpa Barton many thanks. I'm Humphrey Banfield, by the way. Everyone calls me Hump."

"What's your room number at the Aberdeen, Hump?"

"I'm in one of the private cottages. Cottage five."

I found a shady place to deposit Hump and felt a small weight lift from my conscience. "I need to run, but I'll see you around five thirty at the Aberdeen tomorrow, okay?"

"Sounds delightful."

I programmed the appointment into my phone. Hump waved as I drove away, and I couldn't help but notice a satisfied grin punctuating his round face.

CHAPTER 11

Early the next morning, I stopped in to check on Grandpa. I held his hand and talked, the words reaching at least his ears, maybe deeper. My cell phone buzzed with two incoming texts. The first was from my lab friend, who characterized her results from the photo analysis as bad news/good news, although I read it as bad news/worse news. First, she'd verified that the mailed photos were genuine, not manipulated into existence by some bipolar lunatic with a hankering for haikus, and second, the fingerprints hadn't matched anyone in the system. She considered the latter conclusion a plus, but to me, it just meant some bipolar lunatic hadn't been caught yet.

The next text was from Sophie Andricola: *Come now, please. I have created something that may or may not be to your unwanted expectation.* Both promising and dire—a trick Sophie probably pulled off all the time without even trying. I texted back that I'd be over in half an hour. After kissing Grandpa on the forehead and promising to return soon, I headed to the elevators. When the doors opened, out stepped Detective Wexler with two coffees in hand.

"Wexler, what are you doing here?"

"Just finished a case two blocks over. Nicholls said you were here, so I figured you might appreciate a morning jolt."

I gratefully accepted the quality beverage that put my morning libations to shame. "Wexler, you are the man."

"And you the lady," he said matter-of-factly.

"As my brother would tell you, I'm no lady; I'm just a drag on a campaign."

"I doubt that. He plays off the twin angle every chance he gets."

I didn't hide my surprise at Wexler's sudden interest in my brother's campaign habits, and he didn't shy away from continuing.

"Did you know there's an unfortunate number of babies born to mothers like yours, but you two are the only twins?"

"Curiosity killed the cat, Wexler."

"This cat's just trying to figure you out . . . Perkins."

There was that tingle again.

"Have you heard from Sophie yet?" he said.

"I'm on my way there now."

"I'd like to go with you."

"Why?"

"Just a sense I get and always trust."

"But you don't even—"

"I concede everything you're about to say. You only know me professionally and I learned most of your family history yesterday. But I have this trip wire inside of me, mostly dormant and quiet, until it's not. Every so often, it vibrates."

"And you react?"

"Wouldn't you?"

"This wire—it's related to me?"

"This time."

I assessed the museum piece before me, wondering if I'd ever crack its protective glass.

"You're wired differently, Wexler. That's for sure."

He gazed back straightforwardly, having long ago embraced whatever made him tick, and awaited his invite.

"Let's go," I said.

CHAPTER 12

Wexler offered to drive. I could see why. His Lexus was immaculate, not a cat hair or used tissue in sight. Not even a loose thread from one of his tailored suits caught in the grooves of the floor mats.

"What was your case this morning?" I asked.

"Too bad you weren't there. Dizzy the Drug Lord's mother."

"Mrs. Dizzy bought it, too?"

"Neighbors called it in for the smell. Two hundred fifty pounds of fun in a muumuu dress and ginger wig. She was supposed to serve as a warning to Dizzy a few days earlier, but I guess he failed to get the message."

"Yeah, corpses don't come with a blinking red light."

"You know what bugged me the most, though?"

"What?"

"She was in a recliner and hadn't reclined. There she was, a TV remote balanced on the arm of the chair, surrounded by cheese cracker crumbs and beer cans, and she hadn't even reclined."

"I'm with you. Who sits in a La-Z-Boy and doesn't recline?"

"Nobody."

Had I been there, I would have been tempted to yank the wood handle and put her in a more comfortable position, but the sudden shift would have messed with her softening body, maybe even melted it into oblivion. I knew what I would have done, though, had the coiled knot of desire in my gut grabbed hold. It would have been too tempting to ignore. I would have grabbed a book off Mrs. Dizzy's shelf, maybe a copy of *The Five People You Meet in Heaven*, and set it on her lap. Her head, surely sunken forward, could easily have passed for someone reading an inspirational tome. I'd have captured it at a forty-five-degree angle from above. A premium addition to my collection—and a far better ending for Mrs. Dizzy.

"Sounds like one of the gangs has gone rogue," I said. "Thought they had an unwritten code that included scruples like not shooting a drug guy's mom."

"Task force thinks it's this new guy in town, Rocko Mania."

"Professional wrestlers taking over the drug game now?"

"Why not?"

"You ever wonder how many other people are lying dead and unnoticed in their homes, their absence only noticeable by an odor?"

"Not really."

"There's this cat, Percival, that climbs the fire escape and taps my window for food. He'd probably be my only hope if I keeled over tonight. I'd be lying there for a week until he shed five pounds and the neighbors would finally realize that *that photo lady* had stopped feeding him."

"It would take a cat longer than a week to lose five pounds," Wexler said with no hint of sarcasm. "There are mice around, you know. You could be lying there for a month."

"You wouldn't stop by in a whole month to bring me coffee, Wexler?"

He glanced at me. "I might."

He almost ducked while parking beneath Sophie's encroaching trees. "Is she as weird as they say?"

"Weirder, and a tad macabre."

"Excellent."

Sophie opened the front door before we reached it. Dispensing with common courtesies, she nodded at Wexler, then aimed her eyes at me. "Upstairs. I stayed up all night."

I glanced at Wexler, suddenly doubting my decision to bring him along. Should I allow him to witness the moment when Sophie's interpretation slapped me across the face?

He met my eyes and his calm confidence gave me strength, but who knew what the hell his trip wire was doing back there? Either way, I decided his presence was a plus.

"My studio," Sophie said, leading us in and gesturing to a tight spiral staircase, its wrought-iron balusters an unexpected tribute to the male form in all its naked glory. I hadn't noticed it on my first visit but as I climbed the stairs, cavorting men with metallic members accompanied my ascent. When I completed one turn and faced Wexler from above, I didn't know whether to resent or be amused by the grin on his lips as he appreciated my discomfort.

Sophie's high-ceiling, exposed-beam studio with ample skylights made me forget about the orgy in the balusters. A lovely space—half of it open, inviting, and pristine, and the other half crammed with sophisticated lab equipment, printers, books, and art supplies— probably a good reflection of Sophie's mind. The place gave off a warm, inviting vibe. But that ended when Sophie dimmed the lights and hit the switch on a projector. The moment I saw what she'd done, all logic and functioning brain circuitry ceased to exist. She had merged the two photos into one seamless image. Staring back at me was my dying mother, her eyes huge and open, in unreserved shock, lying in a near life-size, 3-D rendering of my childhood living room. It was only an artificial projection on a wall—of an image I'd already seen—but my jaw still went slack as I experienced the uncanny sensation that I'd traveled through time and landed in my own past—on the one night I'd least like to experience. Wexler instinctively inched up behind me and placed a supportive hand on my lower back.

Sophie had scanned, digitized, and enhanced the images to a stunning degree, and while she'd mentioned extrapolation, she'd failed to convey the scale and depth. With significant effort, I tore my eyes from my mother's and noticed that Sophie's work had made the hazy bumps on the bottom of the second photo both prominent and definable. I just wasn't sure I wanted to know how she'd defined them.

Protruding two inches from the wall, fine strands of twine spread out like a fan. They ran from the center of my childhood living room and extended downward, beyond the borders of the original shots. Each strand—and there were dozens of them—was held fast to the wall with a pin. It reminded me of the string method the forensics guys used to analyze blood spatter, creating awesome mini-macramé projects that revealed the distance and direction blood had traveled to its eventual destination. In this case, however, Sophie wasn't interested in blood.

Between the bottom of the projected illusion and its newly imagined baseline several feet below—where the twine was ultimately pinned—remained an empty space crying out to be populated, to be filled in with the missing pieces of whatever was causing the bumps along the base of the combined images.

"Accounting for the warped dimensions of a photo shot at such a close angle," Sophie said, "its slight downward trajectory, and the measurements of the room available in the county records, I considered multiple human body ratios—such as, from the bottom of the nose to the outside corner of the eye is equal to the length of the ear, that sort of thing—and I analyzed the available statistics from thirty years ago based on the Bertillon system of anthropometrics. From that, I was able to complete the picture for you. Twice."

Despite Sophie's original protests, she apparently did use that arcane skill known as *thinking*.

"First version," she continued, "as it came to me without preconceived notions, and then, incorporating the information and possibilities you shared on your visit. The results are behind you."

Wexler and I turned to the large, sheet-covered canvases behind us and waited, assuming Sophie would do the big reveal. But for all her peculiarities, she wasn't one for drama.

"Whenever you're ready," she said quietly.

I stepped toward the painting on the left, the echo of my boot heels against the floor emphasizing the vastness of the studio.

"That's the first one," Sophie said.

I took a breath and grabbed the sheet by the upper corner, pulling it off in a diagonal fashion, wishing I were alone, while simultaneously wishing I were not here at all. I sucked in a breath at the sight of Sophie's work, but refrained from gasping aloud, hoping that the twitch of my shoulders hadn't betrayed my alarm.

According to Sophie's rendering, Bridget Perkins's eyes that night had been gazing at a broad-shouldered, tall man lying in a crumpled mess on the floor in a perfectly pressed white shirt. No blood stained him, although the accumulating pool seeping from my mother's head had branched out into what looked like accusing fingers pointing in his direction. His glossy, brown hair lay perfectly styled in a longer cut than would be deemed professional today. The merest flecks of gray framed the temples and sideburns. Unbelievably, Sophie had sketched a man lying on his side, as if the photo had been taken from above and behind his right ear. You could see the brow, the top of the cheekbone, and the jaw.

She got all this from a few smudges along the base of an old photo? I forced my eyes away and glared at Sophie, knowing she would see anger, if not rage, in my expression. She remained utterly, irritatingly neutral.

I turned back. Allowing one inhalation and exhalation, I braced myself for the second portrait, already suspecting what I'd see. As I lifted the sheet, Sophie became quite animated in her description, almost defensive.

"I used my knowledge of forensic facial reconstruction," she said, "the principles of facial symmetry and lack thereof, incorporating what I could from the body dimensions, and created one possible face."

I removed the sheet completely. A striking, albeit distorted version of Grady McLemore's face filled my visual space. I swallowed hard, my jaw and neck so tight, I almost hoped they'd cut off circulation to my brain.

This time, Wexler placed a firm hand on my shoulder. "You okay, Janie?"

"No," I said, spinning to Sophie with venom in my eyes. "What did you do, look up the case? Search for old images of Grady McLemore?"

"No," she said, as if I'd asked if she wanted honey with her tea.

"What are you trying to say with this? That the second photo shows Grady McLemore lying on the floor, unconscious, when the picture was taken?"

"I'm not saying anything. The photo is."

"Impossible."

"Why?"

I pointed accusingly at Grady's image. "Because he's the only one who saw her like this. He made her like this! Unless my grandfather took time to snap a keepsake photo before trying to save his daughter's life."

The more I ranted, the calmer Sophie grew, until she somehow ended up seated on a chair carved from a burnished log with spindly branches for arms.

"You take crime scene photos, Janie," she said. "You notice when things are askew."

I felt Wexler gazing at me as surely as I felt myself melting into a puddle of denial and victimhood.

"You're trained to look at crime scenes with a cold, hard eye," she continued, "to see things clinically and to photograph what matters and what's out of place. Your eyes become the jury's eyes. Your story becomes the prosecutor's story and the defense's albatross, or maybe their blessing."

"What does that have to do with anything?"

"You're not looking at this as a crime scene. How could you? You see nothing beyond your dying mother on the floor, beyond your life inside her, and the story that led to this point. You can't see anything in those photos except your future without her. That's why you're denying what's right in front of you."

"I wouldn't miss an entire body lying on a floor. Those were somebody's fingers, or a smudge on the lens. How in the world do you get a whole person out of a smudge?"

"And how could you hope to focus on the outer details of an image when the eyes of your mother call to you like a maternal siren? There's such clarity in them."

Clarity? Was it supposed to comfort me that my mother was fully aware of her impending death? I blinked away hot tears while the smudge savant continued. "You brought these photos to me because you knew something was off. All I did was rip away the blanket you were too scared to look under." She leaned forward but remained seated, nonthreatening. "In a way, we just handed the defense its magical moment in the sun. If Grady McLemore is lying on the floor, and someone else was in the room taking this picture within moments of the fired bullet, then there *was* a third person in the room, a person who for some reason wanted a picture."

"A trophy," I said, my voice cracking despite its whispering tone.

The next few minutes whooshed by. Despite the conversation's potential importance, I couldn't recall a single word exchanged between the three of us. When it was time to leave, Wexler led me out the door, but I stepped back to have a final word with Sophie.

"You're wrong about one thing," I said.

"It wouldn't be the first time."

"I don't look at crime scenes with a cold, hard eye. I look at them my way."

"And what way is that?"

"However I want them to be."

She cocked her head as she contemplated my words, the snake on her neck wriggling for an instant. When she narrowed her eyes and nodded, I felt she understood.

As I stepped into Wexler's car, pixels swirled in my mind, the enlarged ones that had created Sophie's magical movie set on a wall, and the ones she had inferred to breathe life into the image of Grady McLemore.

"A trophy," I uttered again without thinking. Wexler knew to stay quiet. If the Haiku Killer had been at my home that night, and had considered the mess of a situation another notch in his belt, then maybe he did take a photo to commemorate it. Was that his weak spot? Serial killers usually chose something physical—an article of clothing, a cutting of hair, or even a body part—to hold, smell, stroke, or manipulate, something to invoke the visceral sensations of their deeds. If the photo was his trophy, would he be so demented as to mail it to the daughter of the victim? Were all of his victims' relatives receiving mementos of their own? And God forbid, was he still active, minus the haikus?

No one ever knew whether he kept trophies, but I knew as well as anybody how carelessly crime scenes could be treated, how even the lowly photographer could enter a scene, rewrite it, and never tell a soul. The police could have missed a skin scraping or a clipped fingernail—or the one thing that could surely be taken without leaving evidence: a photo. Its only evidence was itself.

And now I owned it.

CHAPTER 13

Janie and Jack Perkins, Age 10

"That's where Mom was shot, you know," Jack said, pointing to a spot on the green-and-maroon Persian rug. "Grandpa was talkin' to Aunt Louise about it."

Janie stared at the spot on the rug. Sure didn't look like a place for a mom to get shot. It looked like a place to lie down with a cozy pillow and snuggle up with a book. In fact, Janie had done just that on more than one occasion when Grandpa had a fire going.

She interrupted Jack as he landed a plane on the rug's green stripe. "So where's the blood then?"

"The what?"

"Mom's blood. In Grandpa's movies, there's lots of blood when people die."

"Ha! You're not supposed to watch those movies. I'm gonna tell."

"Then I'll tell about you sneakin' extra cookies for school."

Jack scowled. Even though he was better than Janie at most things, she always seemed smarter when it came to getting away with stuff.

"The blood's under the rug, stupid."

Janie backed away, as if believing there was nothing between her bare feet and her mother's corpse but a few shreds of wool.

Jack landed another plane and crashed it into one that had inexplicably parked in the middle of the runway.

"Planes park in hangars, Jack. You're such an idiot."

"Shut up."

Janie looked back and forth between Jack's planes and the spot on the rug where her mother's blood was stuck to the underside. "Have you seen it?" she asked quietly.

Jack turned around slowly, realizing his advantage. "Course I have. Who hasn't?"

"Me," she said. "I mean, I knew it was there and all, but—"

"No, you didn't. I just told you. You're totally scared of it."

"Scared? I'm not scared of stupid old blood. I scrape my knee all the time. And I squash a hundred more spiders than you."

"Spiders don't bleed," he said, and Janie couldn't recollect her spider victims clearly enough to refute his claim.

She crossed her arms and scowled, desperate for a retort but coming up short.

"Go ahead," Jack said. "If you're not scared, why don't you look at it?" The grin on his face screamed victory—his sister would be moving furniture and rolling back that rug in a matter of seconds.

Janie froze in place a moment more, steeling herself for a task she'd never considered before. At her hesitation, Jack shrieked with excitement. He rolled back until he was balanced on his buttocks, his hands grasping the underside of his thighs while his feet kicked wildly in the air.

"Go ahead! Look at it! Look at it!" he shouted. "Unless you're too chicken." He rolled forward again and pointed at his sister. "Chicken, chicken, chicken! Can't even look at a little blood."

"Can, too. Just don't know if I can move that chair by myself."

Jack couldn't have risen any faster. He rushed over to the velvety chair whose thick legs left indentations in the carpet. He scraped it mercilessly across the floor and shoved it against the wall. "There. Go ahead."

He crossed his arms, grinned, and raised his eyebrows so high that he looked like a badly carved jack-o'-lantern.

Janie sucked in a gulp of courage and stared down the rug like an enemy. Its patterns took on a movement all their own, the lines crisscrossing and dancing until she was sure that something alive—or dead—was rising up from the thick wool stitches. A deep red stripe ran into specks of the green *S*-swirls until it all formed a nauseating mishmash of pigment. She wanted to look away, but the gyrating, pulsating thing on the carpet wouldn't release its hold on her. In her mind, it assumed a three-dimensional shape, twirling up like a genie and forming a garish apparition that rose almost to the ceiling. She followed its eyes. They were nothing like human eyes, more like vacuous holes of shadowy evil. They drew her own eyes far away from that hideous spot below. Perhaps the specter would keep going and take her mother's blood with it. Perhaps it would spare the daughter. And just as she grew certain that she could make the blood disappear, her brother knocked her to the side. She lost her footing and fell on the carpet. Jack's voice penetrated her haze. "You're such a baby!"

A frenzied expression had replaced Jack's haughty one as he rolled back the carpet, desperate to show his sister the spot. And despite her fear, Janie knew she'd look—and never forget.

Jack got to within a millimeter of the claimed exhibition. "There! It's right there! Go ahead! Look!" And he flipped the carpet back in one fell swoop, hoisting the accumulated dust and making Janie choke and sputter as she gazed at a perfectly normal plank of wood flooring.

No blood. No stain. Her brother had tricked her.

"Ha!" he screamed. "You were so scared! Are you really that stupid? There used to be a different floor here, you idiot. They weren't gonna keep bloody old boards around. I don't even know where she really landed."

Janie fled toward the back door, the one that led to the deck. Despite the expansiveness of the room, the walls closed in on her and she needed to escape. But Jack got to the door a split second before her and blocked her exit.

"Let me out! Let me out!" she screamed, turning back to make sure the thing hadn't rematerialized. Despite no evidence of its presence, she felt it looming, ready to swoop down to take her to the place where it had stowed her mother's blood.

"Let me out, Jack!" She clawed at him wildly, reaching for the handle but denied at every turn by her more athletic brother.

"Not until you admit you were scared!" He laughed and teased her by allowing quick chances for the doorknob before cutting her off again.

"It's coming, Jack! It's coming! Let me out!"

She shrieked then. A painful, screeching wail that must have penetrated Jack's head like a dagger. When Janie sucked in an agitated breath to let out another, Jack stepped aside, a panicked realization growing on his face. Had he gone too far?

Janie screamed again, each howl layering atop the other. Jack pulled the door wide open, but it was too late. Janie was transfixed by the void between the carpet and the high ceiling, hyperventilating until she flung her head forward, fell to her knees, and got sick all over the floor and Jack's shoes.

The long silence was punctuated only by Janie's rattled gasps for air. Still on her knees, Janie lifted a haunting face to her brother. Her green eyes, shaded by dark brows and lashes, threatened a lifetime of pain as they seemed to hang in the air, detached from her body. "Don't you ever trap me in a room again, Jack Perkins."

Jack steadied his breathing and refused to relinquish victory. "You coulda gone out the front door."

She reared up and, from her low vantage point, launched a fist toward his face, catching him off guard with a solid strike to the jaw. It was the first time she'd ever hit someone and it didn't feel good. But she didn't regret it. Jack never locked her in a room again—and he helped her clean up the mess.

CHAPTER 14

I cursed myself again for wearing a dress. Why did I choose something uncomfortable for a situation that was bound to be unnerving under the best of circumstances? And why hadn't Emily Post ever advised what to wear while visiting your alleged father after having visited exactly *never* while he served time for murdering your pregnant mother? Then again, even Anna Wintour might have been stumped by that one.

I'd gone with the stupid outfit because I wanted to feel professional and grown-up, but now, covering the last few miles to Everly State Prison, I felt the zipper carving a Frankenstein tattoo along my spine. And the sick feeling I'd battled all afternoon felt like a hernia ready to burst. That was as good an analogy for Grady McLemore's existence as any: a massive, hibernating presence that gained advantage when I felt weak.

When Jack and I were little, Grandpa Barton hadn't held back on the particulars of our mother's demise, so Grady had not only become our personal Boogie Man, but something crueler, because he didn't become a childhood memory—he stayed real. The terrors ingrained in a child went deeper than any anxiety acquired as an adult. The fear bred itself right into growing bones, mellowed into hatred, and became part of the DNA. In my case, it laced the edges of every cell, like heroin and equally addictive.

The prison came into view, propped against an artificial-looking sky that seemed to reflect the pigments of the dying leaves on the autumn trees. Everly hardly looked like a prison. More like a Civil War relic, barricaded solely to keep graffiti vandals out, not murderers in. With each rotation of my underinflated tires, my desire to turn around grew stronger. I gave in—almost—by pulling over twenty feet from the entrance.

Lowering my head against the steering wheel, I let its pressure relieve the pounding in my brain. This couldn't be worse than the nightmare scenarios I faced on the job—an emaciated child tied up in a closet, found three days too late, or the starving dogs with burns on their skin that looked healthy in comparison to their methed-out masters. For God's sake, I could face one lousy politician, a man who hid his pregnant girlfriend from the world while preaching morality to *the people* whose feeble voices could only be amplified through *Grady McLemore—your bullhorn in Washington.*

My brother had called last month and asked my opinion on reviving the slogan for his own campaign—*your bullhorn for justice.* I'd slammed the phone down and ignored his calls for a week.

Knuckles rapped on my window and I jerked up to see an armed guard standing there. *Lenora Dabney* read her name tag. A woman of mixed race, strong and stout, with a belt cinching her waist so tightly it made me thankful for my dress.

"Help you, ma'am?" she yelled through the window.

"No," I snapped. "I'm fine."

"You can't loiter here. Prison property. We gotta check the ID of everyone on the grounds."

I lowered my window. "I'm about to enter. I'm visiting some-one."

She looked me up and down as best she could and smirked. "Oh . . . You one of Grady's Ladies?"

"Excuse me?" The tone conveyed my answer.

"Sorry. It's just you're the type that usually shows up." She filled the ensuing pause with an amused stare. "You look more like 'er than most. Course, we got some new ones coming in now that he's getting out soon." She shifted her stance, settling in for a chat, like we were old pals shooting the shit in the prison yard. Yes, let's yuk it up about the assorted neuroses of needy, self-loathing women.

"Some of the old faithfuls," she said, "they stopped showing 'bout six months ago. Reason they showed up in the first place was 'cause he was incarcerated, right? Least that's my theory. Puts them in charge. Once he's out, he's just another wife beater, am I right?"

If she next slapped the top of my car and doubled over in laugh-ter, I'd have to run her over. Some people shouldn't be left to work alone all day.

"You're talking about Grady McLemore?"

"Uh, yeah, sorry. Figured you knew. Who you here to see?"

My teeth clamped so tight I wasn't sure I could utter the name without cracking my face. "Grady McLemore."

Her little grunt begged me to step on the gas and aim the tires in her direction. How dare she assume I was some psychotic groupie? I had my own insane admirers and, for the first time, had to resist bragging about them.

My white knuckles on the steering wheel beamed out at me like four sets of accusing eyes. "Can we just proceed as if we didn't have this conversation?"

She shrugged and kept grinning. "Sure thing. I'll meet you there by the booth."

I immediately regretted my snappishness to a fellow member of the law enforcement community, but come on, she needed to reel in the enthusiasm. By the time I freshened my appearance and pulled up to the booth, she'd made her way back in.

"Can I help you?" she said. Well, at least she was acquiescing to my wishes, but really, this was like slicing through a scar.

"As I said, I'm here to see Grady McLemore." I rushed out the last two words lest they tattoo themselves on my tongue.

"Grady McLemore," she uttered to herself while scanning a list. "Let's see . . . Grady McLemore, Grady McLemore."

After the third utterance, I helped her out. "Murderer. Lying sack of shit. You seemed to know who he was a minute ago."

"ID." She extended her hand toward me while staring off at an angle like a pissed-off dog that didn't like being put in its place.

I handed over my driver's license, the one with the distorted picture that made my face look red and angry. She wrote down my name, returned the license, and then examined what she'd written, as if reading each letter individually. "Ohhh," she said, drawing out the syllable for the entire length of her exhalation. "Right."

Yes, that's right, genius. I'm Bridget Perkins's daughter. Usually, I had no problems carrying the burden of my last name. It was common enough and didn't cause people to jump to conclusions. But tied directly to a small blonde with green eyes and a bitchy attitude visiting Grady McLemore, there was little room for doubt. I probably needed to tone it down or this chick would be on the phone to TMZ and Homeland Security before I reached the parking lot. I forced a slight smile.

"You go right ahead, Miss . . . *Perkins*," she said. "Park there to the left. And if you don't mind my saying so, Senator McLemore isn't nearly as bad as you think. I work inside most weeks and I've gotten to know him pretty well. You might be in for a bit of a disappointment."

I wiped away the smile, letting the full brunt of my personality regain strength over the wishy-washy childhood bullshit that had built up on the ride here. "It's *senatorial candidate*. And I do mind."

I parked my car, slammed the door, and strode toward the double doors, fully prepared to meet the man who'd murdered my mom. For the first time.

CHAPTER 15

Bridget Perkins, 30 Years, 8 Hours Ago

Bridget Perkins arrived at Field Diner thirty minutes late. While such tardiness might spell trouble for Lucinda, the bucktoothed, oft-bruised waitress, Bridget knew that Mickey the manager would merely give her a half-eyed leer while checking to see if the thirtieth week of pregnancy had added any bulk to her swelling breasts. While Bridget unwillingly provided material for Mickey's jerk-off fantasies, all the employees knew that Lucinda didn't do it for him, because he declared it every time she screwed up an order. *Christ, Lucinda, bad enough I gotta keep you from poppin' into my head when I'm doin' the dirty, but you're a sucky waitress on top o' that.*

Sadly, all the waitresses also knew that for Mickey, *doin' the dirty* meant a solo event. None of them knew what he called the duet version—and doubted they'd ever find out.

Bridget didn't appreciate Mickey's special treatment. In fact, she treated him worse than any of the other girls did, but guys like Mickey, threats egged them on. They lacked that sense that distinguished between flirtation and repugnance. Bridget's rejections excited him, often sending his fingers on extra trips through his greasy mop of hair. It was his sexual tell, those slippery fingers. Not much of a stretch to imagine that if he wasn't in public, he'd be using them to stroke a different head.

Lately, there'd been disturbing rumors that his misdeeds were escalating, so on the nights Bridget closed the diner by herself, she double-checked the parking lot in case Mickey had doubled back from his mouse-infested trailer to stare—or worse.

"Hey, Mickey," she said. "Sorry I'm late. Car trouble again."

Mickey's eyes licked her body—slowly—from the ankles up. She could practically feel him tongue-lashing her thick, straight hair into a bouffant. Lucinda, who was filling lemonades for some boys in booth eight, gave Bridget a sympathetic wink before glancing at a waiting customer—her way of saying, *Get moving, we're busy.* Bridget felt a little better about her earlier fib to her dad when she saw that both of Lucinda's eyes looked bright and fresh today. Maybe she'd finally thrown that boyfriend of hers to the curb.

The next few hours saw a hungry crowd, including a soccer team, a group of septuagenarians who'd skipped their weekly bridge game, and kids who wanted milk shakes that had to be mixed on the slow machine Mickey refused to replace. Its grinding gears competed with the din of the customers, but the night went fast and Bridget liked fast. If things slowed, her extra weight took more of a toll, so when Lucinda sat a party of one at the small round table in her section, Bridget skedaddled over. She checked out the customer's reflection in the window as she approached: short and compact with keen eyes, a snub nose, and a head of light brown hair that was just starting to make itself scarce on his globe of a head.

"Hi, how ya doin' tonight?" she said. "Saw you in here last week, didn't I?"

His darting eyes found hers for a flash, then rushed back to the menu. "Yes, oh yes. Very kind of you to remember." His voice came out tinny, closer to a whisper than anything resembling sonorous tones. "I'd like the turkey Reuben tonight, if you don't mind."

"Sure. Anything to drink?"

"Oh, yes. A glass of your sweetest lemonade, please."

Bridget swiped his menu. From his startled reaction, she may as well have torn away his security blanket. "Did you want to hold on to the menu?"

He looked flustered. "Oh, no, no. You take it. It's fine."

Bridget spun around to put in his order and nearly tripped over her own feet when she saw Lucinda leading another customer to her section. When the customer raised his head, Bridget's shimmering eyes became trapped in the slow, syrupy gaze of Mr. Abner Abel, neighbor, meat trucker, slow driver, and semi-absentee father—except when it was time to knock up Mrs. Abel and add to their passel of brats. Quite a machine, that Mrs. Abel, outlasting Fords, Chevys, and wobbly delivery trucks.

Mr. Abel nodded at Bridget as his lanky body flowed toward the table like an unfurling flag in a mild breeze. Bridget had never realized how short he was, but as he stood next to Lucinda, it became obvious. The height illusion must have come from the skin and bones, with little to fill the spaces between.

Bridget forced a quick smile and tried to catch Lucinda's eye, but she was deep into a story that required wild gesticulations as she sat Mr. Abel two tables down from turkey Reuben guy. Bridget handed in her order to the kitchen and geared up to wait on Mr. Abel, willing herself to remain composed.

"Evenin', Mr. Abel," she said. "No Mrs. Abel tonight?"

"Hello, Bridget," he said. "Little Annelise is down with an ear infection and I just got back from a day-long haul."

Bridget knew he was lying, and for a split second her face betrayed her. She tried to cover it up quickly—she sure didn't want to be the one admitting they'd passed each other on the road earlier—but Mr. Abel had caught her reaction.

"What I mean is," he said, "I got back from a long haul earlier and then had some local deliveries."

His sentences seeped out as if a fine-tooth comb had been run through them, the words separated uniformly, delivered in their own sweet time. It made Bridget feel spastic by comparison.

"Of course you did," she said. "Sorry to hear Annelise is under the weather."

"How is your father?" he said. "Haven't seen him in a while."

What Mr. Abel meant was that he hadn't seen Barton Perkins in church lately, but Bridget glossed over the dig. "Daddy's fit as a fiddle and stayin' busy. The insurance game is goin' well, but I tell you, the man works from sunup till sundown."

"And on Sundays, apparently."

"Seven days a week, yes, sir."

"Work is good," he said, turning the simple statement into a grand proclamation. "Keeps us out of trouble." He turned his head decidedly toward the menu and away from the *trouble* growing in Bridget's uterus.

"What can I get for you, Mr. Abel?"

As he swung his long head back toward her, an eerie smile crossed his face, although it carried little of a smile's usual connotations. "Did I see you earlier today, Bridget? In a fancy black Mercedes 300?"

Bridget nearly dropped her pencil.

"Um, no, I don't think so, sir." She hated lying to him. His attitude always made her feel like a trembling girl with impure thoughts and accompanying actions, on display for the world to see. "You need a moment to look at the menu?"

"Very odd," he said. "Because I'd swear on a stack of Bibles that I saw you out on Cumberly Road, in a Mercedes, with a man."

Bridget remained rigid and silent as he reached a long-fingered hand out to push the menu away like it was a distasteful woman of the night. "I'll have a cucumber sandwich on white bread with mayo, a cup of coffee, and half a grapefruit."

Given her delicate state—as some in town called it—the order made her stomach turn. At the same time, she felt another urge brimming inside her, one she'd need to vanquish soon in order to calm down and regain control after this uncomfortable encounter with Mr. Abel.

"I'll get that goin' for you." She jotted down his order as fast as she could and headed to the kitchen. Turning back around, she became acutely aware of a persistent gnawing in her stomach, one that had nothing to do with the twins or Mr. Abel's order. It was the bedevilment, as she liked to think of it, and she needed something solid in her hand to quell the churning gush of desire welling up inside her, cresting and teasing. She'd need to ride the wave until it crash-landed on shore, lest it overpower her.

She glanced from Mr. Abel to her other lone customer. Both easy. Both distractible. Either one would do.

CHAPTER 16

Seriously? This guy was like a walking Viagra ad. Had to be mid-sixties but would look great on the arm of any thirty-year-old. Full head of hair, less than half gray, with shoulders and pecs that put the guys I dated to shame. Even the great Grady McLemore must do nothing behind bars except lift weights and ponder how to spend his weekly dollar from doing prison laundry. Then again, with his reputed charms, he probably supervised the other inmates while demanding starched collars for his own jumpsuits.

Grady turned to the guard who'd shown him in. "Thanks, Al, I can take it from here."

Damn. His voice. It reverberated like an entire string section and filled places in my ear I never knew existed. No wonder Mom had swooned over this guy. Couldn't have been many like him coming into Field Diner on a regular basis.

And then I noticed something I hadn't thought about in years: the cleft in his chin. Sure, there'd been photos forced upon me over the years, and I knew it was a dominant trait that guaranteed passage to offspring, but I hadn't realized how perfectly his would match mine. Slightly off center with a particularly deep spot three-quarters of the way down, as if some master seamstress had flinched, pulling one stitch too tight. My brother shared the same feature, though it wasn't as prominent.

I rose from the table, my chair grating against the floor, my height dwarfed by his. He hovered over me as he had my entire existence, an indiscriminate cloud too heavy to move, too porous to touch. I looked down, hoping the moment would evaporate into nonexistence, but I could feel the radiance of his gaze on my face. No wonder he'd been touted as a sure thing. He mesmerized without even trying.

As I reprimanded myself for having given the elevator nurse such a hard time, I raised my face to—undeniably—my father's.

"Hello, Mr. McLemore. I'm Jane Perkins."

His smile conveyed the frivolousness of my words. They were practically an insult.

My hands stayed glued to the small, clear purse I'd brought solely for the purpose of clutching in case he reached out to shake my hand. He didn't.

"Janie, what a joy to finally meet you." He'd changed *Jane* to *Janie* as naturally as breathing. So much for my attempt at maturity.

His voice really was ridiculous. What must it have been like to see him on the campaign trail? Supposedly, he was a rock star, but I'd attributed the trumped-up accounts to the public's shallowness. Now I understood. I'd met only one other person who held this kind of immediate sway over people—a suspect in an insurance case for which I'd been hired to take pictures—and he'd turned out to be plotting his mother's murder after hiding three bodies in her basement. Still, I had enough practice in keeping my distance and detaching from situations. In this case, I needed only remind myself that the strong hands clasped together in front of me had pulled the trigger on the gun that cost me a mother.

We sat down, nothing between us but a shoddy table onto which someone had scratched the words *This Sucks* with a sharp object. The message's existence didn't bode well for the prison's security screening system, but the sentiment made me feel less alone.

"I need to talk to you about a photo," I said, cutting hard to the chase.

For all the attention he gave my declaration, I might as well have announced he'd be getting an extra pudding with dessert tonight.

"You look so much like your mother," he said. His doleful expression coated me, but not in a good way. More like toxic paint. He raised one hand quickly to his mouth, then let it drop again. "It's extraordinary."

"I've heard about the resemblance," I said, "but of course, I never met my mother and only know her through photos, one of which I'd like to show you."

That oughta dump a load of antifreeze on his warm, familial bullshit.

He nodded, closing his eyes to add sincerity to the gesture, but the cluster of freckles on his eyelids pissed me off to no end. Was he whiling away his punitive years in the sun, stretched out on a lounge chair while sipping tea with lemon? Did the guards grant him special privileges? Of course they did. No one looked this good in prison unless the people in charge were complicit in his upkeep.

"Janie, your attitude is completely understandable."

If only I had an engraved plaque to hand him. It would read *Understatement of the Century*.

"I wish we'd gotten to know each other all along," he continued, "although the logistics would have been tough." He grinned and damn if it didn't make him more likable. "I know how lucky I am that John has allowed me to be part of his life. I can't tell you what that's meant to me."

John? Really? Nobody called my brother *John.* Would he next break out the full *Jane Elizabeth Perkins?*

"I've never asked the same of you," he said.

"You're not really in a position to ask me for anything, are you, Mr. McLemore?"

The *Mr. McLemore* part got to him. It showed in the horizontal creases near his eyes. "I've kept a personal vow never to intrude in your life. But that doesn't mean I didn't want to." His fingers touched each other periodically, as if he wanted to reach out and hold someone's hand while delivering this tripe.

There'd be no offer from this side of the table.

"I've followed your schooling and career," he said, "and John keeps me up to date, but, if I'm honest, the emptiness haunts me. Because you were the girl. I should have been around to protect you."

I raised one hell of a dubious brow. With that kind of protection, I'd be better off living under the care of Dizzy the Drug Lord.

And then he released tears, as if commanding a small cadre of laborers in his amygdala to unleash the waterworks. This guy was unreal. But then, why did I feel myself swallowing back a rush of emotion? Why did I want to reach out and reassure him and catch him up on the entirety of my existence?

I didn't do it, of course. An unyielding silence gripped me as I focused on something—anything—less cloying. I noticed the protrusion of his cheekbones and the angle of his nose. He'd be the rare perfect subject for a Rembrandt portrait, where a light source above the head makes the nose's shadow fall toward the cheek. Not every face could pull it off. It needed a particular bone structure. The effect was a triangle of light below the eye, surrounded by shadow. Some photographers felt it gave the subject a sophistication and gravity. I always felt it suggested a dark intelligence and a calculating precision to every move and emotion.

While he got himself together, apologizing here and there, I observed how his shoulders slumped forward now, as if every part of him were reaching out, giving its utmost. Those selectively benevolent shoulders had probably worked in his favor when he leaned down to shake a frail constituent's hand. Maybe an old woman with a cane or a veteran in a wheelchair.

I saw him once again for who I knew him to be—a heartless, spineless cad who, when push came to shove, couldn't act out the Superman role he'd been born to play. If there had been a third person in the room that night, Fate's central casting had put Grady in the right place at the right time to save my mother, but it hadn't given him the right set of tools.

"Mr. McLemore, as I—"

"Please, call me Grady. That's what your brother calls me."

"We're twins, not robots."

Another crack in his handsome armor, evident in the tightness of his lips. "Whatever you're comfortable with."

"Someone mailed me pictures of the crime scene. Did you have anything to do with that?"

"Your mother's crime scene?"

"Of course my mother's crime scene. The one you staged for all of us." Despite evidence to the contrary in my possession, I still needed to say it. Thirty years of coarse, DNA-entangled hatred didn't just evaporate overnight. I reached into my bag and slapped the photos in front of him like an accusation.

He gazed at them and I'd never seen anything like it. No shock, no horror, no regret. An actual smile crossed his face.

"I'm sorry," he said upon realizing his expression. "It's just that"—and here came the tears again—"I haven't seen a picture of your mother in so long. I'm sure when you look at it, you see—"

"A recurring nightmare? The brutal shortening of a vibrant life—and almost two more?"

Grady reached across the table to touch me, only to be throat-cleared into submission by the guard, not to mention the abrupt removal of my hand. He retracted the offer smoothly, as if it had never been made. "I see the woman I loved, the woman who was going to give me the life I dreamed of but didn't think possible, considering . . ."

"Considering what?"

His sigh came out with more timbre than most people's voices. If he vocalized a glitch at the end of it, I might lose my shit. He didn't.

"Considering the life of a politician," he said, "a public figure. I didn't think I'd have a normal shot at it. Assumed everything would be manipulated for maximum advantage."

"Why?"

Grady chuckled. "You never met my mom. No *first comes love, then comes marriage.* It was *first comes achievement, then comes status, and finally, power.* Only heard the word *love* when I brought a girl home for Easter one year. *Don't go falling in love with that opportunist, Grady; she is not daughter-in-law material.*"

I suppressed all thoughts of Grady's cold-hearted mom possibly being my grandmother.

"You wouldn't believe it," he continued, "but there are lots of politicians out there with fixed marriages to cover for their true preferences—or arrangements where trusts are traded for social status. But with Bridget, I had it all. I didn't need anything from her except to be with her. I could give her everything, and I loved doing it." He let out a short exhalation through his nose. "I sound like a dime-store romance novel, but she made my life whole. We were in love."

Hell, I wouldn't pay a nickel for that schlock. "What must your mother have thought?" I said. "Or were you planning to deliver the knocked-up waitress to her like a dish of cold revenge?"

"We'd stopped speaking by that point, although Bridget had planned to remedy that."

Hadn't known my mom was the let's-all-get-along type, but given her own experience, she probably couldn't fathom a cold relationship between parent and child.

"This is eye-opening and all, Mr. McLemore, but I didn't come here to climb the old family tree. I need to know one thing: Who took this photo? Because these smudges down here are supposedly you."

He squinted and zeroed in on the base of the photo.

"Even through your crocodile tears, you must be able to see that this was taken before my grandfather traipsed over your collapsed body to save my mother."

The words were meant to sting and they did. His brows formed a *V.* "Forgive me, I . . . I . . ."

"Yes, shocking. I understand. But I'd like to get your answers quickly, before you can shellac them with lies. It's been so long. Why not come clean?"

He took a long moment to gaze at the photo, his eyes slowly widening as they showed a combination of surprise and disbelief. "Janie, if your assessment of these photos is correct, then they're proof of the third person. Whoever injected me."

"Then who the hell was that? Someone you hired?"

His expression dimmed. "You know as well as I do. The Haiku Killer. To this day I have no idea who he was."

"A lot of people—twelve in particular—think the Haiku Killer's only role in this case was as an excuse."

Grady shook his head, but his face showed patience. "My old handler, Sam Kowalczyk, looked into it for years. He investigated dozens of people, but no one panned out. He looked into local folks, guys passing through town, customers at Field Diner, people who resented me, supporters, ex-cons, even people who might have known about your mother and me."

The last one caught me off guard. "Who else knew?"

"Sam knew, of course, and it's possible a few hotel employees put two and two together." He gazed upward for a moment, thinking. "There was one other man your mom was worried about, but Sam couldn't come up with anything concrete on him."

"Who was that?"

"I can't remember his name. A neighbor of hers. I'll get the name from Sam."

"Did Sam share his findings with the police?"

"Never came up with anything solid enough. Besides, case was closed. They had their man. Me."

I leaned back, listening to the grinding gears in my head as I shifted from hating this guy to viewing him as a potential resource. But the clutch stuck and I couldn't get there yet.

"What did my mom say to you that night that made you rush to her house?"

"It's in the police files. Haven't you read them?"

I shook my head. "Until now, I assumed they were filled with fabrications."

A glimmer of hope flickered in Grady's eyes, turning them a sparkling russet. Come on, did he really think a couple blurry photos extrapolated by an eccentric in a log cabin would exonerate him? Then again, what the hell was I doing here if they hadn't?

His expression mellowed then, as if enough years had passed that he could now look back on the dreaded night with a degree of peace. "Bridget called shortly after I left the diner. Sam had dropped me back at the office and I was polishing a speech. She sounded panicked, very unlike her, and she said she had a haiku, a real one. I asked why she thought it was real, but she was too flustered to answer. She was worried the guy would double back and kill her. She said she had to get out of there. I told her to stay put, that I'd be right over, but she was breathing fast and all she said was, 'I've got to go,' and then the connection went dead."

"What happened?"

He stared not *at* me, but *through* me. "I don't know. That's when I panicked. I didn't like that diner manager and for all I knew, he was somehow involved. I should have called the police but I was only a few minutes away, so I raced over. Darkest night I'd ever seen—no moon—and no one else on the road. I got there within five minutes, but she was nowhere to be found."

He paused, breathing hard, his body recalling the adrenaline rush.

"When I couldn't get inside the diner, I snapped. I was about to smash the window with a bench when I finally noticed her car wasn't there. I jumped back in my car and raced to her house. Must've been going ninety on those curvy roads." He stopped suddenly and looked at me with concern. "Are you sure you want to hear this?"

Not at all. "Yes, go ahead."

"Crazy ideas flew through my head. By the time I got there, I was ready to take down the first person I saw. I grabbed my gun—I always kept one in the car—and I swear, even from outside the house, even though I'd never been there, I knew something was wrong. I walked into the living room and Bridget was . . . She was just standing there. In the middle of the room. It was . . . eerie. Like she was frozen, but in a dream. She had this bewildered look in her eyes and I realized the guy was already there. She had to be incredibly scared for you and John."

"Did she say anything? Nod to you or something?"

"There wasn't time. It was pitch black behind me and I don't know if he had a gun aimed at her head or what, but before either of us could say anything, I felt a sting in my neck and my knees hit the floor."

Grady leaned forward, his hands on those same knees, his face splotchy. So much for the peaceful recollection. "I never heard him, never got a good look at him. It was so unlike me. I used to be a hunter, for God's sake." He jerked his head up. "Have you ever had a panic attack?"

"No."

"Even before he injected me, weird things were happening to my body. I couldn't breathe right, I had tunnel vision, my heart was racing. It was bizarre. My whole life, I'd never flinched or backed down. First shot at a buck, I was fifteen, didn't hesitate. But this time it was Bridget in the crosshairs and I lost it. I was down before I could even tape up my gloves for the fight."

"But you didn't bring gloves, Grady. You brought a gun. Do you take any responsibility for walking into a volatile situation with a loaded gun?"

"Of course! Why do you think I'm here? I never denied what I did, but I sure as hell disagreed with the how and why that the prosecution claimed." His voice held remarkably little anger for an innocent man, but after thirty years, even a boiling cauldron of anger could run dry—or at least satisfy itself with a steady simmer.

His words came out all crumbly. "I thought I could save her—and I was a damn good shot."

"Apparently."

He took his medicine.

"If I had it to do over again—"

"No," I said. "Sorry. You don't get to give that speech. Not to me."

He cast his eyes down and in that single gesture, I sensed thousands of lonely nights spent reliving the nightmare of the shooting. Suddenly I was whirling in a riptide, getting pulled into a vortex where Grady controlled the outcomes. I needed to remain neutral, to swim parallel to the shore, the way Grandpa Barton had taught

me. He'd made me fight vicious undertows at the beach to be sure
I wouldn't get sucked into a questionable situation—one with no
answer but death.

I swam parallel now. "Assuming the mysterious third party is
still alive, why did he mail this photo now, after all this time?"

Grady's stunning eyes opened wider and I could see him as a
younger man, before the lids had grown heavy and the skin had
succumbed to age, albeit gently in his case. The appearance rattled
me as a resemblance to Jack flashed across his face.

"As I'm sure you know," he said, "I'm getting out next week.
Despite your moving letters."

I dropped eye contact, but refused to apologize. Was I supposed
to feel guilty that every few years, I'd crafted a stirring missive to
remind the parole board that the man before them was a heartless
killer, not some handsome charmer? I'd laid it on thick, reminding
them of the sad life of half a twinset who'd become less of herself
each year for lack of a mother and father—thanks to the selfish
actions of a wheeler-dealer who took advantage of a young woman
and then discarded her like a torn campaign poster.

Now, with these damn pictures, I had to question whether I'd
kept an innocent man in jail. "I didn't put you in here," I said. "I
wasn't even born."

Grady gazed at me until I lifted my eyes to his. I lost myself in
them—a cold heart warmed by a crackling fire.

"Janie, I wasn't implying that you did. I can't imagine how difficult this all is for you."

What was I supposed to do with a free, possibly innocent Grady
McLemore? He'd never been anything but a pixelated planet in my
universe, one that included my 3-D, full-color mother as the sun.
Grady had been the dark to her light, the bottomless evil to her infinite love. In my mind, the two of them only existed when I wanted

them to, when I needed someone to adore or despise. The energy I could muster from either emotion was often the only thing that kept me going.

"If the Haiku Killer mailed this because you're getting out," I said, "then he's been following your life all this time."

"Not just mine, Janie." He looked genuinely concerned. "He mailed them to you."

"So what am I supposed to do?"

He smiled, a mixture of sympathy and pride on his face. "I have good instincts about people." His eyes, not so unlike my brother's, constricted to razors and cut to the chase. "You're going after the Haiku Killer."

CHAPTER 17

At least my dress still looked good. Come on, I urged myself, just do it. It had to be fate that their house was within newspaper-tossing distance of the road that led home from the prison. The worst they could do was boot me out and tell me to get lost.

I climbed the creaking steps of the porch and surprised myself by wishing Wexler were here. The thought of his composed self-control gave me strength, so I raised my hand and knocked on the door.

A guy answered. A hot guy. A really hot guy. *That* hadn't shown up on my smartphone when I verified the owner of the home as Melinda Biedermann, widow of Professor Jason Biedermann, the Haiku Killer's first victim.

The hot guy's shirtless torso stared back at me with bumps and valleys made of pure muscle, and it took me a good five seconds to rip my eyes away and find his. He had to be Professor Biedermann's son. The professor had been half-Spanish and it looked like Junior here had inherited all the good parts, including wavy, dark hair that he wore long, like a hipster skater, despite an age north of thirty.

"Hi, there," I said. "My name is Ja—"

"Yeah, uh, my mom's at a retreat and she usually gets her makeup from those pink car ladies."

"Oh, no, I'm not—"

"You wanna come in?" he said. "I was kinda in the middle of something and I don't want it to burn."

"Sure," I said. "I'm Janie Perkins, by the way."

He reached his hand down and shook mine. "Nice to meet you, Janie. I'm Jason Biedermann. The third. But we don't acknowledge the second very much." It was then I caught a whiff of something earthy and mellow, and noticed pink lines running through the whites of my host's glazed eyes. Of course. Jason Biedermann the third was stoned out of his mind.

He gestured for me to come in and led me to the kitchen.

Despite being alone with a strong, high stranger, I sensed no threat. After all, I was the one barging in on him.

"You're not a narc, are you?" Jason asked.

"No. In fact, I've partaken a few times myself."

He nodded approvingly, slipped on a muscle tee—which seemed redundant—and muttered, "Cool."

He turned off a few pots cooking on the stove, but I didn't ask. I was more curious about past crimes, not potential new ones.

While he tended his *project*, I sat down at the modest kitchen table and jumped in. "Jason, my mother may have been an indirect victim of the Haiku Killer."

"Shit. Like, recently?"

"No," I said. "She died years ago, not long after your father."

"Oh, gotcha. I mean, why do you think my mother's at a retreat, right? Not only a widow, but man, when the stuff came out about my dad, it freaked her out. She's never been the same. I mean, what was he doin' with all those chicks, right? They were like teenagers."

"A few might have been in their twenties," I said lamely.

Jason's dad, philosophy professor Jason Biedermann of Eastern Virginia College of Liberal Arts, had been the Haiku Killer's first victim. The haiku found at the scene had read:

Death greatest of all
Busy yet barren am I
Blest be as I deem

Several experts had convened when the case was fresh. The consensus was that since the victim made his living as a philosophy professor, the words held a direct tie to Socrates, the subject of Biedermann's thesis years earlier. They posited that the first line referred to the Socrates quote *Death may be the greatest of all human blessings.*

Since blessings were normally bestowed by God, the experts agreed that the killer—sans nickname at that point—viewed himself as God, and death as a blessing. While the killer was comfortable taking life, he nonetheless framed it as a good deed, because a professor who worshipped Socrates would surely agree that death was a blessing. Perhaps the killer thought he was doing the professor a favor?

The second line—*Busy yet barren am I*—was one of the reasons Mrs. Biedermann needed a retreat. The professor had often been too busy to see students during regular office hours because, as it turned out, he was busy seeing particular students who boasted Ds, not As—in bra sizes, not grades.

Sadly, in death, the professor was outed as a prolific philanderer. The investigators uncovered disturbing photos of the professor with more than forty female students. He took the pictures himself, the camera found within reach of his office chair—the one where he hosted the majority of his students. Apparently, his personal philosophy included no objections to oral sex. Out of courtesy to the girls, or due to their facedown positions, he kept their recognizable features out of frame; it was only from the girls' varying hair colors and styles that the police ascertained a number north of forty.

Jason sat down across from me and lit a joint, offering me first dibs, but I refused. "Before my brother killed himself"—Jason drew long and hard on his blunt—"he would refer to our dad as Professor Fellatio. He used to wonder why Professor F. couldn't at least take the girls to his couch. Laziest fuckin' philanderer ever."

I was no philosophy student, but I could think of one Socrates quote that would fit Professor Biedermann to a tee. Unfortunately, it would also insult the long-suffering Mrs. Biedermann: *By all means marry; if you get a good wife, you'll be happy. If you get a bad one, you'll become a philosopher.* Or a dirtbag.

After the photo discovery, the investigation into Professor Fellatio's murder focused on his sexual liaisons, because the authorities had no idea that his death marked the beginning of a serial killer's legacy. The unsolved case was tucked away until seven months later, when the second murder occurred. And that's when the local case of the promiscuous professor became national news, apparently sending Jason's brother to an early grave and mommy to therapy.

"The worst part," Jason said, "was my dad's gawping, over-the-moon expression in some of those photos. He looked like a monkey in a science lab who'd been taught to press a button to get an orgasm, like, both enthralled by the button and unable to believe it existed." He took another hit and laughed. "Guess he was ahead of his time with the selfie, though, huh?"

I nodded. Busy yet barren. Of morals.

After allowing Jason this questionable trip down memory lane, I came to the purpose of my visit. "I'm here because someone sent me photos of my mom."

"Oh, shit. Don't tell me my dad did your mom back in the day."

I almost laughed. "No, nothing like that." I explained my receipt of the photos and my mother's link to the Haiku Killer. "What I need to know is if you or your mom received any photos in the mail recently. If these were mailed to me by the Haiku Killer, he might have mailed photos to all his victims' families."

Jason looked horrified. "No, man, no. We haven't received anything like that. Can you imagine?"

Obviously, I could, but I let it go. "You live here with your mom?"

"Not officially, but I've been here for like a year, so I guess I do for now."

"And you'd definitely know if a photo came in the mail? Maybe from Ridge, West Virginia?"

"Absolutely. I always get the mail. And I'd totally show you the photos if I had 'em. You're smokin' hot, you know what I'm sayin'?"

I wanted to be flattered, but I knew Jason would have said the same if a female orangutan was sitting across from him. I smiled anyway.

"Help you with anything else?" he said.

"Just, um, I guess you and your family never sat around the kitchen table and came up with connections to the other victims, did you?"

"Naw," he said, drawing out the syllable in a sad way that implied he didn't want to disappoint me. "As far as I know, my dad didn't know that priest or that doctor. He didn't go to church or have a heart problem or anything. Of course, I barely knew him, but I'm told when he wasn't teaching, he was either cooking or researching recipes."

Or getting his jollies from the mouths of babes.

"He used to host a lot of dinner parties here," Jason continued. "And he liked to read and collect Roman shit. Weren't those other murders in like totally different parts of the state?"

I nodded.

"My dad was a homebody. Didn't get around much—at least geographically."

Surprisingly, Jason made a good point. It wasn't the victims who got around, but rather, the killer. And with no signs of forced entry or struggle in any of the cases, the Haiku Killer could have been somebody the victims knew and trusted, someone who established himself in their lives, appearing with such regularity that they didn't even consider it unusual when he came to kill them.

The question was, who could do that and also walk into my old living room in Caulfield?

CHAPTER 18

Bridget Perkins, 30 Years, 2 Hours Ago

The turkey Reuben guy at table two was proving just enough of a challenge to satisfy Bridget's urges. He'd been shielding something with his hand for the last ten minutes, puzzling over it, communicating with it. If Bridget didn't know better, she'd think he was sneaking bits of his sandwich to a pet mouse. But then she spotted his pen. An elegant pen that clashed with the man's blue-collar appearance. It was gold, shapely, substantial. For all Bridget knew, it might be a knockoff, but something about the way it acted as a counterweight to his pudgy hands told her it was the real thing. Had he purchased it himself? Or had he held on to it since high school graduation years ago with hopes for a future that would merit such a pen? Bridget suddenly had to know what that pen was writing.

"Hey there," said Lucinda, pulling Bridget from her thoughts. "Just what has gotten into you lately? You seem distracted and happy at the same time, and there's only one thing I know can do that to a lady, and that's a good man."

"What's that, Lucinda? You have a new man in your life?"

"No, but I'm sensing you do." Lucinda winked, but it was a graceless gesture on her.

"Oh, Lucy, you're so funny," Bridget said, a line that had worked once before to brush off Lucinda's mild obsession with Bridget's personal life. Although she thought of Lucinda as a big sister, and would do anything for her, she had to keep her at bay now and again.

"I'm just sayin', you have a glow—"

"Tell you what, we'll talk about it over the breakfast shift. Plus, I have some ideas about helpin' you boost your self-esteem so you'll finally believe you deserve a quality man. You do, you know."

Lucinda touched Bridget's arm, her eyes welling. "Thanks, Bridget. I think I'm finally ready to listen."

"I know you are." She stroked her friend's arm. "Oh, table two is ready for dessert. Be right back."

When Bridget got three steps from the table, she saw the customer shove his shielded item back into his blazer pocket. The blazer was worn, with thin elbows and threads fraying at the wrist, but most important, the pockets no longer held fast to the jacket. They gaped open, sloppy and wanting, like baby robins awaiting a worm. Perfect. After all, she wasn't a professional like those overseas kids that got training the moment their pincer muscles scooped up a grain of rice. Bridget was just a good old-fashioned kleptomaniac, and if that meant the occasional pickpocket job, then she was up for it. Her preferred method was a distraction-swipe, a simple placement of one hand on the table while leaning toward the menu, allowing the other hand to sidle away with the *objet du désir*. Sometimes she'd just knock something to the ground and strike at the moment of clatter. Despite promising herself she'd stop—heck, they were her fingers at the end of her hands—she didn't want to, not yet, not with the fabulous crescendo inside of her and the intoxicating provocation of this customer's mad scribblings.

Bridget looked the small man right in the eyes, at least for as long as he would raise his, and smiled. "We've got a fabulous custard cream pie tonight," she lied, knowing it tasted like watered-down milk, "and a chocolate mousse that's out of this world." She shifted a plate and saucer on the table as if preparing them for bussing. "Or at least they're pretty darn good, if you're interested in some dessert."

With an imperceptible flick of her pinkie, she knocked his pen to the floor, knowing he'd cross hell or high water to keep ahold of that thing. His eyes nearly poked out of his head as he watched the precious implement cascade toward the grimy tiles below.

"Oopsie daisy," Bridget said, crouching down as if to retrieve the pen, knowing the customer would waste no time leaning over to reclaim his prized possession. With the two of them in that awkward position, Bridget took pleasure in the fact that the eyes of several customers were on the tiny commotion and yet she'd still be able to pull off her heist without fear. Even if anxiety did rear its intrusive head, she'd channel it to enhance the experience and make the high that much sweeter. This triumph would last her a good long while.

The customer's pocket opened wide and said *ahhh*—or maybe *AHHH*—as it sensed a pending violation. Her slim fingers did their dirty work before the poor man could even reach his precious pen. As he finally grabbed it from under the table, Bridget slipped the procured item into the side pocket of her apron, the one where she kept personal items properly separated from everything else. Meanwhile, the poor customer never did get to ponder the dessert decision the way he wanted to, because at that moment a grand Mercedes pulled up to the front of the diner and drew everyone's attention.

Flashes of the lighted *Field Diner* sign glinted red off the Mercedes's shiny black paint. The *F* in *Field* had been threatening to burn out all week and its flickering indecision now played off the vehicle's roof, giving the impression of an upscale police car on a mission.

Bridget sucked in a panicked breath, forgetting all about her swipe. Her heart pounded as she hoped Mr. Abel wouldn't notice that the car outside the diner was the same Mercedes he'd passed on the road earlier.

When Sam Kowalczyk got out of the driver's seat to open the door for the passenger in back, the interior lights illuminated none other than Grady McLemore. While Bridget was thrilled to see Grady again, her primary concern was the driver.

She glanced at Abner Abel, who had halted midbite, a chunk of grapefruit en route to his mouth. He curved his long face into a distorted mask of concentration, and when he finally placed the wolfish face of Sam Kowalczyk, a window shade of realization lowered itself over his countenance. He swiveled his scraggy neck and Bridget suddenly felt like he was peering into the depths of her deceptive soul.

The item in her apron pocket, evidence of her most recent sin, burned against her skin.

CHAPTER 19

When I arrived home, somewhat woozy from Jason Biedermann's secondhand smoke, I spotted a package outside my door. No biggie—I was not above ordering batteries or pancake mix via laptop—but this particular parcel threw me for a loop. My brother's publisher must have printed up huge, full-color address labels for him; they matched the cover of his book. I glanced around the empty hallway, my stomach turning at the thought of passing neighbors having read the book's title: *My Life as a Harried Haiku Twin*, by John B. Perkins.

The cover photo, in keeping with Jack's ego, showed his fat, well-nourished hand peeking out from the yellow blanket in which Grandpa Barton had wrapped us when we departed the hospital at ten days old. Baby Jack practically waved to the crowd, and the reporters had eaten up every wiggle of his fingers. I was surprised Adult Jack hadn't Photoshopped a tattoo on the chubby palm: *Vote for me!*

I grabbed the box, shoved it under my arm, and rushed inside. A scraping sound from the fire escape made me jump, but then some brain cells kicked in. "Hey, Percival. Give me a heart attack, why don't ya?"

I tossed Jack's book on the couch, let in my green-eyed feline friend, and opened a can of cat food. As I heated water for tea, a reminder dinged on my phone: *Meet Hump Banfield 5:30—Bring scanner.*

Damn, I'd completely forgotten about my wheelchair buddy. I checked the time. If I left in half an hour, I'd make it. In the meantime, I grabbed my tea and hardened my psyche to read the book exploiting my mother's murder. Pulling my legs beneath me on the sofa, I tried to discern Jack's marketing angle. Did he envision people leaving this five-pound monstrosity out as a casual conversation starter? *Have a seat! Cheese and grapes on the way—and feel free to lose yourself in the illustrated story of a pregnant woman shot in the head by her secret lover. Bon appétit!*

I cracked open the stiff, glossy pages, so laden with full-color photos that a heavy ink smell wafted up, blocking out the usual new-book scent. Jack had taped an extra picture on the inside front cover, just for me. It showed us wrestling on the floor in front of the Christmas tree, torn wrapping paper covering our feet. He'd written a note on the page opposite: *Love ya, Sis, even if you do wrestle like a girl.* I was pretty sure we were fighting over whose Cabbage Patch Kid was uglier. He'd won.

I flipped through the pages, lingering on some, rushing past others. Either short on story or desperate for visual impact, Jack had included large photos on most left-hand pages, with close-ups of selected areas on the right, as if he were a cartographer detailing the busier parts of a slaying while highlighting the smaller roads that led to votes. Apparently, voters needed to know such trivialities as the titles of the books on the shelf behind my mother's unconscious body.

They needed to see the neatly arranged photos on the marble table in the back of the room and the grate of the barren fireplace as it awaited winter's wrath. Little Bro had clearly gotten *his* harried hands on the police file, given the clinical nature of some of the photos.

I flipped to the centerfold and nearly spit out my tea. No wonder Jack hadn't been that upset by the two photos I'd shown him. He'd taken it to a new level of perversion by dedicating the center spread to a close-up of my mom's body as EMTs crowded over her, followed by detailed shots showing a Texas-shaped mustard stain on her uniform; her scuffed, thick-soled, white shoes; her shimmering blond hair; and, of course, the baby bump with the protective, ringless left hand flung across it. It was Jack's first true close-up, and he would never have let a book go public without it, even if it was in utero and shrouded by a dirty uniform.

Whoever had taken the police photos must have arrived at the same time as the medics. They'd managed to get a more distant shot that showed a bare-chested Grandpa Barton still hovering over his daughter. He looked so vulnerable, so wrecked, it broke my heart. He'd been strong all his life, callous even, and maybe too direct, but always full of good cheer—rarely with a tear in his eye or a regret in his heart. But here he was, cast upon the world with his body and soul exposed, swaddled in so much grief that he appeared shattered from the inside out. His body pointed in four directions as emotions pulled at him from every corner. His swollen eyes stared at the approaching ambulance technician. His right hand held his own shirt against his daughter's bleeding head. His left pointed accusingly toward the kitchen, undoubtedly at the prone man still holding the smoking gun, but the main of Grandpa's body draped his daughter, shielding her from harm while the futility of that effort glared back at him through a blood-soaked rag.

When my own tears crashed down on the page, I forced myself to buck up. After all, this was what Jack wanted: sympathy that would be converted into votes. Part of me hoped his strategy would backfire, that people would be so horrified at his heartless manipulations that they'd give their vote to the person who didn't choose tragedy as a tool. But I knew most readers would run to the election office blubbering, asking to cast their vote early.

Despite my disgust, something bigger bothered me. This *wasn't* our first close-up. I possessed that photo. I lurched from my reclined position, letting my tea grow cold. From my bag, I extracted the mailed photos and placed them side by side with the book. I tried to detect which details were different, to see if anything would provide a clue about the Haiku Killer. None of the inanimate objects in the room had been touched; it was only Bridget Perkins who was different—and she was damn near inanimate herself. It stirred me again to realize that Jack and I were fully alive in there, the only ones unaware of the preceding moment's impact. Heck, we might have been pawing at each other like hungry kittens, vying for nutrition or more space, or maybe even to get out and be. Who knew?

I gazed at the picture in the book, then at the picture taken by someone who'd made a serious clusterfuck of my decades of misdirected anger. Something bothered me, but I couldn't place my finger on it. As a crime scene photographer, I couldn't always look for the best angle or lighting. Rather, I needed facts. Cold, hard, brutal, and undistorted. I needed to produce when the coroner asked to see the body's position in relation to the blood spatter. I needed to capture the bruises when they were fresh, the blood before it thickened, and every finger and toe articulation. If I missed the shot that showed where the knife lay in relation to an arm, or how the head took a chunk out of the coffee table on its way to the floor, I'd be out of a job. But when I looked at these photos, I felt blind, incompetent. Grandpa Barton hadn't changed a thing in that room for years, except to put in new flooring and a huge carpet. And here I was, with the unique advantage of unlimited playtime in an actual crime scene, unable to figure out what was calling to me. It felt like the pinprick of a misdirected eyebrow hair, where sensation could be isolated to a single follicle because it pointed one way its entire existence and now it didn't.

Maybe Sophie Andricola was right: I was too close to the situation to see anything clearly.

I flipped through the rest of the book, disgusted by my voraciousness. I was as bad as the readers of the celebrity rags who cackled when they saw the sunbathing celebrity who had gained five pounds at age forty. *Fat Fat Forty, No Longer Sporty.* They forgot that the woman in the photo read the papers, too, just like they forgot there was a little girl in that womb who didn't want her picture splashed on a tabloid cover when her brother's book became a bestseller. *The Harried Haiku Twins—Where Are They Now?*

The aggressive knock on the door startled me, but then I got pissed. Tenants weren't supposed to let salesmen into the building, and salesmen weren't supposed to claim they didn't see the *No Soliciting* signs. I yanked the door open and my fed-up expression immediately transformed into one of surprise.

Hump Banfield was smiling and waving at me from his wheelchair.

CHAPTER 20

"Surprise!" Hump said, his smile growing clown-like.

I couldn't have been more surprised if it had been Grady McLemore with a Father of the Year pin on his lapel.

"Hump, what are you doing here? I was—"

"The Aberdeen has that shuttle service and I thought, since it was getting close to five and I hadn't heard from you, I'd save you the trip."

"How did you know where I lived?"

"My niece knows where you live."

The hell she does. But then I remembered two occasions when reporters had staked out my apartment for comments. The first, when it looked like Grady McLemore might get of prison five years ago, and again when Jack was hired by the attorney general.

"I said I'd come by at five thirty, not call."

"I know, I know. Hope you don't mind."

He rolled in, forcing me to the side, then pivoted his chair around and closed the door. When he also turned the deadbolt, a pang of alarm went off in my brain, but I forced it down to a dull buzz in the back of my head. There were plenty of ways out of my fourth-floor apartment: the fire escape, the small window in the bathroom beneath the neighbor's balcony, the bedroom window. I really wasn't a big fan of enclosed rooms with strangers—unless they were already dead.

"Lovely place, Janie. Lovely. Very practical. Not as much as you want, but as much as you need, plus a dash more to make it home. Gosh, if all Americans lived this way, the landfills would go out of business."

I really didn't give a damn about the landfills as I tried to wrap my mind around this visit. For a moment, my thoughts jumped to the gun I kept loaded and ready—but I quickly followed it with the embarrassment of an imagined headline: *Haiku Twin Slays Wheelchair Veteran*. Definitely wouldn't play well with the public.

"Listen, Hump, I wasn't expecting—"

"Told the shuttle driver to pick me up in an hour. Not that I'd intrude on you for a full hour. I'll wait on the street, maybe get a few people to throw coins at my chair." He chortled. "People do that, you know. They literally throw money at chairs! It's a wonder there aren't more scams."

"I think there are," I said, feeling more discombobulated with each animated sentence he delivered.

"I brought the war photos," he said. "I've just been so excited since we met."

I flicked on a lamp, realizing how dim the room had gotten as the sun sank behind some buildings.

"Isn't that delightful?" Hump said in response to the lamplight. "I remember the long nights spent in the trenches in my early military years. We would have been thankful for a candle back then. The only light came from the landmines we didn't see in time; you'd be amazed how brightly a body can burn."

The comparison jarred me. Maybe it was the way he conveyed it like a fond reminiscence. Hump had wheeled himself to a snug spot between the couch and chair, as if it were his usual spot.

"You have your photos, then?" I said, swallowing away my unfounded anxiety.

"Here they are." He handed me an envelope much like the one I'd received in the mail. "I'm eager to see your reaction."

The burden of having to react to his photos weighed on me. I was good at a lot of things, but being phony wasn't one of them, and I didn't have the energy to feign interest in his predictable war-buddy scenes. I pulled them out.

No feigning needed. These images weren't predictable. In fact, they were disturbing. I glanced at Hump and then at the locked door. The hairs on my arms stood up and my heart raced. Here I was like an idiot, locked in my apartment with a man I barely knew, and no one within a two-mile radius who even knew my name. My cop buddies would skin me alive for this genius move. Then, feeling Hump's eyes on me, I realized how he must feel every day—confined, limited, trapped. The thought calmed me. These were just photos, no worse than the ones I took on the job, and he was a lonely old man. Besides, I could surely take a guy in a wheelchair. Look at his feet, for God's sake, turned in toward each other—probably hadn't felt solid ground in years.

The image in my hand stared back at me with empty eyes. It showed a man, midthirties, in a hospital bed, pale as a corpse—because he was, in fact, dead. His slightly open, dehydrated lips and gaunt face seemed to form a sound—*eeeeh*—like the screech of an unwilling door forced open by the hand of death.

"That's my friend," Hump explained, inching closer and tapping the photo. "Harry West. Begged me to capture his soul leaving his body. Said it would be fifteen minutes after he died because he'd be bidding farewell to the memories in his heart and brain. So I sat with him all night. He passed at 2:15 a.m. and I took the picture at 2:30. Injured by a grenade, you see."

"I don't mean to be forward, Hump, but in this photo, it looks like he's been dead for more than fifteen minutes. You took this shot in profile and you can see all the blood pooled at the base of his neck. It's called livor mortis." In death, blood no longer enjoyed the thrusting pump of a heart to help it defy gravity. It settled to the bottom like everything else. I'd seen one guy lying facedown for four days in an alley during a particularly hot August. Between decomp and livor, we couldn't even tell if he was black or white.

"Oh, gosh, Janie, I forgot how much you deal with this stuff every day. Well, you know how I am."

No, I didn't. Hump spoke as if we shared a long-established bond rather than a one-minute roll across a parking lot. I found it disconcerting and the room seemed to grow smaller. The smells of an old man in such close quarters suddenly became more concentrated—his old-fashioned aftershave, the bad breath from a rotting tooth he'd tried to cover with minty toothpaste, the bits of mud caked in his wheels that provided a gritty tone to the palette of odors. It all combined to make the oxygen in the room more difficult to access.

"Your friend here . . ." I said, not sure where I was going with the words.

Hump touched my arm. His hand was cold. "Just between you and me, Janie—I've never told anyone this—but I may have drifted off for a few hours while waiting for Harry to pass. I'm afraid I broke my promise." His small voice fell to a shameful whisper. "His soul slipped out while I was snoring at his side." Hump removed his hand, held up a crooked finger and shook it. "In my defense, I'd been feeling ill, and the air in that hospital was hot and thick. Could have lulled a warlock to sleep."

I gazed at him sympathetically. He'd been carrying that around for a long time—the sin of sleep while a friend died alone. Was I his sole confessor?

"I think Harry would have understood, Hump."

"Thank you, Janie. That means a lot."

"Still, do you think this is an appropriate picture to share with your grandnephews?"

"Oh, yes," he said, perking up. "Right now, they think war is aiming a gun with a plastic controller and watching blood spurt out like a fountain. I want to show them reality, make an impact. Don't you think that's noble?"

Noble, sure—or warped. I flipped through more photos: a damaged tank with a streak of blood on its side, four smiling men with missing limbs, a close-up of a foot with four toes and an inelegant scar, a portrait of a woman in uniform with the reality of the world weighing on her narrow shoulders. The dreariness continued. I couldn't. My surroundings grew tighter. There wasn't even a back door to escape through if the rear windows were jammed shut. And what if the fire escape was blocked or corroded?

My inner voice, the one I so often stifled when it warned me of danger, had gone from nibbling at my core to chomping at my brain. Weighing my options, I decided that scanning the photos and wheeling him out of my life for good was the way to go. Hell, I'd even throw dollar bills at him.

"Let me grab my scanner so you can get on your way."

"That would be lovely," he said, "absolutely lovely. And . . . might I trouble you for a cup of tea?"

I looked at him like he'd asked for roasted duck, then forced myself to get a grip. It was an old man who wanted tea. I should be embarrassed for not having offered.

Ah, screw it. I'd make his tea lukewarm, let him gulp it down, and shoo him out.

"Sure." I shoved a chipped mug of water into the microwave and set it thirty seconds less than usual, then headed to my bedroom to get the scanner and flash drive. By the time I returned, Hump's chair was facing away from me and his head was sunk down. *For God's sake, please tell me he's not dead.*

"Hump, you okay?"

I went rigid when he didn't answer. I was fine with stiffs, but not in my apartment, and not ones I'd just been chatting with. I dropped my things on the coffee table and rushed toward him just as he whistled in appreciation. "My goodness, Janie, is this the house where you grew up?"

Relief and agitation washed over me. "What are you looking at?"

He spun his chair around in a remarkably deft movement, Jack's book on his lap.

"Oh, jeez, Hump, let's put that away. It's my brother's debut as an author, of sorts."

"You've clearly cracked it open," he said, a hint of accusation edging his voice. "It didn't make that new-book creak, the one that quality hardcovers make when you spread the pages for the first time, as the smell of the virginal paper wafts toward the reader."

His tone gave me chills. Did he think I'd raped the book—or denied him the pleasure?

"Looks like you spent a lot of time on *this* page," he said, tapping it with his pudgy finger.

So now he was a literary forensics expert? The page showed multiple photos of my mother with her parents, mostly on her birthday or holidays. In the largest image, she wore a pretty lace dress and a salmon-colored bow, the same color as the paint in her childhood room. That page had bothered me because it seemed to hold a clue I couldn't decode.

"I can tell," Hump continued, "because the book wants to go

there, offering itself to you. Was there something unique—or disturbing—about this page, Janie? Or had you just not seen many photos of your mother when she was young?"

I wanted to slap him and say, *It's disturbing because my mother was killed in that room, dumbass*, but I went with, "I don't know. The whole book is tasteless and manipulative."

"Ah, how Machiavellian," Hump mused. "Well, your brother is a politician. It's in his blood, one might say."

"Or one might not."

"Problem accepting a politician as your father, Janie?"

"Look, Hump, I'm trying to be nice here, but my hang-ups are my own."

"You know, I learned a lot from others in the chair. Repression has its merits, but denial, no. It's one thing to accept a reality, make it small, and stick it in a corner, tend to its needs when its cries become relentless. But denial? That hoodwinks your mind into believing that something you know happened didn't happen. Look at motion sickness. Your eyes tell your brain you're moving, but your body tells your brain it's sitting still. It doesn't compute. Imagine what happens to the poor brain when its master processes two opposing facts as true. This happened; this didn't happen."

"That's all well and good, Hump, but if you don't mind, my family dynamics are—"

He put up a hand to stop me. Almost immediately, his eyes swelled and the telltale tensing of the neck followed. "I'm sorry, Janie, so sorry. Lifelong tendency of mine." His voice caught. "*Big buttinsky*, my parents called me. Please forgive me. You've been nothing but kind, and I've taken advantage. I get too . . . enthusiastic with new friends. It's a phenomenon that as we prepare for the solo journey to meet our maker, life readies us by making us more alone with each passing year." He pressed his finger to his lips. "I guess I'm not quite ready yet."

Oh for shit's sake, why didn't I just kick a puppy? I went to the microwave and gave his tea an extra thirty seconds. I'd offered this deed in the first place to make up for my lack of time with Grandpa. The least I could do was see it through pleasantly. I set down his mug and even brought along some old gingersnaps, hoping he'd dip them so he wouldn't realize they were stale.

Having returned my brother's book to the coffee table, Hump accepted the tea and immediately dunked a cookie.

"Sorry I was short, Hump."

"You had every right. We'll just get those photos scanned and I'll skedaddle."

"By the way," I said, "that *was* the house I grew up in. It's kind of painful to see those photos because the house stayed like that most of the years I lived in it. Right down to the ugly papier-mâché gargoyle my grandmother made in an art class."

"And where is it now? Still there?"

"Probably not. Grandpa overhauled the place about ten years ago to impress a lady friend."

"Oh, my. What did he do with the old things?"

"Not sure. Probably put them in storage."

"But they must hold rich memories for you, Janie. You'll find when you're my age that solid links to the past can be valuable, restorative really."

I sighed. "I guess I should find out, especially with Grandpa being sick." I opened the book to point out the gargoyle, but stopped at an earlier page to show him the tall tree outside the huge living room window. "See this magnolia?"

He nodded with an encouraging smile.

"I used to hide there during hide-and-seek. Jack never found me when I used that spot."

"My spot was a divot in a giant evergreen where a branch had rotted and fallen. It offered the perfect indentation for a small boy to blend in if he crouched just so."

"Things don't change much between generations, do they?"

"Not as much as we think." Hump picked up his envelope to remove the remainder of his photos. "All right, Miss Janie, show me how to scan one of these things." He pulled out a photo and gasped. "Oh, my! I'm so sorry! I don't think you meant for me to see this." He thrust the photo of my prone and bleeding mother at me.

"Jesus, Hump, sorry," I said, stashing the photo out of sight. "Thought those were on the far side of the table."

He tilted his head at me. "Well, now it makes sense."

"What does?"

"Forgive me, but that was your mother, wasn't it? As she lay dying, as Faulkner might say."

His description gave me the chills and I swallowed hard. "Yes."

"You were trying to find an answer."

"To what?"

He looked at me thoughtfully. "As I told you earlier, my niece let me read her materials on you. Quite the treasure trove."

"Just who is this niece you keep referring to?"

"Jenna, of course. Jenna Abel. She kept her maiden name."

My jaw dropped. Yes, Jenna had become a reporter, one who allegedly wasn't above using her good looks to coax quotes from otherwise reluctant public figures. "So you're *Uncle* Hump? I remember you."

"It's a name that sticks with you, that's for sure, but how do you remember me?"

"From playing at the Abels'." The memory of my first and only childhood encounter with Uncle Hump would stay with me until my dying day. "Can't believe you're an Abel." Accusation colored my tone a murky gray.

"No, I married Abner Abel's sister, Joann, but she passed five years ago. I'm a Banfield through and through."

"That's a relief," I said, not giving a hoot if he was a descendant of Cap'n Crunch, as long as he wasn't an Abel by blood. "How come you only considered staying with Jenna, but not Mr. Abel?"

"I'm afraid Abner doesn't speak to me anymore. We had a rather serious falling-out over the care and treatment of my wife when she was dying. I encouraged her to fight with all she had, to try some experimental treatments, and he grew convinced that's what killed her."

"I'm sorry. He can be rather inflexible, can't he?"

"He doesn't even know I'm in town. Jenna's been helping me out during my medical visits. She's always been kind to me, probably against her father's wishes, but she and my wife had been close." He slapped his hands down on his thighs. "Enough about me. Seems like you've got more interesting things on your plate."

I studied the old man for a moment. Yes, his war photos were of an eerie variety but they'd also been of a superior quality, and I respected anyone who could draw story and emotion from a single frame. Maybe he could help. "Okay, Uncle Hump, I'm curious. What exactly do you think I was trying to answer with those photos? Because I've been a bit stumped myself."

Hump looked at me with suddenly shrewd eyes. "You're looking for an explanation, Janie, an explanation that finally fits. Certainly both the prosecution and the defense came up short in providing a satisfactory story, one that filled all gaps and allayed all doubts." His voice grew soft and hypnotic. "You're seeking to understand why your mother died in that living room, why she ran home at all, why she thought she had a real haiku, and if she didn't, why her boyfriend marched into her house and ended up taking her life. No matter how you dissect the situation, no single explanation really suffices, does it? At least not one that's been speculated to date. And I can't help but think that this absence of an actual answer has pecked away at you your entire life on some subconscious level. We both know what the pecking of a persistent notion does to us. It demolishes fragments of our nature before we've even had a chance to gain familiarity with the whole. And so we keep searching, searching for the answer that finally fits, finally fills the jagged void the pecking has wrought, with the dream of one day, maybe, putting it all to rest."

His tea had grown cold. I had grown warm. My heart had slowed. I felt lulled, pacified. No one had ever expressed it so ominously yet so succinctly.

"You need to dig, Janie. You need to find the answers, for your own sake." He touched my arm again. "Let me help."

CHAPTER 21

Janie and Jack Perkins, Age 13

Annelise Abel turned the hose on young Janie and sprayed so hard that the water shot up her nose. At first Janie giggled to maintain the illusion of fun, but Annelise stepped close enough that Janie thought the metal nozzle itself might be searing her skin.

"Stop, Annelise! Cut it out." Janie kept her voice light so the older girl wouldn't banish her from their yard again. Annelise was one nasty bugger. If she told her siblings to make life hell for the Perkins girl for the entire summer, those devilish minions would take her orders to the nth degree. Three of the minions—Annelise's sisters, Jenna, Mary, and Maureen—giggled inanely as Annelise taunted Janie with the hose. Meanwhile, two of Annelise's brothers stayed busy filling water balloons at the spigot behind the house.

Janie tried to outrun the reach of the hose, but Annelise's spindly legs could cover a lot of ground. She was an expert at concentrating the stream into razor-sharp lasers, leaving red trails up and down Janie's back.

"Don't be a baby, Janie! It's just water."

Suddenly the sound of the gushing liquid halted and the pain ceased. Janie spun around to see her brother, Jack, behind Annelise, the tube made pinched and powerless by his strong grip.

Annelise wheeled, ready to verbally thrash whoever had interrupted her fun, but upon seeing handsome Jack Perkins, she lowered her head into her shoulders like a turtle in retreat. "Oh, Jackie, it's you. When did you get here?"

"Why don't you cool it, Annelise?"

Annelise held the nozzle behind her with both hands, swaying her hips and acting like the most misunderstood gal in all of Caulfield. The pose made her tiny breasts stick out through her cousin's ratty, hand-me-down bathing suit. "I didn't mean nothin' by it, Jackie. We was just playin'."

"Didn't look like Janie was havin' much fun."

"Course she was. Weren't you, Janie?" Annelise turned to Janie with viable threats looming in her close-set eyes. The threats spelled weeks of being *it* in all games and future dares, like putting sausage just beyond the reach of Mr. Clark's dogs and ringing old ladies' doorbells—things Janie hated but did anyway to stay in the good graces of her only playmates. A lapse of loyalty here would mean a lonely summer, especially with Jack being so busy and popular.

"It's okay, Jack," Janie said. "You can let go." Her body shivered at the thought of being attacked again, but luckily, she and Jack—despite plenty of sibling animosity—shared an unshakable mental conduit, as if the normal twin bond had multiplied exponentially when they'd been denied attachment to actual parents.

"I don't think so," Jack said. "Give me the hose, Annelise."

Annelise hesitated only a moment before strutting over and relinquishing the hose to the boy she'd had a crush on for two years. Despite being older, Annelise would have given anything, including her not-so-sought-after virginity, to Jack Perkins at the snap of his fingers. Luckily, Jack had the wherewithal never to snap his fingers in her presence.

The next twenty minutes held shrieks of delight, with Jack using the hose as a toy rather than a weapon. But when a strange car pulled into the Abels' driveway, all the kids ducked down and watched. Visitors were a rarity and the ultimate excuse for spying.

"Let's go," Annelise commanded as her father, Abner Abel, came out on the porch.

To Janie's young eyes, Mr. Abel always looked ill, but since he'd looked that way forever, she figured some fickle disease must've wasted him into a sunken-chested, hollow-cheeked man and then up and left. The boys looked the same way. Maybe it was destiny for Abel males to look like death had painted them with a soft brush and then moved on in search of meatier subjects. Not to say Mr. Abel wasn't strong, though. His power multiplied tenfold when he took a switch to his sons' bottoms.

Mr. Abel waved to his guests—a short, chunky man and a slim woman in a hat. When they entered the house, the kids skedaddled toward the cellar doors that lifted up from the ground and offered entry to the cool sanctuary where they all told ghost stories on Saturday nights.

Janie loved the cellar because anything could happen. Imaginations ran wild and morals flew out the spiderwebbed windows. Annelise had gotten her first kiss down here, and Robbie Abel—dumbass that he was—had inhaled his first cigarette at the bottom of the stairs, letting the telltale smoke travel straight to the kitchen. His first ciggy had been followed by his hundredth belt whooping.

Annelise settled herself on the tall, creaky chair that Janie and the younger Abel girls had garbage-picked two years ago. They'd carried it clear back home, getting splinters and sweating up a storm, only to have Annelise commandeer it for her personal throne.

As she wrapped herself in a towel and assumed her position on high, the rest of the girls squirmed on the floor, trying to find the thicker parts of a thin rug that smelled like rotten eggs.

Annelise caught Janie's eye and pointed to a white stool in the corner that was missing the bottom quarter of one leg. "That's where our daddy got whooped by his daddy. He'd sit in that stool bare-backed and if he yelled out while getting thrashed, his daddy started all over again."

"Why you tellin' me that?" Janie asked.

"Daddy says punishments must fit the crime. You keep actin' like you did outside, we'll have to put you in that stool, and I don't think that lily white skin of yours would look so good with whoop marks on it, do you?"

Janie hugged her knees and shivered, wishing Jack was within earshot, but he and the Abel boys were piling crates so they could uncover the ceiling hole they'd drilled last month. They used it to listen to adult conversations above.

"I didn't know y'all's dad grew up in this house," Janie said.

"Course he did," Annelise said. "We Abels been in this house over a hundred years. When I grow up, I'm gonna live here, too."

Janie couldn't imagine a worse fate, especially if Mr. Abel was still around.

"Who are the visitors?" Janie asked.

"Aunt Joann and Uncle Hump," said Jenna, two years younger than Janie and by far the prettiest of the bunch, not that the competition was real steep. "Aunt Joann's real nice and all, but Uncle Hump, he'll look at you funny and give you the heebie-jeebies sometimes."

"What kind of name is Hump?" Janie said. "It sounds plain wrong."

Annelise put a hand up to keep her sisters from answering. "Janie," she said, "don't tell me you don't know what humpin' is."

The other girls looked at Janie pitifully, and she gave thanks for the bad lighting that covered the blush of her cheeks. "Course I do," she said. "I didn't fall off the turnip truck yesterday."

"Tell us, then," Annelise said. "Tell us what humpin' is."

"If you don't know, it's not for me to say." Janie thought herself pretty clever for that one, but Annelise came back fast. She feigned a hurt look and leaned down with a desperate whisper.

"Please tell me, Janie. I'm serious. I'm real embarrassed 'cause I don't actually know. I heard the boys talkin' last week and they was goin' on about humpin' and I felt stupid 'cause I didn't have the slightest idea what it was. Please?"

"Yeah, we don't know, either," said Jenna, apparently forgetting how she'd just laughed at Janie's ignorance.

"Well," Janie said, enjoying her moment of superiority, "it's when two animals go courtin' one another, and the male animal tries to impress the female, so he struts around like he owns the place. And that's when people say, *Look at that raccoon, humpin' for that lady raccoon, tryin' to get a date.*"

Annelise burst out laughing, emphasizing it with a point of her prominently knuckled finger. The sisters followed suit. Their peals of laughter sounded like the jeering scorn of an entire town, and Janie felt like the hot one at a Salem witch trial.

"That's peacockin'!" Annelise said. "You have no idea what humpin' is, and I don't think you ever will, not with that indented chest of yours."

Janie curled her legs in even tighter. "You don't know what it means any better than I do." She realized as she spoke that Annelise had known all along.

"Lemme tell you something, Janie Perkins, I know for sure that you *should* know about humpin'. It's what your mama did to that lyin' murderer in jail. She humped on him sum'n good and then got herself knocked up with you and Jack there." Annelise glanced lustfully at Jack, who had his ear pinned to the ceiling. "I guess one good thing came out of your mama's mortal sin."

"My mama was no sinner."

"Look it up, Janie. Your mama was the worst kind. And now you and Jack, you're stained forever. It's like a bad birthmark only God can see."

"I'm not stained any more than you, Annelise Abel."

Annelise began chanting and pointing at Janie. The younger sisters joined in. "Stained, stained, stained, stained." The sound exploded in Janie's head and before she realized what she was doing, she rushed Annelise, toppling her and her throne to the ground. Annelise's head smashed into the rough wooden stairs and landed with an ugly thunk on the cement floor.

Everything went silent and even the boys stopped their eavesdropping to take in the drama.

The blood running down Annelise's head sent Janie into a shocked frenzy. She took off, lifting those thick cellar doors like they were tissue paper. By the time they slammed shut, she was halfway across the Abels' backyard, the woods ahead a blur of rage and tears. But when she got twenty feet from the shortcut to her house, she ran smack into Mr. Abel and the infamous Uncle Hump. A compact camera stuck out of Mr. Abel's pants pocket—he often carried one to photograph birds—and each man held a pint of fresh-picked raspberries in pink-stained fingers.

"Slow down there, young lady," said Mr. Abel.

As Janie skidded to a stop, the hot air molded to her body and she felt exposed in her flimsy two-piece. Her legs shook beneath her.

"Young lady," said Mr. Abel in his sticky, molasses voice, "where are you running to?"

Uncle Hump chortled. "Might be more appropriate to ask what she's running *from*, Abner."

Abner must have fixed Uncle Hump with a measured glare, for the latter stopped laughing abruptly while his stubby fingers found a loose button on his shirt to fiddle with. That was all Janie could see of the mysterious Uncle Hump, because she refused to lift her eyes to either man.

"I asked you a question, Miss Perkins," Mr. Abel said.

He never called her *Janie*, as if the utterance of a familiar moniker would signal approval of her existence. "I was runnin' home, Mr. Abel, sir. I needed to use the bathroom."

"I see."

"This ain't one of yours, Abner?" asked Uncle Hump.

"Heavens no," said Mr. Abel, the two words smothered by the shame of the suggestion. "She belongs to the neighbors. And enough said about that." Leaning down, he breathed in and out slowly, his sour breath making Janie's nostrils flinch. "Where are my children? They need to say hello to their uncle Hump."

Janie refused to be the tattletale on top of being the idiot. "I don't know, sir."

"Weren't you just playing with them?"

"Yes, sir." She was shivering and dizzy from her mad sprint.

"So you're lying. If one of mine lied to me like that, it would mean the belt and no supper. Punishments must be exacted. But then, we don't expect much from the likes of you Perkinses, do we?"

"I don't know, sir."

Just then, the basement door opened and Jack emerged, followed by the lanky Abel brothers.

"Ah, there they are," said Mr. Abel to Uncle Hump, adding quietly, "along with this one's bastard brother."

With that, Janie had about had her fill of the Abels, because she sure as hell knew what a bastard was. She stomped down hard on Mr. Abel's bad foot and sprinted away for dear life, heading for the safety of the woods and her own house.

"You'll pay for that, young lady!" Mr. Abel shouted. "Sinners always pay! Just look at your mother!"

Despite the circumstances, Janie turned around, cupped her hands to her mouth and shouted, "Grandpa says you're a big, ugly blowhard, Mr. Abel, and everyone in town knows you're a two-faced humpin' bastard!"

As she turned and ran, the wind whooshed past her damp ears and a smile lit up her face. The whoop of Jack's laughter and the rapid cadence of his footsteps running behind her in support added the only sounds that could have made the moment any better.

CHAPTER 22

The morning after my unexpected visit from Hump Banfield, Jack and I paid a quiet visit to the hospital. Not wanting to mention Grady's name in front of Grandpa, I dragged Jack into the hall to talk.

"Listen," I said, grabbing his phone from his hand as he tried to check a text, "I need to say something."

"Not like you to preface anything you have to say, Janie. I can't imagine."

His snippy attitude wouldn't make this easier, but I wasn't entirely sure I deserved an easy go of it. "You might have been right."

"Hold the phone!" Jack yelled, and then he glanced at my hands. "Oh wait, you already are. But do tell. What was I right about, and to what do I owe this miraculous turn of events?"

I explained to him about Sophie's work. He looked surprised and impressed.

"So you actually believe Grady now?"

I shook my head. "There's still a lot that needs to be figured out, but, uh"—my mouth went dry and my head felt hot and woozy—"I did go visit him."

Jack's face showed a true, unfiltered, unrehearsed reaction. "Damn" was all he said, and I felt our gap shrinking a few precious millimeters. Until he ruined it with, "You know, the timing of this could be awesome. I could work it into my stump speech."

"I've got to go," I said, firmly entrenched on my side of our chasm. I handed him his phone.

"Wait, I need more details."

"I don't have time right now. Why don't you call Grady? He loves hearing from his precious John."

I returned to Grandpa's bedside to kiss him good-bye. "Hey, Janie," Jack said as I reentered the hall and strode past him, "you'll call me if you need help, right? Or if you just want to talk?"

I harrumphed and looked back. "I wish I could, Jack."

The slight change in his posture betrayed his disappointment. "Well, at least don't do anything dangerous."

The huge, messy can of worms I was about to open filled my mind. "I'm afraid I already have."

I left the hospital and drove straight to the police station to ask a favor of Detective Wexler. I found him crouched beneath his desk.

"Hiding?" I said.

He glanced up, not the least bit startled by my sideways appearance or my ponytail nearly brushing the floor.

"My sister had a toy horse like that," he said. "Your hair, I mean. She cut it off one of her dolls and glued it to her horse's butt."

I threw my ponytail behind me as I stood back up. "Thanks?"

"Well," he said, crawling out from his protective lair, "your hair would have made that horse envious."

He dusted off his jacket and held up the tiny screw he'd retrieved from the floor. "Dropped something."

"Yeah, his pants," shouted a passing senior detective I despised. "Dropped 'em to his knees, then crawled under there to take care of business."

"Lovely, Detective Schwank," I said. "But not everybody conducts their love life the way you do—cowering in a dingy corner, alone and afraid."

Schwank flared with anger; I'd clearly struck a nerve. "Yeah, Perkins? Why don't you let me show you how I do conduct my love life? Maybe knock you up with some twins—like your mom."

Detective Wexler slowly reattached the screw to his three-hole punch. Without raising his eyes to Schwank, he spoke in a clear voice no louder than the hum of a ceiling fan. "Detective Schwank, if I ever hear you speak to Ms. Perkins like that again, I will not only file sexual harassment charges against you on her behalf, and drag your ass through Internal Affairs for all the laxity in your recent investigations, but I will give you ample reason to bring me up on assault charges. Of course, you'll be doing the latter from your hospital bed."

Schwank sucked in a bitter gulp of air, letting his chest puff up almost as big as his gut. It gave him a moment to make sure he'd understood Wexler correctly, but he still didn't look too sure about what had just transpired. He stood a good four inches taller and forty pounds heavier than Wexler, but the meat on his bones was discount ground chuck, while Wexler sported Grade A filet mignon.

"Listen here, newbie," Schwank wheezed—his asthma tended to act up when his facial capillaries bulged—"I'll say what I want when I want, to whoever I want when I want."

The lameness of the comeback made me smile and I didn't attempt to hide it.

"Excellent," said Wexler, taking a seat and gesturing for me to have one, too. "I look forward to more of your profundities. Now be on your way."

Schwank kicked the garbage can of the clerk whose desk he was passing. Papers flew everywhere, and it occurred to me that a waste-basket would be a fine place for my brother's paperweights.

"Well, well," I said to Wexler as I glanced at his matched set of bulging biceps and sculpted shoulders through his white, button-down shirt. "Look at you, going all Dirty Harry over li'l ol' me."

"I do what needs to be done," he said, brushing off the front-and-center display of chivalry. "What can I do for you, Janie?"

"I had a heck of a day after we left Sophie's yesterday and I'm on a serious mission today. Since you've become my unwitting ally in the mysterious photo caper, could you lend a little detective help?"

"Name it."

"Any way to find out who mailed the photos?"

"You have the envelope?"

I laid it on his neat desk.

"Ridge, West Virginia," he mumbled. Tapping his computer, he called up information on Ridge's lone post office. He picked up his phone and got the postmaster on the line. The man's loud, choppy voice came through clearly. After a short conversation, during which they mentioned surveillance cameras and two mailmen, Wexler gave the postmaster his phone number and hung up.

"He'll get back to me this afternoon."

I grinned. "I feel like I could have done that."

"But you didn't. Had I realized ten years ago that most detective work is dialing a phone, I might have reconsidered my career choices."

"Which would have been . . . ?"

"Chef or pilot."

"You've thought that through."

"Hasn't everyone? I'm halfway to becoming either/or."

The comment hit me like a sneaky slug from a smart bully. Wexler hadn't intended anything by it, but a sadness washed over me. I barely had a plan for the next week, let alone alternate career paths mapped out with courses on standby to launch me on the way.

"Janie, you okay? You look . . . confused."

"I'm fine. Can I trouble you to do something else for me?"

"Of course."

"Could you look into a guy named Humphrey Banfield and make sure he's on the up-and-up?" I explained about my two encounters with Hump. "I keep getting mixed signals, and now I've lent him my brother's book."

"Why?"

"Long story, but I knew I'd be busy today and figured it wouldn't hurt to have another pair of eyes helping me out. Plus, he kind of pleaded for it. I think he fancies himself a detective with a unique perspective."

"Don't we all?" he said with an implied wink. "And yes, I'll check him out for you."

I scooped up my bag and turned to go, but spun back around, leaning one hand on the far corner of his desk. "By the way," I said with a nod toward the still-red Detective Schwank, "could you?"

Wexler grabbed a triangular paper clip and spun it slowly between his fingers. "Absolutely. He'd need stitches above his left eye, a reset of his broken jaw, lots of bendable straws since he wouldn't be able to eat solids for a week, and a year to heal his inexplicably huge ego."

I smiled, believing every word. "Bigger ego, bigger target."

"It's what brings them all down," Wexler said. "Eventually."

CHAPTER 23

Lucinda Lowry, a waitress who had worked with my mother, lived with another woman she referred to as her *buddy*. After a string of abusive boyfriends, Lucinda had wised up and married the innocuous Ned Farting, a diner regular with a steady job as a traveling salesman and enough money to set her up in a three-bedroom ranch house. She had two daughters with him before a woman showed up on her doorstep one day with two boys who bore a striking resemblance to old Ned. The woman arrived with three bits of news. The first: her marriage license was dated two years before Lucinda's. The second: Ned Farting's last will and testament left everything to his legal spouse. And the third: Ned was killed the night before when a tractor trailer overturned and squashed his Volkswagen like a bug. The last bit was delivered with a sinister grin.

Lucinda had mourned like a real wife, given thanks that she'd been persuaded by a Helen Reddy song to keep her own last name, and took over Ned's sales route. She'd made good money, met up with her buddy somewhere along the way, and retired a happy woman with two lovely daughters. She welcomed me with open arms.

"Look at you, darlin'! Haven't seen the likes of such beauty since your mama and I worked together for that disgusting Mickey Busker."

"Sorry I haven't been in touch much, Lucinda," I said. "Thanks for seeing me."

"Nonsense. We both have lives to lead. Tell me, you got a man in yours? What's his name, what does he do, and are you sure he doesn't come with a ball and chain already attached?"

I laughed or groaned or some combination of the two. "More men in my life than I care to mention. Some of them coworkers, one of them my brother, and most of them corpses."

"Oh, Lord, don't tell me this visit has to do with police work. You still workin' those crime scenes?"

"Yup, and I pick up freelance work on the side."

"For the life of me, Janie, I don't know why a pretty thing like you gets involved in that stuff."

Was it just me or did pity cloud her gleeful expression? It passed quickly. "I made us some sandwiches and tea," she said. "Come on in."

We settled into her cozy kitchen and I realized I hadn't eaten a homemade meal in ages, even if it was just sandwiches. Turkey, Gouda, tomato, and avocado on rye with a dollop of mustard hit the spot. When she pulled out a concoction called Cocoa Bomb for dessert, I about exploded, but it tasted so good, I asked for seconds.

"Good to see you eat, Janie. You could use a few pounds. Now tell me, to what do I owe this visit?"

I apportioned the story into digestible chunks and let her take her time with it. It had surely been a while since she'd thought about the events of that night.

"I remember it like it was yesterday," she said, surprising me.

"Your mom was the closest thing I had to a sister, even if she didn't feel the same way about me."

"What do you mean?"

"Don't get me wrong. Your mom was sweeter than anyone else at that diner. We'd laugh and make fun, and she'd let me ramble on about whatever. And heck, I'd confide things to her I never told another living soul, but she never let me get too close. Played her cards close to her vest, and, well, she knew I was itchin' to find out who your daddy was." Lucinda glanced down apologetically. "I was a tad nosy in those days."

Where was that understatement plaque I'd planned to give Grady? Everybody in Caulfield knew Lucinda was still unduly curious about others' personal lives, but she was so open about it—and not a spreader of acquired gossip—that it actually endeared her to folks.

"Lucinda, do you have any idea how my mom might have gotten her hands on a haiku?"

"Oh, Lordy, no. It was busy that night. How truly frightening to think that a killer might've been in the diner."

"Any customers stand out in your memory?"

"Let's see. We had a soccer team in from Goodland. Their coach was odd, but mostly 'cause he collected dead animal tails; he died in a boating accident years ago—engine sucked up a beaver tail, believe it or not. And we had a lot of old folks in, some families with kids. I remember it being loud, and your mom was late 'cause her car broke down."

Lucinda strummed her fingers on the table. "The thing I remember most is when Grady McLemore came in, unannounced and all. Course, it makes sense now, knowin' about the two of them, but it was unexpected then. He chatted it up with the customers. A couple ladies asked him to sign autographs and one even asked him to sign a cheap dinner napkin!" Lucinda giggled. "That man had such a pull on people."

"So I've heard." I'd swear she blushed.

"And then he went over and made a big to-do about some shy customer who worked for him. I tell you, that poor man turned the same color as his name." She slapped the table in amusement.

"What was his name?"

"Rusty! Least that's what Grady called him. Said this Rusty fella had fixed up some stuff at Fourth and Eastman, the makeshift campaign office. Humble little thing. Thin brown hair, pale, and he sure didn't like bein' the center of attention. He was in your mom's section." Lucinda nodded as details flooded back. "Yup, she gave him a free piece of pie. I remember 'cause we were almost out and he got the last piece."

I jotted down notes. *Grady, Rusty, repairman, pie.*

"Any other customers my mom interacted with?"

"Well, sure. She had a nice chat with Mrs. Murphy about her flower garden, but that old biddy kept glancing from your mama's belly to her left hand, which bore no ring, of course, and I wanted to go over and slap that three-chinned wonder 'cause I knew good and well some secrets about her that wouldn't cast her or her late husband in too fine a light."

Lucinda took a big breath after that one while I wrote down Mrs. Murphy's name. Hard to imagine a jiggly widow wreaking havoc around town, plus I had a vague recollection of reading her obituary.

"Anyone else?"

"There was a chatty, older couple who Grady sat down with, and, oh, Abner Abel, of course."

"Mr. Abel, my neighbor?"

"That's the one. He'd come in now and again when he got back from a long haul. Parked his meat truck across the street from the parking lot 'cause Mickey would yell at him for hogging up spots otherwise. And you know what I heard?"

She waited for me to answer, so I shook my head.

"Heard he was a different man out on the road, driving all through the state and up and down the East Coast, delivering fresh kills to butchers and grocers. Friends at every stop."

It jumped unbidden into my head that Mr. Abel might have been enjoying other forms of fresh meat out on the road, considering what was waiting for him at home. The Mrs. Abel I knew had spent most of her life pregnant or miserable—or both.

"And he would chat nonstop on his CB radio," Lucinda continued. "Can you imagine? I heard tell his CB handle was *Big Ham*."

"Good Lord, no," I said, unable to conjure a more disappointing serving of ham than Abner Abel on a plate. *Junior Burger* or *Veggie Pattie,* maybe, for a man who floated through Caulfield like a bedraggled ghost, but not *Big Ham*.

"It's true," Lucinda continued. "Here's the best part. Apparently, he was some sort of CB counselor, dolin' out advice to other truckers. Can you imagine?" Lucinda lifted an imaginary CB radio to her mouth. "'You've got Big Ham. What can I cure for ya?' That's what he used to say! I swear!"

Seriously? A CB counselor with a specialty in meat issues and a penchant for puns? I could only imagine the calls. *Hey, Big Ham, I just overpaid for some diesel. You think I have a bone to pick?*

The new image made me shudder. Did Mr. Abel, in hammy advice mode, speed up his verbal delivery from his syrupy fifty words per minute to the standard hundred and ten? Or were those truckers so bored, they'd hang on for ten miles to get a four-sentence answer from the guy? I tucked the information away and hoped never to retrieve it.

"And my mom waited on him?"

"She sure did. And you know, they had some kind of fallin'-out."

My ears perked up, pleasing Lucinda. She loved an attentive audience. "Go on."

"Well, I always sat Mr. Abel away from the kitchen so he wouldn't hear any of the cursin' or carousin' back there. Told me once he didn't approve of the devil's music they played. And I sure didn't want him overhearin' any of Mickey's tall tales. That Mickey would lie to Saint Peter himself without battin' an eye."

Mickey—pathological liar, I wrote.

"Your mama about handed me my head later that night, tellin' me never to put Mr. Abel in her section again. I don't know what all went on. I would've asked her the next day, but, well, you know."

Yes, comas put a serious damper on gossip. And this story put a serious footnote on Mr. Abel.

I wondered if Mr. Abel was the local who knew about my mother and Grady, the one Sam Kowalczyk had investigated and dismissed. If so, maybe there were more layers to that man than seemed possible for his slight body. Would he have considered my mother's sin so vile, so contemptible, that he'd have taken it into his own hands to do something about it, to clean up a little mess for the Lord?

Lucinda and I chatted for another twenty minutes before her buddy, a genial woman who ran a history-tour company, arrived home. She was lovely and it warmed me to know that at least one of Mickey's waitresses had attained happiness. Unfortunately, though, based on what Lucinda had said, I now had to seek out a much less happy duo: the vile Annelise Abel and her upstairs tenant—that humping bastard, Abner Abel.

CHAPTER 24

Bridget Perkins, 30 Years, 90 Minutes Ago

Grady McLemore walked into the diner, all shoulders and swagger, power and charm, a grand grin showing everyone the miracles that fastidious orthodontic care could accomplish. In a weird occurrence that Grady probably considered normal, the diner went silent upon his entry. Not even the clink of a spatula against the grill in the back. Bridget knew instinctively that the underpaid kitchen workers were poking their heads through the order window or pressing their noses against the greasy panes of the swinging doors. There was just something about Grady.

Comfortable as ever in the spotlight, he let loose with a big "Hey, folks! Lovely evening out there. What a night!"

Bridget wished she could agree, but Mr. Abel's eyes were still peeled on the window, watching Sam Kowalczyk's Mercedes drive off, the same Mercedes he'd seen earlier when Bridget was the passenger.

Mr. Abel caught Bridget's eye and lifted his arm like a tin man in need of oil. He beckoned her over.

She froze for only a moment. Oh well, nothing to it but to do it; she hoped he'd show some tact. She smiled to indicate she'd be right there, then glanced down at her other party-of-one customer, the turkey Reuben guy. He was the only person not staring at Grady. Instead, he clutched his treasured pen so hard that his index finger looked like a barbershop pole, flashing red and white as blood fought through his rigid grip. Grady might have a tough time switching this guy's vote to his column.

Bridget felt sorry for the lone man and felt doubly bad about her earlier heist from his pocket. "How 'bout some pie on the house?" she said, leaning over him. "Since I knocked down your pen and all?"

The man nodded, just barely, and Bridget wasn't even sure he'd processed her question.

While Grady signed autographs and chatted up customers, Bridget forced herself to step lively to Abner Abel's table. "Yes, Mr. Abel? What can I get you?"

"You know," he said, his demeanor smug, "the missus found out *she's* pregnant with a little one." He looked pointedly at Bridget's belly.

"How wonderful for you both," Bridget said, wondering if her words sounded as flat as her reaction to his non-news.

Mr. Abel turned his eyes to Grady just as laughter erupted from a group of admirers forming near the door. Then Mr. Abel glared at Bridget, making it clear he knew the truth.

"Be a shame if that McLemore gentleman loses his election."

"What makes you say that?"

"Humility. It's both a gift and an obligation. Those who feel superior, who try to pull the wool over the eyes of the flock, they suffer the wrath of the Lord in unexpected ways."

Bridget stiffened. "And you think Mr. McLemore has not humbled himself before the Lord?"

"Not my place to say, now, is it?"

"On that, we agree, Mr. Abel." She forced a smile. "You interested in dessert this evenin'?"

"I hear the pie is sinfully delicious but . . . it can be a bear payin' for sins down the line. Don't you agree?"

Bridget delivered her rebuke with a joyful lilt in her voice. "Kind of makes you wonder, doesn't it, Mr. Abel, about what past sin *you* might be payin' for, given how your children behave half the time. Children can be a bear sometimes, don't you agree?"

Mr. Abel practically breathed fire from his narrow nostrils. "How dare you? Barton made a big mistake not encouraging you more strongly to get baptized. I tried to spread the Good News to him, but he failed to hear."

Bridget could put up with a lot, but she wouldn't allow anyone to disparage her father, and she wasn't about to start with this pastor wannabe. "The only thing you're good at spreading, Mr. Abel, is your seed. And poor Mrs. Abel, she bears the brunt of the results, doesn't she?"

Mr. Abel jerked up from his seat, scraping his chair and making Bridget jump. He leaned toward her, his breath tinged with alcohol, and his taffy-stretched face testing the limits of elasticity. "For you may be sure of this, that everyone who is sexually immoral or impure has no inheritance in the kingdom of Christ and God."

"Ephesians, Mr. Abel? Thought you'd be more of a Corinthians *flee from sexual immorality* type."

With nostrils flaring and lips quivering, he shoved his hand into his pocket and cast his money down on the table without breaking eye contact, as if a steady glower could excise Bridget's sins. Two quarters clanged to the floor. "I warned Barton. I warned him what would happen."

"And he warned me—to watch out for those who drape their beliefs over others. Usually means they're too afraid to draw back their own curtain."

Grady suddenly approached the table to save his damsel in distress. Mr. Abel reared his head back to sneer at the sinner. As Grady opened his mouth to speak, Mr. Abel put up a hand to shush him. He shook his head in an *X* pattern, like he was warming up for a boxing match, then thinned his lips into a satisfied grimace, directing his words at Bridget. "Sins come full circle," he hissed. "But all who receive Christ as Lord can receive forgiveness."

Grady, undaunted as ever, extended a hand. "Hi. I'm Grady McLemore. And you are?"

Mr. Abel jerked away, turning his linear form into a curve as he veered away from the practiced politician and stormed out the door.

With most patrons' eyes upon her, Bridget forced a smile.

"He didn't want dessert, after all," she said, getting a laugh from several relieved customers. She grabbed what Mr. Abel had thrown on the table and shoved it into the first pocket she found in her apron, hoping her hand wasn't trembling too visibly. After clearing his plate and shaking off the encounter, she went and got the final piece of pie for her other customer.

Grady, the master of smooth in all situations, acted like nothing had happened. He chatted with two older women, who used any excuse to touch him, then put his arm around a blushing Lucinda—insisting that everyone tip her well—and finally headed straight to the table where Bridget was setting down the pie for her turkey Reuben customer.

"Rusty!" Grady said, patting the customer's back in recognition. "Didn't know you frequented this thriving establishment. Best milk shakes in town, wouldn't you say?"

Bridget glanced back and forth between her customer and Grady, surprised they knew each other.

"Hey, there, Mr. McLemore," Rusty said, turning to shake hands while keeping his eyes low, a slight tremor evident in his fingers now.

"Rusty here is the best handyman around," Grady announced, riveting everyone's attention. "He's only been in town a few weeks, and already he's fixed the dripping faucet in my office, patched a hole in the roof, and silenced a radiator that squealed and kicked like a toddler every time I was on the phone."

"Simple adjustment, simple adjustment," Rusty mumbled, staring at his pie as if it held the secret to the universe, his face the color of the ketchup bottle.

The female half of an elderly couple, seated a few tables down, chimed in and wagged a finger at Rusty. "Sir, if that's true, I'm gonna have you over to my place. The radiator and refrigerator have been on the outs with each other all week. When one works, the other doesn't. I've either got cold milk or cold feet all day long!"

Her husband released a hearty chortle and Grady chimed in with a laugh.

"I remember you," Grady said in a teasing voice as he suddenly focused on Bridget. Now it was her turn to make like the ketchup.

"And I, you, Mr. McLemore," she said, giving as good as she got. "You campaigned here—what was it—ten months ago?"

Grady's lips twitched in amusement. "Longer than that, I'm afraid. Closer to a year and a half. Just kicking off the campaign back then."

"That's right," Bridget said. "You ordered a fruit salad and scrambled eggs—and something else that wasn't on the menu."

"That I did. All of it well beyond my expectations."

"Makes one wonder why you waited so long to come back."

"Well," he said, "I do think about this place every time I'm ravenous."

Rusty cleared his throat and shoved a too-large piece of pie in his mouth, clearly uncomfortable with the odd exchange going on above his head.

"Awfully long campaign," yelled the husband of the cold-footed woman. "Over a year? Back in my day, they kept the campaignin' to a minimum, the work to a maximum."

Grady knew an opening when he heard one. He strode over to their table and, within a minute, was seated in their booth, fork in hand, scooping a chunk of the woman's mashed potatoes into his mouth—at her insistence, of course.

Bridget slid the repairman's check onto his table. She noticed him glancing at Grady periodically with an expression she couldn't quite distinguish. Distress? Awe? Jealousy? Usually she could decipher others as easily as breaking down a recipe and detecting an extra sprinkle of cinnamon, but this fellow was so twitchy and reticent, she couldn't get a solid read on him, as if he were wearing a mask. Well, she'd gotten what she needed from him anyway; her craving had subsided. Let him retreat to his life in the shadows, fixing faucets and radiators, with circuits and sounds for company.

Suddenly she remembered that she needed to return his item. It was buried somewhere in her pocket and she hadn't even read it, let alone had a chance to return it, but she didn't want him to leave without it. That preachy Mr. Abel had thrown her off her game, but all was good; the act of the taking had been precisely the thrill she needed. She'd drop the item on the floor and pretend to find it for him.

But before she could, the man stood and paid with cash on the table, swiftly, as if he'd had the money counted out in advance. Leaving half his pie uneaten, he strode out, head down, looking at no one, hands tucked firmly in his pockets. Slightly emptier pockets.

So distressed was Bridget by his sudden exit that she never noticed the lit cigarette across the street from the parking lot, traveling up and down in a smooth arc, from thin lips to narrow hips, far too fast for a leisurely smoke. Occasionally, its flame reflected against the grille of the truck where the smoker was leaning.

CHAPTER 25

Janie and Jack Perkins, Age 15

The sun made steam rise off the dark roof shingles, so Janie and Jack grabbed towels before climbing out.

"Did you get 'em?" Janie asked.

"Course I did," Jack said. "Got a little something else, too."

"What? Marijuana?"

"No, idge-head." It was his word of the month for *idiot*. "What does Grandpa Barton always have when he's smoking?"

"Brandy or whiskey or some god-awful smellin' thing."

"Exactly." He held up his knapsack in triumph. "Got us some mulberry wine from Mrs. Peckinpaw's."

"How'd you do that?"

"Old Lady Peckinpaw's deaf as a doorknob, so last night I snuck into her canning shed and took two bottles."

"Two?"

"The Haiku Twins do everything in twos."

Janie nodded in simple agreement, then smoothed her towel so she could stretch out her legs. She loved looking out over the yard.

If she angled herself just right, she could block out everything, including the distant smokestack from the Lucky Strike plant, leaving her with only trees, sky, and hawks—three of her favorite things.

Jack reached into his back pocket and pulled out the coveted pack of smokes and handed them to Janie. She peeled the red string from the cellophane and stuffed the crinkly cover into her pocket.

"We'd never get away with this if Elsa was still here."

"Elsa the Terrible!" Jack shouted. "Why'd Grandpa even need a housekeeper?"

"They hired her when Grandma got the cancer. Guess she just ended up stayin'."

"She was plumb nuts, rearrangin' the pillows on my bed for ten minutes at a time, makin' 'em into perfect squares and facin' 'em all the same direction. She about pulled her hair out once when I jumped on the bed and messed 'em up."

"You were what they call a Grade A pain in the ass."

"Finally faked a sneezin' fit and convinced her I was allergic to the stuffing in the pillows. Showed her an article on dust mites and everything."

"You can talk your way out of anything, Jack, unless you're wantin' to talk your way in, of course."

Janie held the cigarette pack to her nose and let the sweet scent coat her brain. Then she smiled, her teeth even whiter than her hair.

"You gonna smell 'em or smoke 'em?"

She slid the first one out and slipped it between her lips like a pack-a-day smoker, lighting it with ease, and inhaling as if it might be the last breath she ever took.

Jack lit one up and took out the wine. Five minutes later, they were lying back on their towels, staring at the sky, woozy and happy.

"You know why mulberries are blood red?" Jack asked.

"'Cause they ain't green?"

"No. It's 'cause of this guy Pyramus and his girlfriend, Thisbe."

"Weird names."

"They're Greek. See, Pyramus and Thisbe loved each other but they weren't allowed to date 'cause their parents hated each other."

"That sucks."

"Their houses were attached, like apartments, so they'd talk through this crack in the wall, and one day, they decided to meet in secret at this white mulberry bush."

"White?"

"That's what I said. So, bein' the girl, Thisbe got all prettied up and put on her nice clothes and got to the bush early. But she got scared when she spotted a lioness walking by with blood all over its mouth, so she ran away to hide. But in the mad dash to escape, she left her cloak behind."

"Uh-oh," Janie said.

"Yeah, well, when Pyramus arrived, he saw the cloak and by then, the lioness had got all up in it and it was mangled and bloody. Pyramus thought for sure Thisbe was dead and decided he couldn't live without her, so he pulled out his sword and hari-kari'd himself right there."

"That's horrible!"

"It gets worse. Thisbe came back to the mulberry bush, but it was too late."

"Pyramus was dead?"

"Not quite, but he was on his way."

"Kinda like Mom was after she was shot."

"Yeah, well, I guess we should be glad Grandpa Barton didn't do like Thisbe, because when Thisbe saw Pyramus dying, she whispered sweet nothings to him, and then she took up the sword and killed her own self. They died together next to that bush."

"That's awful. Why are you tellin' me this?"

Jack lifted the stolen bottle from Mrs. Peckinpaw's shed. "'Cause we're drinkin' mulberry wine. The story goes that it's Pyramus's blood that stained the mulberry bush and turned the berries red forever."

Janie shook her head. "I can't imagine bein' that much in love."

"You seen Carline Waters's bosoms lately? I could definitely imagine bein' that much in love."

Janie smacked her brother. "Well, I guess it's how much I would've loved Mom if she'd lived."

"Nah, you'd hate 'er for curfews and such. And who knows? Maybe Mom would've been a real witch."

Janie flicked her brother with her finger. "Promise not to laugh?"

"No."

"Sometimes I pretend Mom's in one world and I'm in another, and they bump up next to each other, and there's this vicious storm that rips a hole between the worlds."

"Like the cracked wall between Pyramus and Thisbe?"

"Yeah, but this crack is big enough for a whole person to squeeze through. And Mom does, and she's all beautiful and wearin' this white dress that blows in the wind, and she has gorgeous hair, you know, the way long hair looks underwater."

"Ever hopeful, Janie."

"Anyway, she tells me all the things a mom is s'posed to tell a daughter."

"Like what?"

"I don't know. Stuff a girl should know."

Jack looked sympathetic. "Yeah, guess you never had anyone to teach you that stuff, did you?"

"Picked up what I needed to."

"So what happens at the end of your colliding worlds?" Jack asked.

"Mom goes back before the crack closes 'cause she can't survive in our world."

Jack laughed. "Why don't you change it? It's your thing. Make it so she can stay."

"Then it's too disappointing when she's not really here. This way it's still possible, you know, even if the chances are like one in a billion."

Jack sipped more wine and gazed out over the expansive back-yard. "I think this is what they mean by the good life."

"I'm hopin' it means a little more than this," Janie said, "but this ain't bad."

"Heard Jenna Abel teasin' you the other day," Jack said.

"She's gettin' as nasty as her sister. Said I'll be the fourth Perkins woman to die young and tragic."

"What'd you say?"

"Pulled her hair. Told her she'd be the first Abel girl to die young and tragic if she didn't shut her trap."

"Nice."

"Grandpa Barton says snotty retorts are my *for-tay* or something." A mellow silence floated between them. "You think it's true, though? You think the Perkins women are cursed?"

"Nah. We all create our own fate, like that poster in my room with the motorcycle dude and that long stretch of road. He's goin' wherever he wants. Like for me, I'm gonna be president. Otherwise, why bother, you know?"

"You will go all the way, Jack. Just don't forget about me."

Jack directed a confidential sideways glance at his sister. "Speakin' of goin' all the way, I heard Annelise Abel started doin' it recently."

Janie came to full attention. "With who?"

"Not sure. Fella a couple towns over. Now they call Annelise *ready, willing, and Abel.*"

"Wow," Janie said, "that's not good."

They stayed silent for a while, both half-dozing off, until a sharp rustle in the woods made them jerk awake and sit up.

"Shit," Jack said, swiping away the cigarette that had fallen onto his jeans. "What was that?"

Janie frowned, looking at the tall tower of ashes on her cigarette, piled like a stack of fanciful wishes. She crushed them into a roof shingle. "You ever see things in those woods, Jack? Think maybe someone's watchin' us?"

"No. Do you?" Jack gave her a cautious, questioning look.

"Just a feeling I have sometimes. And it's always about those woods."

"Could be reporters, but they're pretty scarce lately."

"Maybe."

Jack narrowed his eyes. "You think he's still after us?"

"Who?"

"The Haiku Killer," Jack said.

Janie pshawed. "Grady McLemore made up that story."

"What if he didn't?"

Janie pictured Grady McLemore rotting away in a cold cell, breathing through a single tiny hole, one teenager-on-a-dare's finger away from his air supply being cut off. "He made him up. He had to."

"But what if? What if he was in our house that night and he's decided to come back for us?"

"Stop talkin' crazy, Jack."

Janie swallowed away the sick feeling in her gut and lit another cigarette. The match's flame quivered in her hand.

CHAPTER 26

I drove three miles to confront a guy who'd surely be less reliable than a blind drunk with a cockeyed imagination and grudges to settle. Come to think of it, that was a pretty good description of Mickey Busker, whose rusting trailer loomed in front of me.

One of my mother's plain-talking aunts once told me a story that she swore came straight from my mother's lips. She said Mickey reveled in the greasy cacophony of the diner kitchen because he didn't have to watch his mouth and could pinch the waitresses' asses out of sight of the customers. After Bridget's first week there, she'd arrived home with a stain on the back of her uniform resembling an infinity symbol—Mickey had branded his property with thumb and forefinger in a highly inappropriate place. Bridget knew she had to take a stand if she wanted a finite end to the infinite sleaze. The very next day, with a full tray in one hand and a soda pop in the other, she caught sight of Mickey's dirty fingers approaching her backside, so she spun around and tossed that pop right in his face. He tried to make some macho comments, but Bridget got up in his business, as close to his stained teeth as she dared, and delivered her warning in a whisper. "Next time, Mickey, it'll be acid. But there won't be a next time, will there?"

I remembered my aunt adding a luscious detail that, in retrospect, was highly inappropriate to share with her sixteen-year-old niece: "Of course, Mickey needed to get to the bathroom anyway, to take care of the burgeoning hard-on in his pants. Just the way he was, I s'pose. Rejection erection, we called it. But at least your mama redefined their relationship that night and he never touched her again. You keep that in mind, Janie, if any boys ever give you trouble."

I hadn't been sure which part to keep in mind, but suffice it to say that my ass remained unbranded. After that story, I'd understood why Mickey never looked Jack or me in the eyes when we were children. I used to think it was regret over letting Mom close the diner alone, but it had to be shame through and through. At least, I hoped it was. Either way, I'd been under strict instructions as a child to never be alone with the guy.

I was about to break all the rules.

I knocked on his trailer door.

A woman answered, an unlit cigarette in her hand. She looked like an actress who'd been freshly tousled for a spent-hooker scene in a Hollywood shot—parched hair pointing in six directions, great skin made sallow by off-color makeup, big eyes made tired by dark bags—but with no director or makeup artist around, I assumed the look was her own and that it was permanent. She introduced herself as Glassie, held the door open for me to enter, and made no effort to move the barrel-chested pit bull blocking my entry. The place was small and smelled like grease. Maybe the diner had permeated Mickey's pores and become part of him.

Glassie pointed behind her, but it wasn't hard to find Mickey. He was lounged out in the space to my left, watching old reruns. Apparently, the same director who'd ordered Glassie to look worn-out and defeated must have ordered *zombie* for Mickey. *Just grab a dead guy, prop him up, and paint some half eyes on 'im, the kind you see on a late-night fast-food worker who doesn't give a damn if you want fries with that.*

Mickey turned his head, easy and calm, as if people came and went all day, paying him social calls.

"Shit," he said in a gravelly voice. "You look just like her, but not as pretty."

"Mickey, you dumb fuck," Glassie said with less judgment than one might expect with that brand of sweet talk. "You don't say that to a lady."

"Guess I shoulda said it to you, then."

Glassie frowned, then padded back to the kitchen in her faded blue slippers, lighting her cigarette on the way. It smelled minty and I wished she'd wave it around Mickey to mask his odor.

I sat, without being invited, on the edge of a faded aqua otto-man and faced my repellent host directly. Last I'd seen him, about fourteen years ago, he'd been in his late forties, but he'd aged in dog years, putting on at least seven for every one of mine.

His eyes stayed glued to the TV while I gave him the bare pre-liminaries. He finally muted the idiot box and looked at me. "So, Mickey," I said, "tell me everything you remember from that night."

His eyes shifted to an even lower gear, and he grumbled before he spoke. "I don't know. Who remembers a thing from that far back?"

"You do." I decided to treat him like a sideshow hypnotist's mark. I'd seen some of the guys at the station do it with drunk wit-nesses. I kept my voice steady, the phrasing repetitive. "An employee you had the hots for was killed that night. You've thought back real hard to that night. Bet you could draw me a picture of the diner that night if you wanted to, with every customer in place, every employee in the kitchen, and every order on a plate."

He waved away my comments. "I was in the kitchen most of the time."

"But you came out some, didn't you?"

"Nope. Only went out to have a smoke after that Grady feller showed up. I liked smokin' in the fresh air, but I saw that ever-complainin' Abner Abel leanin' against his truck smokin', so I went back inside to avoid that preachin' prick."

Interesting. "What else do you remember?"

"Nothin'. Don't remember nothin' else 'bout that night."

I kept up my entrancing tone. "We remember trauma, Mickey, and maybe joy. The rest fades into a kaleidoscope of glossed-over garbage, but we remember the things that leave a scar."

"What the hell you talkin' 'bout?"

"The bad stuff gets vaulted in our brains so it can't go away. But you know the combination to your vault, Mickey. Couldn't forget it if you wanted to. And we both know that Bridget Perkins getting killed was bad stuff for you. It's why you never looked Jack and me in the eye. It's why you never spoke to our family. You feel guilty about something, don't you, Mickey? Ashamed. Tell me about that night."

He almost leaned forward, but the demand on his flaccid abdominal muscles was too much. He settled for a quick lurch, followed by his usual recline. "You know how much I drunk between that night and today? You got any idea?"

Yep. A shitload.

"Talk to the poor girl, Mickey," said Glassie, appearing at the entryway, her cigarette now half its original length. "It ain't like you got a reputation to protect. Tell her how you was watchin' her mother that night. Tell her."

Watching? Where? When? I held my questions—and my horror—while Mickey went mute and shaky, seeming to undergo a set of DTs despite smelling like whiskey and clutching an open beer. Was he reliving the evening? Was he on tape delay? After half a minute of crushing silence, he wheeled—as much as a seated drunk can wheel—on his woman. "Shut yer trap, Glassie. 'Tain't none of your business nohow." He sucked on his beer. "Why don't you take that goddamn dog out for a walk 'fore he pisses the floor again?"

Glassie, unfazed by Mickey's bravado, shook her head and grabbed the leash.

I stayed focused on my mission. "When were you watching Bridget, Mickey? Were you watching her that night?"

He chucked his beer can across the room and looked like a sullen child.

"I know you liked to watch her, Mickey. And the police have uncovered new witnesses who are implicating you and putting you at the scene. It'll be a lot easier if you talk to me now."

"What witnesses? Is it that damn Lucinda runnin' her trap? She was always such a pain in my ass."

"I'm not at liberty to say, but I can tell you the sooner you come clean, the better. Come on, Mickey, you remember. When were you watching Bridget?"

His hand squeezed at empty air, craving his tin can back.

"After," he mumbled, his head sinking, rolling around his chest.

"After her shift?"

"After *my* shift. Wasn't the first time, neither. Sum'n 'bout her bein' pregnant. I dunno. Women give off different hormones when they're knocked up. She was so full, and sum'n 'bout the way she smelled, and her face was . . . I dunno. How's a man s'posed to control himself, that's all I'm sayin'."

If my fetal presence in my mother's body had made her more attractive to this letch, I really needed to paste his picture above the medicine cabinet of every woman in the country, with the caption *Don't Forget Your Birth Control*. Then again, maybe it hadn't been my mother's pheromones, but rather the scent of a bathed woman, that had done it for him. Hard to imagine he'd been around many.

"Did you control yourself, Mickey? What did you do? Did you threaten her? Did you follow her?"

He jerked away as if I'd grabbed him. "What are you talkin' 'bout? I ain't never said that to no one."

"Just because you didn't say it doesn't mean it isn't true."

"Don't go tryin' to confuse me with fancy talk. I been interrogated for all sorts of misdemeanors, mostly drunk, and they ain't been able to trip me up yet."

Mostly?

"When did you watch Bridget, Mickey?"

He stood up with tremendous effort, shoved at the air like it was biting him, and turned his back to me. "I was in the parkin' lot, that's all. I done it plenty o' times. Didn't hurt no one."

"You liked to watch her when she was alone in the diner, on the nights she was closing?"

"Who wouldn't?"

Normal people. Nonperverts.

"Didn't she see your car? Didn't she know you were out there?"

A tight fear gripped my chest. Fear for my young mother, laboring in the spotlight, unaware of her starring role in the porno in Mickey's head.

"How stupid you think I am? I rode my bike. Wasn't but a mile or so from my trailer."

He whirled then, suddenly angry at me for making him admit to something he was ashamed of. His close-set eyes became two enflamed slits. Combined with the red veins traversing his nose, they reminded me of a bloody sheet, stretched thin as a desperate man wrung it out, trying to hide the evidence. But Mickey couldn't hide anything anymore. Any character he once possessed had been whittled down by alcohol, his moral fiber shredded into wispy filaments barely holding him together.

I could see the moment when he changed his mind, when he decided to wallow around in his guilt and go for the shock factor, to make it my burden instead of his. A single spark lit his eyes.

"Heh, this must be eatin' you up 'cause you were there that night, weren't you? I guess in a way, I was gettin' my jollies off of you, too. And it was sweet. All I needed was my spyglass and a tree to lean on." He held up his right hand, its palm remarkably clean, and shoved it toward my face. "And this, of course."

So Mickey was a voyeur, getting off in the parking lot with a pregnant waitress as his muse. Was that all he was, though?

"You ever done it standing up?" He was on a roll now. Might as well get it all out. "It's harder 'cause your legs get weak, and you gotta stay upright at that moment when all you wanna do is collapse and explode. I mean to tell you, shit. Ain't never had it as good as when I was young. And your mother . . ."

If he dropped his pants right here and started whacking off, my surprise meter would jump to zero. But since I had no desire to stand in for my mother in this particular role, I shut down all emotional attachment to the situation and tried to bring Mickey back to cold reality. Cold-shower reality. With a lie.

"And then you followed my mother home and broke into her house. That's what the police think, Mickey. Did you know that? They wanted to haul you downtown to talk to you, but I begged them to let me handle it first."

The police barely knew Mickey was alive—except when they were failing to befuddle him with their fancy talk—but I needed to find out if he knew anything about the third man, or, God forbid, *was* the third man.

Mickey looked hurt, like my comment had blunted the erection struggling to form in his trousers. "How do they know I followed her home?"

Holy shit. The shock I swallowed formed a lead ball in my stomach. Mickey really had followed her home? Why did I keep ending up alone with the unstablest people in town? I glanced around for support. Where was Glassie? How long did it take to walk a damn dog, for God's sake? You let it pee, you bring it home.

"Who told you?" he shouted. "No one ever knew I was there."

"The police told me. They have new photos that don't look good for you," I said, letting him infer what he wanted.

"I knew it! I knew someone was takin' pictures. What else could those flashes have been?"

Inside, my stomach performed wild gymnastics, but I stayed calm, not wanting to halt the flow of information. Mickey turned oddly contemplative, his intellect perhaps stimulated for the first time since he'd had to decipher a thorny episode of *The Simpsons*.

"Who was taking pictures?" I said, my own intellect on edge, along with every nerve in my body.

"I dunno." He shrugged, looking like he could transition into a nap with minimal effort.

"Mickey, this is important. Who did you see taking pictures?"

"I didn't know who it was back then. I sure as hell ain't gonna know now."

"Are you talking about Grady McLemore?"

"No, the other guy."

My eyes went wide and I became as still inside as I'd ever been. Finally, an eyewitness to the mysterious third person—and it turned out to be this vermin?

"Pretty sure I saw that Grady feller, though. Came in with a gun." Mickey cackled, but it caught in his throat and turned into a wet cough. "Wasn't long before that haughty bastard was down for the count."

"You saw another man at my mother's house that night and you never told anyone?"

"Right," Mickey said, lacing the word with sarcasm. "Like I was gonna tell the police I was at Bridget Perkins's house jerkin' off in a tree the night she got shot. What are you, stupid? Yer mother sure as hell weren't stupid. She kep' secrets and stuff real good."

"Yes, I'm sure she wishes you gave her eulogy."

His eyes went to half-mast as he sat back down and reclined, the confession having lifted a burden from his wrecked soul. Meanwhile, his inexcusable silence had wreaked havoc with mine. It had kept Jack and me from having a father. It had kept Grady in prison. It had allowed another man to go free. I could barely process the unfolding tidal wave of implications as I saw the pages of my life flipping backwards from this moment to my birth, each page with an alternate floating just out of reach in some unattainable abyss, containing a story that could have been written, a story that could now never be told or experienced. Even in a man like Mickey, the consequences of his inaction must have created a fetid hollow in his heart, one he'd been trying to fill with alcohol ever since. I couldn't help but wish it had already drowned him. But my rage had to wait, at least until I got more information.

The next sentence in my mouth tasted like bitter fruit. "You mentioned a tree at my mom's house, but I thought you were . . . pleasuring yourself against a tree at the diner."

"I was, but then yer ma was gettin' ready to leave, so I hightailed it to her house before she could get there. I was in good shape then. Wasn't no big thing to bike a few miles. Hell, I had nothin' to do and I'd done it once before, besides. Used that big tree in her backyard. Easy climbin' and lots of places to . . . get comfortable."

I wanted to curl up and make myself so small that my brain couldn't function, with all memories squeezed out and destroyed. Because no way could I process the image of Mickey Busker jerking off in my favorite magnolia, the one where I'd hidden from Jack, where I hosted make-believe parties with imaginary friends and magical fairies. When I envisioned how my mother's old bedroom could clearly be seen from that tree, it was all I could do to keep from knocking Mickey unconscious and setting fire to his trailer.

"Let me get this straight," I said. "By the time you biked to the house"—I couldn't think of it as *my* house for the moment—"and climbed the tree to get a good look, Grady McLemore was already there?"

"He was just gettin' there. It was him, your mom, and some other guy I never did get a good look at. I couldn't tell what all was goin' on, and I was wonderin' what in the hell Grady McLemore was doin' there in the first place, when all of a sudden he crashed to the floor. Looked like that other feller bashed him in the head or sum'n. Then a gunshot went off and that's when I started scramblin' down those branches 'bout as fast as a hunted squirrel. Right after, some headlights shot into the backyard and I knew I had to hightail it outta there, and just as I'm ready to jump to the ground, that's when I seen them flashes go off."

"And you think they were camera flashes?"

"Sure looked like it. Quick, you know, kind of blindin', goin' in different directions. Maybe a dozen or so. Then the back door flew open and I figgered I'd best set my ass in place on that low branch. And good thing I did, 'cause someone came crashin' out that back door and down the steps and run across that backyard into the woods. Had kind of a giddyup in his step, I remember that."

"A giddyup?"

"You know, a hitch, but he ran pretty fast besides, like it wasn't nothin' to him."

"Which foot was it?"

"Shit, how should I know? I was tryin' to zip up and whatnot. Didn't know I was witnessin' a damn crime."

"Yes, gunshots usually suggest good times all around." I shook my head, trying to reel in my horror over Mickey's arboreal antics. "Which direction did the man in the woods run?"

"Weren't but so many ways to go. Toward the Abel place, I guess."

"Did you hear a car start up after that? Anything?"

"Nah, but I wasn't exactly listenin' for nothin', neither."

"Did you follow the guy?"

"You nuts? I wasn't gonna go chasin' after some phantom in the woods while I was trespassin', sportin' a woody, and voy-errin' on one of my waitresses."

"So you took off on your bike and never said a word to the police?"

"Now you got to realize, I had no idea Bridget was lyin' in there bleedin' half to death."

"Otherwise I'm sure you'd have run in to save her."

That got him out of his reclining position again. "Don't go gettin' all high and mighty on me, little girl. I'd argue till my dyin' day that any normal guy in that situation woulda turned tail and ran, just like I did."

I stood and leaned in as close as I dared to this animal. "No *normal* guy would've been in that situation."

"You weren't there. You don't know."

"Normal guys don't climb trees and get their jollies off a pregnant lady in the middle of the night, and then run into the woods like little babies with their dicks hangin' out of their pants."

"Now yer just puttin' things in a way that don't seem right."

"*Don't seem right?* What'd you do, Mickey, run home and find the third time was the charm? Did you finally finish the deed, you sorry-ass deviant? Jerking off to a dying woman instead of saving her life?"

I didn't know if that last bit was even possible, but I never wanted to hurt someone as much as the pathetic, cowering loser in front of me. "You put Grady McLemore in jail for thirty years! A man who could've made something of himself. A man who could've done some good for the world. What have you done with thirty years, Mickey?" I gestured around the dreary trailer. "How do you live with yourself?"

"I done some good for the world."

And with that, Glassie returned, the short butt of another cigarette hanging out of her mouth, the pit bull straining at the end of his leash to rip apart the small woman berating its master.

"Tell her, Glassie, tell her," Mickey implored.

"Tell her what, Mick?" she said, disinterested as all hell.

"Tell her I brung some good to the world."

Glassie lifted her weary eyes to mine and shook her head.

CHAPTER 27

My cell phone rang as I drove down the road, trying to cleanse my soul of the visit with Mickey. I wanted to shower but water didn't come hot enough to remove the stains of depravity he'd inflicted on me. I sure didn't like the way my mother's final hours were panning out. Seemed like she was in trouble everywhere she turned, and calling the one person she did trust had turned out to be the worst move of all.

The ringing wouldn't stop. I didn't like talking on my cell while driving, so I pulled into a roadside farm stand.

"Hello," I said.

"Hey, Janie. Alex Wexler here." It was the first time we'd spoken on the phone, and the first time he'd announced himself. It was endearing that he'd said Alex instead of Detective, but it left me at a loss.

"Hey, Wexler, not to usurp the conversation, but you will not believe what I just found out."

"Do tell."

The horror of Mickey's silence, not to mention the apelike images of him defiling my favorite tree, darkened every nook of my mind. "You know what? It's best not discussed over the phone, but if the words of an inebriated reprobate are to be believed, then the mythical third person is quickly morphing into a flesh-and-blood entity."

"Does the entity have a name?"

"Not yet. But you called me. What have you got?"

"I heard back from that postmaster who's probably also the mayor and premier watchmaker of Ridge, West Virginia. Ridge is one of *those* towns."

"Says the man who's a detective, a chef-in-training, and a defender of poor maidens threatened by psycho cops."

"I know you can handle jerks like Schwank, but an overwhelming sense of courtliness came over me. Hope I didn't go too 1800s on you."

I laughed as I got out of my car and scanned seven bins of apples, knowing I'd end up with premade apple butter and a loaf of bread baked by someone else. I'd become that kind of country girl. "Your chivalry was refreshing. Remember, I'm used to the likes of Nicholls."

"If that's where the bar is set, I'd like to think I cleared it long ago."

"By several yards. Maybe miles."

The pause on the other end of the line allowed me to imagine Wexler's full lips framing his crooked smile, and my heart fluttered as if feeling the softness of those lips on mine. I dispelled the image quickly by shoving a tiny sample of applesauce into my mouth.

"So I have a name for you," Wexler said. "They think it was a local woman that mailed the photos. Elizabeth Fitzsimmons, known around town as Betty. She handed the envelope to the mailman herself. I checked online to see what I could learn about her, but only came up with a letter she wrote years ago to the local paper about animal cruelty. Then I called the Ridge Police Department."

"What'd they say?"

"They were closed for lunch."

"Closed? What if I was mugged at lunchtime in Ridge?"

"A lovely woman by the name of Florence would take your call. She said a black-and-white could be dispatched if I was lying in a ditch bleeding to death, but, otherwise, I didn't meet the criteria for disturbing the sheriff during his ribs and slaw. She took a message."

"At least we have a name. Betty Fitzsimmons. I can't wait to find out how she got her hands on those photos."

"The postmaster knows Betty, of course. Said she was born and raised there. Still lives in the farmhouse where she and her brother were brought up by a widowed dad who doubled as preacher and farmer. Keeps to herself, works for a vet, bit of a packrat."

"How old is she?"

"About sixty, although the postmaster hinted she looks older and acts like something out of the nineteenth century."

"Ah," I said, "a woman who would appreciate your knightly gestures."

"My nightly gestures? Like gargling with Listerine?"

Was he making a joke, or had he actually misunderstood? "Knightly—with a *k*," I said through a smile. "I don't know anything about your nightly gestures—with an *n*."

"Oh," he said. "Would you like to?"

My stomach flipped. In a good way, not the nauseating way it had in Mickey's trailer. And then I fumbled and couldn't come up with a single damn thing to say in return. Figured it was best to move on. "Did you find out anything about my buddy Hump Banfield?"

"Running a search now."

"I owe you."

"Tell you what," he said. "If you're not busy later, you can buy me a drink. Maybe the sheriff will have finished his ribs by then, and I can update you."

Despite myself, I bubbled over with nervous anticipation. "Sure, yes," I blurted. "Where and when?"

"The Shell Place, on Garrett. They have a great bar and small, quiet booths. Say . . . six o'clock?"

"See you there."

"And Janie?"

"Yes?"

"I brush and floss before washing my face, and usually read a magazine before I fall asleep."

A grin slowly overtook my face and I wished he could see it. "Those are some fine nightly gestures, Wexler. I'll see you later."

CHAPTER 28

Ridge, West Virginia, Present

Sheriff Tucker picked the last of the sinewy ribs from his teeth. Ralphie's BBQ + Beer provided toothpicks free of charge on the way out the door, but they might've done better to serve a higher grade of rib in the first place. The sheriff, only two years from retirement, tossed the toothpick onto Betty Fitzsimmons's front yard, hoping she wasn't peeking out her window and tsk-tsking. For all her slovenly stockpiling of useless junk, Betty tended to be fastidious about two things: her lawn and her hair. Both were done up fine and right, the former trimmed to within a quarter inch of its life and the latter combed into a tight, neat bun that glowed with cleanliness.

Sheriff Tucker had already stopped by Doc Mason's on the way over to see if he could catch Betty at work, but the doc said she was home sick. Had been for a couple days. And her brother, Leroy, the local fix-it man who kept to himself more than a zebra in a tiger pen, was out of town on a construction job. Poor Betty must have been tending to herself. The sheriff felt right bad that he and his wife hadn't heard about Betty feeling under the weather. Hadn't even brought her a pot of soup, and now here he was, about to bother her over some photos she might have mailed. The city fella on the phone hadn't gone into specifics, but Sheriff Tucker sure hoped it wasn't something as trivial as Betty putting on postage a few cents short. That Betty, she could save a mangy, tick-infested hound and have him doing new tricks in two days' time, but she couldn't mail a dang envelope without getting the law involved.

He knocked twice on the front door, then brushed away a cobweb thick as a long drip of syrup to find the doorbell. He pushed it but heard nothing. It was likely gunked up with dead bugs from when it used to illuminate. Betty and Leroy got so few callers, they probably didn't even know the bell was broken. He knocked again, louder, with a good eight raps. Nothing. Now, that was weird. Maybe she was too sick to answer. He couldn't exactly bust in, though, not over postage. He'd try back later, maybe have Florence give her a call.

Grumbling about wasting his time, the sheriff turned to go, but then he heard a thump against the dining room window.

"Betty? That you?" He couldn't see through the grime on the pane. With all the cats Betty took in, the layer of filth probably consisted of tongue slime and fur, nothing the sheriff felt like taking a close look at.

A second thump came. "Now, Betty!" he shouted. "I'm gonna have to come in there unless you can answer me."

He waited, then knocked one more time. In the heavy hush that followed, he walked over and placed the edge of his hand against the window and pressed his face close, only to leap back in shock as a cat plastered its body against the window in what seemed like a desperate bid to escape. Sheriff Tucker didn't cotton much to cats, being more of a hound person himself, but he could tell that cat was none too happy about its current set of circumstances.

Knowing the feline would take a break before its next launch, he pressed his face to the window again.

"Lord have mercy," he said. Then he turned around and threw up exactly eight dollars' worth of Ralphie's BBQ + Beer lunch special.

Poor Betty. She sure would be displeased with the appearance of her hair in the next photos taken of her.

CHAPTER 29

Janie and Jack Perkins, Age 16

"Come on! Hurry up!" Jack yelled, his newly low voice still freaking Janie out. But in truth, both twins were changing. Jack got all the height, breadth, and muscles, while Janie got thick hair, an angular face, and a figure that got her voted *Most Wanna Get in Her Pants* by the varsity football team.

Janie entered his room, a sketchbook and pencil in her hands. "What is so dang important, Jack?"

"Janie, we're not saying *dang* anymore, remember? We're removing all twang and colloquialisms."

"Yeah, why is that again?"

Jack sighed while he gathered his patience for his less bookish sister. "Southern twang doesn't play well on the national stage. No more *ain't* and *y'all*, either—unless it's called for."

"Clinton's got some kind of accent. Worked out all right for him."

"Regardless, I need to be able to eliminate it if necessary, so help me practice."

"Fine. Now what is so *damn* important?"

"We've got to get on the roof before Mr. Abel gets here."

"Mr. Abel? He's never set foot in our house."

"Robbie called and said I was in deep shit." The grin on Jack's face said it all; he might be in deep shit, but he was quite comfortable there and could always find his way out.

"What'd you do now?" Janie asked.

Jack raised the window and climbed out. Above the expansive front porch, the roof flattened just enough that if they stayed face-down near the edge, no one could see them. They lay head to head, their feet pointing in opposite directions. As they got situated, they heard the crunch of the rocks when Mr. Abel's truck turned down their long driveway.

"Does Grandpa know he's coming?" Janie asked, overemphasizing the *g* at the end of her sentence.

"Nope," Jack said, lifting his head and peeking at the truck. "Holy shit! Annelise is in the passenger seat. This oughta be good."

Janie gasped. "Did you do something with her?"

"Please," Jack said.

Mr. Abel got out of the car while Annelise stayed rooted in her seat, a stubborn, snotty look on her face. Mr. Abel turned back when he got a few feet in front of the truck and realized he was alone. "Get outta that car this instant, young lady. When we have problems, we address them and accept whatever punishment the Lord doles out for us."

Janie watched Annelise exit the truck, slam the door, and sneer at her father. Her upper arms looked mighty red, like someone had grabbed her hard, and everything on her face looked puffy. She was a plain mess.

"She lose a fight with a Dumpster?" Janie whispered, having written Annelise off as a friend long ago.

Below them, the screen door opened. "If it isn't Abner Abel," said Grandpa Barton. "Need an insurance policy, do ya?"

"I've got my insurance agent, Barton, and I visit Him every Sunday morning. Wouldn't hurt you to do the same."

"How you doin' there, Annelise?" Barton said. "You must be drivin' by now. Need yourself some good insurance?"

Janie and Jack rolled their eyes simultaneously, but then grinned. Grandpa Barton may have been a relentless salesman, but you'd have to search far and wide to find someone who didn't like him—aside from Abner Abel, that is.

Annelise's response, if there was one, was drowned out by her father's heavy, arrhythmic footsteps as he climbed onto the porch. Normally, he wore a brace that helped his left leg compensate for a childhood malformation of his shinbone, but when he didn't, he tended to limp. It sounded as such now with each heavy footstep followed by a lighter one. Jack and Janie used to scare one another with made-up tales of Mr. Abel, ax in hand, sneaking up on small children in the night, their only warning the slow thumpety-thump of his approach.

"Barton," Mr. Abel said, "we got a serious issue to discuss with you. It's about your boy, Jack."

"You don't say. You want to come in, have some tea, and talk about it?"

"We're fine right here, thank you. Here's the thing. I found an empty bottle of whiskey in my cellar this morning, so I went and smelled the breath of each of my children before they woke up. I'm an early riser, as you know."

"Can't say I knew that, Abner. Good for you."

"Annelise here was the guilty party," Mr. Abel said. "Now this next part's hard to say, but I, uh, I also found evidence of other sinful goings-on in the basement."

Janie and Jack took mutual pleasure in imagining Annelise squirming on the porch. Two grown men talking about her misdeeds while she was forced to stand there like a dolt and take it.

"Annelise tells me that not only did your boy, Jack, steal the liquor from your very own house, but he got mighty fresh with her down there in the cellar."

"I see, I see," Grandpa Barton said, probably having entire conversations with himself during the gaps between Mr. Abel's words. "You'd be talkin' of a sexual nature now, Abner?"

Jack and Janie exchanged a look of shock and pure frustration at not being down there to witness the look on Annelise's face. And Mr. Abel had to be turning eight shades of crimson at the mention of sex. Oh, this was the stuff of soap operas and they were missing it.

"Come on," Jack whispered.

Janie understood and followed. They climbed quietly through the window, raced down the stairs, and were out the front door in less than a minute.

"Oh, hey, there, Mr. Abel," Jack said. "Hi, Annelise. Thought I heard someone out here."

Janie joined in. "Jack and I are heading to the general store on our bikes. Pick you up anything, Grandpa?"

"As a matter of fact, kids, Mr. Abel here has something he'd like to talk to Jack about."

Annelise, humiliated and perspiring heavily, turned her toes in toward each other, lowered her head to her chest, and crossed her arms tight enough to wrap around her back.

"How can I help you, Mr. Abel?" Jack said. "You need some yard work done, or some of the young'uns need watchin'?"

So much for the national stage. Janie imagined this must be one of those situations where a *colloquialism* was called for, because Jack was laying it on thick. He'd helped with the Abels' yard maybe one time six years ago, and he'd never once watched the Abel *young'uns*.

"Uh, no," Mr. Abel said, torn between thanking Jack and continuing with the angry intent of his visit. "Did you bring alcohol into my home last night?"

"No, sir, I did not. Did someone say I did?"

Janie wanted to catch Annelise's reactions, but she actually felt sorry for her ex-friend. The wretched girl seemed humbled for the first time in her life.

"Why should I believe you?" Mr. Abel said, sticking out his slight chest, which paled in comparison to Jack's.

"Why shouldn't you?" Jack said.

"Annelise here says you forced yourself on her in the cellar last night."

Jack glanced at Annelise, a practiced look of innocence coating his handsome features, then back to Mr. Abel. "What do you mean, sir? I'm awfully confused."

"You know exactly what I mean, boy."

"Daddy," Annelise murmured.

"Shush, now, child." Mr. Abel turned his attention to Barton. "You know what I believe, Barton. Swift and severe punishment never did no child no wrong. This boy's lyin' through his teeth."

"You sure it's Jack who's doin' the lyin'?" Barton said with a smirk.

"My children know better than to tell me tales," Mr. Abel said. "Perhaps if you'd brandished a little more discipline with your daughter, like I've done with Annelise here, things mighta turned out different for you."

Barton was as steamed as he'd ever been. "What are you implying, Abner?"

"You know exactly what I'm saying. Your girl Bridget made herself available to all manner of—"

The cross punch that Barton threw never landed on Mr. Abel's jaw because Mr. Abel demonstrated remarkably fast reflexes. He blocked the incoming fist and instinctively struck the old man in the gut with a short jab. Of course, it wasn't as powerful as it could have been since Mr. Abel had trouble putting rotation behind it with his bum leg.

Mr. Abel, immediately regretful, reached out to support Barton, but Jack got to his grandfather first. With his other hand, he grabbed Mr. Abel by the shirt.

When Barton muttered that he was fine, Jack tightened his grip on Mr. Abel and pulled him in until their faces nearly touched. "Listen to me, *neighbor*, and listen good. I wasn't at your goddamn house last night. I was here with my grandfather working on his truck. So why don't you take your lying sack-of-shit daughter and find out who really boned her in your cellar last night before making false accusations?"

Mr. Abel tried to pull away, but Jack held tight and continued. "You wanna talk about someone making themselves available to all manner of creepy perverts in this town, well, as the Bible says, you might wanna put your own house in order first."

Jack shoved Mr. Abel away, not hard enough to send him careening down the stairs, but not real gently, either.

Annelise turned tail and ran, all the way up the driveway. A silence hung over the porch, broken only by the distant sound of Annelise's sobs and punctuated by the steady crunch of rocks beneath her feet.

Mr. Abel bucked up, walked down the stairs, then turned back to the Perkins family. "I'm right sorry 'bout this, Barton. I was wrong to strike you. Reflex from my boxing days, I'm afraid." He lowered his head, but he wasn't done yet. His voice came out softly. Combined with its interminable slowness, it sounded hypnotic. "I will wait and see what the Lord has in store for me now. He's worked in mysterious ways with me many times. Very mysterious indeed."

As he took off in his truck, Jack grinned. "It ain't real mysterious," he said. "You stick it in and the sperm fertilizes the egg."

"Jack," Grandpa Barton said, his tone holding no admonition.

"Thought we weren't saying *ain't*," Janie added.

They went inside together. It was nine months later that the three of them stood on the porch again, gifts in hand, as they started their trek to the Abels' house to welcome Annelise's baby boy.

CHAPTER 30

Someone had scrawled *WASH ME* a few feet to the right of the Abels' front door. A shirtless boy with a sunken chest answered after I rang the bell a second time. Before he could speak, a familiar twang scraped at my ears from the kitchen.

"Jedediah Jr., I done told you to put a shirt on. You want the neighbors thinkin' we run around here like animals?"

He wiped sleep from his eyes despite the late afternoon hour and addressed the source of the voice. "It ain't no neighbor, Ma. It's some short lady with blond hair."

I could practically hear the intake of breath, the muzzled reprimand of the son, and the fluffing of the hair as Annelise Abel tried to make herself presentable. Yes, the unannounced visit was rude, but I didn't want Annelise to have time to ensure her father's absence. As hard as it was to wrap my mind around the idea of Abner Abel having anything to do with my mother's death, some interesting cards were stacking up in his favor: his telltale limp and his heretofore unknown presence at Field Diner on the infamous night. At a minimum, he might have noticed something unusual at the diner. At a maximum, he was a ruthless, demented son of a bitch with nothing left to lose.

The boy disappeared, leaving the door ajar and me on display. I felt like the awkward middle-schooler leaning against the wall while her prettier friends accepted dance invitations. Finally, the door was pulled wide and Annelise Abel stood before me. The hair could have used more fluffing, or at least a style, and the growing wet spot on her peasant skirt, where she'd unsuccessfully tried to wash out a swipe of chocolate, should have been turned to the side, but other than that, Annelise didn't look half bad. She had color in her cheeks and well-applied lipstick, almost enough to make her look refreshed. Unfortunately, no concealer could hide the dark bags of an overwrought mother living with her father while her husband made cross-country jaunts in his semi.

"My heavens!" Annelise said. "I thought it might be little Janie Perkins. Goodness, I haven't seen you in years."

Thirteen, to be exact, if that was the age of the charmer who'd answered the door.

"How is that handsome brother of yours?" she continued. "He came on TV yesterday and I hushed the kids straightaway. Told them how Jack and me were almost sweethearts. He has such a nice voice, let alone the rest of him."

I repressed my awkwardness and amusement as she both lusted for my brother and lied through her teeth. "He is on TV a lot," I said lamely.

"Come on in," she said, gesturing big, as if she'd read that pretending you lived in an estate worthy of giant arm flourishes was half the battle. "You remember the place. Haven't had much of a chance to straighten today, of course. Makin' a cake for my daughter's birthday."

The place was a disaster. Toys, magazines, clothes, mud flecks, dirty dishes, crayons, empty soda bottles . . . you name it, it was scattered. Of course, I'd rarely been inside the Abels' home as a child, except for the cellar. Maybe it had always been like this. Couldn't imagine the ever-slouched Mrs. Abel had kept a tidy homestead.

"How many children do you have, Annelise?" I fully expected to hear *twelve*, given the quantity of socks on the floor, but Annelise had limited herself to four.

"There'd be more," she said, "but Jed is always on the road, if you know what I'm sayin'."

I did know and really wished she hadn't put that image in my head. Jedediah Matheny had been three years ahead of Jack and me in school and was the boy who'd stolen the Jack Daniel's, along with Annelise's alleged virginity. Hard to reconcile how Annelise could have been attracted to my brother while allowing the likes of Jed Matheny to bed her. He was everything Jack wasn't, and that was the biggest compliment I could pay my brother.

We filled the next ten minutes with the ages of her children, their questionable accomplishments, and a full recitation of Annelise's local activities, including her initiative to stop bullying in the schools. If I had to suppress an ironic guffaw at that one, I really deserved a pass.

I worked the conversation around to her dad and asked if he was home. "You know," she said, "Daddy got Jed his truckin' job and now he makes a pretty fine living. He even took on Daddy's role as a sort of talk-show host to other truckers over his CB."

"Isn't that something?" I said. "What's his handle?"

"Oh, he just took over Daddy's, Big Ham. Like when Dear Abby took over her mother's column and neither of them was really named Abby?"

The columnists would be so flattered by the comparison. "So your husband delivers meat, too?"

"No, he just uses the handle. 'You got Big Ham. What can I cure for ya?'" She giggled a little too hard. "See? It's funny 'cause it works two ways."

I tried to smile but I no longer had it in me. Didn't surprise me that Jed Matheny couldn't come up with an original handle. In high school, he could barely rub two sentences together. On the rare occasions he had, they'd invariably included the words *tackle* or *boo-ya*.

"Is your dad around? I actually—"

"My dad? I'm afraid he's—"

"What is it you want, young lady?" came a voice that couldn't be mistaken for just any old humpin' bastard.

I turned to see Abner Abel. Except for some gray around the edges of his brown cap of hair, he looked the same, but since he'd looked prematurely old my whole life, maybe he and time had finally met in the middle.

"Mr. Abel, how are you?"

"The Lord sees me through each day, and I'm blessed at least four times over living here with my grandchildren."

As we all entered the kitchen, two of the blessings sprinted through, squirting water pistols. I wondered if Annelise recalled any water incidents from our own childhood. With her lips pulled tight and a quick, nervous glance at her father, she wiped up the puddle on the floor. It would be interesting to see when she would actually inhale again.

"You must have a lot of grandchildren by now, Mr. Abel," I said.

"Fourteen. Hoping for more, of course."

"Aren't we all, Daddy?" Annelise chimed in. "Aren't we all?"

She tied an apron around her waist and wore a tight grimace-smile as she iced the cake. A wave of pity washed over me for my childhood bully. Here she was, the doting mom, the bridge between generations, the daughter who'd replaced the mother, and the dutiful wife to a guy she'd been forced to marry. Heck, back then she'd gone from bathroom to bride so fast, she'd probably had to hide the pregnancy test in the shoddy bouquet of white carnations her brother had picked. Jack and I had spied through the hedges on her wedding day. The younger Abel girls had pulled out their fiddles to play some screeching excuse for a bridal march while the local pastor pretended to be thrilled for the happy couple. Mrs. Abel had wailed and nearly sunk to her knees in despair while Mr. Abel had looked like he wanted to impart only the shotgun part of the shotgun wedding. As soon as it was over, Annelise had vomited, blaming it on morning sickness, but we all knew better.

"Mr. Abel," I said, "some information has come to light about the night my mother was shot."

"Has it, now?"

"Yes, sir. Apparently, you were at Field Diner that night."

Annelise sucked in a gulp of air, surprised at the revelation, but she immediately returned her attention to the cake as it collapsed in on itself under the weight of her drippy frosting. Did she spend every day either cracking eggs or walking on their shells?

"Not that it's any of your business," Mr. Abel said, "but yes, I went to Field Diner that night. What does it matter?"

"I've been told there was an . . . altercation between you and my mother that evening."

He twisted his features into something sinister. "Your mother lied to me."

That wasn't what I was expecting. "About what?"

"Said she hadn't been in a black Mercedes earlier that day, but I knew she had. I saw her. Turned out it was Grady McLemore's car. And let's just say, I put two and two together."

"When did she lie to you? Did you ask her about it when she waited on you?"

"Of course. She got downright smart-alecky about it."

"Perhaps she didn't want to discuss it in a public place." You dumb proselytizing fuck.

"Well, it became pretty public when Grady McLemore and his driver showed up at the diner a few minutes later."

"And that's when you put the two and the other two together and came up with a pregnant waitress?"

His glare made it clear my sarcasm was unwelcome. "Didn't take a rocket scientist."

"I hear you stormed out of the diner. Why was that?"

"I merely stood my ground when she got mouthy. I demanded the respect I deserved. She was rude and obscene so I took my leave. There was no *altercation*, as you call it."

"How did you happen to see my mother in that Mercedes? Was it when she was returning from the Aberdeen Hotel?"

"The Aberdeen!" Annelise said, desperate to lighten the mood. "What a place! You used to deliver meat there, Daddy, remember?"

Mr. Abel fixed his daughter with a glare that would sterilize a stray, but she was too busy trying to thicken her icing with additional sugar and flour.

"I don't recall," he said. Each word dropped into the room like a time bomb.

"Sure you do," she said, working that smile overtime. "You used to bring us those little soaps with the fancy *A*s on them that the manager, Moss Wise, gave you. I remember him because we called him Most Wise. And one time, he gave you a whole sheet cake left over from a meeting and you brought it home, remember?"

In contrast to Annelise's prattling, Mr. Abel sucked in the slowest breath of air since Methuselah drew his last. "I had many stops on my routes, Annelise."

"Very true," she said. "You know, Janie, my dad has kept up his trucker's license all this time. Still picks up jobs now and again. Must know every back road in the entire state."

A lightbulb went off. "Did you see my mother at the Aberdeen, Mr. Abel? Is that how you knew she was with Grady McLemore?"

"No. I told you. I saw her in a car with Mr. McLemore's driver. Why are you twisting what I say?"

"It's just that you seemed awfully interested in my mother that day. And Lucinda Lowry, the other waitress, said you'd just returned from a long haul. But if that were true, why were you driving around town hours earlier, passing my mother in a car?"

"What's your angle here, young lady?"

"I've got a dead mother in the game, Mr. Abel. What's your angle?"

"I will not be spoken to this way."

Annelise accidentally dumped a whole cup of flour into her icing. She tried to beat it but it was like trying to whisk a wet beach.

"Did you see anyone suspicious at the diner? It's possible the Haiku Killer was actually there."

"What are you playin' at? Grady McLemore shot your mother. There was no Haiku Killer. Is it such a stretch to believe that a grave sinner like McLemore would also be a liar?"

"As I said, I'm privy to new information. Did you see anyone unusual or suspicious? Someone my mother may have encountered?"

"Absolutely not." He'd given the question no thought at all. "I was minding my own business."

"And my mother's."

He tried to silence me with his eyes, but his ability to intimidate me had evaporated as surely as water from a hose on a hot summer day.

"Since you were keeping such a close eye on her, monitoring her sins and all, did you see her pick up a note from a customer at any time during the evening?"

He looked uncomfortable, the tendons in his neck twitching. "This is crazy. You mean like a haiku? You're spinning some wild yarn in your head, young lady, but it's come unraveled. Of course I didn't see your mother receive any kind of note."

"After you stormed out of the diner," I said, playing off something Mickey Busker had mentioned, "you stayed and watched my mother from the parking lot across the street. Did you see her take a note from anyone then—or do anything out of the ordinary?"

Abner Abel sucked his cheeks into his teeth. It made his chin pucker and point. He held the pose for a prickly moment while Annelise compulsively smeared her lava-like concoction onto the cake. "Your implications offend me to the core," he growled. "I enjoyed a smoke now and again after my supper, and I might have stayed around for a cigarette, but that doesn't mean—"

"Now, Daddy, don't get yourself—"

"Quiet, Annelise!" he said, keeping his eyes on me. "That doesn't mean I was watching your mother. Who's spreading these lies?"

Annelise dropped a blob of icing on the counter and stared at it like it might burst into flames.

"Where did you go after the diner, Mr. Abel? Did you follow my mother home?"

"We lived next door to each other! If we had left at the same time, it certainly would have looked that way, but I left before her. You have some cheek, young lady, suggesting anything sordid. It was late and I had children to tend to."

As if Mr. Abel ever did *the tending*.

Annelise lifted her head and looked a few Prozac short of a dose. "I think it's best if you got on your way, Janie. It was so nice of you to stop in like this."

"Sure, Annelise, no problem." But I turned back to Mr. Abel, his defensiveness spurring me to dig deeper than I'd intended; besides,

I had nothing to lose. "Mr. Abel, I apologize for upsetting you. You must understand, if I didn't ask the questions, I'd never forgive myself."

He closed his eyes and let out a sigh that lasted longer than most yawns. "I understand, Miss Perkins, and I feel for what you're going through with Barton. Despite our tensions over the years, he's always been a good man, a better neighbor than I deserved."

"That means a lot. Thank you." The mood had shifted, so I went for it. "Speaking of neighbors, my ambitious friend Stephanie"—the one I was making up on the spot—"plans to be a farm vet. You used to pick up from some of the big farms, didn't you?"

"Yes. In fact, some of those farms go from sow to slaughter. Do the raising, killing, and processing all in the same place. Did pickups like that all the time."

"They have vets on staff, then?"

"Got to. Those animals spend half their lives drugged up. It's the reason I became a vegetarian. Wasn't about to put that stuff in my body."

But would he put it in someone else's?

"Just delightful to see you, Janie, really," Annelise said, her voice now shrill. "You'll have to stop around again." I said good-bye to Mr. Abel and let Annelise lead me through the living room. "Do give my best to Jack," she muttered out of earshot of her father. "I sure let that one slip through my fingers, didn't I? Can't believe he's still single."

I wondered if Annelise knew she was living in some kind of Twilight Zone. As I exited, I glanced back at Mr. Abel, who was sitting stiff as a board on the kitchen stool, staring at nothing. Two steps from the door, I accidentally kicked a toy delivery truck into an old radiator. I let the ping reverberate through me in sync with my distaste for him; he'd unnerved me my entire life and now I knew he'd haunted my mother's final hours. But at least I'd uncovered something interesting. Mr. Abel knew about the illicit affair, had access to animal tranquilizers, and made regular stops at the Aberdeen.

I didn't like coincidences. Annelise should have kept her big mouth shut. But most wise, she wasn't. And you can't cure that, Big Ham.

CHAPTER 31

I arrived at The Shell Place before Wexler, allowing enough time to quell my nerves by ordering a Shell-acked Martini, a strange combination of pear vodka, bitters, simple syrup, and essence of ginger, topped by a shelled shrimp on the rim of the glass. It struck me as disgusting at first, but the bald waiter had raved and I'd been anxious enough to listen. Even the shrimp went down easy.

It isn't a date, I repeated to myself as I ordered a second drink. It's a work meeting to discuss Betty Fitzsimmons and all the sickos in Caulfield. Besides, Wexler was standoffish, meticulous, and far too sartorial for a girl who wore tight jeans and loose shirts as a second skin. We'd mesh about as well as UGGs and a cocktail gown.

A year ago, asked to label myself as an extrovert or introvert at a county team-building exercise, I'd sidestepped the question and jokingly opted for *non-detail-oriented perfectionist with ADD tendencies*. I'd been more than a little appalled when everyone in the room agreed. The paid psychologist conducting the session had asked to see me afterward under the pretense of discussing my job's discordance with my personality description, but I could tell he only wanted to get me in bed. I declined. If there was one type I didn't like, it was tall, dark, and psychologist. Either way, I was pretty sure Wexler was a detail-oriented perfectionist with OCD tendencies, and between us, that was one too many acronyms for a normal relationship.

Wexler materialized in front of me. "Hey, Wexler," I said, realizing the strength of my first drink when my lips were a half syllable behind my words. "Have a seat."

"Why do you call me Wexler?"

I glanced around, seriously wondering if I'd mistaken some guy with unwavering eyes, a strong neck, and a slightly hunched, muscle-laden back for Wexler. No, it was definitely him.

"That's your name," I said. "It says so on your Fight Club card."

"You just broke the first rule of Fight Club."

"Eh, so did Brad Pitt eventually."

"Touché. But what I meant was, why don't you call me Alex?"

"Same reason I call Nicholls *Nicholls*."

"Oh," he said, his mouth scrunching in disappointment. "I hoped our relationship might be . . . a step above that."

And what did *that* mean? If he'd said *more professional* or *more romantic* or *more filled with wild, rampant sex*, then I'd know where we stood. But no, he'd laid a big pile of ambiguity on my lap with his *step above that* crap. I opened my mouth to demonstrate an example of direct communication when the waiter interrupted. Good thing, too, because my comment might have included something about the rampant sex.

"Another Shell-acked Martini for the lady," the waiter said, his pate as shiny as the silver tray holding the drink. Suddenly, I felt embarrassed and remembered that I'd eaten only that early lunch with Lucinda and one drunken shrimp all day.

"Actually," I said to the waiter, "I ordered that for my guest."

The waiter knew I'd made a face-saving decision on the fly and, in the interest of hefty tips, went with it. "You said as much earlier, ma'am, and I've quite forgotten your water." He placed the drink in front of Wexler. "For the gentleman."

We ordered a couple plates of appetizers and got down to business. I filled him in on everything I'd learned from Lucinda, Mickey, and Mr. Abel, and then gave him the floor.

"I finished my homework, too," Wexler said, "but I'm not sure you're going to give me an A when you hear the results. First, your friend Hump Banfield checks out. He is Jenna Abel's uncle and he did serve in the military. No brushes with the law. Worked as an occupational therapist until a car accident ten years ago. That's what put him in the chair."

"Weird. My spidey sense was all a-tingle, especially when he showed up at my door. And the dire theme of his photos freaked me out. So hopeless and bleak."

"Guys in wars, they see things differently. Violence scars them, even if it's not always physical. You ask me, it creates entirely new ways of processing information, like your brain needs an escape hatch."

"And nothing is appreciated the way it was before?"

"Exactly. Dark filters drape your senses, and everything you see, hear, or touch gets sifted through that shadowy, sometimes jittery gloom."

"Wow, Wexler," I said. "Do you know how much I want to dissect the skeletons in your closet right now?"

"My dad was in the military. But we're not here to talk about me. I've got bad news about Betty Fitzsimmons, the woman who mailed you the photos."

"Shoot."

"As I mentioned earlier, Betty was a bit of a spinster, who lived with her brother, Leroy, on a dusty, nonworking farm."

"Uh-oh. You're speaking in past tense."

"She was found dead this afternoon by the sheriff. Really shook him up. Said she'd been lying there for days, a cat clawing at her hair and face, trying to get food from her. They're not entirely sure this cat didn't eat a chunk or two of her body."

For a single tipsy moment, I didn't want to focus on what it meant that the lonely old woman who'd mailed the photos was dead within days of doing so. Instead, I spoke on autopilot. "Postmortem predation, it's called. Fancy way of saying, *When you're dead, you're food*. Cats will sometimes go for it after only a day or two."

Wexler didn't miss a beat. "Better than siafu—those ridiculous army ants. They just wait until you're weak to enter your lungs and suffocate you. And then they eat you."

I yanked myself from my detached state and turned hyperfocused eyes on Wexler. "What did she die from?"

He shrugged but his face contained traces of sorrow that I appreciated. "Waiting for the coroner's report. No sign of trauma. Could be anything, but they can't rule out foul play yet."

"And where was brother Leroy while Betty was feeding the cat?"

"Left Ridge a few days ago for an out-of-town job. He's gone a lot, apparently."

"How convenient. Betty mails the photos and immediately meets her maker, and her brother has skipped town. You have a photo of either of them?"

He pushed across a few pictures of Betty, who I didn't recognize. She could have been any stout woman with a neat bun of gray hair.

"And her brother?"

"Sheriff said Leroy did all the picture-taking in town and rarely got in front of the lens."

I felt a kinship. "What about a driver's license photo?"

"That's all I got. It's seven years old." He pushed a fuzzy image of Leroy toward me. Even blown up, it showed nothing more than a middle-aged guy with small eyes, a plump face, longish, graying hair—what was left of it anyway—and a bushy beard and moustache.

"Great," I said. "This narrows it down to the entire population of Appalachia and the members of ZZ Top."

"Nice reference," Wexler said, "and that's coming from a sharp-dressed man."

Despite the circumstances, I smiled. Then my face soured as I realized that the mailed photos now carried more weight, including that of a dead body. "I don't mean to jump to conclusions, but do you think Betty found her brother's pictures and mailed them? Then her brother found out and killed her?"

Wexler took a sip of his drink. "You not only jumped—you vaulted over the high bar with that one."

"How so?"

"Betty could have found those pictures at a yard sale or while rifling through someone's garbage. They could have been left there by a renter or a drifter they let in. Heck, Betty could have found them under a pile of cat litter somewhere and been trying to return them to you as a courtesy. From what I gather, she wasn't all there."

"You're right."

Wexler leaned toward me. He smelled good, fresh. "But I do think it's worth taking a drive to Betty's and looking around. No offense to the sheriff, but the worst they've dealt with in Ridge this year was a guy keeping six Rottweilers at his house. Know what the problem was?"

"No."

"That's one over the legal limit." Wexler took a swig of his martini. "I'm off tomorrow. I could drive you. Might help to have a detective along. And I don't want this Leroy fellow showing up if you're snooping through the attic and come across a creepy mannequin that looks like you."

"Thanks for that image! And why would a Janie mannequin be creepy, by the way?"

"They're all creepy, even the pretty ones." He locked on to my eyes with the last part of his comment and only tore his gaze away when a text came in.

"Yeah," he said after reading the text, "you're gonna want me to go with you."

"Why?"

"We were wrong about the attic. They just found a box of Haiku Twin memorabilia in Betty's basement."

CHAPTER 32

Bridget Perkins, 30 Years, 30 Minutes Ago

Bridget Perkins listened to the lanky teenager suck down the last bubbly bits of his shake. He had the woeful disposition of someone who'd been ditched by a longtime crush. At least his broken spirit made sure that he failed to notice the prominent political candidate sitting in the far booth, quietly working on a speech for the Women's Auxiliary. Those dang women had the vote now, as Grady often joked, and he knew how much influence they wielded.

The skinny kid threaded his way out of the booth and left with a half-hearted wave. Bridget watched as his car took him home to a pity party for one. She turned away just before his headlights illuminated a dark car in the back corner of the lot. Had she been looking, she would have seen no driver behind the steering wheel—because the driver wasn't stupid. He'd ducked down in plenty of time.

The much-ballyhooed fix-it man that Grady had called Rusty watched the teen depart. Kid looked like he'd been put through a stretching machine, then starved for six months. But Rusty didn't care about him. No, his subject tonight was—he let his internal voice enter game-show announcer mode—*the incomparable, insatiable Grady McLemore! Better than everyone in his constituency and ever hungry for affirmation of that very fact! Let's hear it for future Senator Grady McLemore!*

The perfect man to take down, he thought, returning to his sedate inner voice and rising from his crouched position.

As Bridget walked to the register, Rusty wondered whose idea it was to leave a pretty thing like that to close up a place like this. Just imagine what could happen to her. And why hadn't thickheaded Grady McLemore taken the hint yet and hauled his ass out of there so the waitress could get home and put her feet up? Was he waiting for a special dessert? Rusty pushed the thought from his mind, but it persisted like a stubborn headache. A special relationship between the two of them *would* explain the showy arrival of the pseudocelebrity at a place with few constituents present. It would explain the weird conversation they'd carried on while flanking his head.

Rusty wanted the lurid thoughts in his mind to be wrong, but when Grady sneaked up behind the waitress, spun her around with a twirl, and planted a kiss on her lips, he knew matters had just grown more complicated. Damn.

He watched Grady back her up against the counter. In a flash, she was seated atop the surface where people would eat their lunches tomorrow, her legs wrapped around the lustful politician. Grady pressed hard into her bulging midsection with a steely disregard for the life inside. Was it his kid in there, or was he taking advantage of some poor working girl in a pathetic situation? What a lowlife. But that would hardly be news to anyone.

Rusty thought back to the conversation he'd overheard in Grady's office. He'd been long forgotten down there on the floor—just the way he liked it—so he lingered longer than necessary while adjusting the radiator's lockshield valve. Grady had been on the phone suggesting *a getaway before you're too big to get away.* Rusty had taken it to mean that the person on the other end of the phone was about to become famous, and thus too well-known for a simple getaway, but watching McLemore paw at the pregnant waitress made him reassess his conclusion. That same day, McLemore's right-hand snake, Sam Kowalczyk, had called the Aberdeen Hotel and made reservations under an alias—Mr. and Mrs. Eugene Purvy. No doubt the reservations were for Grady and his paramour. Only someone with McLemore's unbridled ego would have the audacity to check in under a name like that without a wink or a blush—especially given the condition of *Mrs. Purvy.*

Rusty had trouble repressing his repugnance. Certainly wasn't how he'd been raised. But then, things didn't always work out the way parents intended. In Rusty's case, he took a slanted pleasure in disappointing his father—he of the straight and narrow, of the Bible Belt, of the belt and fist.

He returned to his unintended voyeurism. What fools! Even the densest of passion-blind morons should know that the interior lights of the diner shined a glaring spotlight on their illicit behavior, even in this remote edge of town. But these political types had no qualms sending those under their command into mortal danger to be treated worse than dogs; why should they care about the consequences of a scandal for an underpaid, overworked waitress? Still, what about the career implications for the mighty Grady McLemore? Quite the risk, indeed.

Rusty smiled to himself as he realized that both *quite the risk indeed* and *Grady McLemore* contained five syllables. Like poetic bookends framing a central tragedy yet to be written.

Ah, well, he'd be doing that waitress a favor.

A car approached, riveting Rusty's attention. Its headlights swerved into the parking lot and made a beeline for the diner's front door. It was Sam Kowalczyk, Grady's driver, staring straight ahead like the submissive sycophant he was, feigning blindness to the amorousness playing out inside.

Grady appeared hesitant to leave but the waitress shooed him out, jingling the diner keys and gesturing around with a smile. *Go on. There's no one here. I just have to lock up.* Grady's head tilted, still deciding, then he blew her a kiss and slithered out to the car. The interior light of the Mercedes bathed the hook-nosed, mouth-breathing Sam in unflattering light.

Rusty always thought Sam looked like a starved wolf, lips pulled back and parted, ready to clamp his teeth onto the first weak rabbit that ventured by. Sure, a sinus problem accounted for Sam's rabid appearance, but it didn't excuse the aura of sleaze he emitted, as if the only actions worth taking in life were those involving covert exchanges of crumpled cash in neglected alleys. Grady, by hiring such a scoundrel, became the moral equivalent.

Amazing, though, how careless such people became when they failed to think of the low-level help as humans with brains. Rusty didn't need an alley to complete his transactions.

The Mercedes took off, its occupants so self-involved that they didn't give a glance or thought to the extra car in the lot.

Time to move, but surely he'd lose nothing if he just watched the waitress one more moment. She was so pretty and he didn't often get to stare unabashedly at beautiful things. He would hate to see her hurt, but what could he do? Things were out of his control, really. He glanced skyward and lamented the situations in which he always became entangled. It was as if someone else controlled his tattered strings and he was the stupid, powerless dummy at the end, with ridiculous button eyes permanently open, forced to watch the horrors that fell before him. And they always did. Right before his stupid button eyes.

He watched now, all alone, and felt a mild stirring in his pants. But no worry. He'd learned to suppress those urges long ago for fear of a snapping belt. It settled back down, deep inside him, where it would channel itself in other ways.

Time to move. But he stopped when he heard something. Was he not the only one observing the goings-on in the diner tonight? Through his slightly lowered windows—he always cracked them so he could hear people sneaking up on him—he heard a metallic squeal, followed by a rustling in the nearby woods, accompanied by a string of discontented grunts.

Rusty pulled out the binoculars he kept in the glove compartment. His lenses found the gaunt form of that repulsive maggot, Mickey the diner manager, a bike on the ground near his feet. He was leaning against a tree, holding a small telescopic device, which he aimed at Bridget like a depraved pirate. For God's sake, did this woman attract any normal men? At least Rusty had a valid reason for his spying.

Mickey moved one hand up and down the long lens as he watched Bridget bending over and pushing in the chairs.

Rusty turned away in disgust, knowing what would come next. But when Bridget reached behind the counter and grabbed her purse to leave, Rusty heard a distinct "Dang it!" as Mickey yanked his dilapidated bike from the ground and pedaled into the darkness, the rhythmic squeak of his brakes fading into the distance.

Rusty savored his final seconds alone with Bridget, he unknown, she unknowing. She'd been so nice, giving him that free pie, but then again, she'd been klutzy about his pen. As she reached to turn off the lights, she suddenly changed her mind and a mischievous grin lit up her face. She leaned back against the counter, set her purse on a stool, and reached into her apron pocket, pulling out something small, square, and white.

"What do we have here?" Rusty said quietly, his voice tinny and thin, even to him. It was the reason he'd acquired a reputation as a man of few words. Words got people into trouble, at least the spoken ones, while the written form contained beauty, proving so much more effective.

He refocused the binoculars on the object in Bridget's hands and his whole body stiffened. "Oh, no, no, no." His voice filled the car with a trembling dread. "No!" He cast the binoculars to the side and frantically patted his pockets. He came up with only his pen and some blank scraps of paper.

"Damn her."

In a rare impulsive move, Rusty's left hand shot out to open the car door, his knee and hip already turned to make the hasty exit, but he stopped himself. The moment he opened the door, he'd be revealed, and by the time he reached the locked diner door and figured a way in, the waitress could be on the phone to the police, or worse, to Grady.

He let his head fall against the driver's side window, hoping its coolness would calm the frantic scenarios rushing through his mind. They all contained nuances of darkness, tainted as they were by the actions of this waitress waif, a player so insignificant in the grand scheme of things that her absence would scarcely register on the scale of humanity. In fact, he'd be doing her a favor if he went in and put a bullet through her skull right now.

CHAPTER 33

Wexler's text, in keeping with our medieval theme, read: *Your char-
iot awaits.* I peeked through my blinds and spotted his double-
parked Lexus below.

The Shell-acked Martini had taken its toll and my eyelids felt
leaden. While wandering the apartment at two a.m., I'd consumed
a huge bowl of cereal and spent two hours soaking up everything
the Internet had to offer on Abner Abel, Mickey Busker, and Betty's
brother, Leroy. Not much. I'd filled the rest of the time covering the
innumerable conspiracy theories surrounding the Haiku Killer.
Apparently a lot of people spent their nights online, feeding the
monster of paranoia. With two pages of self-assigned tasks jotted
down, I'd finally drifted off on the couch.

I texted Wexler to see if he wanted a to-go cup of coffee, but he
replied that he'd already *java'd up* for both of us. That put a smile
on my face. I opened a can of cat food and shoved it onto the fire
escape for Percival, managing to drop my keys twice. I really didn't
do well without sleep.

Three minutes later, I was sipping hot, strong coffee, knowing it wouldn't keep me awake. "Did you get my message about stopping at the Aberdeen?" I said, having texted the request at three a.m.

"Sure did. I thought it was a little forward of you to suggest a hotel, considering we've only had one Shell-acked Martini together, and not so much together as consecutively."

"Ha, ha," I said, reaching into the bag for the orange scone he'd brought me. "I need to pick up my brother's book from the infamous Hump Banfield. I swear, I don't know whether to listen to my gut or my brain with that guy."

"Gut. Always," Wexler said with unexpected intensity. "Brains are secondary, the product of a long evolution. Gut instincts are what allowed our ancestors to survive so we could evolve at all."

"I read once that the gut has half a billion neurons. It's like a second brain."

"It's the one I trust most. Given some of the weirdos I'm sure you've dealt with in life, you should, too."

"There was this one group, when Jack and I were twenty. Called themselves the Psycho-Ticks—a play on the word *psychotic*."

"Sounds like a sixties rock band."

"More like a warped cross-section of degenerates and geniuses who claimed they wanted to understand serial killers, but actually emulated them."

"Sociopaths can be quite the charmers."

"I've always thought of them as actors who are on all the time. Scripted, phony, perfect. It must be exhausting. But if it's all acting, maybe it becomes their norm."

"Except for the part where they torture and kill. That's their personal intermission, when the curtain gets lowered on someone else but they finally get to be themselves."

"Gotta wonder what makes them . . . wait for it . . . tick."

"It's that damn first brain. The wiring's all screwed up."

"Absolutely," I said. "But there are upsides, right? No guilt to clog a performance, no attachments to botch up judgment, no inferiority complexes, no worrying what others think."

"I'd rather live with attachments and love and a conscience, and all the mess that comes with it." He glanced at me when mentioning the mess part, and I found it oddly flattering.

"Not them," I said. "They learn the lines, smile on cue, throw in a little humility, and voila, score an Oscar."

"Or at least a fan club of lonely hearts and ne'er-do-wells."

"What a turbo-charged ego boost, though, right? They're the only ones who know they're pulling it off, and inside they laugh at the audience for being such suckers."

Wexler pulled into the Aberdeen's long entryway and headed toward the cottages. "So these Psycho-Ticks were into the Haiku Killer?"

"I guess. The Baltimore police made us aware of it. Along with pictures of the real victims and my mother and Grady, they had school pictures of Jack and me. Kindergarten through senior year, laid out all nice and neat on their website, in computer-generated frames."

"Even my parents don't have that," Wexler said.

"I should probably look up the site. My grandfather never bought our yearbooks."

"Check the Internet. There are tons of pictures of you growing up."

I stared at him, grinning, until he realized he'd just revealed his own snooping; then I tossed him a lifeline. "I prefer pictures where my hand's not blocking the lens and Jack doesn't have that *Ta-Da! Aren't I grand?* expression."

The Aberdeen came into full view. It hadn't changed much over the years. It was one of those old standbys that survived more on its past reputation than current service or quality. In its heyday, it had stood as a testament to the Old South. Thick, white porch pillars, wide slabs of painted oak leading to the grand entrance, a front door that could accommodate a truck, and bellmen dressed to the nines. Its thick and luscious red carpet had announced to guests that they'd truly arrived. It had even sported a reputation as a retreat for DC bigwigs seeking rejuvenation. And if the *juven* part of rejuvenation came in the form of barely legal company with slender legs and welcoming hips, well, no one need be the wiser. Bellhops made a killing keeping their lips zipped about the unzipped; a quick twenty ensured they went on their way until summoned to return with postcoital martinis on a silver tray.

The stand-alone cottages where Hump was staying had been built years later for extended-stay guests. Several novelists had penned works in them and, to my recollection, only one dead prostitute had ever besmirched the Aberdeen's reputation. That unfortunate episode had been swept under the carpet by rumors that the victim was a runaway who'd wandered onto the property uninvited. When the truth came out fifteen years later, the judge who'd strangled the poor girl was six feet under, and hotel management had disavowed all knowledge of the incident. Smooth place, the Aberdeen.

Just as Wexler pulled up to cottage five, two deer soared in front of his car. He slammed on his brakes and my remaining coffee splashed onto my shirt. Guess I should have left the lid on, but scones shouted out for dunking.

"I am so sorry," he said before pulling out a clean rag from his console. Then he reached into his backseat and conjured a white shirt, still in its bag from the store.

"Seriously?" I said.

"Doesn't everyone keep a spare? Tell you what, let me get the book from this guy while you clean yourself up—if you don't mind changing in the car. The windows are tinted."

I looked around. Not another person in sight. "That's fine, but I should really get the book."

"I'd like to do it. I want to see what my gut says about this guy. Besides, it would hardly be chivalrous of me to allow a lady to enter a cottage alone with a man who gives her the heebie-jeebies." With that, he winked and was down the path to Hump's front door in a few short strides.

Hump wouldn't like it, given his warped interest in me, but I was curious to get Wexler's impression. I let the situation play out. When the cottage door opened, Wexler's broad shoulders blocked my view of Hump. He disappeared inside and the door closed behind him. Three minutes passed. Then five. Then seven. I was about to join them in my oversized, high-thread-count shirt when Wexler emerged, book in hand. I lowered my window to wave at Hump, but the door slammed shut, as if a scorned lover were sending a defiant message.

Wexler got in and assessed my new look with a flick of his brows—either approving of either his *wardrobe* or its wearer.

"That took a while," I said.

"I don't know what was going on," he said. "But definitely heebie-jeebie-worthy. He claimed he couldn't remember where the book was, then disappeared into the bedroom to look. I took the opportunity to snoop."

"You didn't."

"I'm a detective. I detect." He said it without a grin, making me wonder if he ever used that line seriously when serving search warrants and shoving protesters aside.

"And what did you detect?"

"The guy has allergies, doesn't like scented deodorant, wears name-brand socks, and had your brother's book under a couch cushion."

"What?"

"Must have hidden it so he could hold on to it longer or something. I don't even want to think about what he was doing in the bedroom."

"What did he do when you found the book?"

"Don't know. I shouted to him that I found it, and before he could get his chair turned around, I thanked him, told him I had an urgent call to make, and took off. He was scooting after me as I left."

"Very odd."

"Certainly ambiguous."

"Ha!" I proclaimed. "That's the complete opposite of what a gut would say. Guts, by their very nature, reek of disambiguity. They go one way or the other, and usually negative."

"Exactly," Wexler said. "So since my gut instinct didn't tell me to cut and run—"

"Although you kind of outran a man in a wheelchair, with pride."

He smiled. "Well, I didn't want you sitting out here detecting anything in my glove compartment."

"Now you know I'm going in," I said, reaching for the glove compartment. It was locked and when I glanced at him, he was smiling. I'd walked right into it.

"Anyway," Wexler said, "maybe Hump was bummed because he was hoping to see your pretty face."

"Compliment accepted, thank you."

"Compliment intended, you're welcome. I mean, you do meet most of the qualifications to be considered universally attractive."

"Most?"

"You're lacking facial adiposity."

"Fat?"

"A little fat in the face is considered attractive, healthy, good for breeding."

"Anyone ever called you a romantic, Wexler?"

"Not that I recall."

"Shocking."

He merged smoothly onto the highway. My thoughts grew tangled as yet another layer was added to my strange perceptions of Hump

Banfield. After a few minutes, I opened my brother's book and examined the photos again, completely unaware that when Grandpa Barton's face melded into Grady's face, which morphed into a third man's shadowy image, it was my first dream inside a Lexus.

I woke up an hour later when the book crashed to my feet. "Please tell me I wasn't drooling."

"In the interest of finding you attractive in the future, I didn't look. But you do snore like Anne Bonny after a bottle of rum."

I smacked his arm, impressed by its firmness, and then reached down for the book. It had fallen open to the page where my brother had taped the extra photo and written his note.

A panicked tension flared behind my eyes. "Oh, no."

"Something wrong, Rip?"

I held up the book so he could see. "My brother wrote an inscription on this page."

Wexler looked and saw a blank page. "I don't see anything."

"This isn't my book."

CHAPTER 34

Percival screeched at the intruder, showing his claws and rearing back with his hair in full *bring-it* mode.

"Get outta here, fleabag!" said the short intruder, swatting at the cat until it leapt to a neighboring fire escape and disappeared. Then he turned to whisper to a guy down in the alley.

"She ain't home," he said as he lifted the unlocked window. "Meet me at the door."

The brawny man in the alley ambled to the front of the building, resembling a mobile letter *A* as he tried to keep his gargantuan thighs from rubbing against each other. He took the elevator up and waited by the door of Janie's apartment. When a neighbor passed by carrying a bag of trash, he nodded politely and knocked on the door. "Hey Janie, you in there? It's me."

The door opened and the man in the hallway slipped into the apartment before the neighbor could see that the person answering the door was a far cry from the pretty blonde who lived there.

"So this seems like a weird search," said the cat swatter. "A fuckin' tennis ball?"

"Rocko has a picture of her holdin' it, and he's got a gut feeling it's where Dizzy hid the combination for the safe."

"Rocko and his fuckin' gut. Ain't nothin' good ever come from that guy's gut."

"Yeah, but it never steers him wrong. Now get lookin' but don't be an asshole about it. He don't want her knowing we were here."

CHAPTER 35

Wexler and I listened to the sound of Nicholls's ringing desk phone as it blared through the car speakers. Six rings and nothing. Glad we weren't calling in to report a mad shooter on the loose. Finally, a gurgle of static came through the line and we knew Nicholls had pressed his unreliable speakerphone button.

Detective Schwank's voice shouted in the background. "You gonna answer that phone, Nicholls, or you like the song it's playing?"

Sounded like Schwank had four inches of an eight-inch cruller in his mouth.

After a hesitation during which Nicholls must have flipped off Schwank, a voice came through the speaker. "Chase Nicholls, Kingsley Police Department."

"Nicholls, it's me," said Wexler. "I need a favor."

"Ain't it your day off?"

"Can you get over to the Aberdeen Hotel and check something out for me?"

"Aw, Christ. You leave a dead hooker over there?"

"Not today. Need you to check on one of the guests. Hump Banfield, cottage five. Rile him up, then follow him to see where he goes. I need to know who picks him up, what he does, that sort of thing. He rode the hotel shuttle the other day so he might leave that way. It's possible he's a reporter."

"Sure thing," Nicholls said. "Slow around here anyway. Ah, shit! Frickin' Schwank throwin' donut sprinkles at me."

I didn't want the whole department thinking I was crazy, so I'd asked Wexler to keep our trip to West Virginia on the down-low, but Wexler filled Nicholls in as best he could.

Nicholls laughed when Wexler finished explaining. "I knew you were more interested in that haiku story than you let on, Wexler. You got the hots for little Janie, don't you?"

"What are you talking about?"

"Come on. You act all weird around her, like, weirder than your usual self." Nicholls's donut chomping filled the hollows of the car. "Lemme tell you something. If I didn't think of her as a little sister, I'd be all over that. Doesn't get any better than—"

The speaker cut off abruptly.

I turned to Wexler. "You cut him off."

"What? No. Bad connection. And trust me, no earth-shattering comments were imminent."

"Maybe not for you, but I was curious. Weird, indeed."

Three millimeters of Wexler's cheeks turned red. It was all I needed.

"Forget him," Wexler said. "Betty's house should be coming up any second. You sure you're up for this? It might be disturbing."

"I've had a lifetime of disturbing."

"Okay. And I'd like to clarify for the record that I am not weird around you."

"I'll be the judge of that."

Wexler turned into Betty and Leroy Fitzsimmons's driveway. "Sheriff's gonna meet us here."

I gazed at the home of my alleged photo mailer. Either my head wasn't screwed on straight, or Betty's white, clapboard farmhouse was sinking into the ground.

"How the hell is that thing standing?" Wexler asked.

"Crookedly?"

"Makes me want to run over there with some two-by-fours and prop it up."

I squinted and tilted as Wexler parked. "Actually," I said, "it's an optical illusion. See? The roof on that side reaches lower to act as some sort of shade for that chicken coop. Looks like they added it on later so rain would run off and fill the water trough." I pointed to the high side of the house. "And the mud has built up in a gradual slope over there. From a distance, it looks flat, but it's angling toward the roof." I adopted a children's storyteller voice. "And that, children, is why the house looks so dang crooked."

Wexler nodded in agreement. "You do have that eye for all things slanty."

"I have a feeling I'll need it today."

We clambered out into the unusually hot day, kicking up dust that rose in the air to coat the calves of our jeans. The sheriff pulled in behind us. Ridge must be one of those *Twin Peaks* towns where folks knew the moment a stranger entered. But when the thin sheriff smiled like we were old friends, all hints of insular freak-town went out the window. He looked like a well-aged Barney Fife who'd wised up and lost the doofiness.

"Welcome to Ridge, folks. Glad you found us. I was at the post office when you drove by. Figured the Virginia plates might be yours. Got some cold drinks in my car if you'd like one."

We accepted an iced tea and a soda from his cooler and he led us to the front door.

"Now, of course, Betty's body is no longer here, and you probably don't need the details of that mess—smell alone would've given you nightmares—but I guess you want to see the stuff in the basement. A bit more relevant to you, ma'am, since you're the Haiku Twin and all."

I appreciated the lack of eggshells he walked on. "Great place to start, Sheriff. Thanks."

"I ain't touched it. Figured we might bring in the FBI if this case is somehow related to your mother, but Detective Wexler here was pretty persuasive, so I promised you first dibs."

I smiled at Wexler, who humbly avoided my grateful eyes. "Thanks again, Sheriff. I know you didn't have to do that."

"Well, if it'd been my mother and all . . ." His voice faded off.

As he led us through the house, only two words came to mind: holy clusterfuck. No wonder Betty Fitzsimmons had come across photos of my mother's dead body. I felt sure I could find pictures of John F. Kennedy slurping a Jell-O shot out of Marilyn Monroe's belly button somewhere among the piles, along with enough rubber bands to make a bouncy ball bigger than Connecticut. I stepped over bundled newspapers from the 1970s, four full litter boxes, and three containers of coupons for products that didn't exist anymore. Dino Pebbles, anyone?

The odor, despite the removal of Betty's body, reminded me of a crime scene two years ago where a four-hundred-pound informant had been slaughtered like a pig, his intestines braided like pork sausage—a warning to would-be informants that if you talked to the pigs, you got treated like a pig. I doubted many of the would-be informants had been clever enough to interpret the message, but I did admire the killer's handiwork in a perverse way before excusing myself to be sick.

"'Scuse the mess," the sheriff said in an understatement so massive, I guffawed in its wake. Wexler managed to keep a straight face—and to breathe through his nose, something even I found impossible. It was all I could do not to pull out my bottle of Blunt

Effects spray and hit the house with a squirt. That stuff could block out *parfum de putrefaction*, but it was no match for the local feline posse that had found a friend in Betty. Smelled like one of them had lost a battle with a skunk.

"Sheriff," I said, "why do you think Betty mailed me the photos with no note of explanation?"

The sheriff chortled. "Wouldn't surprise me in the slightest if Betty wrote you a note but forgot to stick it in the envelope. She could tell you the quirks and ailments of any animal in town goin' back years, but she sent out Christmas cards more than once without the card. Just an empty envelope. Course, we appreciated it just the same. One time she invited a slew of us over for a cookout, and when we arrived, she'd plum forgot about it. That was Betty, God love 'er."

Betty's state of mind might explain the address on the envelope that had been missing a few pertinent points.

"Now, these stairs here," said the sheriff, opening a door that promised a basement full of creepy-crawlies, "they're a bit rickety. Be careful going down."

I flicked on my heavy flashlight and took the lead. The first stair let out a pained moan, clearly mistaking me for a sausage-intestined drug informant. I continued anyway, my torch illuminating the mostly barren space below.

"Must have been Leroy who used the basement," said the sheriff. "He was a bit tidier than his sister. Used to tell her she was puttin' all the landfills out of business by keepin' most of the garbage herself."

A dizzying sensation overwhelmed me. Was I having déjà vu? Where had I just heard a similar sentiment?

"It'll be over to your left, there, ma'am. Exactly where we found it."

I negotiated the final step and spotted the box on the floor, a location that had probably rendered the bottom inches of content unusable due to moisture. Then something reached out and stroked my face. After an embarrassing gasp, I pulled the offending string, which turned on a single forty-watt bulb overhead. It cast just enough light to be both helpful and eerie. My shadow fell squarely on the overstuffed box, dimming my final hope that the mailed photos might prove to be a big hoax by the Psycho-Ticks or their ilk.

"How much do you know about this Leroy Fitzsimmons?" I asked the sheriff.

"Knew him as a kid somewhat. He was older than me, but I used to go to his daddy's church and he helped out there. Quiet kid, unless he was onstage. Had a little acting bug and usually got a good part in the church productions, until some other kids made fun of his voice."

A niggling uneasiness tapped at my brain.

"Leroy came off as real smart," the sheriff continued, "but maybe that's 'cause he was smart enough to keep his mouth shut. Sometimes, you'd get the feeling he was judging you, but not too harshly. Just sort of makin' up his mind."

"What about as an adult? Same way?"

The sheriff scrunched his lips together and thought about that one for a moment. "Now this ain't a real big town," he said, "but I can't say as I've seen much of Leroy as an adult. He joined the military right out of school, then made his way back, oh, musta been twenty-five years ago at least. Took jobs wherever he could get 'em. Handyman, electrician, general fixer-upper sort. He'd stay away for a week or two, finish a job, then come home. Tell you the truth, I don't think Betty knew where he was half the time."

"Either of them married?"

The sheriff suppressed a laugh. "Uh, no. I wouldn't say either Betty or Leroy was the marryin' type."

I sifted through the box while Wexler checked the rest of the basement. "Why's that?"

"Well, you might say they were just a little off, bein' raised by their daddy and all. He was one of them strict, by-the-book preachers.

Not sure how he was at home, but church sure wasn't much of an uplifting experience when Preacher Fitzsimmons took the pulpit."

"Fire and brimstone?" Wexler asked.

"To put it mildly. But he died long ago. His wife had passed when Betty was just a baby."

I came across a pile of palm-size marble notebooks—miniature versions of the type kids used in math class. Releasing them from their purple rubber band, I opened the top one to see pages upon pages of tiny calligraphy, of such high quality it could have been printed by a computer. Several of the notebooks contained sketches, mostly of animals, and illustrations that could only be described as word sculptures, like the individual letters of *detachment* written over and over in a spiral that led to a fancy *A* in its center. It was titled on the bottom in a careless scrawl: *Attachment*. Another one showed random letters in a three-dimensional pyramid, topped by the head of a sphinx. Something told me the letters weren't random, but damned if I knew what they meant. A third consisted of twelve synonyms for *deceitful* written in green and squeezed in between red-lettered synonyms for *honest*. He'd pressed so hard with the green pen that it had torn through the paper at one point. Of the dozen or so notebooks, most spilled over with letters and illustrations, but a few remained half-empty, awaiting Leroy's next mishmash of dark verbal conceptions.

"Was Leroy some sort of artist, Sheriff?"

"I believe he fancied himself such. Can't say as I ever saw his work, though. Maybe upstairs?"

I set the notebooks aside, wondering what it must look like inside Leroy Fitzsimmons's mind.

I picked up the next item in the box and unfolded it to its considerable size. A blueprint.

"Oh, my God," I said.

"What'd you find?" Wexler said, holding a stack of papers he'd retrieved from a worktable in the corner.

I showed him an architectural plan depicting the rear of a three-story structure.

"You know the place?" he said.

"This window," I said, pointing, "allowed the sun to shine in on my dollhouse, and over here"—I pointed to the next window—"is where Jack would lean out and toss me a tin can so we could play telephone."

"You think Leroy was planning to break into your house?"

I frowned. "Or he already did. This box goes way back and stays current. He has stuff about Jack's recent campaign stops and articles about Grady getting out of jail. This guy had far more than a passing interest." I looked at Wexler with controlled panic. "You think he was the third man?"

"Could be. Look what I found." He handed me a stack of papers. "His laptop is missing, but he'd printed these out recently."

It was information on the Abel family from one of those genealogical websites. In addition to the primary members of the Abel family, like Abner, Annelise, Jenna, and the rest, there were sheets on aunts, uncles, and cousins, including an obituary for Joann Banfield, *wife of Humphrey "Hump" Banfield*, whose survivors had included many nieces and nephews, including a special niece, Jenna. "Was he stalking my whole neighborhood?" I said, too overwhelmed to put the obvious together.

Wexler's phone rang and he glanced at the caller ID, his face tightening. "Let me take this." He walked over to a corner to speak while I sorted the contents of the box in a daze. I knew what I was looking for now. Betty had sent me just two photos, but Mickey Busker claimed to have seen about a dozen camera flashes while getting his jollies in my childhood tree. I kept digging, placing a printout of Jack's latest speech to my right, followed by a *People* magazine photo from when he dated a reality show star last year. Next came a photo of me that I'd submitted to an online photography group. Below that was a Google Earth shot of Field Diner, now converted to a convenience store, and blown-up photos of the diner and my house.

With the next treasure to emerge from the box, everything in my body sank an extra inch toward the floor. I felt like a melting Popsicle as a shiver pulsated from my neck to my feet, where it turned around and rushed back up as a hot flush of anger.

In my hand, I held the negatives of the two photos mailed to me, along with three of the kitchen, two of the far living room corners, one each of the flowered couch, the marble table, and the fireplace, and then one that made my jaw clench—a close-up of the apron covering my mother's pregnant belly. The final negative showed a perfectly focused half of Grady's collapsed body, just as Sophie Andricola had sketched it.

I shoved the negatives back in their envelope and stood, fighting a severe bout of light-headedness. So Leroy Fitzsimmons—a man who meant nothing to me, from a town that meant even less—was the person responsible for tipping the first domino in the long and twisted path that had uprooted and toppled the Perkins family tree. But who the hell was this guy? Just some aimless drifter, some fly-by-night worker for hire? Could he actually be the Haiku Killer? Then again, weren't they all nobodies until their vile actions became the stuff of public obsession, the next hungry monster to be fed and nourished by the sleepless and paranoid?

Wexler emerged from the dark corner where he'd taken his call. Unaware of my discovery, he launched into his own update.

"Bad news," he said. "Nicholls checked out Hump Banfield's cottage at the Aberdeen. The place was almost empty, like no one had been staying there. The clerk at the front desk said they didn't even have a guest registered in cottage five."

"What? How could that be?"

"He must have broken in and made himself at home. It was pretty remote over by those cottages, and I don't think they rent them out much anymore. Who would have noticed?"

"That is bizarre," I said, fighting a truth I already suspected.

"There's more. Nicholls drove over to the newspaper where Hump's niece, Jenna Abel, works."

"Good. She'll know where Hump is." Doubt filled the gaps between my words, and even I could hear how lame they sounded.

"She hasn't seen her uncle Hump in two years."

Even though I hadn't smoked since my teens, I'd have given anything for a long, slow cigarette right about then, just to give my body something to do besides panic. I leaned against the splintery post at the base of the stairs, wooziness coming on full force. "Did Jenna have a picture of her uncle Hump, by any chance?"

"Nicholls sent one to my phone. That man in cottage five was not the real Uncle Hump." He showed me the photo and I agreed. "Whoever he was, the man did his research and simply borrowed Hump's identity for a while."

"Sheriff," I said, "do you have a recent picture of Leroy Fitzsimmons?"

"Not offhand, no. I could look through old church and festival photos, or we could search upstairs."

"No need," Wexler said. "I think I have a picture of Leroy Fitzsimmons right here on my phone."

"How?" I said.

"When Hump Banfield answered the door at his cottage this morning, I took his picture. Just a hunch. He had no idea I did it." Wexler flicked to the photo and held his smartphone up to the sheriff.

The sheriff leaned in close to the four-inch display of the man I'd known as Hump. "Well, dang, that's Leroy, all right. Sure as I'm standing here. But what the heck's he doing in a wheelchair?"

I let my face fall into my hands as I sat down on the bottom step of the creaky staircase. At least my palms muffled my shout. "I am *such* an idiot! Leroy Fitzsimmons was impersonating Hump?"

Wexler sighed. "The wheelchair was the only thing left in cottage five."

So *Hump*, aka Leroy Fitzsimmons, could walk. Hell, he could probably run—he'd run circles around me, anyway. Once again, Mickey's words haunted me. "Sheriff, did Leroy have a limp?"

"Matter of fact, he did have a little hitch in his step. Lost a couple toes in a tractor accident. Not real noticeable, though, unless he got runnin' at a real good clip, which I only saw him do once, in an egg-carryin' race. Fund-raiser and all."

It was all I could do to raise my eyes to Wexler. "Leroy Fitzsimmons was the third man . . . the Haiku Killer." My voice found both strength and shame. "I let him into my apartment! I made him tea!"

Wexler sat next to me, our legs touching, his arm tight around my shoulders. I'd never felt smaller or stupider. "Janie, come on, you had no way of knowing."

"He tricked me from that first day at the hospital. It was all a setup."

"Betty must have found the pictures down here and sent them, maybe to warn you about her brother."

"Jesus," I muttered, "he must have killed his own sister."

I could feel the wheels turning in Wexler's head. "All this just to get his pictures back?"

"No," I said, shaking my head. "It wasn't about the pictures. He could have taken those; he had them in his hands at my place." My eyes doubled in size. "He's after the haiku. That's why he has all the pictures of my old house. He must think it's still there."

"You're right," Wexler said. "It would be evidence against him. He must have figured that once Betty mailed you the photos, you'd start believing there was a third man, and you might start looking for that haiku."

I smacked myself in the leg. "With everything I told him, I probably already led him to it."

"Impossible," Wexler said. "You don't even know where it is."

"Well, one of us is going to figure it out. It's a question of who gets there first."

"Excuse me," the sheriff said, almost laughing with incredulity, "but what's this all about? Y'all can't think Leroy was tied up in that Haiku Killer stuff. Come on."

The sheriff came across as someone who wanted to appear skeptical but was secretly hoping it was true. A direct connection to the Haiku Killer would be more exciting in Ridge, West Virginia, than having the fattest pig at the county fair.

"He wasn't *tied up* in it, Sheriff," Wexler said.

"He *was* it," I finished.

CHAPTER 36

"How were you supposed to know?" Wexler said after my hundredth lament. "The guy's been fooling a lot of people for a long time."

"I'm supposed to have radar for these things. I'm supposed to spot things when they're off, remember?"

"Why should you expect more from yourself than everyone else?"

"Because I've been dealing with it since I was born. Since a month *before* I was born. This guy played me. Played on all my weaknesses and I never even saw it."

"You did. Otherwise, you wouldn't have mentioned him to me. You wouldn't have gotten those negative vibes. You knew something was wrong, but maybe you wanted to believe that not everything in your life revolved around this Haiku mess."

It had been a rough ride home for Wexler, between consoling me and barking out orders to the police force back home, but he held it together like a symphony conductor. With his phone as a tool, he set up BOLOs—Be on the Lookout alerts—arranged a wall-to-wall search of cottage five, convinced Nicholls to interrogate all staff and guests at the Aberdeen, and dispatched two officers to question hospital staff about the day Leroy Fitzsimmons intercepted me in the parking lot.

In between Wexler's controlled but energetic directives, I wailed out random things: *There wasn't even a niece! What was with the war photos? Did his feet really turn in like that, or was he wearing prosthetics? How did he get a copy of my brother's book before me?*

The last question gave Wexler an idea. He called the IT guys to track down all the sales of *My Life as a Harried Haiku Twin* to see if they could discover where Leroy had purchased the book. Unfortunately for the investigation, but fortunately for candidate Jack Perkins, the book had been preselling well for two months. Over ten thousand copies had been shipped the day it became available.

Wexler then pulled out a small tape recorder and recited everything he could remember from his visit to cottage five while Leroy was sequestered in the bedroom doing God knows what. Maybe loading a gun to kill the detective who was a little too close for comfort.

To really top things off, I returned home to find my apartment had been rifled through. Leroy had been here—on foot this time. Anyone else would have disagreed that my apartment had been searched, but *anyone else* didn't live here. Everything was off just enough to make the entire scene wrong in my head.

I checked the front door inside and out. No sign of forced entry. No unusual smudges or marks on the white paint. I marched to the back window, confident that the intruder had left long ago. The window was unlocked and I cursed myself for not being able to remember if I'd locked it after feeding Percival.

I glanced around. What had Leroy been looking for, anyway? The damn haiku? Didn't he know that if I had it, I'd have gone to the police long ago? Was he looking for something I hadn't even thought to look for? Maybe Annelise Abel had been right all those years ago. I was nothing but a naïve hick fresh off the turnip truck.

And then I let out a low grumble filled with self-disgust. I'd had thirty years to look for that stupid haiku and I'd never done it. Sure, I hadn't believed it existed, but that was no excuse.

My brother appeared at my open door. "Janie, don't you know any bum could walk in off the street?"

"Too easy," I said. "What do you want?"

"First, I want to thank you for this." He held up the cover of *Crime Time* showing a picture of me giving the world the bird.

"Not bad for an out-of-focus picture through a screen," I said. *Crime Time* was a free rag that flew off the shelves in Kingsley because it contained two weeks' worth of perps every time it came out. Kingsley locals delighted in searching for felons they might know—some sort of bingo for the warped.

"Somebody took this picture at Dizzy's crime scene," Jack said, "and unfortunately, it's good enough for people to know it's my sister."

"Want me to get it framed so you can hang it across from your desk?"

He sneered.

"Don't worry about it, Baby Bro. You're about to have much bigger issues hogging the front page."

"Like what?"

While making us tea, I explained about Leroy Fitzsimmons. Jack's mouth remained slack most of the time.

"How did I not know about this?" he said.

"You're the deputy AG. They bring you in later, not when the manhunt's just getting started."

"I've got to get my staffers on this. This is awesome."

"Awesome?"

"The pursuit and capture of this Leroy Fitzsimmons guy will be front-page news every day. Perfect timing. Only two weeks till the election."

This version of Jack was so familiar by now that his comments barely fazed me. "I've got a bone to pick with you," I said. "How come you never looked for the haiku?"

The incredulous look on his face was complemented by a scowl. "*What* are you talking about?"

"You and Grady. You were so tight all these years. If there was a third person in the room and Grady believed Mom had found a real haiku, why didn't he ask you to find it? Or at least ask Grandpa?"

"Right," said Jack, his tone mocking. "The guy who shot his pregnant girlfriend was going to call her dad and ask for favors. Come on! Grandpa hated Grady's guts. And in case you've forgotten, it wasn't until after I moved out of the house that I struck up a relationship with Grady—nineteen years after the shooting—a bit late to start a search for some stupid scrap of paper that was probably in Mom's pocket or purse."

I detested logic when I was steamed up, female, and full of emotions. Jack knew it, so he continued. "Besides, Grandpa wouldn't have allowed it. It would have lent credence to Grady's version of events. When Grandpa found out about the first time I visited Grady, he was so pissed he didn't speak to me for almost a year."

"What? When was that?"

"You were off at school, and then you took that internship in North Carolina for the summer. You probably didn't notice that the three of us hadn't been together from one Christmas to the next."

I thought back. He was right. I had chalked it up to busy schedules, but there had been serious tension and an endless string of excuses why Jack couldn't come home for holidays and breaks.

"Speaking of Grandpa Barton," he said, "I'm as shaken up as you are about the whole situation, but if Grandpa doesn't make it, you have any idea where all the old stuff is?"

Apparently Jack hadn't yet reached his low in my eyes. I smirked and shook my head at him.

"I'm just saying, what if?"

"What *stuff* are you talking about?" I said.

"All the furniture and stuff he got rid of when he redecorated for that dog trainer lady he was dating."

"Why?"

"Uh, I can't exactly have a random storage locker showing up on some crap reality show ten years from now, revealing personal details about our family."

"Ironic, coming from a guy who puts out a biography at age twenty-nine and thinks it's newsworthy every time he farts. Tell me, Jack, do you describe your own ass on those occasions, or does your ghostwriter do it for you?"

He sighed. "Get away from those cops, Janie. They're turning you into a pig." He pressed a button on his phone. "I'll take care of it." Into the phone he barked, "Randall, can you troll around the local storage places, find out if they have a contract with Barton Perkins? . . . Yeah, there's at least eight of them in the area . . . And, Randall? Come down hard if you find the unit, in case the owner gets ideas about cashing in on my name."

As nauseating as his last sentence was, I ignored it and grabbed my brother's arm. "Jack! The stuff!"

"Yeah, I'm on it. Did you not hear the conversation?"

"No. What if the haiku is in storage? If Mom hid it in a couch cushion or under a pillow or something, it might still be there."

"We don't even know if there *is* a storage unit. Grandpa might've sold the furniture or given it to Goodwill. I never even asked. Remember we came home for Christmas that year and everything was different?"

I did remember, and I recalled the unexpected feeling of relief, as if the burden of living in a shrine to Mom and Grandma had been lifted. Every room had a fresh layout, new floors, and a cheery, bright decor—except for Mom's bedroom, of course; that had never been touched. Grandpa's dog-training girlfriend could have bribed him with a trapeze in his bedroom, complete with whips and ropes, and he still wouldn't have allowed her to change Mom's room.

"Let me know if your guy finds the storage unit," I said. "I'd like to search it."

"For God's sake, Janie, it'd be like looking for a particular grain of sand on the beach. You're nuts. Let it go. The cops will find this Leroy Fitzsimmons and we can bask in the limelight."

"You can bask alone."

Jack shook his head. "Do what you want, but I'm moving forward. I can't wait for Grady to get out."

"Jesus. When is that?"

"Final paperwork needs one last signature, but they're keeping the details quiet to avoid a bunch of reporters."

"This is going to suck."

"Are you serious? Look at your life. You're employed and talented, you've got a brother on his way up, you're considered attractive from what I hear, and you're famous. Most people strive for that last one their whole lives. You had it handed to you, and you've never once used it to your advantage."

I spun on him, the frustrations of my day mounting. "You're so twisted, Jack, it's like you believe your own spin. You can't even see what you are because you're one with this sickness you've become."

Jack kept his cool. "You know why you don't like me anymore, Janie? Because every time you want to hide behind your lens and cry, *Woe is me, my mommy was killed, my daddy's a murderer, and people take my picture when I don't want them to*, I'm the perfect counterexample. There's nothing you can claim you went through that I didn't experience—and I turned out pretty damn awesome. I'm the living counterpunch to every sucker punch you ever tried to land."

I huffed and puffed but couldn't have blown a single house down, not even one built on excuses and resentment.

"If you think about it," Jack continued, "you pulled off a pretty neat trick. By digging into those two photos, you exonerated Grady. Can't wait to see how you handle that one. It'll be like one of those films of a building collapsing, the kind they play in slow motion so you can see every splinter of the termite-eaten wood crumbling to the ground." Jack rubbed his fingers together as if discarding specks of dust. "And nobody really remembers the old building when the shiny new one is built." He strode to the door, its creaky hinges contrasting perfectly with the well-oiled spring in his step. "See you later. I've got a press corps to manipulate."

I threw a pillow at the door as he closed it. All it did was give off dust. From down the hall, I heard a distant, haughty bellow. "Love ya, sis!"

"Love you, too," I mumbled.

I hated when he was right.

CHAPTER 37

I stayed up late, touching base with Nicholls and Wexler on the massive search for Leroy. They'd wanted to send an officer for my protection, but I felt confident that Leroy wasn't after me. He knew everything I knew, and if he'd wanted me dead, I'd already be dead. My body could have rotted away in cottage five for months until some ninety-year-old ex-senator got horny and hit up the Aberdeen for a quickie. Besides, Leroy needed me alive. He was after the haiku and figured I had as good a chance of finding it for him as anybody. I wondered how my mom had come across it. Didn't seem the type of item a killer would leave lying around.

I grabbed my brother's book. It had a chapter on the Haiku Killer, complete with photos of the corpses—treated respectfully enough, despite the pesky fact that they'd been murdered—and images of the hand-printed haikus. Looking at everything anew, with Leroy in mind, perhaps I could uncover some fresh detail.

I already knew Professor Biedermann's haiku:

Death greatest of all

Busy yet barren am I
Blest be as I deem

The second line could actually be about Leroy himself. Declaring himself a busy man—an in-demand contract worker—who found life barren, with a father who berated everything he did. According to the 24-7 retrospectives now playing on TV, Leroy had stayed busy through the years. Grew up in Ridge, helped out at the church, rose at dawn to take care of the pigs and chickens, and kept house with his sister. He'd gotten in minor trouble with the law—stealing gas for a friend's truck, graffiti, and public drunkenness—but nothing to keep him from getting drafted in the final years of conscription. He was sent to Vietnam at the end of 1970, got involved in the troop expansion into Laos, and then captured—details about this remained sparse. He was released from a prisoner of war camp two years later when the peace agreement was signed in Paris. Before his capture, he really had been his regiment's unofficial photographer, as well as a decent soldier, taught to kill efficiently and without emotion. Was that a natural fit for Leroy, or a mind-altering ordeal?

In the years following his discharge, either life or the service had taken its toll and Leroy had finally sought help for his demons.

"Sure, I remember him," said a bespectacled doctor on TV, whose scattershot hair made Einstein look fashionable. "I wanted him on antipsychotics. He thought everyone was after him, from the grocery cashier to the paperboy. He didn't act on his paranoia, but that can change, as I predicted it would. No friends to speak of, unless you counted his sister. And the conspiracy theories in his head, I mean, it's no surprise to me it all caught up with him."

I wanted to kick the television. Not only was this quack revealing confidential information, but he seemed the type that would stick an old lady on antipsychotics to monitor changes in her knitting habits.

"I honestly don't remember him," said another psychiatrist, calmly confident, distant, and cold, "but according to the file, we thought we were dealing with PTSD, or stress response syndrome, as we called it then. He had residual family issues and showed classic signs of depression, anxiety, and mild increased emotional arousal, where the patient is always on guard. We put him on anti-depressants and low-dose anti-anxiety meds."

Back to the eager Einstein-haired doc: "I wanted to blue-paper him, but no, the big shots didn't think he was a threat to himself or others. Of course, as I became a big shot myself, I got more patients committed than any other doctor in the history of that hospital"— he leaned into the camera—"and I'm feeling rather vindicated today. What say the naysayers now, as they hunker down, trying to avoid the Haiku Killer?"

Anyone watching who didn't want to slap the arrogance right off this guy's face had to be schizo themselves.

The program cut to a mousy administrator, her greasy hair highlighted by a chipped bobby pin flattening her cowlick. She chewed gum and couldn't have conjured one shit about her hospital's shoddy recordkeeping if a bipolar ex-con with homicidal tendencies had pressed a gun to her head. "I guess they lost track of him. There's no record of any return visits or follow-ups, so they'd have had no idea if he continued on his prescribed regimen or not. Doesn't sound like it, though."

According to an assortment of people who'd encountered Leroy, he became a drifter, but never a beggar, picking up manual-labor work where he could, renting rooms by the week or month. One reporter dug up people who'd hired him; they all said the same, predictable thing—seemed nice, quiet, did his work, kept to himself, almost obsessively so—except for one woman who said he freaked her out. Said he muttered to himself all day, his lips moving with no discernible words, and he was always jotting things down in a tiny notebook that he'd protect like gold in his pocket. She fired him after one day because he wouldn't look her in the eye. Oddly, she looked a lot like my mother might have at fifty.

I muted the TV, read the bios of the victims in Jack's book, then glanced back up to see the harsh, taciturn eyes of Leroy's father staring at me through an old photo on my high-def screen. The digital rendering made him look stern and soulless—or was it a realistic depiction of the man who'd raised Leroy? If so, the apple hadn't fallen far from the tree, but it did make the apple more pitiful.

The pretty news anchor transitioned viewers to teenage photos of Leroy, always in the shadow of his lanky father, like he was just a whisper of a person, so dominated by his surly elder that he seemed less than a beaten dog, expected to perform without an ounce of pride. And if it felt that way to me, how must it have felt to Leroy? No wonder he'd tried to fill his emptiness with others' blood, others' lives. Yes, busy yet barren was Leroy.

My cell phone rang. "Hey, Wexler, you catch him single-handedly?"

"I wish. I'm outside your apartment. Can I come up?"

The idea of Wexler in my apartment made me panic. Not only was there something intimate about it, but the guy was a neat-freak. I dusted as often as I cleaned my fridge—and my fridge had three-year-old ketchup spills in it. I buzzed him in, although the building lock was broken half the time.

He got to the door quickly and seemed distracted. "Hey, Janie, everything okay here?"

"You could have asked me that over the phone. What's up?"

"There was activity at your house."

"At Grandpa's? Was it Leroy?"

"They think it was neighborhood kids messing around. Found some eggs thrown at the windows, but I felt uneasy about it."

"The old trip wire going nuts in there?"

"Something like that."

"Grandpa said there'd been problems lately. Bunch of new houses have sprung up since a neighbor subdivided his land last year; the kids smoke and drink in our woods now."

"Okay, well, it still felt wrong for you to be here alone."

I touched his arm. "Thanks, Wexler. Really."

The next moment became awkward as I let my fingers linger too long and neither of us had a thing to say.

Finally, he pointed to my brother's book on the couch. "I haven't had a chance to look at that thing yet. You mind?"

"Not at all."

I grabbed two beers and caught him up on the first haiku. Together we tackled the second one. It was found with Dr. Columbus Cardiff, a cardiac surgeon who'd had a run of bad luck. His stellar reputation had been called into question by the family of a wealthy seventy-six-year-old man who'd died on the table. Evidence showed Dr. Cardiff had performed high-risk surgery against his better judgment, succumbing to pressure from the hospital and the family to try a controversial new procedure. Things went from bad to worse when a nurse claimed the doctor had wine on his breath and showed signs of fatigue while scrubbing up. The lawyers pounced, and the whole thing played out like a cheap soap opera. It was in the midst of this drama that the cardiologist met his unfortunate end at a remote hunting cabin. He'd been strangled with fishing wire. The haiku had read:

Suggest such counsel

Be ashamed as I would be

Above all, you should

The experts agreed that it referred to a version of the Hippocratic oath taken by most doctors. The only catch had been that the references were pulled from two versions of the oath, an older one and a modernized one.

The first line, *Suggest such counsel*, directly contradicted a line in the oath that read: *I will give no deadly medicine to any one if asked, nor suggest any such counsel.* The haiku was saying, *Yes*, do *suggest such counsel—give that deadly medicine.*

The second line, *Be ashamed as I would be*, referred to a line in the oath that read: *I will not be ashamed to say, "I know not," nor will I fail to call in my colleagues when the skills of another are needed for a patient's recovery.* The haiku suggested that the doctor *should* be ashamed to admit he didn't know something, ashamed to call in colleagues.

"It's godlike again," Wexler said. "The killer views himself as omniscient and, therefore, as someone who would be ashamed to admit ignorance."

"He's a god with no faults. Why would he ever call in a colleague?"

Wexler raised his beer bottle. "To being human," he said.

"And riddled with deficiencies," I added.

"And feelings and desires and all that goes with it."

A smile worked its way up to my eyes. I clinked his bottle with mine and we drank.

The third line, *Above all, you should*, set the killer's psyche on center stage in Broadway lights. It referred to the modern Hippocratic oath: *Above all, I must not play at God.* The haiku directly contradicted that statement with *Above all, you should.*

"This guy's got a real hard-on for himself," I said, before remembering I was in the company of someone with couth. "Sorry."

"No need," Wexler said. "I'd go so far as to call it raging."

I grinned, not quite able to meet his eyes, and he continued. "So Leroy Fitzsimmons rocked a serious God complex, or at least used it to justify his slaughter of two somewhat innocent human beings."

"Good observation," I said, slugging down the remaining third of my beer and opening another for each of us. "Both victims were flawed—Professor Biedermann by his sexual liaisons and Doctor Cardiff by his recent lawsuit and possible drinking on the job."

"Who was up to bat for number three?" Wexler asked.

The final haiku was found floating in a plastic toy ship in a bin of holy water near a dead priest, Father Jonathan Santiello. He'd been found with his white collar crushed into his neck, strangled by his own stole—the long silk scarf priests wear to symbolize their rank in the church. It also symbolized being attached to the Lord, to show that the Lord shared the priest's burden, which said almost as much about the killer as the haiku:

Collar of harsh white
man of the people of God
Almighty be damned

This haiku had offered the biggest challenge to the experts, with its lines tying together in various formations. It could be read: *Collar of harsh white man*, *White man of the people*, *People of God Almighty*, *God Almighty be damned*, or *People of God Almighty be damned*.

The experts had vehemently disagreed.

"What do you think, Wexler?"

He leaned back and gazed upward, the beer exacting a price from his carefully calibrated personality. "No matter how you slice it, I think Leroy was symbolically going after his own father."

"But his father wasn't Catholic," I said. "He was a preacher at Ridge Chapel."

"Could represent all men of the cloth. Some would argue that priests are the closest connection we've got to God." He tapped my brother's book. "The first line, *Collar of harsh white*—he didn't say *starched* white or *bright* white. He said *harsh* white—and even Sheriff Tucker remembered Preacher Fitzsimmons's fiery sermons from childhood. Sounds like Leroy didn't hold a favorable view of the white collar, the item that often symbolizes a man of religion."

"And if you read it as *harsh white man of the people*, it could still be a dig at his father."

"Even if you read it as *man of the people-of-God-Almighty be damned*, he's damning the man."

"With death."

"The awkward little farm boy taking revenge against the father with the very thing that attaches the father to God. More than Mr. Fitzsimmons was ever attached to his son."

"This haiku seems more sophisticated than the previous two."

"Serial killers evolve, Janie." He turned sideways to face me fully, the book balanced half on his knee, half on mine. If either of us moved, it would fall to the floor. He moved closer. The book fell. Neither of us cared.

"You know what else evolves, Janie?"

"What . . . Alex?"

His eyes smiled when I used his name, then he stroked my cheek. "Relationships."

Our eyes remained locked while a long, silent conversation took place. My final offering was a resounding yes.

His lips grazed mine as our knees overlapped. Then he wrapped a strong arm around me, pulling me in close. I felt safe for the first time in years and let the feeling wash over me. I stroked his smooth face, smelled his skin, listened to his lips finding mine again. I felt his softness, his strength, and his wanting. The taste of his hoppy beer on my tongue gave the world a sweet, stimulating flavor, and I gave in, body and mind and body again.

We made love late into the night, tremulously transporting ourselves to the bedroom sometime after midnight. Perhaps not surprisingly, Wexler approached sex with precision and passion, treating me much like his piece—the .357 SIG sitting on the bedside table: with care and respect, but fully in control, maintaining power with no safety, instead relying on timing, good action, and precise finger control. No subpar excuses for Wexler. Because it was his first time handling this particular piece of equipment, he focused all his attention on getting it right, the intensity of his gaze reaching deep, the caress of his sure hands as gentle as it was meaningful. Eventually, we lay back and he pulled me in tighter than I already was, sending me off into the deepest, most gratifying slumber I'd experienced in years.

Hours later, showing his softer side, between bouts of laughter and warm intimacy, he got up and fed Percival, who tapped on the window just after dawn. Covering himself with a towel, probably more out of locker-room habit than modesty, he strutted with confidence across the room as he kowtowed to the demands of a feline. The gesture struck me as sweet and humble, considering the formidable, unrestrained talents that lay beneath the cotton threads.

"You know what sucks about this?" I said when he returned to the bed, filling the void that had always existed but had only become evident in his absence.

"Nothing?" he said.

"Close," I said, pressing my mouth to his warm lips. "What sucks is that Nicholls was right."

"You're bringing Nicholls into bed with us?"

"Sorry. That is gross." He stroked my cheek, and despite our bodies already touching in dozens of places, the additional contact made me flutter.

"What was he right about?"

I rose up on an elbow so I could tease him directly and monitor his reaction. "About you having the hots for me. Now he's never going to let us hear the end of it."

"No. Sorry, but Nicholls was way off base."

I narrowed my eyes at him playfully, embracing the feeling of pure security. "How so?" I said, lying back.

"I don't have the hots for you." He rose up to gaze down at me, his defined shoulder muscles in full flexion. "That would be cheap and coarse. It would degrade the sweetness that is you." From his elbow perch, he leaned down and pressed his lips to mine. It made me feel vulnerable, and I relished it. "What I have for you is something much classier, more dashing, and far deeper than the hots."

"Oh, Wexler, my gut is telling me something very definite."

"Oh, Perkins, never listen to your gut—"

"But you said—"

"Never listen to your gut when your heart is drowning it out."

We disappeared under the covers together.

CHAPTER 38

Grady McLemore knocked on my door just the way I'd have predicted. Three perfect raps, rhythmically spaced and confident. I'd been dreading the visit since Jack's seven a.m. call, five minutes after Wexler's departure. Grady had been released before dawn, complete with decoy cars to evade reporters. He'd surprised Jack at his condo by announcing through the intercom, "I'm sprung! You got anything to eat?" The release had been all hush-hush, and I suppose I should have felt honored that Grady's second order of business was to visit me, but instead I found myself jittery and unsure. And one minute ago, I'd watched Jack drop Grady off while he went to park.

With a sharp, deep breath that startled my lungs, I wrenched the door open to see the ex-con standing there, grinning from ear to ear, a grocery bag at his feet. He looked more like my brother than ever, wearing a black sweater and pleated khakis that Jack must have lent him. They wore the same size and had similar physiques, although Grady's chest filled the sweater more broadly—because who wouldn't expect a sixty-plus man living on white bread and meat mash for thirty years to be in better shape than a twenty-nine-year-old guy who hit the gym almost daily?

"Grady," I said too loudly, "this is . . . weird, isn't it?" I couldn't help it. I was punchy, nervous, and on a contact high from ample contact with Wexler.

His grin disappeared and he blinked like doe-eyed prey that had been spared a bullet. "Janie, this is a moment I never envisioned." As he extended his right hand, the accompanying extension of his left arm made it obvious that he was hoping it would evolve into a hug, but it didn't. My deeply embedded, highly nurtured emotions couldn't just turn on a dime . . . but parts of me were definitely coming around.

We got through the greeting and I waved him in. I went to lock the door but decided to leave it open for Jack. When I turned around, Grady was in the exact spot that Leroy Fitzsimmons's unnecessary wheelchair had occupied a few nights before. It felt like someone had pumped a load of helium into my head as the parallel images clashed. The last two men who had seen my mother alive and kicking had now occupied the same space within a few days' time.

Grady saw me noticing. "Everything okay, Janie? You look spooked."

"I am, a bit. Can I get you something to drink?"

His eyes sparkled. "I brought something." He pulled champagne, orange juice, and strawberries from the grocery bag he'd brought, and just like that, the tension between us reduced tenfold.

"Perfect," I said.

I took the bag and headed to the kitchen, unexpectedly relieved to put a little distance between us. I'd gotten so accustomed to barbed wire, steel bars, and fifty miles of road as our barriers that even the length of the living room felt too intimate.

Jack barreled in, slamming the door behind him and extending both arms outward. "Isn't this awesome?" he announced. "Janie, can you believe this?"

His blatant, unguarded enthusiasm made my greeting seem downright funereal, but from courtroom to podium, Jack rarely found an occasion to choose muted tones over bright, loud proclamations. I gave him a grin rather than my usual sneer and it felt like a step forward.

"Nothing for me," he said without having been offered anything. "Unfortunately, I've gotta dash. Down to the final month of campaigning and Randall is not letting me off the hook." He whipped out his cell phone, slapped an arm around Grady's shoulder, and held the phone out in front of the two of them. "Get in here, Sis. This is one for the memory books!"

I froze, unsure whether to be more upset that Jack's first impulse was to commemorate this moment of *family togetherness* with a cliché and vulgar selfie, or that he thought my joining in was even a possibility. The frown between my eyes fought it out with the bursts of confusion in my heart as I mentally framed the photo that could have been, one that included my mother and perhaps a smiling daughter. For the first time, I felt the loss of the last thirty years in a new way; although the possibility of Grady working his way back into the equation seemed to remotely exist now, my mother would never find her way back into the picture, no matter how hard I tried to stage it.

Jack took a few shots, the matching grins obvious. The two of them stood, shoulder to shoulder, similar chins and noses reaching toward the lens, eyes equally perceptive and sharp. Jack even dwarfed Grady by an inch or so, as if showing off the flourishing health of the next generation, the way it should be in any normal family.

"I don't have any makeup on," I said lamely by way of excuse, though my mascara and blush were obvious. "Maybe later."

Jack heard something in my voice that made him lower his smartphone and return it to his pocket. A pleasant surprise, but I was more taken with Grady's reaction, as he seemed to perceive my discomfort, also. His shoulders lifted just enough, and his head cocked ever so slightly, as if to say, *I'm with you, Janie, but what can we do? Just Jack being Jack!*

Jack then made a show of patting his pockets to find his car keys. "Listen, I've got to get going, make a quick stop at the hospital, then it's off to the races. Give you two a chance to catch up."

I swallowed hard and my neck tensed—Grady and I would really be alone now—but Jack had met his quota of subtle perceptions for the day.

"Can you make sure they keep Grandpa's pillow flat?" I said. "He prefers it like a pancake and some nurse keeps fluffing it."

Jack snorted a bit and gave me a look: *You know he's in a coma, right?* I smirked back: *You'll do it anyway.*

With some jolly words of departure, he gave Grady an embrace, full and manly. The image floored me. It had been a long time since Jack and I had hugged, and I couldn't recall a single image of him wrapping Grandpa up in his strong arms, though I was certain he'd done it regularly. As my eyes welled, I turned to the kitchen, ingredients still in hand.

"See ya later, Janie. Love ya!" I knew Jack was waving his hand over his head as he made his way to the door, but I didn't turn around.

"Love you, too," I said, opting for more hushed tones. By the time the door slammed, I was at the kitchen counter, but by turning my head right, I could see into the living room. "Make yourself at home," I said to Grady, the words sounding strangely disjointed.

"Thanks. You need some help?"

"No," I said too urgently. "I'm good."

He sat down and picked up my brother's book while the muted TV screen flickered in front of him. I'd forgotten it was on, and unfortunately, the local news channel was showing the retrospective on Leroy Fitzsimmons again, flashing recent images, which meant they'd loop back to kindergarten-Leroy soon, followed by those weird adolescent shots with his father. Then would come the awkward senior class photo where Leroy's eyes were lowered, as if sorry that anyone had to look at his pale mug.

As I turned to slice the strawberries, I heard Grady utter a couple *wows* and *oh, my gosh*es, but I wasn't prepared for his final exclamation: "Holy shit!"

I came in carrying the drinks, expecting him to be looking at the centerfold of my mother, his bullet not doing wonders for her hair. But no . . . he was standing up and staring at the television, at Leroy Fitzsimmons's downcast eyes and shy smile. Age twenty-five, fresh out of the Army.

Grady glanced at me, then back to the TV, concern pushing his features into a tightly knit ball of anxiety. "I know who that is."

"Yeah, that's the guy who injected you. Leroy Fitzsimmons. He's been all over the news."

"If that's Leroy Fitzsimmons, he was at the diner the night your mother was shot."

"Leroy Fitzsimmons was at the diner? Impossible. Someone would have mentioned it."

My landline phone began to ring. I ignored it, as hardly anyone I knew called that number.

"I can't believe it," Grady said. "I mean, I knew the guy, but I never knew his real name. We called him Rusty. Rusty the Repairman."

My answering machine clicked on and Lucinda's voice came through, sounding frantic. "Janie, are you there, honey? It's Lucinda and I've just about had myself a heart attack. I'm watching TV and they just flashed a picture of that Leroy Fitzsimmons on the screen when he was a younger man. Honey, that is Rusty, the customer I told you about from the diner. Oh, my word, I sat a murderer in your mama's section. I'll never forgive myself." Lucinda's voice cracked and she made a few more muffled sounds before muttering, "Call me," and hanging up.

Grady and I stared at each other in some sort of mutual shock. I handed him his mimosa. In sync, we both plopped down on the couch and gulped half the drinks. So much for a celebratory toast.

"My mother gave free pie to the Haiku Killer," I said faintly, "and I gave him tea and cookies right here in this room."

Grady smirked, apparently amused by my take on the situation. "Well, no one can accuse the Perkins women of being ungracious." He reached over and clinked my glass lightly. "To fine Southern hospitality." We drank.

"At least now we know how my mother got the haiku. Leroy must have left it on the table or dropped it or something, and my mom picked it up."

Grady looked at me, weighing his options, hedging his bets. A hint of pity marred his handsome features.

"What?" I asked. "Did I say something stupid?"

He exhaled, then bucked up. "I doubt he left the haiku on the table."

"How else would she have gotten it?"

"There's something about your mom you don't know." He looked pained, but also charmed. "Your mother was an occasional pickpocket."

CHAPTER 39

Bridget Perkins, 30 Years, 28 Minutes Ago

With shaking hands, Bridget Perkins read the haiku several times before laying it down on the counter. She sat on one of the stools, rested her chin on her hands, and thought hard. No. No way that little repairman could be the Haiku Killer. What had Grady called him? Gus? Dusty? Whatever, it didn't matter. That man couldn't hurt a fly, and she was rarely wrong about people. But then, hadn't she wondered about the way he'd gazed at Grady, the way he'd been hiding something, and the way he'd left in such a huff? And what had Grady said? That the little repairman had drifted into town out of nowhere and shown up at his office looking for work. When was that? A few weeks ago? Yes, she was sure of it, because she remembered Grady complaining about that stupid radiator noise. It had squealed while she and Grady were on the phone, and he'd compared it to the noise she made during sex—and when comparing her to the broken appliance, she hadn't come out favorably. But he'd said it with a chuckle in his voice and it had made her laugh.

It had been a few days later that Grady had gotten the radiator fixed, because he'd joked about missing the noise, not to mention the memories it elicited.

When had the Haiku Killer last struck? Hadn't it been just over a month ago? That poor priest, the one with the Italian name. Maybe he'd hired that same repair fellow to fix something and as soon as he'd turned to face the altar—*wham!* The repairman had risen up and strangled him with his own stole.

Bridget shivered and felt the walls of the diner closing in on her.

From his car outside, the repairman had picked up his binoculars again. He watched the waitress read the item in her hands. He felt sure it was his, but he couldn't be certain. Maybe she swiped personal items from all her customers, the little thief.

At first, she'd seemed to relish what she was reading. He'd recognized the expression immediately: pride. Pride and haughtiness over her acquisition. He always could sense others' kinks—some sort of mirroring skill—and he'd just spotted a klepto who got off on the mundane. Kleptos didn't usually care what they took; it was the thrill of the taking, the art of the gotcha, that did it for them.

Well, this gotcha would come back to haunt her.

He watched as her look of pride morphed into fear.

How could he have been so stupid? He should never have taken it out in a public place.

Would she remember him? Of course she would. That scum Grady McLemore had made such a production of pretending to care about *Rusty the Repairman*, like Leroy was supposed to delight in some stupid name usually assigned to gum-smacking, redheaded teens. He pushed out an angry breath. At least the nickname had maintained his anonymity in town.

Inside the diner, Bridget bit down on her lower lip. She didn't know what to think. The killer had been moving all around the state. First the Eastern Shore, then the mountains near Skyline Drive, then up north by DC. It seemed fitting that he'd strike near Kingsley next. Was it really possible that she, Bridget Perkins, had intercepted a murderer as he plotted his next crime? The way he'd left in such a hurry and gotten himself all in a dither when Grady entered the diner—so odd. Bridget gasped. Was it possible he was planning to take out a politician next? To take out Grady? She picked up the haiku and read again:

Public Serve-ant Slave

Pandering gratuity

To none you serve now

Public serve-ant? That would describe a politician—and be an insult, suggesting Grady was as low as a common ant. And *pandering?* Wasn't that how Sam Kowalczyk described what Grady needed to do with certain constituencies to improve poll numbers? *To none you serve now.* Pretty self-explanatory. No politician could serve well after death, though some would argue the public would be better served.

Bridget pressed the haiku to her chest, her heart thumping. Grady had been naïve for perhaps the first time in his life. It hadn't been a random laborer looking for a job at his office three weeks ago; it had been a killer targeting his next mark. He'd gotten to know Grady's routines, his habits, his vulnerabilities. And if that fellow was in the campaign office enough, listening through vents and whatnot, he probably knew about her and Grady. She started again. That man had not been in the diner tonight to eat Mickey's soggy turkey Reuben and bland pie; he'd wanted to learn more about Grady's biggest vulnerability—her.

Both babies kicked at once and the sensation didn't subside. Bridget's stomach remained in knots, her breath coming in short bursts. Frantic, fearful, she raced to the back, through the two swinging doors to the kitchen.

Outside, Leroy's insides tightened when the waitress bit down on her lower lip, paling it. Oh, yes, she knew what she had in her possession now. Coupled with the odd customer from earlier, she was reaching a conclusion that wouldn't bode well for anyone.

He watched as she pressed her hands to her chest and glanced toward the swinging doors to the kitchen. With only a moment's hesitation, she rushed to the back.

The thought of the note in her ignorant hands made him sick. She . . . the most ignorant of all. What did she plan to do? Call the police? Call her *boyfriend*? This was his only chance. He might be able to exit the car and get to the diner door before she saw him, but what if she panicked or pulled a gun before he could get in? Oh! None of this was part of the plan. Ever since the misfire with the professor, he hated disrupting plans. But what choice did he have? It wasn't him. *She'd* upset the scheme. He was certain this time. It was not *paranoia*, or part of some conspiracy theory or the result of chronic anxiety or whatever else they wanted to label it! He was as certain as he'd ever been—a characteristic those doctors would have used to further their case against him—but he knew this time. He knew.

His insides churned into a thrashing turmoil of rage. The feeling was foreign to him because even when he slaughtered and killed, he managed to keep emotions at bay. Except for that one time— that first time when his father had forced him to drown those puppies. His *father*. The word crossed his mind with such bitter vulgarity that he had to jerk his head and spit to get rid of the taste.

The tall, hawk-nosed intimidator, preaching to the masses about the sanctity of life and the value of all things created by the Lord. Puppies must have been the work of the devil, then, because his father had showed them no mercy. Nor did the widower-cum-preacher display that trait to his children. No matter how hideous the punishment or bizarre the chore assigned to Betty or Leroy, Daddy Fitzsimmons could always justify it with a verse or two. A twisted interpretation of the Good Book—or just things he felt *deserved* to be in there. He'd elevated himself to saintly status, so why shouldn't he be granted poetic license over the book itself?

Kill those puppies now, son. We can't afford 'em and their barking reminds me of your mother.

Kill something that sounded like Mom? Young Leroy had prayed endless times to be gifted with *anything* that reminded him of his mother. He had not a single memory or trinket or photo of the woman, only a pen and a soiled death certificate he'd stolen from Daddy's desk when he was eight; he'd risked his hide stowing it between his mattress and box spring all those years.

Daddy was all he and Betty ever got—and that man came up short six ways from Sunday.

But we could slaughter one pig and feed the puppies off the bacon for a year.

Don't defy me, son. Do I need to remind you of your commandments?

No, sir, no! Thou shalt honor thy father and thy mother.

But wouldn't it dishonor his mother to obey his father in this case? Leroy didn't actually know if his mom had liked dogs, but it'd be nice to think she wouldn't have approved of killing them. Worst of all had been the expression on his sister's face while mandates of death passed from father to son. Icy, hot fear. Immobilized horror. Frozen disbelief. Like her mind had left her body to escape the unfathomable reality. As Leroy had departed to carry out the command, his sister's body had shown signs of life again. She'd started trembling near the utility sink, where she'd brought one of the puppies to wipe its paws.

Now drown those puppies and—

Leroy drowned the memory by humming loudly and rocking himself back and forth in the front seat of the car. He had saved the one. He had saved the one. But the rest . . . still too fresh to remember.

By the time he'd pushed the episode to the back of his mind, his opportunity to rush the diner had passed. Bridget was back in view. She yanked the diner keys from her purse, dashed through the front door, locked it, and ran to her car before Leroy could decide on a plan of action. He couldn't be sure, because he'd ducked down, but he thought she might have looked directly into his car.

Her car swerved past and he knew. He knew she'd called Grady. And suddenly, Leroy saw it all play out and knew what he had to do. Of course! He'd visited his sister at work last month, as if he'd known this day would come. Thank God he was prepared for any eventuality—and those doctors had always thought him crazy. Who was crazy now?

"Leroy," Betty had said. "What are you doing here? You never come by Doc Mason's."

"Can't a brother take his sister to lunch when he's home? Besides, you told me it was going to be slow today. Give me the grand tour. I want to see everything, Betty. Everything."

Betty had been so delighted. She'd made sure to show him a new puppy that was in for its shots because she never liked to let Leroy forget his childhood sins. But then they'd moved on, and Betty had even shown him the locked cabinets and secret storage compartments where Doc Mason kept all the farm animal medicines.

CHAPTER 40

"What do you mean, my mother was a pickpocket?"

Grady smiled. "She didn't think I knew, but I did."

"You were dating a thief?"

"I wouldn't call her that. I'd say she had a penchant for . . . pilfering things. Bit of a kleptomaniac."

I swigged my drink, then finished it altogether. How had I not known this about my mother? I got up and mixed two more mimosas.

"Bridget took insignificant things," Grady explained. "Trinkets, scraps of paper, an earring post, things like that. No idea why, but the desire overwhelmed her, like a craving where she'd get physically ill if she didn't satisfy it."

"She stole," I said, calling a spade a spade. "Is that how she came into possession of the haiku?"

"It would make sense, wouldn't it?"

"Well, damn," I said, because really, what else was left to say?

"I looked into the psychological components of kleptomania while I was in prison. They think it's a form of OCD, and her only relief from that pent-up feeling was to pocket an item, even if it meant nothing to her. Sometimes, I saw the tension percolating, although we never discussed it, and she was clever with her heists."

"Not clever enough that you didn't know."

"I watched her once through a peephole," he said proudly. "We were at a hotel in DC."

The image disturbed me, but I hid it behind my second morning cocktail.

"She was in the hall, stalking the cleaning lady."

I grunted. "That's lame, even for a klepto."

"No, she took a key right out of the woman's pocket. A master key that opened a small compartment in each room where the staff kept decorative knickknacks. The hotel had a policy of changing things up so even if a guest requested the same room, it felt new with each visit."

"And you embraced her behavior? Seems risky, given the spotlight you were destined for."

"Somehow, on Bridget, it was adorable—and worth it. Besides, she returned the things. If she were a real thief, she'd have taken the silver ashtrays and copper drink holders. She left that key on the bedside table for the cleaning woman to find."

"So she enjoyed—what?—a quick vacation in other people's lives? Lived for the thrill of being intimate with their possessions?"

He shrugged while I grew angry with this version of my mother. "Sounds like it's only a stone's throw from how a serial killer needs a trophy to be reminded of the high," I said.

Grady stared at me like a father deciding the best way to handle a testy toddler. "That's quite a leap."

"Well, the whole thing's weird. Her doing it and you enjoying it. But it does explain some things."

Grady downed his second drink.

"Lucinda told me how you raved about Rusty that night at the diner. Why did you call him Rusty?"

"When he first knocked on our office door, he was wearing white painters' pants with rust stains because he'd been working on some old pipes. Sam called him Rusty and the name just kind of stuck."

"Sam was your driver, right?"

"More than that. An odd bird, but he was my savior. Probably the only reason I polled as well as I did."

"Thought you were a shoo-in."

"Partially Sam's doing. He stayed in the background, working his magic. And his own background wasn't any better than mine is now, I'm afraid."

"Ex-con?"

"Involuntary manslaughter. He was driving his mother to the hospital after she'd fallen down drunk and hit her head. On the way there, he hit an old guy on a bike and killed him. He was slightly over the legal limit himself, so they threw the book at him. Just a kid, really. Soft in the middle, but the time made him hard."

Lines like that must have made the ladies go all gooey in the center over young Grady McLemore. More than one weak-kneed woman had supposedly fainted at his campaign stops.

"As clever and well-connected as Sam was," Grady said, "I can't believe he missed the Leroy Fitzsimmons connection all these years."

I drew back in surprise, still finding it hard to adjust to a world where Grady McLemore was the good guy trying to solve the crime. "Sam looked into Rusty? I mean, Leroy?"

"He must have. I told you when you visited me. He looked into everyone who had a link to your mother or me. Customers at the diner, employees at the Aberdeen, the people who saw me speak that day, you name it."

"Does Sam still have his files? Maybe he'll have insight as to where Leroy is hiding out now."

"Of course. It's never stopped being an active investigation. The fact that the guy who killed my future wife was out there for three decades while I sat behind bars—that's a scenario that didn't sit well with me. I hired Sam, and Sam hired others. The thing was, we had almost nothing to go on. The police never believed there was a third person, so they never treated that living room like a crime scene. And this was before DNA evidence. I mean, what'd the police have? Leaves on the floor? A mishandled blood sample that showed only traces of the drug in my system? A bruise? I doubt they even checked for fingerprints."

"I didn't tell you," I said, almost cringing. "I dug up a witness who saw the third person leaving that night."

Grady's head shot up. "Who?"

"Mickey, my mom's manager."

"Come on. That guy's as reliable as a jailhouse snitch."

"I believe him. The things he told me were not the types of things you'd fabricate to make yourself look good. He says he saw you fall to the floor—and he heard the gunshot."

"That's impossible. Sam would have talked to Mickey. He would have uncovered that."

I frowned. "No offense, but Sam seems to have come up a few clues short of a solution."

"Sam is thorough and loyal to a fault."

I posed my next question gently. "Have you been . . . paying Sam all this time?"

"Every month. My lawyer set it up from a trust I have."

"For thirty years?"

Grady nodded.

I looked at him with ample cynicism but didn't push it. "I think I should talk to Sam. He might have some insights."

"He hasn't been answering his phone."

"Maybe it's time for a visit?"

"You read my mind. I'm driving to his place this afternoon. Just need to hire a driver."

"Let me take you. I want to see everything he's dug up over the years."

Grady looked surprised, yet delighted, surely envisioning that big hug he'd been denied earlier.

"Where does he—"

A vicious kick to my front door snapped the deadbolt like it was a toothpick. I spilled my drink on the couch and jumped up. The perpetrators weren't even in full focus, but I did catch the steel glint of a nine-millimeter gun aimed at my head before spinning around, dropping to my knees, and pulling my own loaded .45 from beneath the couch cushion, only to face a bleak situation. I was in a standoff against three thugs, one of whom had a massively muscled arm wrapped around Grady's neck and a muzzle pressed to his head. I shifted my aim from one punk to the other.

"Get out now and nobody gets hurt," I shouted. "I'm with the police."

"Who the fuck is this?" the guy holding Grady yelled. "Thought you said she was alone."

"She is," said the short guy. "Almost always."

I decided to be insulted later. "I'll ask one time," I said, "and then I start shooting. What the hell do you want?"

"Where's the ball?" said Shorty. "We know you got it."

He may as well have spoken Russian for all the sense he made. "Does this have something to do with Leroy Fitzsimmons? Did he hire you?"

"What the fuck you talkin' 'bout, fucktographer? We want the combination and we want it now. Who you workin' for, anyway? You better not have opened that safe."

The third man, who'd temporarily lowered his gun and remained mute so far, began kicking things over in a slow, deliberate manner, making a controlled threat of sorts. He started with my cheap end table, progressed to my cheap chairs, and finished with a cheap lamp. Meant to be intimidating, it was merely loud. He worked his way to me, raising his gun within inches of my head. That proved more intimidating.

I faced him, my own gun leading the way. He was giving me free license to shoot him—at the expense of my own life, but he sure as shit knew I wouldn't. The trembling hand at the end of my arm told him as much.

His tired blue eyes showed thin red trails of blood and it made me feel better. Perhaps we were equals—both performing suboptimally.

"Janie Perkins," he said, making it clear this was no case of mistaken identity. "I'm going to give you the benefit of the doubt and maybe even spare you and your guest serious injury." His clear articulation and accent-free voice surprised me. "You took a tennis ball from Dizzy's apartment, did you not?"

What the hell? How in the world—

"Did you not?" he repeated, the threat in his voice needing no volume.

"How did you know that?"

"Is that some quirky thing you do?" he said. "Take souvenirs from crime scenes? Are you a thief, Miss Perkins?"

Now he'd pissed me off, laying bare my sinful soul in front of Grady after I'd just accused my mother of no better. I channeled my anger to the ends of my arms, forcing my hands to be steady. "Screw you," I said. "I took the stupid ball by accident."

"Fine," he said. "Where is it?"

"If everyone will lower their guns, I'll be happy to get it for you."

"Gentlemen," came Grady's voice, sounding like a restaurant host offering the best table in the house. It was the most melodious thing I'd ever heard. "I'm afraid there's been a misunderstanding. Perhaps I can help clear this up."

The gorilla-armed man yanked Grady's neck tighter, pressed his mouth to his ear. "What kind of misunderstanding, old man? The kind where you end up dead?"

"Quite the contrary," Grady said. "The kind where you do."

With that, Grady backfisted the thug's face, disorienting him enough that he was able to grab the gun. After relieving the gentleman of his piece, Grady slammed the guy's head into the tipped table and knocked him out. The gushing blood would do a number on my cheap area rug, but the fifty bucks to replace it would be worth it. Shorty used the opportunity to take a shot at Grady, who hit the ground and rolled out of the way just in time. When Grady rotated onto his stomach again, he raised the gun he'd confiscated and took an immediate shot from the floor, catching Shorty in the shoulder, which was enough to make him drop his gun and wail like a baby. That's right, Shorty, bullets hurt.

Grady kicked the loose gun across the room.

I held my .45 firmly on the articulate third man and he kept his on me, remaining silent and calm despite the abuse his cohorts had taken. The scene was the most surreal of my lifetime—and all over a ball that meant no more to me than a housecleaner's key had meant to my mother.

The calm man now trained his gun on Grady.

I had to put an end to this before more blood was shed. "Everybody, stop!" I shouted. "I'll hand over the tennis ball. It's in my bedroom."

"I'm sorry, Janie," Grady said, his tone laced with controlled menace, "but this behavior cannot be rewarded. We have two guns against his one. He assumes I care if I die. Which I don't."

The man turned his gun back to me, waving it like a conductor's baton, his composure rivaling Grady's and the whole situation playing out like a sequence in a gritty noir film. I caught a glint in Grady's eye and suddenly saw how it all would end—with a corpse lying next to me and Grady being carted off to jail. Damn testosterone. Why couldn't they just let me get the ball?

The composed man started to speak. He'd be dead before he finished his stupid threat; he started it anyway. "Well then, perhaps you care if she—"

I shot him in the leg and followed it with a well-placed, rigid kick that knocked out his wind and flung him onto the couch to recuperate. My childhood with Jack had finally paid off.

Grady instantly relieved Calm Guy of his gun and pinned him to the couch.

Suddenly everything went silent and still. A hollow loudness filled my ears and my body shook uncontrollably. As my heart rate caught up to where it should have been all along, sweat flowed from every pore and I dehydrated drop by drop. Grady flipped the intruder onto his stomach while Shorty, spotting an opportunity to get the hell out, bolted through the back window and clattered down the fire escape, still whimpering.

After Grady secured Calm Guy by crisscrossing his arms behind his back, he used his own shirt to stanch the bleeding. Despite the insanity of the last few minutes, I couldn't help but notice three scars on Grady's back, two long, one blunt and triangular. Something told me he'd have more on the front. Perhaps prison hadn't been all sipping tea and lounging in the sun.

He turned to me. "Janie . . . Janie! Keep it together!" He was shouting for my sake while remaining perfectly calm himself. "Bring me that tennis ball and then call the police."

Like a zombie, I shuffled to my bedroom, removed the floor vent whose air flow I'd blocked with an old shirt, then pulled out the small plastic bin that contained my personal album of altered crime scenes. I grabbed the tennis ball and returned to find Grady and the man finishing up a conversation.

The man turned his head as best he could from his prone position and sneered at Grady. "Yes, I understand," grumbled the man.

"Repeat it to me."

"We had the wrong address. Supposed to be picking up some money we were owed."

"Good," Grady said. He took the tennis ball, squeezed along the ripped seam, and pulled out a small slip of paper tucked inside like a fortune from a cookie.

"What the hell?" I whispered.

"You good with numbers?" Grady asked the man.

"Yes."

Grady read from the slip of paper: "Fifty-two, ninety-seven, twenty-nine, eighteen, three. Got it?"

The man repeated it back. Grady shoved the combination in his own pocket and the tennis ball into the man's. "Maybe they'll let you bounce that around your cell. If not, you'll get it when you pick up your possessions in five years. But at least you got the job done, so Rocko will let you live. I met him on the inside. Do give him my best."

Wexler and three uniformed officers barged in, breathless but calm. I hadn't even called, but a neighbor surely had. *Something's going on in that lady's apartment. Joanie or Janie or some such person.*

"All clear, officers," Grady said. "There were three of them. One on the ground there, one took off out the back window, and this guy on the couch. Miss Perkins and I are fine."

At a nod from Wexler, two of the officers tended to Muscles while the third approached Calm Guy and called for an ambulance.

Wexler, seeing a pale, trembling version of the woman he'd spent the night with, grabbed both my arms and sat me down. "Janie, what happened? You okay?"

"Yes, yes, I'm fine."

He crouched down, keeping his eyes locked on mine, looking for signs of shock, as Grady approached.

"Detective, thanks for getting here so quickly. I'm Grady McLemore."

They shook hands and Wexler introduced himself, maintaining a rigid professionalism. If not for the circumstances, I might find it adorable that my new boyfriend was meeting my new dad.

"Janie and I were talking," Grady said, "and the next thing you know, three hoodlums barged in screaming about a meth payment. They had guns, all three of them. I disarmed one and knocked him out, then used his gun in self-defense on the second man. Janie disarmed the third man, getting off an accidental shot in his leg while doing so. She was about to call the police when you got here."

How could he be so cool and smooth?

Wexler looked at the scene, at the perps, back to Grady, and then at me. Doubt filled his eyes.

Not knowing what else to do, I nodded to affirm Grady's version of events.

"Mr. McLemore," Wexler said, "you mind coming down to the station and giving your statement?"

"No problem, Detective," Grady said.

Wexler put his hands on my knees, cueing Grady to make himself scarce. "Janie, I know these guys. They work for Rocko Mania, the drug dealer who probably ordered the hits on Dizzy and his mother. They don't get addresses wrong. Want to tell me what really happened?"

Any remaining fortitude within me collapsed. I leaned in close, picking up a hint of nervous perspiration from Wexler. It mingled with the scented soap he'd used in my shower earlier. "The tennis ball in the guy's pocket," I whispered. "It had something in it. A combination for a safe. They were here to get it back."

Had to give Wexler credit. He put it together in no time flat, and I couldn't have been sadder when I saw his perception of me change. "You took the ball from Dizzy's?"

I nodded. "It was a mistake, I swear."

All the implications instantly merged in Wexler's head. If word got out that I'd manipulated a single crime scene, every conviction that had ever involved my photos would be in jeopardy. The defense attorneys in town would dine out for months on the appeals bonanza. Everything I'd ever touched would be tainted, and forget about keeping my job.

"Grady's story is cute," Wexler said, "but what are these guys gonna say at the station?"

"Grady worked something out with them about sticking with the mistaken address."

Wexler stood and addressed the room. "All right, guys. Let's keep things moving. Looks like a case of the bad guys getting a bum scoop."

Grady's eyes met mine. I didn't know whether to thank him for saving my life, curse at him for lying to Wexler, praise him for covering for me, or pat myself on the back for keeping him from killing someone on his first day out of prison. I settled for returning his gaze.

CHAPTER 41

The immediate aftermath of the break-in was horrific and nauseating, and it sucked up the entire day, but things had worked out. Calm Guy had given his weak story. Shorty had been arrested and corroborated the story, while Muscles was in the hospital with a serious concussion. Wexler leaked the tennis ball information to let Rocko Mania know I'd relinquished the ball and the safe's combination. Yes, my new lover was keeping me safe, but would he keep me as a lover? He hadn't returned my calls yet this morning.

As I waited in my car to pick up Grady from my brother's place, I grabbed the third newspaper I'd bought and read another front-page article feting Grady as a hero. They couldn't get enough of the irony of the story. *Grady McLemore failed to save the love of his life thirty years ago, but arrived in the nick of time to save the life of his estranged daughter.*

Hm, I'd take Haiku Twin over *estranged daughter.*

According to one ridiculous opinion piece, he'd saved my life twice: *Thirty years hence, the nimble, sure-footed Grady McLemore* rose as if from the ashes to save the life of the daughter he never knew. *Yes, fans of literal interpretation will argue that Mr. McLemore's intervention decades ago cost his daughter a mother, but without his heroic deeds on that dire evening in a dark living room, when a public panic over a perilous serial killer was the prevailing sentiment of the land, the Haiku Twins may well have lost their lives before they'd even begun. Luckily for them, McLemore stepped into harm's way.*

Who wrote this stuff? Clark Kent on an alliterative high?

My favorite was the one by a fawning journalist who believed my mother was the Haiku Killer's target all along: *His actions spared the next generation, who surely would have perished in the Haiku Killer's mad rush to murder his first female victim, embodied by stunning waitress and art student Bridget Perkins, who died in the very uniform that may have made her a target. And now, Grady McLemore has done it again.*

I wanted to throw up, but settled for throwing the papers in the back. Suddenly, a glaring flash hit me in the eye. Not a camera flash—I knew those backwards and forwards, professionally and personally—more like a piercing beam. It flickered from one eye to the other and when I threw my hand up to block it, it traveled to my steering wheel and then my lap. When it started making a dash-dot-dash pattern, I knew exactly what was going on. I smiled and lowered my hand. The light flashed four times, paused, and flashed again, followed by a longer flash, a quick flash, and two longer flashes. I could predict the flashes that would follow, and they did. Jack had just sent me a Morse code message: *Hey, Sis!* Even with rusty translation skills, I got it. We'd mastered only a few basic phrases as kids.

I glanced up at Jack's third-story condo window to see him holding a mirror, which he lowered before any of the lurking news-hounds noticed. Some of the reporters—in wrinkled clothes and generally unkempt—looked like they'd camped out overnight, desperate for a glimpse of their new hero. It'd be a jackpot day for them if they got a shot of Grady and his handsome son together. But Jack and Grady were probably waiting for the pivotal, maximum-advantage moment to stage such a shot; otherwise, they'd be pulling a Michael Jackson right about now—Grady dangling Jack from a window with a wool blanket over his head.

Jack next held up a can of soup and wiggled it to make sure I'd see. I grinned, but finding myself without a trusty tin can and string, I opted for calling.

"Hey, Sis," he said upon answering. "Grady will be down any minute. He's just brushing his teeth."

"Wish you could come."

"I would, but there's a huge development in one of my cases. Looks like we might be turning a guy, bringing down a whole heroin operation that's been under surveillance for months. Besides, I think you should let the police handle this whole Leroy situation."

"I know, but I want to talk to this Sam guy myself."

"Well, sorry I'll miss it. A family drive in the country would have been so us."

I glanced up at the window to see him smirking playfully.

"Actually, the drive will give me a chance to talk to Grady," I said. "We kind of got cut off yesterday."

"You sure you're okay after all that? Can't believe you wouldn't stay here last night."

"I refuse to be cowed by the criminal element. But thanks for sending dinner over. That was sweet."

"Ordered it myself. Didn't even have Randall do it."

He was so proud that I couldn't even muster any mockery. "You know, Jack—"

My passenger door suddenly wrenched open. An old man in a floppy rain hat and sunglasses threw himself into the seat, a heavy cane in his hand. I gasped. "Leroy?" Reaching for my door handle to escape, I shouted into the phone. "Jack! Call the police! Are you seeing this?" But then I heard a resonant laugh—in stereo—as both Jack and Grady—the man in my passenger seat—had a good chuckle at my expense.

"Seven reporters outside your brother's building," Grady said, "and not one of them gave the old man with the bum leg a second glance."

Grady, still laughing, flashed camera-ready choppers as he cast his props into the backseat. I had trouble deciding between punching Grady in the arm and flipping off my brother, so I dropped my phone to my lap and did both.

Jack laughed and waved from his perch while Grady feigned pain and rubbed his arm. Then I noticed some of the reporters catching on to the antics and running toward my car. I started the engine, gunned it, and turned the corner before any flashes went off.

"Maybe we should start again," I said. "Good morning, Grady. You have the address?"

He waved some papers fresh off my brother's printer. "If you get us to the town of Stuart, I'll get us to Sam Kowalczyk's."

I got us out of the city in eight minutes and the scenery changed dramatically. Central Virginia was like that. City and country, pavement and pastures, sometimes butting up against each other, but always finding a way forward. Grady seemed to enjoy being out in the open, a delighted grin playing on his lips every time I glanced over. "Would you do me a favor, Grady?"

"Anything."

"Would you tell me something nice about my mom? I need to replace the pickpocket image in my head."

He laughed before launching into ten minutes of breathless wonder. He told me about my mom's penchant for hoop earrings, her adoration of animals, mysteries, and chocolate, and her abiding love for blueberry cobbler. "She'd eat enough to turn her teeth purple," Grady said. "And here's something else. She was determined to master the unicycle after you kids were born."

"Why?"

"She loved trying new things. Told me she was going to be the most well-rounded first lady in the White House."

"She believed in you."

"Like no one ever had—and I wasn't exactly lacking for support. But when Bridget Perkins believed in you, you felt it. She had this radiance; able to entrance people without trying."

"Like a vampire?"

He grinned. "She was a night person, that's for sure. She'd work late, then stay up till the wee hours sketching, sculpting, or writing in her journals."

"Journals? I've never seen any journals."

"She kept them since she was fifteen, I think. Maybe they're still tucked away somewhere."

I felt cheated, like he'd confided that a piece of my mother still existed but no one had thought it worth mentioning. All I had were a few old sketches, some school papers, a small collection of her clay sculptures, and my childhood fantasies. If there was a journal somewhere, I'd sure like to see it.

"If my mom had all this ambition, why was she working in a diner?"

"She wouldn't take money from your grandfather or me. Insisted on putting herself through school, because that's how the Perkins family had always done it. You know she was studying art, right?"

"Only a few credits to go."

"The rote book stuff didn't come easy to her. Her mind was all over the place, like a bullet ricocheting around a steel room."

"Speaking of bullets, where'd you learn to shoot?"

"Summers with my grandparents in South Carolina. They had a little land and a lot of bullets. Learned to shoot before I was potty trained."

I laughed at the exaggeration.

"I swear. There's a picture of me in a diaper, wearing gigantic earmuffs and shooting a twenty-two."

"You did well yesterday," I said, avoiding mention of how he didn't do so well thirty years ago.

Grady sighed. "In prison, a them-or-you mentality takes over. You don't act, you die. No two ways about it."

"You were in with some hardened criminals, I guess."

"Why not? I was a murderer in the public's eyes."

His statement hung in the air between us like an unexploded grenade, and then he exploded it.

"I was responsible for the death of a guy inside, about fifteen years ago."

I glanced at him, desperate to gauge his intent by sharing that bombshell, but his eyes were distant, his fingers covering the corner of his mouth as he decided what to share.

"We didn't hit it off, to say the least," he said, "recognizing characteristics in each other that were bound to conflict. I was a leader on the inside; earned it the hard way. It's the reason I can barely lift my left arm over my head, and you don't want to know about the scars under this shirt."

"I saw them yesterday."

"Anyway, this guy didn't fit in the hierarchy and my guys picked up on the tension."

He left it there, turning his attention to a sticky spot on the passenger window.

"Sounds like your guys were hired killers, instructed by you."

"Not at all. Things happen in prison without direct communication. There's an undercurrent. You know how women get on the same cycles when they hang around each other?"

My cheeks burned. Had the female prison guards left issues of *Cosmo* lying around? "Yes."

"It's the same with men. Every inmate picks up the same vibrations when their hands are on the bars long enough. Your feet are touching the same concrete when those metal doors slam at night. The reverberations tear through your body like a recurring nightmare. I didn't issue any orders, but the disharmony between me and this other guy, it was tangible."

"And the guy with the sharpest shiv picked up on it?"

It came out more accusatory than I'd intended, but not as pointed as the weapon used on Grady's enemy.

"He bled to death in the shower."

I couldn't mask my horror.

"Come on, Janie. I never even knew who did it."

"But you knew why."

"It was understood."

I suddenly saw Grady as a child, a gun shoved in his hand, a toughness preached into his core with a drive instilled by a cold mother. Born with thick coats of veneer, he'd struggled to peel them away to reveal his heart, his compassion. Maybe it was my mother, she of unicycle dreams and deft fingers, who melted his layers enough to allow his heart to beat loudly and to love. And when the time came to don the layers once more, in prison, it was easy for him, like slipping on a familiar coat. I didn't know. But how else to understand a man who went to prison unjustly for murder, only to become a violent leader inside? Would Grady's layers melt again? If what I saw in his eyes yesterday was any indication, he still had some work to do.

The mood in the car took its cue from the heavy clouds above as we climbed the mountain toward Sam's place.

"I won't tell anyone about your crime scene quirks, Janie. Don't worry. But doesn't it put your job and reputation at risk? Maybe the apple didn't fall far from the tree."

"I'm no klepto!"

"Didn't say you were. But if you're stealing—"

"I don't steal. I . . . restructure. It's my own thing."

"Okay," he said, his voice pleasant and light.

I sighed. "Look, I don't mess with crime scenes. Not enough to matter, anyway. And it's wrong, absolutely, but taking that tennis ball was a bad mistake, a panicked reaction to a photographer." I smacked the steering wheel like a petulant teen. "You know what? Rocko's gang probably figured I had that tennis ball because of that photographer's picture—and people wouldn't be taking my picture all the damn time if it weren't for you, so gimme a break here, okay?"

Out of the corner of my eye, I thought I saw him grinning, but I refused to look. Was he enjoying a taste of the fatherly role he'd wanted to play for decades? Maybe so, but I wasn't yet accustomed to playing the daughter.

We entered the area where Sam lived and nausea overtook me as the road wound tighter and the cliffs grew steeper. My tires hugged the center line as Grady directed me to an isolated home at a crisp elevation in the Blue Ridge Mountains. When we got out of the car, I sucked in deep breaths to clear the nausea while he seemed in awe of the view, taking in eyefuls of everything he could.

"I'd forgotten," he said simply. And I understood.

We walked past two cars in the driveway, an old Pontiac and a compact SUV with a nursing school sticker on the back. "Sam's been really ill the past few months," Grady explained. "COPD."

"Might be why he's not answering his phone."

We trudged up the dozen slate steps to the front door. Before we could ring the bell, a small Hispanic woman, about forty, pulled it open and nearly dropped the box in her hand. "Lord have mercy! Didn't hear you pull up."

Grady smiled and put out his hand to hold the door for her. "I'm so sorry," he said. "You must be Sam's nurse, Millie."

Sam had probably mentioned the name in his letters, and Grady, like any good politician, had tucked it away for future use.

"Yes, sir, I am." She seemed flustered. "You here to see Mr. Kowalczyk?"

"We are. I'm Grady McLemore and this is Janie Perkins."

From her full-on blush, I figured she'd mistaken us for the king and queen of England. "Oh, yes, I know. An honor to meet you, sir. And you, ma'am." She'd added the last three words as a rushed courtesy. "Mr. Kowalczyk worked for you back in the day, didn't he, Senator?"

"Sure did," Grady said, showing no hesitation in responding to the *Senator* label. "Really helped me out."

"I'm afraid Mr. Kowalczyk isn't here." She looked genuinely distressed, not so much because Sam was absent, but because she didn't want to disappoint her idol. "I come by twice a week, but he's not here this morning. I'm a little worried."

"Does he normally go out?" I asked.

"Not in his condition. Hard for him to stay gone long, but it's strange because his car is still here. He can't walk but a quarter mile or so, and that's on a good day without a mountain for a backyard. I was going to come back in an hour and call the police if he wasn't back."

"Would you mind if we looked around?" I said. "See if we can figure something out?"

She seemed hesitant, but when she glanced at Grady, he worked his magic and she stepped aside. "Sure."

"Thanks, Millie," Grady said. "By the way, Sam mentioned you several times. Said he appreciates everything you do, and that you even laugh at his Polish jokes."

"Sometimes they're actually funny," she said, her face glowing. Grady really had been born for this crap.

We entered Sam's home. It was decorated in predictable mountain mode: dark beams, mounted animal heads, Southwest-themed furniture, rustic wall hangings. It smelled stagnant, though, as if Sam rarely let in fresh air, perhaps feeling he only deserved the bottled-up staleness of his own exhalations. It was an immediate, dour impression of a man I'd never met, but it hit me hard. A sudden pang of jealousy washed over me. Even this man, who I instinctively didn't like, had known my mom as I never had—living, speaking, enchanting, thieving.

I tried to focus on the task at hand—learning what this ex-con could contribute to the current craziness in Caulfield.

The tiny kitchen gave off an air of loneliness. Four of everything, with a single dirty dish on the counter, a congealed, crusty egg yolk covering it. Was it just me, or was the dried yolk flipping me off? The sink was bone dry, as if the faucet hadn't been turned on for days. Millie's duties must not have extended to housecleaning.

I wandered to the bedroom. The comforter was freshly fluffed, but the whole ensemble smelled sweaty, and the contents of the coffee mug at the bedside had partially evaporated, a dark ring hovering above the current level of liquid like an ugly halo. "Looks like he hasn't been here for a while."

"What was your first clue?" Grady said. "The stale smell or the complete lack of life?"

I glanced at Grady. He'd spoken sarcastically, but he might have hit the mark.

"Think he went on a trip?" Grady asked.

"Without telling his nurse? And without his car?" I wandered to Sam's desk in the corner of the bedroom to examine the scattered files. "Looks like he was getting ready to give you a final report," I said. One folder was open, filled with photocopies of canceled checks from a lawyer's office, drawn from Grady McLemore's account. "You were generous."

"You want results, you pay for them," he said. "I wanted results."

I picked up a thick green file that contained dozens of manila folders labeled with names, including Mickey Busker, Lucinda Lowry, Doris Murphy—the judgmental customer who'd chatted flowers with my mom—and Abner Abel, along with a bunch of people I didn't know. I peeked inside Abner Abel's file first. It included a copy of his birth certificate, an ancient photo of him as a child, church bulletins where he was listed as a deacon, his tax records, and several candid shots taken by someone—probably Sam—who must have followed him.

This Sam guy was good. The photos included Mr. Abel leaving Field Diner two weeks after the shooting, exiting church with his family, shopping at the hardware store, and making a delivery to a butcher at least twenty miles from Caulfield. Next was a clumped collection of photos, taken through a window, of Mr. Abel meeting with other people in the dimly lit basement of an old building, followed by a picture of the building itself—a crumbling warehouse in Kingsley that had recently been converted to condos. What the hell kind of weird cult had Abner Abel belonged to? I swear, if it was some branch of the Psycho-Ticks, I might flip out. I turned the photos over. All were dated twenty years ago or more.

"He had quite the file on Abner Abel," I said to Grady.

"That's the name! That's the guy your mom said might know about us. Nasty piece of work. He and your mom had words that night at the diner."

Even though I knew the story, I wanted Grady's version. "What about?"

"I guess he'd seen her in a car with Sam when they were returning from the Aberdeen and didn't appreciate our . . . I don't know . . . duplicity. He took off without it coming to anything, but it left your mom shaken up, not that anyone else could tell."

"How could *you* tell?"

Grady smiled. "She had systems for everything, from the way she did her laundry to the way she arranged things in her apron pockets."

I smiled, remembering Jack's childhood penchant for sorting and labeling his Hot Wheels and plastic dinosaurs.

Grady continued. "She would keep customer orders and bills in one pocket, payment and change in another, tips in a third, and personal items in the fourth. After Mr. Abel threw his crumpled bills on the table and huffed past me, I saw her put that money in the wrong pocket, and that's when I knew how flustered she was."

"What a detail to remember."

"The things I remember about your mother could fill a book."

"If you write it, I'd like to read it."

He glanced up and we shared a moment; it felt like my mom was in the room, linking us together. I returned to the files and opened the one on Mickey Busker, the tree-jerking loon. According to Sam's notes, Mickey had shit for brains, no friends except his right hand, and a chip on his shoulder the size of Mount Rushmore. There was a record of a short jail stint for indecent exposure, and two DUIs, which might explain his two-wheeled mode of transportation between trees. Maybe Sam Kowalczyk wasn't so bad, given our similar conclusions about Mickey.

The other files covered people from campaign stops—some of them real crackpots, one with a serious gun fetish—and vendors in town that Sam and Grady had worked with, as well as Aberdeen Hotel employees and Field Diner workers.

The last file was empty except for a chintzy key, the type that came with bargain luggage and could be bitten in half by a toothless man. I glanced around for anything lock-worthy, and finally noticed the top right-hand drawer of Sam's desk. Without weighing the morality of such an action or the chances of Sam walking in and catching me red-handed, I opened the drawer. It was crammed full of boring files: tax receipts, bills owed, bank statements, and dozens of things in life that should come with a pocket CPA. I'd have kept that drawer locked, too, just to keep from looking at it. I almost closed it, but a slight pull beyond its natural extension revealed a cluster of files stuffed behind the regular rack. I yanked them out.

The first was labeled "Family Photos" with a pink tab. It contained a slew of old, faded pictures that Sam's parents must have passed on to him. The way they stuck together indicated Sam didn't waste much time reminiscing. The sight of the second file elicited a gasp from my throat, one that failed to draw Grady's attention. He was on the bed paging through old campaign photo albums.

"Grady," I croaked, "you need to see this."

He didn't respond.

"Grady," I repeated sternly.

"Yes, sorry," he said. "There's a picture here with your mom in the background. Sam took it the day we met."

The great orator's voice cracked. If Jack were here, he'd record that crack, practice it, and break it out at the next campaign stop. Grady was barely holding it together, but I knew my news trumped anything he had.

He wiped his face with his hands as he crossed the room, then leaned one hand on the desk and the other on the back of my chair, like Nicholls did when examining crime photos at my desk; the implied camaraderie felt good, but made me regret what I had to show him.

"What've you got?"

"Sam had this file hidden." I flipped it open to reveal four photos of Leroy Fitzsimmons. "These photos were taken at Leroy's house in Ridge, West Virginia, so Sam did know Rusty's real identity. He knew exactly where Leroy lived and what he was up to."

"But Sam had files on lots of people," Grady said. "It doesn't mean he thought that Leroy Fitzsimmons was the Haiku Killer."

I closed the file and showed him the label: *5-7-5*.

"Five-seven-five," I said. "That has to be code for the Haiku Killer."

Grady put on his reading glasses and took hold of the file. "It's got to be a coincidence. Sam was a loyal friend."

"Sam needed your money."

Grady turned the file to get a better look at the tab. He read the tiny date scribbled next to the 5-7-5 title. "If you're right, Sam's known for over twenty years that Leroy was the Haiku Killer."

CHAPTER 42

After recovering from the shock, Grady and I dug deeper into the 5-7-5 file. Despite Grady's determination to examine everything, catching his most loyal friend in a decades-long act of deceit took its toll.

"Sam was my friend," he mumbled periodically in meek protest. It was enough to break the coldest of hearts.

The file included photos of young Leroy Fitzsimmons outside his house in Ridge. The bushes in the front yard were small and new and the house hadn't yet begun its illusion of sinking. The grass was neatly mown as it had been when I was there, and everything looked younger, more hopeful, including Leroy. In one photo, Leroy was bending down to stroke the back of a dark hound who gazed up at him with affection.

Another photo showed Leroy taking a group shot of the church choir beneath a huge walnut tree. Little did he know that Sam Kowalczyk was snapping away in the shadows.

The next shot, a close-up, showed Leroy staring daggers at the local preacher, jaw tensed, eyes narrowed into precisely aimed slits. With his head low and his pale brows casting a shadow on the bags beneath his eyes, a frightening portrait emerged. What had the preacher done to poor Leroy? Or was residual hatred for Daddy Fitzsimmons rearing its ugly head?

Sam Kowalczyk was no slouch in the photography department. He'd enlarged that particular photo and laminated it. If the case had ever come to court, Sam was ready to show the jury this likeness of Leroy. It would have circulated on newsstands nationwide and gone viral on the Internet, with only one headline possible for such a wanton image: GUILTY.

I thought back to the wartime photos Leroy had shown me. Seemed that from either side of the camera, the man's dark impulses shined through.

"Something doesn't add up," I said. "Sam knew you were getting out of jail. He knew you would come see him and he's not in good health. Since this file wasn't hard to find . . ." I waited to see if Grady was getting it; he wasn't. "Do you think Sam left it as . . . an offering? An act of contrition?"

"Too little, too late," Grady mumbled. "All this time, we could have gotten justice for your mother. And who knows how many more victims there were over the years?"

"Yes, but . . . I think Sam wanted us to find it."

Grady shrugged.

I looked toward the woods behind the house. Dense, murky, private. A perfect place to atone for sins. I stood up and glanced at the empty gun rack by the fireplace. "We need to find Sam."

"With COPD, he couldn't have gotten far."

"I don't think he wanted to get very far."

CHAPTER 43

We came to a fork in the trail behind Sam's cabin, one side looking unkempt and leading downhill, the other flat and worn. "Let's head down," I said. At Grady's questioning look, I shrugged and added, "It's where I would go . . . if I wanted to be alone."

A pained look shot across Grady's face. "Maybe we should call the police."

"All we have to offer them is an empty cabin."

"And a file on the Haiku Killer."

"And we're certainly giving them that. But let's just—"

A bear reared up on its hind legs forty yards ahead of us. At least, I thought it was a bear. It made a racket scrambling to get out of sight before I could decipher its shape against the trickery of light and shadow in the woods.

"Was that what I thought it was?" Grady asked.

"If you thought bear, then I think so."

The next sentence didn't need saying. The bear had been investigating a mound partially covered in wet leaves. We headed toward the abandoned curiosity and laid eyes upon the body of a small man, no more than 140 pounds, a rifle at his side but no immediate evidence of a bullet wound.

"Sam?" Grady said, as if expecting him to answer.

Sam lay faceup, mouth and eyes open. He still wore his nasal cannulas, which seemed odd, since they wouldn't have aided him on his final trek. Perhaps they'd become such a part of him, attached to his steady flow of oxygen in the house, that he'd forgotten they were there.

"He was so frail," I said, "like just the thought of a bullet could have killed him."

"There's no blood," Grady said. "I don't mean to be crass, but with a gun that big, you'd think his only choice would be to shoot himself in the head while holding the gun from below."

"Maybe the trek here was too much," I said. "He could have passed out and died from exposure."

Grady kicked at the dry leaves that had fallen atop the thicker, wet ones. "Looks like he's been here awhile."

"I'd say almost two days. Rigor mortis is lessening, and look at the pallor of his face." Clumps of fly eggs bubbled out of his ears and filled his throat. At least his nostrils had been spared, due to the cannulas. A bit of detectable movement in his mouth meant life was thriving in there and maggots would emerge soon. I'd seen the sight many times and it always made me think the same thing: death was as ungracious as nature was relentless. I wanted to take his temperature, turn him over, check the lividity, and get the full story, but the medical examiner would have my head if I touched anything.

I leaned in closer as Grady took a step back. Although no one could claim to relish the stench of rotting human flesh, I'd been around enough that I could compensate. Mouth-breathing, ointments, sprays, and focusing with the other senses helped to block out olfactory input—at least psychologically—but today, I relied on a different tool: overwhelming curiosity.

Sam wore a heavy orange flannel, black Dickies pants in what looked to be a slim cut for boys, and heavy boots. No hat or sunglasses.

"Look at this." I pointed for Grady's sake, forgetting that he was probably looking anywhere but at his former friend's body. "A small bruise on the side of his neck." Luckily, the bruise had formed about half an inch above the dark, pooled blood at the base of his neck; otherwise, it wouldn't have been visible. "He might have injected himself and hit a vein."

"Then why the gun?" Grady said.

"To ward off bears?" The irony lay there like a bad joke, perhaps one Sam would have appreciated.

I checked the area for a syringe, brushing away fresh leaves and older, decaying ones, knowing the police would have my ass in a sling if they found out. Seemed the syringe should be lying near his hand, but he could have thrown it, if it existed. I crossed to his other side and repeated the search. Nothing. Either the police would find it or the lab guys would backpedal into the answer.

Grady stared at the bruise. "Same place Leroy injected me. It's the last sensation I remember, that stinging jab out of nowhere."

"Could Sam have been sending a message by killing himself this way? A confession that he'd held back on what he knew?"

"Wouldn't surprise me." Grady sighed. "He enjoyed symbolism, along with his own sense of justice, or so I thought."

"Wonder if he left a note."

Unable to silence the bad angel in my head telling me to search Sam for a note, I picked up a twig and slid it beneath his damp flannel—careful not to puncture his bloating midsection. I lifted, hoping to catch a glimpse of a paper tucked inside. I checked both sides until my good angel—who only made cameos—insisted I stop. The urge to dig my hands into Sam's pockets gnawed at me and I wondered what my mother would have done.

I tossed the stick, glared accusingly at my hands, then pulled out my cell to call the police. When I turned my back to the corpse to give Grady a moment alone with his friend, I saw it. Pinned to a skinny oak tree, protected by laminate similar to that covering the eerie photo of Leroy Fitzsimmons—a single piece of white paper with three lines of text. Seventeen syllables. A haiku.

CHAPTER 44

Nicholls stepped out of his car into a big puddle. He shook his foot, then his head, glaring at me like I'd personally dumped muddy water in his path. "You kidding me with this, Janie?" he said, shoving a handful of potato chips in his mouth. He'd just driven an unexpected two hours after being up all night working the Rocko Mania case, so his mood was understandable. "Gonna start a file on you, the way bodies keep appearing in your midst."

He introduced himself to the officers stationed outside; then we entered Sam's house together. Nicholls went straight for the bedroom. Every officer who had appeared so far, and there were over a dozen, had gravitated to that room immediately, as if they could smell the sick man living, eating, and wheezing in there—doing pretty much everything except dying.

Nicholls wiped his hands on his jacket and said hello to the local officers and chief. Meanwhile, in the kitchen, a beer-bellied, thick-lipped detective peppered Grady with questions, more interested in events from three decades ago than the fresh corpse in the woods, around which the medical examiner and forensic investigators were swarming for clues beneath a tent. By now, they'd have pulled stray fibers from his jacket—some of which would belong to a curious bear—scraped beneath his fingernails, sampled his palms for gunshot residue, and sealed the haiku in an airtight case more secure than the one holding the Declaration of Independence.

Nicholls returned to my side. "What a fuckin' mess. How do we have every uniform in the state looking for Leroy Fitzsimmons, and he waltzes up here, drags this guy into the woods, and leaves him out for deer food?"

"Bear food," I said, "but you bring up a good point. Why did Leroy go after Sam after all this time? I mean, Sam's known Leroy was the killer for years."

"Come on, Janie. Even I can figure that out based on what you told me about this guy."

"I must be exhausted from doing your job, Nicholls. Please share."

He shoved another wad of chips in his mouth—really, didn't most people eat chips one at a time? His explanation came onion-scented. "On the one hand, Sam Kowalczyk was screwing his old buddy there"—he jerked a thumb at Grady—"taking money every month and pretending to be tracking down a killer. And maybe he really did for a while. That would explain all the files you told me about. But when Sam finally tracked down Leroy Fitzsimmons and determined he was the third guy, he decided he didn't want to give up the monthly paycheck from Grady."

"I agree. He let a serial killer go free for a few bucks."

Nicholls licked the salt from his fingers. "Sex, money, and drugs. It always comes down to one. Plus, you gotta look at it from Sam's point of view. Maybe he charged Leroy Fitzsimmons a monthly stipend, too, to keep quiet about the truth. That way, Sam's got two sources of income. But it all came to a head this week because McLemore was gettin' out of jail and Sam was gettin' ready to keel over. Everybody knows that impending death makes a man wanna clear his conscience, so it was only a matter of time before Sam shouted out to the world who the real Haiku Killer was—and Leroy did not want that information going public."

"I owe you a quarter, Nicholls. I think you're right. And remind me to steer clear of your deathbed. I don't want to hear whatever spills out of your conscience."

He grinned and then looked around the scene again. "Who woulda thought a chubby redneck with a limp and an AARP card could outrun the entire Kingsley police force?"

Grady extricated himself from his fans and joined us. "Detective Nicholls," he said, "I've heard a lot about you."

They shook hands, but Nicholls didn't look swayed by Grady's standard charms. "Lemme ask you, Mr. McLemore, what was so urgent you had to come up here and see Sam Kowalczyk today?"

Grady took a slow moment to assess Nicholls. I knew from experience that Nicholls was a hard guy to stare down or make flinch; Grady figured that out fast and answered, "Detective, I've waited a long time to get my hands on whoever was in Bridget's house that night. I figured Sam might offer the quickest route to the guy, maybe even know where he was hiding out."

"So Sam updated you regularly when you were inside?"

"Yes, but the trail ran cold the last decade or so."

"Little did any of us know how hot it would get, eh?"

Grady looked unamused. "Sam's work still has value. I'd appreciate seeing his files when the police are done with them."

"You did pay for them, didn't you?" said Nicholls, ignoring Grady's request. Those files would go nowhere until the case was closed; even then, Grady might never see them. Which was why I'd taken photos of the contents while the police were en route.

Nicholls gestured for us to follow him toward the fireplace, out of earshot of the crowd. With all the commotion, some wily reporters could have sneaked in unnoticed. The three of us settled beneath the horns of a big buck and Nicholls spoke quietly. "You guys saw the haiku, right? What'd it say?"

"It was strange," I said, "but then Grady explained it."

Nicholls shot a cynical glance at Grady, expecting the man whose looks rivaled his own to be condescending, but Grady merely lowered his head, closed his eyes, and prepared to recite the haiku. He looked like a priest about to bless the wine and wafers.

"Horse sedative no
Only stallions merit such
Glutton juice for him."

He opened his eyes but remained silent, a trick surely learned from his political days while waiting for applause to simmer, or in this case, for thoughts to percolate. Somehow, I doubted Nicholls used the time for reverential reflection on glutton juice.

"Well?" Nicholls blurted.

Grady adopted a conciliatory tone. "Forgive me if I'm telling you things you already know, Detective, but the drug I was injected with—"

"The one everyone thought you injected yourself," interrupted Nicholls.

"Yes, exactly."

Nicholls couldn't help himself. He was so accustomed to dealing with pathological liars that it had become his natural tendency to throw off the rhythm of anyone he questioned.

"When I was arrested," Grady continued, unfazed, "I was in shock, accused of everything from premeditated murder to involuntary manslaughter. The police took my statement at the scene, and at my insistence, took me to the hospital for blood testing."

Nicholls grunted. Hard to tell if a chip had lodged in his throat or if he was mocking Grady. Either way, Grady paused and waited until Nicholls had his guttural reflexes back in order.

"The hospital couldn't come up with anything solid, so the samples had to be sent to the state lab. It took over two weeks to get an answer, but the results of the drug test came back positive for—"

"Ketamine, right?" Nicholls said.

"No," Grady said with a hint of condescension. "Ketamine was the drug erroneously reported to the general public during that two-week wait. I thought you'd be up on the file, Detective."

Sometimes, it was fun to see Nicholls flapping in the wind.

"Got enough current homicides to keep me busy. No need to dig up ancient history."

"This history may now be relevant. The police never revealed the actual drug in my system—not because they thought it would exonerate me, but because they wanted to weed out the crazies who might come in and confess."

"Weren't there like thirty of 'em?" Nicholls said.

"Thirty-six," Grady said. "Thirty-six people who wanted to take credit for Bridget's death. To them, it offered a path to notoriety."

"Those damn cops, though, right?" Nicholls said, shoving gum in his mouth for dessert. "Always givin' credit to the guy who wants it least."

Grady acknowledged the slight with a small nod. He'd have doubters his whole life, and Nicholls was firmly planting his flag in the skeptics' camp. No matter how you sliced it, Grady did pull the trigger, and Nicholls tended to be a black-and-white guy. *You pulled the trigger or you didn't. You killed someone or you didn't.* Grady had. But the situation felt awfully gray to me, especially here in the middle of the mountains, in a damp cabin with black clouds outside sinking closer to Sam Kowalczyk's body—another mouth silenced to keep the secrets of a long-ago night.

"All these years later," Grady said, "the tactic the police used has come full circle. You see, I was injected with azaperone."

"A zap of what?" Nicholls said.

"Azaperone. A sedative used to calm pigs when they're being moved."

"So that's the glutton juice the haiku mentions?"

"Yes. Ketamine is a horse tranquilizer. The haiku says only stallions merit ketamine."

"And Fitzsimmons got you with pig juice." Nicholls almost grinned. "Didn't think you were a stallion, eh?"

"Apparently not," Grady said. "It's a direct reference to what he injected me with, versus what was reported in the papers. With today's note, he's boasting that he's the real deal."

Nicholls's head tilted so much, it was almost sideways. "Just what was it between you and this guy? You stiff him on the office repairs or something?"

Grady let his head fall to the side until he and Nicholls looked like they were prepping for an awkward kiss. But Grady seemed to be using Nicholls's eyes more as a mental whiteboard, looking through him and searching for an answer to an unasked question.

"I mean," Nicholls said, righting himself, "this new haiku, along with murdering your buddy out there, it seems personal, angry. Like he has a vendetta against a guy who deserves only glutton juice."

Grady still didn't speak. Instead, he let himself collapse onto the fireside love seat. The great man looked defeated, a condition I hadn't yet witnessed in our short time together. "What if you're right?" he said, almost pleading with Nicholls and seeming ashamed in my presence. "What if Leroy Fitzsimmons was after me that night, or after Bridget because of me? I'd always assumed he was there to reclaim his haiku, but what if . . ."

Nicholls showed his usual self-control and maintained a hard, cynical silence. I, on the other hand, could barely tolerate the suggestion hanging in the air. "No, Grady. No way. You think Leroy somehow tricked my mother into taking the haiku, knowing she'd call you? That he was luring you to my mother's house to kill you? Come on."

Grady swallowed hard, raised his eyes from the cold fireplace. "Maybe not that elaborate, but what if I was supposed to be the next victim?"

"No," I said, "it happened because my mother came across his haiku. It was all a mistake."

"Maybe, but once he knew she had it, he saw an opportunity to enact his plan early. Maybe it wasn't a random coincidence that he showed up at my door to offer his services."

Nicholls and I glanced at each other, reaching the same warped conclusion simultaneously.

"If that's true," I said, "then he's after more than just his old haiku now."

Grady looked up at me, questions brimming in his distraught eyes.

Nicholls answered. "He might want to finish the job."

CHAPTER 45

The husky ambulance attendants carried Sam's wrecked body to the waiting vehicle. He looked weightless in their strong hands, creating only a slight mound beneath the sheet.

I pressed my foot to the accelerator, my passenger quiet and thoughtful. After forty minutes of exacting silence, I broke in.

"My friend Detective Wexler thought the Haiku Killer had a Renaissance theme going."

"How so?"

"The professor, the priest, and the doctor—philosophy, religion, and medicine. If you were a target, would politician have fit his scheme of things?"

"Sure. The ruling class. Instead, with your mother, he got the working class. I guess that stayed within his theme, if that's what it was."

"Wexler and I—and most experts—think the Haiku Killer has a God complex."

Grady looked out the window, pensive. "Maybe. A professor professing to interpret the greatest minds in the world. The priest, a member of an elite group that offers the closest embodiment of Christ on earth, and a doctor, performing what some call the Lord's work— saving lives or causing death, making decisions better left to God."

"It fits with the haikus, too."

"The problem is," Grady said, "I don't believe murderers are jigsaw puzzles. Their motivations are never as tidy and packageable as the experts pretend. You can't just slap the pieces together and get a sharp-edged, full-color picture, like, *Here's Leroy, a psychopath with a God complex.* Instead, it might be as inexplicable as, *Here's Leroy, a psychopath with a penchant for murder.* Maybe all the victims had hangnails that rubbed him the wrong way or he didn't like their voices or he was sent to his room too many times as a child. Who knows what makes them act? I have a sneaking suspicion they don't know themselves. Ted Bundy offered every explanation for his behavior, from too much porn to lack of a father figure to a girl who jilted him. And now they think he was just toying with the experts to amuse himself. These people just *are*, and a universe that makes sense, as our grand vision has it, simply *isn't*."

The lament had grown angry toward the end, but if anyone was entitled to pent-up anger, it was the man next to me.

"I think it's biology," I said. "A billion connections per brain— bound to be some bad circuitry in there. With advanced wiring comes advanced problems, unless there are goldfish swimming around out there with autism, borderline personality disorder—"

"Or kleptomania." Grady had filled the word with equal parts bitterness and affection, as the full consequences of my mother's old habit came to bear.

"Makes it hard to define *normal* when everyone's got something."

"What the hell did Sam have?" Grady said, still disbelieving his friend's deception.

"Nothing atypical, I'm afraid. Self-interest. Greed." I shivered, thinking of Sam's comeuppance. "Grady, what was it like when you got injected?"

"Horrible." The answer came with no hesitation, no wobbliness. "Not because of the pain, but because it compromised my ability to protect your mother. It hit me so fast and created this distorted perception of clarity and confusion, like I thought I had perfect dexterity and coordination while being clumsy as all hell."

"The spastic kid in class insisting he should be chosen first?"

"Exactly. My mind and body were completely out of sync. I was certain I could handle the situation, but I was half-collapsed on the ground and seeing at least two of your mother. Never even got a clear look at the other guy."

"Even when you had the gun pointed at him?"

Grady took a moment on that one, inhaling deeply and shaking his head. "Know what I do remember? The white knuckle of my thumb against the metal of the gun. Clear as day. Must have been the only thing I could focus on."

I pictured my mother at the moment Grady was contemplating his hand. Sober, clearheaded, scared out of her mind, and utterly confused. She'd have been watching her hero, ham-fisted and disoriented, bumbling about with a loaded gun. Had she been calm enough to process what was coming? Did she anticipate the other man's interference, the change in the trajectory of the traveling bullet? Did she freeze, jump, duck, step back? Did she scream? *Did it hurt?*

"I'm sorry, Janie," Grady said. "Have I ever said that to you? I am sorry." The words were so full, they crushed me. They pressed tears from my ducts, blood from my heart, and forgiveness to the surface. I tried to remain silent to avoid blubbering while driving—until I didn't care anymore and let it out. Grady handed me tissues when I needed them.

Gradually, we got into a rhythm, tossing around hypotheses. Unfortunately, none of them got us any closer to determining Leroy Fitzsimmons's whereabouts.

"You got any gum, Grady? This mountain air dries me out."

He patted all his pockets and finally felt something. When he pulled out a pack of gum, a folded ten-dollar bill and a plastic flosser came out with it.

"See?" I said. "You need my mother's pocket system. She'd have had her hands on that gum in no time."

Grady chuckled. "I do need a better system—or at least a wallet."

"Holy crap!" I yelled. I slammed on the brakes and skidded the car into a dirt patch on the side of the road, beneath a jutting precipice of rock.

Grady knew enough to remain quiet, but he must have been concerned that my exclamation might cause boulders to crash down on his head.

"What if it wasn't Leroy Fitzsimmons?" I said.

Grady looked at me like the mountain air had dried out my brain.

"Listen," I said, "you never saw the third man's face, so the possibilities are still wide-open. What if my mother did pickpocket Leroy, but whatever she took from him wasn't the haiku?"

"You lost me at *holy crap*," Grady said.

"You said my mother put Abner Abel's money in the same pocket that she reserved for personal things. Personal things could also mean things that she'd kleptoed."

"Not sure you can use it as a verb, but go ahead."

"When Mr. Abel threw his money on the table, a note could have been folded up in there—a note with an incriminating haiku written on it."

Grady frowned.

"Just listen," I said. "My mother would have scooped it up and put it in her pocket along with his money. And already in that pocket was whatever she lifted from Leroy Fitzsimmons. Later, when she pulled it out to look at it, she thought she was looking at her heist from Leroy, but she was really looking at whatever Mr. Abel had inadvertently thrown on the table."

"Go on."

"I bet if we compared Mr. Abel's old driving routes with the times and places of the murders, we'd find they matched up. He's even got a bum ankle, and Mickey Busker said the third man ran with a limp toward the Abels' house. And talk about somebody rocking a God complex. That guy wrote the book—or thinks he did."

"I don't know. Leroy had those photos that his sister mailed you—and their negatives."

"Leroy *possessed* them, but we don't know where he got them."

"You're suggesting a link between Leroy and Mr. Abel?"

"Until two days ago, I never would have thought there was a link between Abner Abel and my mother other than an occasional wave. And now I find out that he fought with her the night she was shot and that he frequented the hotel where you and she . . . you know."

"Then why would Leroy have a secret box of information on you and Jack—and me? Why would he have stolen your book?"

"Because my mother screwed up just like I did. She thought she was taking something as valueless as an old tennis ball from Leroy's pocket, but whatever she took was valuable *to him*—and he's wanted it back all these years."

"So Mr. Abel would be the one who injected me?"

"He had access to animal tranquilizers and he admitted to hanging around the parking lot after storming out of Field Diner."

"And," Grady said, his head tilting up to the left in a now-familiar way, "he's a deliveryman. People would have let him in, even if it wasn't his usual time."

"The college where the professor was killed got meat deliveries and had an agriculture department."

"What about the church where the priest was killed?"

"I read about it in my brother's book. They had a feed-the-homeless program. Every month, they held a pig-picking."

"But the doctor—he was in a remote cabin."

"And Abner Abel still knows every back road in the state. He could have been lying in wait when the doctor got to the cabin."

"It's worth looking into. One thing's been consistent through all these years. That missing haiku. We've got to find it."

Both my hands reached across the seat and grabbed both of Grady's hands. I didn't realize we were touching until I saw the evidence. He saw it, too. A moment passed—awkward, heartfelt, full—before my phone rang. We glanced at each other and smiled before I answered.

"Hello?"

"Janie, it's Wexler. Where are you?" No small talk, no flirtation. And he was back to being Wexler. It was the first time we'd spoken since the tennis ball fiasco.

"I'm ten minutes outside of town," I said, keeping my voice as distant as his.

"Can you get to Sophie Andricola's? She's okay but she walked in on an intruder."

"Is there a body? Why do you need me?"

"The intruder was Leroy Fitzsimmons."

301

CHAPTER 46

I arrived at Sophie's house alone, having told Grady the call was work-related. Sure, it was an awkward way to start our fledgling relationship, but the last thing he needed to see was Sophie's larger-than-life drawing of him sprawled on the floor while my mother lay there bleeding. I'd dropped him at my brother's and promised to call as soon as I knew anything.

The floodlights and flashing red from the police cars cast Sophie's cabin in a spooky, strobe-light glow. The quiet aura of my previous visits had been displaced by chaos and coldness, the fresh smell of cedar overtaken by diesel fumes.

"Wexler!" I shouted when I saw him on the front steps. "What's going on? You sure Sophie's okay?"

"She's fine," he said, still sporting layers of frost beneath his air of professionalism. "She returned early from a jog after twisting her ankle. Heard a noise in her studio, went up, and saw Leroy plain as day crawling out a back window, a camera around his neck."

I remembered the layout of Sophie's house and frowned. "What'd he do, shinny down the drainpipe like a horny teenager?"

Wexler didn't even grin. This sucked. "The deck is multitiered, so it was only a six-foot jump, then an easy leap to another deck, down a few steps and gone."

"So why am I here?"

"I need your eyes to see everything he saw. Sophie did some new work and Leroy would have seen it. You've got to tell me where it's leading him."

As we talked, he handed me surgical booties to cover my shoes. I put them on while he waited, our silence louder than the surrounding melee. The stairs teemed with CSIs looking for fingerprints and hairs, fibers, and anything else that may have caught on the penis tips of Sophie's sculpted railing—all to close in on the Haiku Killer before he embarrassed his trackers again.

"Wexler, I have an idea about another suspect."

He frowned. "Janie, I don't do open-and-shut very often, but I've slammed the door on this one. Let's go."

Great. What else had he slammed the door on?

As I reached the top stair, a helicopter whizzed by outside the window. As much as I wished it were the police hot on the trail of an old man on a mission, I knew it was a news helicopter. Something about the way it buzzed at a higher pitch, maybe due to the lighter intellectual load on board. I wanted to take solace in the fact that at least they weren't here to steal my soul, but once again, I found myself integral to the biggest news story in town.

As I entered the studio that had previously sent me into a rage, I locked eyes with Sophie. The heavy blanket around her shoulders and the cup of water in her hand suggested either a woman in shock or an overanxious EMT. Her quick engagement with me, accompanied by a lively expression, suggested the latter. Through the bustle of worker bees, she gave off a strong vibe of warning cloaked in excitement, anticipating something. But what?

A uniformed officer urgently pulled Wexler aside, so I approached Sophie on my own. She shook off the blanket and met me halfway with intense regard. "I finished it late today," she said. "I was going to call you after clearing my head with a jog."

A shift in her gaze led me to the same wall where she'd originally projected my mother's crime scene. A dozen new, close-up drawings bordered it, but I zeroed in on one immediately.

"There it is," I whispered.

"Right?" She smiled, big and unguarded.

I spun to find Wexler, but he was involved with two officers now. "Not only that, sir," said the first officer, "we've got a witness outside, says he saw an older man cutting through his backyard and another guy says his son's car was stolen out of the driveway."

Wexler turned, his plate full but his composure intact. "Janie, I've got to talk to these witnesses. Did you see anything that might help?"

A major crack in *the Wexler* had shown itself. He didn't like artificial ingredients in his tea, scratches on his car—or ugly imperfections in his lovers. Too bad I didn't care for those who demanded perfection. The sooner he learned it, the better. Welcome to my life, Wexler. Take it or leave it.

"I'm not sure if there's anything concrete here," I lied. "Let me check something out with my brother and I'll get back to you."

He looked dubious, but sensed that neither his skepticism nor his company was welcome at the moment.

The officers grew impatient. "Sir? The witnesses? You want us to handle it? Put out the APB?"

"Go on, Wexler," I said. "Go handle it. You deal with the unexpected so well, after all."

I dashed out, stunting his retort, and raced toward my car. I knew exactly where Leroy intended to go next. I just wasn't sure he did.

CHAPTER 47

Jack answered his cell on the first ring. "You and Grady catch him in the act, Sis?"

"Go ahead and make fun," I said, sitting in the front seat of my car with pen and paper at the ready. "We almost did."

I told him about Sam's body and the new haiku. From the utter silence on the other end of the line, I realized that for the first time in years, my brother might not have checked his watch while we were talking, or gestured to someone to get him off the phone.

"Wow" was all he finally said.

"Hey, where'd you get all the pictures for your book?" I asked.

"A cabinet in the sitting room filled with negatives and slides. It was a godsend, in chronological order and everything. Elsa must have done it years ago."

"What about the old framed photos? In the same cabinet?"

"No. Whatever's not on display in the house is probably in storage. Grandpa did have a unit. Piece-of-shit place called Stuff-n-Stash on Route 59. Figured I'd wait before raiding it in the hope that maybe he can clean it out himself."

There was hope for Jack yet. "How do I get in?"

"My guy, Randall, got the manager to reset the keyless entry code to 123456 in case we needed to get in. Unit 782. Why? What's going on?"

"Turns out you were right," I said. "There is something in that unit that would have scored record-high ratings for some crap reality show, but I'm going to get it."

"Ah, Christ, did Grandpa make a sex tape? That lady with the zodiac tattoos above her ass? I knew it."

"Yeah, Jack, I'm rushing around town like a madwoman to make sure Grandpa's shriveled member doesn't go viral."

"Too far, Janie. Too far."

"Look who's talking. Listen, can you meet me at the Stuff-n-Stash? It's possible Leroy Fitzsimmons is on the same trail as me and I don't want to be there alone."

"I'm over an hour away, still trying to make this guy our bitch. Good news is, I think we're going to get him."

"Please, Jack."

He hesitated. "All right, I'll slip out as soon as I can."

"Love you," I said and hung up.

I punched the name of the storage facility into my navigation system and took off. It would only take me thirty minutes, but I could use the downtime to make sure no one else entered the unit. With any luck, I'd soon be looking at the haiku that got my mother killed.

CHAPTER 48

The land housing the huge storage facility comprised the former hunting grounds of an old estate. It had been sold by the great-great-grandson of the original owner and converted to Stuff-n-Stash, an architectural insult to the imperial brick home situated in the distance. The bearded man behind the front desk chatted on the phone, his feet propped up, while watching a show about sharks on a ludicrously large TV. I drove by without disturbing him, figuring that's why they had keyless entry codes. He never even looked out.

I made my way to unit 782. No cars or customers in sight. Guess most people repressed the urge to paw through old junk in the dark of night. Knowing what a packrat Grandpa Barton was, I didn't anticipate an easy time of it, but if he'd at least labeled the boxes, the task might not be too daunting. Besides, I just needed one small item. I checked my watch. Jack wouldn't be here for twenty-five minutes, and that was assuming my notoriously late brother had left his meeting immediately.

I looked around one last time. No sign of anyone. Screw it. I was going in. Thirty years was long enough. I got out of my car and entered the code. As the door rose, something crashed. Either Grandpa had literally stuffed this thing and I was disrupting a carelessly constructed house of cards, or I was about to come face-to-face with a big, hairy rat who'd made a nest in Grandma Elizabeth's old wool sweaters.

"Are you kidding me?" I said aloud when the door revealed the mess. It reminded me of our attic growing up—and our attic had been a fire hazard twice over. Couches piled on tables ornamented with precariously balanced lamps next to rolled rugs, canvas paintings, toys, chairs, and boxes upon boxes of hastily labeled junk. Grandpa was not one for discarding anything with sentimental value, but apparently he was not above treating it like garbage.

I flicked a light switch and was rewarded with a single ceiling bulb. For all the illumination it provided, I could have lit a match. As I exhaled, I heard an echo. Did rats breathe loudly? I held my breath and listened. Nothing. *Come on, Janie, keep it together.*

No way to move the heavy furniture by myself, so I decided to mount it and work my way from top to bottom. A tall stack of overstuffed boxes was piled against the wall about three-quarters of the way back, so I planted one foot onto the arm of an upholstered chair, placed my other foot on a coffee table, and worked out the rest as I went along. By the time I reached the boxes, I was coughing up dust and pulling off enough cobwebs to knit a silk scarf. At an altitude of twelve feet—Grandpa had gone for the double-tall unit—I summited. Grabbing a random couch cushion, I set it on a pile of plastic bins, took a seat, and let my feet dangle into a small, steep shaft of surprisingly empty space surrounding a metal support pole. The fact that the pole had rusted did not say much for the moisture-control settings in the unit.

I set my phone on the couch cushion and reached over for the top box, helpfully labeled *Miscellaneous.* The moment I touched it, two hands pummeled my back, casting me down into the narrow chute of darkness, junk encasing me. The pole scraped against my skin and I felt like the victim of a hazing ritual for fire department newbies. I landed hard on my heels, but at least on top of the contents of the box I'd grabbed; *Miscellaneous* evidently stood for throw pillows, providing one bright spot in a very dire and confined situation—one where I was trapped like a kid in a well, with only a maniac for company.

The relief over my intact bones morphed into panic as I scrambled for cover but found no place to turn. I was locked in tight, completely constricted in a straitjacket of random, useless crap. If the person who pushed me down here had a gun, there was nothing between my skull and an impending bullet except my hair—and, horse tail or not, it would not stop a bullet.

I braced myself, but no enemy fire rained down. Then the barest shatter of thin glass sounded and everything went black. The intruder had broken the bulb. It was followed by scampering, a fair bit of muttering, items crashing, and at least one more breakable item shattering against the floor.

"Leroy? Is that you? Please, Leroy! We can work together! Don't leave me here—please!"

Slowly it dawned on me that I was trying to reason with a man who'd been described in recent days as mentally unstable, sociopathic, schizophrenic, abused, irrational, and most of all, desperate enough to kill. My discomfort probably wasn't real high on his list of priorities. But what if it was far more than discomfort? What if I never got out of here?

And then I heard it.

The door to the storage unit lowered and slammed shut. A metallic click followed. Then nothing. Nothing! Not even the breath of a single rat.

My own breathing filled the silent void—short, quick, desperate, my mind racing even faster. What if I suffocated? What if more items came crashing down in the world's most pathetic avalanche, crushing me and cutting off my air? What if no one found me? What if Leroy stole my car and Jack thought I'd never arrived—or had been kidnapped? Would he even search *inside* the unit? Some future bidder would buy the unit at auction and never explore it until I was a pile of bones, hair, and teeth on top of a throw pillow.

I scratched, clawed, and wiggled awkwardly, clumsily, to no avail. I tried to scale the pole pressing into my back, but I could barely bend my knees or lift my arms, let alone make it to the top. The only movement came from my rattling, hammering heart. What if? What if? What if!

Unbidden, I saw the situation for what it was: I was entombed in a vertical coffin of darkness inside a sealed room.

CHAPTER 49

Bridget Perkins, 30 Years, 3 Minutes Ago

Bridget Perkins skidded up to the front of her house, convinced for most of the drive that another car was following her. Was it the strange repairman? Was it Grady, having made it from his office in record time? She'd barely exhaled, driving like a demon, until her pursuer had turned off into the Abels' long driveway. Was it her imagination or had the car shut off its headlights before making the turn?

Damn her stupidity. Why hadn't she just driven to the police station? He'd never have confronted her there. This was insane, but Daddy would protect her.

Her heart leapt in terror. Where was Daddy's truck? Oh, no, he was out with clients. She'd forgotten. Now what? Maybe she should have stayed at the diner? No, she couldn't have lingered there a moment longer. If she was destined to be killed by a psycho, she didn't want her last breath of life to be the stale, greasy air of Field Diner.

She threw aside her coat and purse and dashed to the kitchen to call the police. But wait—if she was followed, if he was close behind, she needed to get rid of the evidence. Where? Where to hide it until things settled down? She glanced around the kitchen. In a drawer? No. The refrigerator? No, too obvious. The whole kitchen was obvious. She spun, searching, her eyes seeing but barely absorbing. She reached into her apron and pulled out the item that might get her killed and rushed into the living room. Her eyes alighted on the gray-and-white marble table in the back corner and she knew what to do. If she had time.

Suddenly she stopped. Dead in her tracks. Her thoughts raced as time slowed and a startling realization overtook her. She flicked on the lamp next to her—two clicks to put it on its brightest setting. Staring at the item in her hand, she ran her fingers over its surface. As she lifted it to the light, tears ran down her face, but her jaw tightened and her shoulders squared in a show of fierce resolve. At the very least, she had to save the twins.

Willing the strength of the mother she was destined to be, she completed her task with only slightly fumbling fingers, then turned around as the intruder's hand wiggled the back doorknob. She turned off the light.

CHAPTER 50

I screamed. Like a panicked, trapped, helpless baby. I screamed like there was no tomorrow, which I was certain there wasn't. And then I screamed again.

It saved me. It brought me back. Somehow, the savagery of the sound, the desperation in my own cry, allowed me to settle into the reality of my plight, to grab hold of it and wrestle it into submission. In fact, I couldn't possibly be safer. No one could get in to hurt me.

Except the brimming psychotic who'd put me here.

Dammit.

Okay, don't think about being trapped in here with the furniture that surrounded Mom as she collapsed, her blood spattering everywhere. Don't think about the specter that rose from that bloodstain and haunted you as a child. Don't believe that Jack might assume you never even got here, or that Wexler has no idea where you are because you were too pissed off to tell him. Wexler had every right to treat you like garbage. You disrespected the job. You put cases at risk. Suck it up! Just get out and you can set things right with him. Get out. Get out. Get out! After minutes of repeating that harsh mantra and forcing my heart rate to a more reasonable level of panic, I got to work.

My phone had been lost in the downward tumble to this hellhole, so it was either beneath my feet or it was still up there on the couch cushion. Good. I had a goal: find my damn phone.

The space in which I was cramped was about fourteen by twenty inches, so I used my feet to feel for the phone. Mostly, I found pillows, but that gave me an idea. I stacked the pillows as best I could with my feet. My hands were level with a shoebox, so I tore at the cardboard and wiggled my fingers around inside. It felt like an old pair of shoes—Grandpa Barton really needed a hoarding intervention. I worked them from the box and cast them to the floor, where I proceeded to step on them. Then I grabbed whatever other items I could reach with barely mobile arms and cast them to the floor. If I couldn't climb out, I would lift myself up on a slowly mounting pile of junk. I just hoped the removal of surrounding items didn't bring the whole mess down on top of me.

By the time I added old place mats, Jack's toy trucks, the legs of several dolls—I had no idea why they were separated—multiple burlap sacks, and an empty spice rack, I was at least a foot and a half higher, and though I could wriggle my arms overhead, I still couldn't bend my knees. I yanked down a Tupperware container, but the heat in the unit must have warped it. It popped open and something spilled from it. A choking powder poured onto my face and I made the idiotic mistake of inhaling; breathing became impossible. Every time I tried to cough, more of the stinging, burning substance worked its way into my lungs, not to mention the number it was doing on my eyes. With my next attempt to inhale, I began drowning from the inside out, with no water in sight. My agitated lungs rebelled against the intrusive matter by forcing a cough but then leaving me even more desperate for air. I grew dizzy and felt my heart pounding against my chest and back. Knowing a full-blown panic attack was imminent, I suddenly got one hint of air and caught the unmistakable scent of curry powder. It filled my nostrils, my brain, my entire being. For God's sake, the Tupperware must have contained the spices that belonged in the rack beneath my feet, and the curry must have been left on *Pour* mode. That jerked me back to a really pissed-off reality.

I could damn well die in this cursed storage unit, but I sure as shit refused to be defeated by a condiment, especially one I didn't like. I embraced the coughing and sputtering and reminded myself I could go minutes without air. I was stronger than this.

Finally, my lungs relaxed and I took a slow, cautious breath. The more oxygen I consumed, the calmer I grew. Trapped like a worm in a greasy straw and coated in curry, I began to laugh, complete with tears, at my sorry state of affairs, wondering if my goose was cooked or just being seasoned for later. I resumed my work, building and riding the slowest, most random elevator in history.

An hour later, I hoisted myself from the hole, vowing to set the entire, hateful unit on fire—right after I found that damn haiku.

I grabbed my phone and saw two missed calls, a text, and a voice mail from Jack, along with six missed calls from Wexler. I called the latter. As I relayed my predicament, the sound of relief and joy in his voice gave me hope. It got me through the next few minutes as I climbed toward the door in pitch blackness. I gingerly descended the unstable mountain, unlocked the door from the inside, and hoisted it open, surprised to see that it was getting dark. As I prepared to call my brother to deliver a much-deserved tirade for being late to his sister's near-funeral, Wexler's car whizzed up; he'd only been a mile away when we spoke. He and Nicholls and the seedy Stuff-n-Stash manager got out and stared, collectively relieved but utterly confused. Finally Nicholls strutted over and sniffed me.

"Yo, Jane Doe, what'd you do? Cook up a little Indian while you were in there?"

"It was tight quarters, Nicholls," I said, "and I had nothing else to do."

Wexler pushed Nicholls aside, grabbed my arms, and pulled me in. He kissed me in front of everyone and didn't even mind the curry. "You never fail to surprise me," he whispered. "And don't you ever do that again."

I smiled, my teeth surely a ghoulish white against my seasoned skin.

"Well, I'll be a one-balled monkey on a teeter-totter," Nicholls said, spitting a pumpkin seed from his mouth. "You two are an item, eh?"

The manager laughed, sticking his tongue through the gap where his front teeth should have been. My brother pulled up a minute later, lamely explaining how he'd taken a wrong turn and ended up on some closed-off construction site where a nail proceeded to puncture his tire. He held up greasy fingers as proof. It was good to see mighty Jack Perkins with a little dirt on his hands again. I finally accepted his apology, but only because his groveling was truly first-rate.

"So, Janie," Wexler asked, "you think it was Leroy in there with you?"

"Had to be, right?"

Nicholls shook his head. "First the guy's rolling around in a wheelchair; then he's breaking and entering, scaling decks, spelunking through a veritable cave of shit in this unit. I mean, what's next for this guy?"

All feelings of lightness and relief dissipated. How long had Leroy been in the unit before me? Long enough for him to have found what I was seeking?

"Janie, what's wrong?" Wexler asked.

Before I could answer, Nicholls got an urgent call on his radio: a shoot-out and an officer with a bullet in his buttocks down near the river; suspect still at large. Wexler and Nicholls exchanged a serious look and both said, "Schwank." A bullet striking any cop penetrated the psyches of all the guys on the force, even if it was Schwank. There was no doubt they were heading to the river, especially with a suspect still on the loose.

"You guys go," I said. "Jack and I will finish up here."

Wexler looked less than reassured, but Nicholls was ready to roll. "Come on, horny boy. Janie's a tough cookie. We'll be back in plenty of time for you to say good night."

I grinned at Wexler, reminded him that nobody had taken down the Haiku Twins yet, and told him to go save Schwank's sorry ass. As they pulled away, I shouted at them to wear their vests—a bit of the protective girlfriend instinct taking over.

When Jack and I were alone, he turned to me, flummoxed. "Okay, Sis, what in God's name were you looking for in there?"

"A picture of Mom on her twelfth birthday, standing in front of Grandma and Grandpa, holding pink, white, and orange balloons."

He tilted his head. "Feeling nostalgic?"

"Mom hid the haiku in the frame."

CHAPTER 51

Jack and I pulled up to Grandpa's house at the same time. He opened his trunk and unloaded the first of the four large boxes that had been labeled *Pix*. I ran ahead and unlocked the front door for him.

"You sure we should be doing this here?" Jack said. "Maybe we should take these boxes to the police."

"Trust me, the police would not appreciate us hauling this stuff in to explore a hunch. Besides, it feels right that it should be you and me, here."

"Yeah, but—"

"Aww, is little Jackie scared?"

"Let's be real. This Leroy guy has been one step ahead of everybody for days now."

"Try thirty years."

"Exactly. What makes you think he's not waiting in there with a loaded gun?"

"Guns aren't really his style. Maybe cyanide or arsenic."

"Comforting."

"Besides, he's probably at your place or mine, or your office, with a syringe at the ready. No way he'd think we'd drive this stuff out to Caulfield."

"All right, but if we find that damn haiku, it's evidence."

"And between the two of us, Jack, I think we know how to handle evidence."

Jack sighed and entered the house, his feet heavy under the weight of the box. I grabbed another box and followed. When we got them all in, we sat side by side on the couch in the living room, where it had all gone down thirty years ago. The boxes sat at our feet, illuminated by the dim lamp Jack had switched on. The stars shined in through the branches of the giant magnolia, its silhouette making me shiver. I'd never be able to wash away the memory of Mickey's actions in that tree.

"Quack," Jack said, pulling me back to reality.

"Pardon?"

"Well, we *are* sitting ducks."

"Would you grow a set?" I said, immediately regretting my tone. I didn't want us to be fighting at a moment like this. "Sorry."

He shrugged it off. "Why are you so sure Mom hid the haiku behind that particular picture?"

"You know how Sophie Andricola did that rendering from the original photos—the ones Betty Fitzsimmons mailed?"

"Yes."

"Well, she also went back and blew up the first photo big-time, the one that was a general shot of this room. She broke it into a dozen separate portions and enhanced each with paint and pencil. It was amazing, lots of freaky detail. In one, she zeroed in on the marble table with the framed photos." I gestured to the table across the room, one of the few items that had survived the overhaul.

"And what? She saw Mom's fingerprints on the birthday picture?"

"No. It was the only photo out of place."

"Elsa the Terrible!"

"Bingo! Elsa treated those photos like soldiers. The ones on the left all tilted uniformly, facing some front-and-center point, and the ones on the right at the same angle, but in the opposite direction."

"Remember that time you crashed and knocked 'em all over?"

"You tackled me."

"You still crashed."

I elbowed him. "Anyway, on Mondays and Wednesdays, Elsa cleaned the bedrooms and the kitchen. On Fridays, she did the living room, dining room, and basement. Mom was shot on a Saturday, so those frames would still have been perfectly positioned."

Jack nodded, infatuated with the power of evidence.

"The birthday photo was off by at least fifteen degrees, and, according to Grady, Mom was standing in the middle of the living room when he walked in."

"So she'd just hidden the haiku in the frame and was turning around when Grady arrived?"

"Not Grady. She'd just hidden the haiku and turned around when someone else came in the back deck door first. Someone who followed her, or who already knew she lived here."

We both looked at that door, holding a solemn, silent vigil. Slowly, deliberately, I stood and walked to the marble table and placed my hands on it as I spoke, my back to my brother. "Mom had just hidden the haiku, her heart pounding, her hands shaking, maybe even sweating. She would have been refastening the backing to the frame, maybe using her dirty apron to wipe away her handprints when the first footstep sounded on the back deck."

I whipped my head around as my mother would have done.

"Stop it, Janie. You're freaking me out."

"She quickly put the frame back in place, but didn't have time to position it just so. The last thing she wanted was to be caught near the table, because then he'd know. So she turned around quickly, trying to make it look like she'd been anywhere but at that table."

I stepped away from the table just as my mother would have done.

"She took a few steps toward the center of the room, with designs on making it to the front door, maybe dashing through it to safety and freedom, knowing Grady would be on his way, but the footsteps grew faster and she heard a hand grasp the knob. It jiggled only slightly, but she knew the door wasn't locked. Nobody locked doors back then. She stopped cold and awaited her fate, desperately formulating ways to talk her way out of it. Then the door creaked open."

"Leroy Fitzsimmons," Jack whispered, his voice as tense as his body.

I stared at the door, half-expecting it to open.

"Maybe," I whispered back.

"What are you talking about? Who else could it have been?"

A footstep suddenly sounded on the lowest step of the back deck, followed by another. Jack and I glared at each other. We quickly became a joint force of one, back to back, defending our territory.

"You carrying?" he whispered.

"No."

The footsteps came steadily, growing quieter as the intruder exercised more caution with every move.

Jack reached over and flicked off the lamp. The last image engraved on the rods and cones of my eyes branded itself there in a photo-negative brain rush: Jack's glistening, dark eyes staring at me, terrified but determined. The Haiku Twins didn't cut and run; they stayed and fought.

I reached over and grabbed a thick glass vase from a table, then took six silent steps toward the door, matching them to the pace of the person crossing the deck. Heavy. Measured.

Jack did the same and took up a crouched position next to the door. Ready position.

"Starsky and Hutch," he murmured, referencing our old childhood game and favorite rerun.

A flashlight beam flicked on outside and pressed directly to the lowermost pane of the door as the knob jiggled.

The door was locked.

I snaked my left arm up to the knob as the beam searched wildly around the room. In one swift motion, I unlocked the bolt and yanked it open as Jack sprang onto the unsuspecting visitor. The audible intake of breath from the intruder was immediately stifled by Jack's hard-charging, full-body assault.

I raced onto the deck, the heavy vase poised and ready to crack a head, but from the excruciating sound of a skull hitting the deck planks, I knew my strike would be redundant.

A second set of arrhythmic footsteps rushed up the back deck stairs, startling both Jack and me and sending us into a flurry of confusion.

"What in God's name?" said a slow, deliberate voice. "Jedediah, you okay?"

It was Mr. Abel, holding a rifle at his side and looking aghast at his unconscious son-in-law. He leaned down next to Jed, laying the gun on the deck.

Jack grabbed the flashlight from where it had fallen and shone it on the person who'd borne the brunt of his pummeling. "Jed Matheny?"

"Annelise's husband," I said in case Jack had forgotten. "From next door."

Jack aimed the flashlight at Mr. Abel. "What are you doing here?"

Mr. Abel frowned and looked embarrassed when he saw the vase in my hand. "I'm awful sorry, Jack and Janie." It may have been the first time he'd ever addressed us both by name. "Guess we scared the wits out of you two."

"Never mind that," Jack said. "What are you doing here?"

"Jed spotted those kids who've been causin' so much trouble around these parts lately. They had a fire going in the woods, smoking, drinking, and whatnot. When he approached them, they ran off in this direction, so Jed came back and got me. Thought we should check it out, what with Barton in the hospital and all. We saw one of 'em near the house, so I went back, got my gun, and we figured we might catch him in the act."

I heard the tale with a mixture of skepticism and fear. As my mind flew in eight different directions, Jack cut in. "Did you ever think to check the front of the house, Mr. Abel, to see if it was Janie or me?"

"You don't know how bad it's gotten. The kids these days are downright delinquent. And with the disturbance the other night and that murderer on the loose, we didn't know what to think. What are you doin' here so late, anyway?"

I noticed Mr. Abel looking beyond me and gazing at the boxes inside. "You'd better get Jed home," I said. "Get some ice on that head. You know the signs of concussion, Mr. Abel?"

Jed helped clarify the answer by coming to and moaning. "Oh, man, I'm gonna be sick. What happened?"

"You let your guard down," Mr. Abel said harshly. "Now hush and we'll get you home."

"Let me help you," Jack said, righting Jed, who looped a long arm over his shoulders. Jed dwarfed both Jack and Mr. Abel and would be a handful to transport. "I'll drive you back," Jack said. "My car's up front."

"Jed," I said, "have you and Mr. Abel been together the past few hours?"

Mr. Abel looked surprised by the question, and Jed seemed too muddled to do anything but give a straight-up answer. "Yeah. We were workin' on my truck for a good while before all the commotion started."

My suspicions about Mr. Abel suddenly dissipated, but if they did prove true, I figured Jack would be safe with Jed as a barrier between them.

"You'll be okay here for a few minutes, Janie?" Jack asked. I assured him I would be, and the three of them tramped through the house and out the front door.

I waved as Jack drove off, suppressing a grin at the thought of Annelise descending the stairs in floppy pajamas and face cream, only to see handsome Jack Perkins—*the one who got away*—in her living room. What a delightful scene it would be.

I closed the door and the silence of the house grew heavy and sullen. I stayed motionless, weighing the idea of facing the boxes without Jack. And then I heard a noise. A creak, a crack, a jarring. Definitely something. I stood there, holding my breath for what felt like a minute, but heard nothing else. *Come on, Janie, you're almost there. It's the same noises you cherished growing up in this old place, the ones that let you know you were home and safe.*

Even in my calmer state, I turned on every light and returned to the living room to face the four boxes.

The birthday photo was in the second box, beneath a cheese grater that had, oddly, worked its way into the Pix box. I stared at it, disbelieving. Here it was. In my hands. I'd found it.

In the photo, the balloons drifted left; there must have been a gentle breeze that day. And my mom looked so happy, like she knew the best secret in the world and she was proud to keep it. The three of them—my mother and Grandpa Barton and Grandma Elizabeth—grinned back at me with delighted expressions that held no warning, no hint of a Perkins family curse. They were simply a family intertwined, touching in as many places as they could through linked arms, held hands, fingers on shoulders, with no idea how violently the links would shatter one day.

The frame was cheap; the photo, displayed with no mat, showed signs of fading. I flipped it over. No back paper to keep out dust and insects or to fight humidity. I hoped the contents hidden within were okay. Slowly, I pried up the small metal prongs that held the coated cardboard in place. Despite my care, one prong snapped off. Had my mother pressed them back too hastily in her panic? With the release of the final prong, the backing came loose and seemed to let out a sigh, relieved to finally share its burden.

I eased off the cardboard to reveal a piece of plain card stock, placed there for its thickness, to keep the photo pressed properly to the glass. Gray and thin, it was utterly nondescript, but I stared at it in awe. There would be no more layers, no more barriers, only this insubstantial piece of glorified paper, and then the reason my mother had died.

I lifted it.

Nothing.

I panicked, stricken with a profound sadness and the utmost rage. I fought the urge to hurl the whole thing, glass and all, across the room, shattering it into a thousand pieces to make it feel as crushed as my soul.

Nothing?

And then it fluttered down. It had been stuck to the other side of the cardboard.

A napkin. A single, square napkin. Cocktail-size. It landed by my feet.

Hands shaking, I picked it up and turned it over.

There it was. In a fine, black ink. The haiku.

CHAPTER 52

Bridget Perkins, 30 Years, 1 Minute Ago

Bridget and her dad—heck, everyone in Caulfield—were so dang trusting that nobody bolted their doors until heading to bed for the night. And even then, they forgot half the time. Bridget knew before the first rattle of the door handle that it would be unlocked, allowing the intruder to walk right in as if invited for tea. Truth be told, she wasn't entirely sure who it would be.

Still in her heavy shoes from the diner, she took four small, silent steps away from the hidden haiku and toward the center of the room before freezing in place. Maybe he wouldn't look this way. Maybe he'd go straight to the kitchen or assume she'd headed upstairs. She'd been a star sprinter in high school; perhaps escape was still an option. But even as the desperate thoughts nibbled at her brain, she knew he'd spot her right away, that he'd have seen the lamp go dark, that he'd sense her fear, her rigidness, her vulnerability exactly where she was, exactly how she was. People like him, they just knew.

He entered, as if her dread had cued him, and turned to her immediately. His tiny flashlight pointed downward and then glided to her feet, her waist, and, finally, her face. The night was so dark and the moon so absent that Bridget couldn't quite make out the details of her visitor, but she knew him now and felt relief that the aura of suspense had been punctured. She turned the lamp back on to reduce the effects of his flashlight. Things were in motion now, things that would change simple events into incidents with aftermaths.

What was the man's name again? What had Grady called him?

"Why?" he said in the trifling voice she recognized from the diner just a short time ago. "Is it some sick thing you do, some game you play?" Then his words took on an omniscient quality, a declarative air. "You take people's things, waitress."

"Yes" was the only syllable Bridget could manage, and its simple utterance—the first time she'd ever admitted her transgression—weakened her resolve, made her feel exposed. "I'm sorry."

"You have no idea," he said, "no idea what you've done."

"I've already called Grady. He's on his way."

"Do you think I don't know that? Do you think I'm afraid?"

"You should be. You know that as well as I do."

"You and I, waitress, we're alike," he hissed. "Both victims. The unnoticed, the underappreciated, the insignificants crawling undetected like dust mites feasting on humans in slumber. You serve your customers and they don't even notice your perfect face." He cast his eyes down, ashamed. "I noticed . . . tonight." He drew a deep breath and then jerked his head up. "I spend days skulking through ductwork, laboring in crawl spaces, stooped low on floors, always discreet in unseen corners, forgotten yet devouring. Not with my mouth, mind you, but with my ears, eyes, brain, and sometimes . . . my fingers. You see, I, too . . . I, too, pilfer, but I suspect you already know that."

Headlights bounced over the bump at the distant top of the driveway and lit up the paleness of the man's face. Twice more as the car grew closer, he stood in brief illumination, flickering but immobile.

From the sound of the engine, Bridget knew the approaching vehicle wouldn't be Daddy's truck. It was a car with an expensive, purring engine, moving fast, frantically, as if a life depended on it.

"Where is it?" he said.

Bridget found the steel within her that had made her so attractive to Grady. "I understand what you go through, how hard it is for you. But this doesn't have to end horribly. I need to protect my twins, and if that means keeping a secret for a short time, I'm willing to do that."

His voice fell to a whisper. "Keep your secret, and God willing—or me prevailing—perhaps *you* won't get hurt."

He stepped back, gliding along the floor into the kitchen, effortlessly slipping into the shadows as he'd done so many times before.

Grady pulled open the front door.

CHAPTER 53

My mother's life for a simple napkin? A napkin that had been in a room with me most of my life? It seemed unfathomable that so much had depended on so little, until I recalled how I'd almost lost my own life over a slip of paper no larger than a cookie's fortune.

I read the haiku, scrawled as it was in a combination of print and cursive:

Public Serve-ant Slave
Pandering gratuity
To none you serve now

I read it again, dismayed to realize I didn't even care about the words. Sick thoughts from a disturbed mind. This ultimate discovery, the big revelation, felt wholly anticlimactic. It could have applied to Grady. It could have been for my mother. It could have targeted anyone in a service or public profession. Whoever it was, their life had been spared by my mother's nimble fingers, the plan diverted, with her life taken instead.

It all seemed so futile, so silly, and yet I knew the importance of the item in my hands. The handwriting could be traced back to the killer and the napkin forensically analyzed. I gazed at it, my eyes seeing the words, my brain hearing their threat, my fingers appreciating the angel-wing texture of their source, but only my subconscious absorbed these details. Most of all, I felt sad and exhausted, beyond repair. Hot tears dripped down my cheeks.

My phone rang, startling me from my curled position on the sofa, lost in the words of a demon, a man who'd lain in wait all this time for the survivors of his massacre to rise up and send him to hell. I hardly felt like a threat.

"Hello?" I said into my phone, scraping together the energy.

"Janie, it's Grady, just calling to check on you, make sure you're okay after our ordeal with finding Sam today."

"Grady," I said, my voice catching. "I'm fine, but . . ."

"You're still shaken up, aren't you? Want to get together? Maybe we could have a drink together without thugs barging in on us."

I took a moment of heretofore unimaginable pleasure in being comforted by my father, and then answered in a whisper. "I found it."

"You found it?" His voice held wonder, delight. "The haiku?" The two words were uttered with such profound awe that my tears flowed freely as I realized I'd not only found the haiku, but the key to Grady's full exoneration, perhaps the catalyst to his future. Could this simple napkin bring everything full circle and provide a worthy ending, if not a perfect one, to a long, dismal story?

I heard Grady swallow back his own tears and sniff away years of pent-up emotion.

"Where are you?" he said, his words barely breaking the surface.

"Grandpa Barton's."

"Oh, Janie, this is . . ." And the resonant voice of the strong survivor faded to blissful silence.

"I know," I said, and we hung up shortly thereafter.

I went to call Jack but saw his cell phone sitting on the couch next to me. Poor Jack, stuck over there with Annelise, unable to use a fake call or text as an excuse to depart. Ah well, it was news best delivered in person anyway, sister to brother.

I forced myself from the couch and walked to the stairs, half-way to the second floor before realizing my destination: my mother's room. I needed to be as close to her as possible, to let her know it was over, but when I entered I was seized with an unspeakable energy, a determination that would not subside until I succeeded.

I laid the napkin on my mother's white desk near a set of art pencils that had remained unused, their sharp points having always offered potential, but never hope. To keep the napkin in place, I weighed it down with my mother's final sculpture, a haunting piece that had hinted at a unique depiction of a man and his much larger shadow. I turned to face the room head-on.

One thought extinguished all others: *my mother had kept journals.* Grandpa Barton would never have discarded them or subjected them to an unforgiving storage locker. I scanned the pristine room, reluctant to disrupt all that Grandpa had fought to preserve, so I sat on the bed and employed the best search tool I owned: my mind.

If my mom and I were so alike in our guileful ways, shouldn't our hiding spots be similar? Somewhere permanent, not a dresser drawer, not anything remotely mobile that could be cast off or stowed. A minute later I rose confidently and approached her closet. I removed the hanging clothes that Grandpa had refused to relinquish, followed by crates of sweaters, shoe boxes, a pack of forgotten lightbulbs, a mousetrap—unused—and some corroded batteries. Then I stepped inside and took full measure of the small space. I knew immediately to turn around and look up. At the top of the closet, above the door frame, near the vent housing was a thin, triangular cut in the drywall, about six inches on a side. A finger-size hole had been bored in its center. Using a crate as a step stool, I climbed up and raised my hand to the triangle. My index finger fit the hole perfectly.

I pulled. My mother had covered the triangle's rough, sawn edges with precision-cut duct tape to keep it from shredding and to make for easier access. I reached into the resulting hole and felt a small stack of notebooks. My mother, reputed to be a technically meticulous sculptor, had measured well, but I finagled the books out at a precise angle, one by one, six in all.

With my new treasures laid out on the bed, I gazed at them with uncertainty. Nothing could please me more than a dose of reality to counter the maternal images I'd crafted, but Jack was right; I'd conceived a princess, a heroine—hazy, mystical beings unsullied by human flaws. Here before me lay the tools to sculpt a real person, untouched by those who loved her unconditionally or romantically, and away from those who knew her as coworker, friend, daughter, niece, or cousin. This would be Bridget Perkins, unfiltered, no pretense.

What if I didn't like what I found?

I stroked my finger along the top journal's soft leather, a deep, inviting red. I hoped Jack wouldn't return yet, as I wanted this moment alone. With stack in hand, I sauntered to the bay window seat and settled in. Illuminated by moonlight, I opened the first journal but immediately put it down. Why not know the person my mother had become? Why not embrace the final, happy days filled with hope and the promise of life?

I picked up the newest journal. It had airy gaps between some pages because my mother had taped in concert tickets, paper programs from local events, a ribbon for a caramel apple pie—all solid memories of vaporous events. Even the Scotch tape had turned brown with little stick left. Flipping to a random page, I found my mother five months pregnant: *Feeling huge! For some reason, Grady calling less frequently. I think Sam K. plans events on purpose so Grady can't ever steal a quiet moment in which to call. He sent roses, though! We are desperately in love and the babies only make our feelings grow stronger.*

On another page: *Grady wrote! It's so rare to get a letter. He says by the time he writes, Sam has him on the move again and never seems to find a post office . . . I question if Sam fails to find them on purpose. I know Grady has a generous heart, but where does he unearth these ne'er-do-wells? Maybe flawed souls are more indebted and grateful to him—not a bad trait in an employee, I suppose, but it sure makes for strange bedfellows. Oh well, far from flawless myself! I shall treasure the letter I did receive.*

I knew there was something off with that Sam Kowalczyk, and I'd never even met him.

My mother had tucked Grady's letter into the page. With its writer on the way over, I would feel disloyal reading it. Still, I opened it for a flash, catching sight of the salutation: *My beloved, bold Bridget . . .*

Ah, an alliterative scribe. Neat handwriting, too. I closed it and read Mom's next entry. Looked like she was back to her klepto ways.

Swiped a real treasure today—a key unlocking all the so-called treasures at the Bellevue near DC—but I must gain power over this bedevilment. A senator's wife cannot be a petty thief. Besides, I'm going to be a mom. Moms don't steal, at least not the best ones, as I intend to be. My kids will become everything they ever dream of, with Grady and me as their invisible, unwavering foundation. Not a traditional, stable foundation, but one that rises to the occasion. They may not acknowledge the support or always want it, but they will know it's there when they reflect on their achievements, when they see our eyes shining with pride, and we will lift them up—always—as high as they want to go.

I pressed my lips together, stifled tears, and moved on to more entries about her future, her plans for an art studio, and the additional children she and Grady would have—*a whole houseful.* She ranged from sweet, sentimental, and funny to crass and skeptical. I experienced a hard pang of regret when I read one entry from a week before she was shot:

Names for the twins . . . can't decide between Jonathan Barton and Jennifer Elizabeth—as a tribute to my parents—or names that speak to me for their strength and beauty: William Blake and Vivienne Louise. Grady says he doesn't care if I call them Twin A and Twin B, as long as they're healthy and happy. Perhaps I'll see what they respond to when I say the names aloud for the first time. One of them just kicked!

I hoped it was me who kicked. I really liked *Vivienne Louise* and could have gotten used to it. I didn't mind *Janie*, but it had occurred to me from time to time that it was morbid of Grandpa to name us after unidentified corpses.

And then came the final entry regarding her night at the Aberdeen Hotel. Just twelve words: *Grand night alone with Grady. He holds the key to my heart.* Taped to the page was a key on a substantial brass key chain with a beautiful *A* engraved on it. I smiled and shook my head as I realized my mom had swiped the rather valuable key to their Aberdeen room, back when hotels trusted their guests.

And then my face fell and my soul disintegrated. Oh, no. It couldn't be. My mind must be playing tricks.

But it kept flashing in my head. When I'd zoned out on the couch, staring mindlessly at the haiku, the words themselves had become meaningless, but a single letter on the napkin had worked its way into my brain and it was all I could see. And suddenly I saw how the whole tragedy must have played out. I understood the alternate route the haiku had traveled. I saw the *servant slaves* doing their menial tasks, from clearing dishes to adjusting valves, all while remaining alert and curious—too curious for their own good. That haiku had changed hands one too many times.

I glanced at my mother's desk where the napkin lay, the confirmation of my suspicions mere inches away. All I had to do was get up and check.

I didn't want to. I flipped back in my mother's journal to check something I'd just read. Damn, it was almost certain now. After a reluctant journey to my mother's desk, all doubt evaporated.

And stupid, stupid me. I'd gone and sealed my own fate, just like my mother.

Thoughts swarmed around me, spelling themselves out, kicking at my brain, each insisting on its own veracity. With the key in my mother's journal, I had unlocked a door in the floor and fallen down the rabbit hole, unable to grasp on to anything solid. I became the central, ultimate letter in one of Leroy Fitzsimmons's spiraling word puzzles as the new reality of my life spun crookedly downward, everything from the past week twisting back in on itself, reversing and flipping before looping back up to push me further toward a truth I could barely acknowledge. But when I landed, cold and irrevocably, my world was not one of insanity, filled with giant rabbits and mad tea parties, but one that finally, ultimately made sense.

Frantic now, but quickly at home in my new reality, I grabbed my phone. It was late, but I didn't care. I woke Sheriff Tucker and requested a favor. He complied immediately and texted me back an answer within two minutes. In the meantime, I followed another hunch. It was the only thing that would make sense, the only window of opportunity.

A quick search for *Lenora Dabney* on my phone resulted in pages of matches. I pared it down and quickly found three social media sites on which the world's friendliest prison guard was highly active. So that's what she did to fill time in her lonely booth at Everly Prison when she wasn't befriending the inmates. Given the sexual nature of most of her Twitter and Facebook entries, I now appreciated why she was so familiar with Grady's Ladies; she was probably one of them. Within her last thirty tweets, I found her Achilles' heel—everyone on social media had one. She'd posted her phone number in code to a guy tweeting as Erudite Earl. By doing it in code, the telemarketing scanners wouldn't pick it up, but she could take her Twitter relationship to a whole new level with chatty Earl.

I called her number. She picked up, answering in a sexy kitten voice. Betting a mental quarter on Nicholls, I employed a tone he would use when in need of information he had no right to request. It worked, threats and all, and within a minute, I had my answer.

A clattering noise rang out downstairs. Jack? No, he would have shouted out to find me.

Another noise. A door opening? Not a big one, though. And then some clicks. Had I even locked the front door after Jack left? Where the hell was my good Samaritan brother, anyway? You ring the bell, you dump the concussed lug, and you make yourself scarce. Annelise had probably yanked Jack in and sunk her claws deep, helping him step over her semiconscious husband and treating him to leftover birthday cake—there was sure to be plenty.

I called 911 and whispered an explanation as best I could, but if my hunch was right, things were about to unfold very quickly, and 911 response time in tiny Caulfield had gone from slow to glacial since budget cuts two years ago. I crept down the hall to Jack's old room to confirm another hunch. Before I even got there, I felt cold air seeping out from beneath his door. I opened it to see broken glass on the floor. It hadn't been a delinquent that Mr. Abel and Jed had spotted on our property. It had been Leroy Fitzsimmons, who'd selected the most discreet roof entrance into the house.

I took a calming breath. If I wasn't careful, this situation could grow very bleak, very fast—and I really wanted out of this rabbit hole.

It seemed impossible, but it was happening. Leroy Fitzsimmons was downstairs and Grady was either here or on his way over. I was about to be in the exact same position as my mother thirty years ago.

CHAPTER 54

I stole back down the hall toward an antique table where Grandpa used to keep a .22. Small but mighty, he would say, just like his Janie. I slid the drawer open. Empty. Damn.

I crept to the top of the stairs. Okay, I just had to—

"Janie?" It was Grady's voice. "Janie, it's me! Where are you?"

Before I knew it, he'd dashed halfway up the stairs. In his hands, a nine-millimeter pocket pistol. He saw me notice.

"It's your brother's," he said, flicking his brows and grinning like a mischievous boy with a forbidden toy. "Never even used. I took it from his apartment."

"A bullet is a bullet," I whispered.

"Figured if you found that haiku, Leroy Fitzsimmons can't be far behind."

I opened my mouth to speak, but a thunk downstairs put an abrupt end to our conversation.

Grady gestured for me to be quiet, then waved me along to follow.

We inched downstairs as he held his gun at the ready. I had no weapon—only a haiku burning a hole in my pocket.

At the base of the stairs, Grady propelled himself around the corner into the dining room, scanning it with alert eyes, his weapon at the ready. Deeming the room empty, he turned back and waved me on. We crept through the foyer. Without warning, he kicked open the French doors to the sitting room. Again, he scanned and cleared it like a pro.

It seemed a lot darker down here now; someone had turned off most of the lights.

As Grady gestured again, I held up a finger to tell him to wait a moment. I entered the sitting room, opened the door of an old corner curio cabinet, and pulled out Grandpa Barton's favorite: an antique Colt .45. Always loaded. Grandpa used to say it felt like a second skin in his large hands. To me, it felt awkward and heavy, but very welcome.

Grady looked surprised and doubtful when he saw the large hunk of metal in my hands, but I held it professionally enough, pointed downward, my finger off the trigger. That seemed to quiet his concerns.

He entered the living room, checking it first, his back to the kitchen—a huge mistake, especially given the last time he'd turned his back on it.

From out of nowhere stepped the short, stout form of Leroy Fitzsimmons. He slammed Grady mercilessly on the head with the butt end of a snub-nosed .38 Special, unleashing decades of frustration. The big guy crashed down in the same place he had thirty years earlier.

It was surreal to see Leroy, the man I'd wheeled across a parking lot less than a week ago, standing upright and able-bodied in a threatening posture. He turned to me, his gun hanging loosely at his side, a smirk on his round face. "This looks eerily familiar," he said.

I smiled, waves of relief, regret, and disbelief bludgeoning me simultaneously from all sides. Talk about overload. My soul simultaneously emptied and brimmed with such a cadre of emotions, I couldn't possibly enumerate them. "Thank God you didn't bring a syringe to a gunfight this time, Leroy."

He smiled, but it was small, quick, and not entirely sure. "So you know, then?"

I nodded, the lump in my throat almost choking out my voice. "Grady McLemore was the Haiku Killer." I pulled the haiku from my pocket and held it up to show him. "The Aberdeen *A* is still visible on the napkin."

"Ah, yes, the subtly raised, Japanese-inspired, calligraphic *A* pressed onto the napkin." His vocal cadence was rapid-fire, unnatural, yet lively, and I realized this was my first glimpse of the real Leroy Fitzsimmons, or at least the Leroy Fitzsimmons he'd become. No more Uncle Hump persona. There was a fleck of irrationality in his eyes, a mark of otherworldliness, and yet, I trusted him. "The Aberdeen put that *A* on everything in the old days, even the toilet tissue."

"And their key chains," I said. "Found one upstairs that my mother had stolen."

"Yes, your mother tended to do that." Leroy's small eyes grew bigger and he bit down on his lower lip, becoming a child asking for a forbidden treat. "May I hold the napkin?"

I flicked on a lamp and handed it to him. He stroked it like it was a long-lost pet. "I didn't think the *A* would survive," he said. "I'm quite glad it did, but had it not, the handwriting would have been enough."

"Yes," I said, "Grady has a distinctive loop on his *d*'s. I saw it just now in a letter to my mother, in the word *Bridget*, and the word *pandering* in the haiku."

Leroy walked across the living room and headed toward the marble table, his limp barely noticeable. Mickey Busker had been right. The man fleeing the house that night did have a hitch in his step; he just hadn't been the Haiku Killer.

Leroy touched the table as I had done earlier, then whirled around, retracing my mother's steps to the center of the room. "Of course, it makes sense now. I didn't think she had time to put it behind a picture frame and reassemble everything, but apparently she did. It was quite a moment watching you find it, Janie. Quite a moment, indeed."

"You must have gotten here just before Jack and me."

"Oh, yes. You're more sentimental than you let on. I knew you'd come here to unearth your treasure. I watched you arrive and observed the unfortunate altercation with Mr. Abel. I do apologize for my eavesdropping, but I had to wait for my prey to arrive."

I picked up Grady's gun and placed it on the foyer table, out of his reach in case he regained consciousness. Jack could use it as back-up when he returned. All the while, I took no chances, keeping my own gun fixed on Grady like a laser. "Did my mother ever know the truth?"

"Oh, yes. Sometime between the diner and her concealment of the napkin, she must have surmised that despite the napkin being in my possession, I was not its author. She must have noticed the *A* and realized that it had been composed at the Aberdeen. Then she zeroed in on the handwriting. You see, the Haiku Killer's notes were all printed in a belabored style, while McLemore the politician wrote almost exclusively in cursive." Leroy thrust his arm into the air and pointed upward like a victor. "However! This note—a first draft for a future kill, no doubt—shows a disjointed combination of cursive and print."

Leroy's eyes suddenly focused distantly, as if watching a scene in his head unfold on a movie screen. His voice grew quiet yet retained

340

its disconcerting animation. "Grady's eyes had likely jerked open in the dark of night—your mother next to him in that slumber known only to children and those with child—and he grew desperate to retain whatever thoughts had startled him awake. He'd have grabbed the first thing he saw—the napkin, of course—and scrawled on it awkwardly."

He gazed at the napkin now with a delighted grin. "Several of the printed letters match the Haiku Killer's notes, while the cursive words match the oddly feminine handwriting used by"—he nodded toward Grady, his distaste evident—"him. Which your mother must have noticed."

The revelation rubbed coarsely against my soul. In my mother's final moments, she understood she'd been played for a fool, a princess no more. "It all fell into place upstairs," I said. "You found the napkin while crawling around Grady's office floor, didn't you?"

"Quite so, Janie. Very astute."

"Then my mother's final words must have been, *Find radiator*, not *Find Grady hater.*"

"Certainly possible, if she was trying to say, *Find radiator repairman.* That's all she knew me as, really. That persnickety radiator had acted up yet again and I was determined to silence it. Grady returned to the office late that afternoon, having stayed with your mother at the Aberdeen the night before. I was fiddling with some settings on the floor when he set his duffel down as he always did, ignoring me, as he always did. The bag gaped open and I . . . Well, I was no better than your mother, I suppose . . . I swiped that napkin. I was so curious. A precise note—on a napkin—in a handwriting that seemed somewhat similar to the Haiku Killer's."

"Bit of a handwriting enthusiast, aren't you?"

Leroy smiled, but it was awkward, ashamed. "You found my basement notebooks. Yes, words have always been my refuge. Not verbal, mind you, but I enjoy playing with them in my head and in my notebooks. They were a distraction, you see, from . . ."—his sparse brows shot high on his head—"from my highly agitated mental state. Much of my life, people hurled words as weapons, when they weren't hurling grenades. They used words to assign nasty labels, but I knew they could be beautiful things—if respected."

"So you went to the diner with the haiku in your pocket?"

"I didn't know what to do. The haiku was such a powerful piece of information. And"—his brows bunched low, his head sinking into his abbreviated neck—"I wasn't entirely sure I hadn't imagined a scenario where one didn't exist. My mind didn't behave so well in those days. Or most days, really. I put the haiku in my pocket, and, quite simply, was hungry. At the diner, I took the napkin out many times, many times, reassuring myself it was real, reassessing the handwriting, deciphering the possibilities—it had so many. I was going to copy it down with my favorite pen, but there was too much commotion and I didn't want to risk a spill, so I put it away, yes, I did."

"And then my mother took it?"

His eyes narrowed and his head shook a few millimeters to each side, his anger fresh, rekindled. "She took it. Yes. She took it. I wish she hadn't. But she did."

"What must you have been thinking when Grady showed up at the diner?"

"That, yes, that," he said, his breathing quick and shallow now. "Well, that was uncomfortable. I already disliked him intensely—I have an immediate sense for evil and he had not treated me well— but then, to discover he was an infamous killer, adored by all, well, you can imagine. He'd never—never—paid so much attention to me as he did that night at the diner. I thought he must know—he must know!—that I'd absconded with his silly napkin. But no, it was all for show, you see, all for show, the big man acknowledging the subservient help so the public could adore his graciousness."

"Why didn't you just go to the police?"

He guffawed and looked at me like I'd suggested he run naked through town. "Oh, no, Janie, no. Oh, no. Are you quite serious? In fact, I can't go to them now. Not while Sam Kowalczyk and Grady McLemore are still alive."

He seemed to believe Sam was still alive. "What does Sam have to do with this?"

He paced now, like an enthused but distraught professor delivering a lecture. "Do you really think Sam and Grady would have let me into their little enclave if they didn't have the goods on me? That quaint story of me knocking on their office door—all well and good, and close enough to the truth—but hardly complete. They hired me for a simple job, yes, but when I asked to be paid in cash and averted my eyes from their gaze, oh, they knew then and decided they wanted to keep me around."

"What did they know?"

"Within days of my arrival in town, Sam confronted me with . . . compromising . . . information from my past. I didn't really see the value to them, but I soon realized they wanted persons in their employ with . . . marred backgrounds . . . scars on their consciences."

I recalled the entry from my mother's journal: *Maybe flawed souls are more indebted and grateful to him—not a bad trait in an employee.*

Leroy's pacing ceased and he stood rigid and taut. "Perhaps they planned to use me for nefarious tasks in the future. A loyal dark soldier. I don't know, but those two, quite a pair. And Sam was gifted—gifted!—in extracting information from others."

"Leroy, what did they have on you?"

His mouth clamped shut and his head kept shaking. I feared it wouldn't stop.

"Leroy, I'm standing here with you, the most wanted man in town, and I've taken the gun away from a man who could have shot you. I think you can trust me."

Leroy huffed several times. "I like you, Janie. I do. Hm. Well, if things go as planned, it won't matter. I'll tell you."

I didn't like the sound of that, but I listened anyway.

He resumed pacing, his words rapid-fire, rising and falling like celebratory bullets.

"Four days out of high school, a friend of mine asked for a lift to Toby's Convenience Store. I obliged, of course, him being my only friend but not a very likable fellow. Unbeknownst to me, he robbed the store and upon exiting, fired his gun back into a random aisle—the dairy section, it was—to emphasize his point to the owner about not calling the police. The shot killed a customer—no milk for him—a professor from a local community college whom I'd once had the pleasure of helping change a flat."

He'd tried to lighten the incident, but its recounting was taking a toll. Every tic he'd ever harbored seemed to come to the fore. From a twitch beneath his right eye to the corners of his mouth widening and narrowing like a horizontal line in flux. The hand that held his gun tensed and released, tensed and released, his words coming in bubbling spurts—a graceless unburdening of guilt delivered in unseemly packets.

"My friend hopped in the car and insisted I drive away. Fast, fast, fast! I took him to a dilapidated warehouse, but no, he was arrested within hours. Miraculously—miraculously, Janie!—he never ratted me out, as they say, but there were rumors, vague witness statements, and a scratchy surveillance video from a nearby bank. If anyone had wanted to pursue it and make a case against me, it was just possible enough. As the driver, I'd have gone to jail, as responsible as my friend who pulled the trigger, unless the jury believed me, and why would they? They wouldn't! My own father never believed a word I said." With his free hand, he pounded his chest. "And I simply did not—do not—will never!—have the constitution for prison, Janie. No, no, no. I paid a heavy price in the war—my penance, if you will—for any dairy aisle sins in which I may have been complicit. My conscience is clear on that front. But even today, unlike your friend Grady here, I'd sooner die than go to prison. Do you hear me, Janie? Sooner die."

"You've lived your whole life under the radar because of that robbery?"

He pulled back, defensive. "I've lived a life where I rarely give out my name or take a formal paycheck. I returned to Ridge to live with my sister a few years after Grady's sentencing, the convenience store episode long forgotten by then. And with Grady behind bars, I knew the world was better served. I saw no reason to share the secret of the haiku. Not that I stopped looking for it, mind you. I knew he'd get out eventually. That's why I took the pictures. I wanted to remember the house and figure out where it was. Oh, how I wanted to search that night—and help your mother—but someone was coming, someone was coming. Your grandfather, I surmise." He looked up at me without raising his head, the bottom half of his eyes cast in shadow, framing his stubby nose. "I came back here over the years, you know. Even sneaked in once while you and your brother were on the roof."

Chills raced through me and I glared at him. All those years I'd sensed a foreboding presence lurking and stalking, I'd been right. But it hadn't been the Haiku Killer coming back to finish the job. It had been an unbalanced little man trying to find his treasure and maybe protect the world from Grady McLemore.

"But Sam wouldn't let me live in peace," Leroy continued. "He and Grady had put two and two together immediately. They knew it was me who'd swiped the haiku—"

"Hold on! Did Sam know Grady was the Haiku Killer?"

"Of course. Probably not until after Grady had killed the priest, but he knew by the time I came along. Come now, Janie. Why do you think Grady paid Sam all these years?"

"He was buying Sam's silence."

Leroy smiled and I'd never felt more disconcerted. "He did have Sam conduct actual investigations, just to make it look good. But it was all a game, all for show, like everything in Grady's life."

"Was my mother just for show?"

Leroy hesitated, not sympathizing, but assessing the possibility. Then, very plainly, he spoke. "I assume so. The pregnancy may have been a rare misstep for the gifted sociopath, but once Grady accepted it, he turned it to his advantage. I'm sure he whiled away the hours imagining his perfect imitation of a life: the handsome politician, the beautiful wife, the successful twins. Probably spent oodles of time constructing the façade in his head, certain, as always, that things would go his way."

"That night at the diner, why didn't you just warn my mother?"

Leroy's demeanor took its most abrupt turn yet, and it had taken several already. "I didn't know she had the haiku until it was too late! Understand my condition, please."

I was beginning to think I understood it all too well.

"They'd put me on dozens of medications, strapped me to a table and sent bolts of Satan through my soul, and then they labeled me! Me! The one they'd done that to. Delusional, depressed, manic, you name it. Half the doctors wanted to commit me and the others wanted an empty bed so they could churn through yet another victim. Today, they'd call it PTSD, but back then I was just another mess back from war, hearing voices and reacting to loud noises like a beaten pup."

"Leroy," I said, wanting to hug him. "I am so sorry."

He wheeled on me, his eyes narrow, almost threatening. "You'd be the first."

I felt both frightened and crushed inside for the life that had been thrust upon the shy, motherless boy from Ridge.

"Don't you realize I'd only had the haiku for a couple of hours?" he shouted. "If I had trouble convincing myself about it, do you really think I could have convinced someone as beautiful as your mother?" He looked ashamed again, punishing himself for admitting to her beauty. "Besides, if she was foolish enough to love that creature"—he gestured to the still-prone Grady—"do you really think she possessed the wits and wherewithal to understand the truth? At one point, I was certain the haiku was about her—that he was scheming to take her out. And if not, *she* was planning a life with a serial killer. Your mother was doomed either way."

He'd hit a nerve now. My mother was not foolish. She'd been sucked in like everyone else. "Maybe, Leroy. But it was you who kicked Grady's hand in order to save your own life. Maybe she wouldn't have been doomed."

He looked at me aghast, his lower jaw going slack. "And this is why I couldn't trust you, either, Janie. Not until I had the haiku in my hands." He changed tone and mumbled, "I'm sorry about the incident in the storage locker, by the way. I do like you, but I couldn't trust anyone who bonded with that man, even if hesitantly." His rage returned. "Oh! His spun tales are maddening, and he is masterful, but *really*, Janie? Really?" He grabbed hold of his own head as if to keep it from shattering.

I was sure of one thing: all of Leroy's mental challenges were not yet behind him.

"Janie!" Leroy shouted as if I'd gone somewhere.

"Yes, Leroy? What?"

His words came fast, high-pitched. "I injected Grady, yes! I couldn't believe how well I placed the syringe—dumb luck—but wouldn't you know, the insane are highly resilient. He fought that tranquilizer harder than any sow I'd ever slaughtered under duress.

He fell to the floor, yes, but—miraculously—he had the strength to raise his gun—directly at your mother."

I felt my own head jerk forward and shake in denial. "No. No. He was trying to shoot *you*. He . . . why would he—"

Leroy huffed, short quick bursts. "She knew the truth. When he entered the room that night, she stood there like a mute idiot, the hurt and accusation screaming out from her face as plainly as a haiku on a napkin. It was only seconds earlier she'd realized who and what he was, and he saw it immediately. It was no doubt a look he treasured on the faces of his victims as they comprehended his inhumanity. I tell you, when he walked in, the horror just shined in her eyes—her brain and heart still fighting it out, her heart losing the battle . . . and the war. That's why I plunged the syringe so quickly. I knew his first instinct would be to eliminate her, the most powerful witness, without a single thought for you or your brother."

"But why would he want her dead more than you?"

"He still had leverage over me, but he had nothing over her. Better to take her out for certain than to allow the possibility that she would produce the haiku and the proof of his guilt. And he certainly didn't want to spend a lifetime being blackmailed by her, receiving threats and ultimatums. No, Grady McLemore would be beholden to no one. You see, Janie, he has always cared first, foremost, and only . . . about himself. He even accepted life in a dirty cell as a martyr because he was still pulling the wool over the world's eyes. Every day in that prison, with his unstable base of groveling fans proclaiming his innocence, with your brother forging a worshipful relationship with him, it fed the voracious ego that consumed him. Rather the nature of the beast, I'm afraid."

Leroy, in another dramatic shift of moods, shuffled over to the couch, took a seat, and slouched back, exhausted. "When Grady raised the gun at your mother, I kicked his hand—that much is true—to try to save her. But she, seeing Grady's muzzle pointed at the very heart that had loved him so foolishly, leapt out of harm's way. And the bullet's path, altered by my kick, found your mother's head. I am more sorry than you'll ever know, Janie."

"It's not your fault, Leroy."

"At least now," he said, his voice barely a whisper, "I've finally, finally set things right."

Grady stirred. I kept my gun on him. He sat up, confused. "Janie, what's going on?" He reached around frantically. "Where's my gun?"

"Out of your reach."

Grady spotted Leroy the same moment he realized my gun was on him. He looked so scared, sad, and confused. It was pitiful.

"Janie, what are you doing? What has he been telling you?"

"Isn't this adorable?" Leroy said quietly, staring through and above us. "A reunion of sorts, if we allow Janie to stand in for her deceased mother."

"I know everything, Grady," I said.

"Everything? What are you talking about? What has he been telling you? How long have I been out?"

"I know you killed my mother. I know you're the Haiku Killer."

Grady guffawed, an expression of genuine shock and disbelief on his face. "What?"

"It was *your* haiku in Leroy's pocket. When my mother called you from the diner, you put it together immediately, realizing Leroy had taken the haiku from your bag."

"Janie, this is insane. Put the gun down."

"I don't think so . . . *Daddy*." I took several steps back, eliminating any chance of him knocking the gun from my hands, while Leroy stayed on the couch, entirely detached, finally unburdened. "You failed to mention one aspect of the shooting—that while you were staring at your thumb knuckle on your gun, with glutton juice coursing through your veins, your gun was aimed at my mother's head the whole time."

"I don't know what he's told you, Janie, but you can't possibly believe I would hurt your mother."

Looking into his eyes, it was difficult to elicit the hatred I should be feeling. I tried anyway. "My mother took the key from the Aberdeen, from the night you two stayed there. It was engraved with an *A*, precisely matching the *A* on the napkin where the haiku was written."

"Napkin? The haiku was written on a napkin?"

He was so . . . believable. I had to remind myself of the monster Leroy claimed him to be.

"You said so yourself," he continued. "Abner Abel was at the Aberdeen all the time. Leroy could have been there, too. It would have been nothing for either of them to grab a handful of napkins."

"It was in your handwriting."

He looked confused. "How would you even know what my handwriting looks like?"

"There's a letter from you to my mother, upstairs in her journal."

Grady looked up and to the left, his signature look of concentration. Then his face grew stern and he gazed at me. "How long has Leroy been here?"

"Since before me."

"Don't you see what he's doing? Please, Janie, step away from him. I can't watch you get hurt. Not here, not in this room. Please!"

I stole a quick glance at Leroy, who was muttering to himself. "What is it that Leroy is doing?"

Grady's beautiful eyes pleaded with me. "He's had thirty years to perfect a story."

"So has he," Leroy said in a singsong tone.

"Think, Janie," Grady said. "He must have found Bridget's journals and copied my letter in his own handwriting so it would match the handwriting on the haiku. *His* handwriting on the haiku. Who knows how many times he's been in this house? He could have done it years ago."

"He took the napkin from *your* bag, Grady."

"There could have been an Aberdeen napkin in my bag, sure. I stayed there a lot. But *he* wrote the haiku on it, not me. Think about his victims. He was a vagrant handyman. He could have gotten into a church or a college professor's office, at any hour, under the guise of being there for a repair."

Leroy spoke up in a bored tone. "Look at his campaign stops, Janie. They match up perfectly with the time and location of each murder."

Leroy's assertions made sense, but so did Grady's. Then I cleared my head and swam parallel to the shore before getting sucked in any farther. I already knew the truth. Why was I still dawdling?

"Tell me something, Grady. When you got out of prison, you went straight to Jack's, but then immediately came to see me, right?"

"Yes, I left with one of the guards at six a.m., along with four decoy cars. The reporters followed the decoys, thinking that the guard was simply leaving after her shift. She dropped me at Jack's."

"Very clever. But in reality, none of the reporters followed you because you left the prison in Lenora Dabney's car—at *midnight*, six hours *before* the decoy cars."

"Midnight? No, that's not right."

"Maybe you're not as good in the sack as you think, *Senator*. You and Lenora may have had a little prison fling, but she gave you up faster than a two-dollar hooker puttin' out for a Benjamin. We had a lovely chat a few minutes ago." Leroy chuckled as I continued. "Lenora dropped you off five miles from the prison, at a gas station where she had a rental car waiting in her name. You had all the time in the world to drive to the mountains and kill Sam Kowalczyk."

Leroy gasped and muttered to himself, "Sam's dead? Oh, my."

I was on a roll now. "You made Sam's files just easy enough for me to find. You killed Sam and framed Leroy while you were at it, making it look like Leroy was gallivanting about, killing anyone who knew his true identity. The beauty of it was that it wasn't even *you* accusing poor Leroy—it looked like Sam's handiwork. You were just the naïve bystander."

"I can't believe this," Grady said. "You can't possibly believe all this."

"Nice touch with the 5-7-5 file. Did you do that before or after you marched Sam into the woods and killed him?"

The upper corners of Grady's lifelong mask curled, as if the heat of being in the spotlight was finally taking its toll.

"And it wasn't just Leroy and the police who knew which drug you were injected with thirty years ago. You knew, too. You wrote that glutton juice haiku and even managed to throw a little pity party for yourself—making it look like you'd been betrayed by your dearest friend all those years while he spent your money and let you rot."

"Janie, you—"

"Your money kept Sam quiet, not loyal."

Leroy piped up, his voice so small it didn't even reach the ceiling. It just hung in the air, searching. "Sam and I spoke when he tracked me down in Ridge. I had caught him taking photos at the church. As horrid as Sam was, he was a spiritual man. He wouldn't have taken his secrets to the grave. Grady knew that; that's why he killed him."

"You really know how to pick 'em, Grady," I said.

And suddenly the façade came tumbling down and the curtain lifted. For perhaps the first time in his life, Grady McLemore showed his real face, and it was something to behold. Evil streaked with ice-cold indifference, shrouded by self-glorification and unreserved hatred. "I picked your mother, didn't I?"

"Don't rise to his bait, Janie," Leroy said. "You've got him where you want him and I'm proud of you. But the cavalry will be here soon, and it's time for me to bid you and your family adieu. I do apologize for the stain."

"What stain?"

"Betty shouldn't have mailed those pictures, but she never did forgive me for those puppies," Leroy said, a mournful smile coating his features. "But I forgive her and I need to go see her now."

Leroy raised his gun to his head, sucked in a defiant gulp of air, and pulled the trigger.

I may have screamed *No!* but I didn't hear it. The deafening shot of the gun pounded against my ears as I watched his round body go limp on the couch, falling gently to the side as if he'd lain down for a nap.

At the same moment, Jack must have returned through the front door, but I didn't hear him, and only Grady would have been able to see him through the archway between the living room and foyer.

Not the least bit fazed by the suicide, Grady screamed to Jack, "Leroy's here! Toss me the gun!" He pointed to the nine-millimeter on the foyer table.

As I turned to shout at my brother, I saw a flash of hard steel fly into Grady's hands. Jack entered immediately after and tried to make sense of the bizarre scene. He ran to Leroy and gently touched his neck to check for a pulse. Not finding one, he looked from Grady to me. "What the hell is going on?"

Reflexively, Jack pulled out his phone.

Grady took aim at my brother's head. "Not so fast, Jack. Put it on the floor."

Jack froze. Had I not been so horrified by the turn of events, I would have enjoyed the expression on my brother's face, but his words sufficed. "No. Fucking. Way."

Anne McAneny

"Afraid so," Grady said, signaling with his gun for Jack to get away from Leroy's body, and away from Leroy's gun.

Jack stepped toward me, repeating himself in a murmur. "What the hell is going on?"

I ignored my brother for the moment and waved my own piece. "Did you forget I'm holding a gun, Grady?"

Grady glanced at me pitifully. "The gun I unloaded before you came down the stairs, Janie?"

Without hesitation, I aimed my gun at the external wall and fired. A disappointing click. Son of a bitch.

"A long time ago," Grady said, "Bridget told me how Barton kept some piece-of-shit gun in an old curio. It's the type of information that's handy to tuck away. And I tuck away everything."

He strutted over toward Leroy's body and shook his head. "What a pain in the ass this guy turned out to be." He sat himself down on the arm of the couch, relaxed and confident. "But at least he can help me now."

"You can't possibly think you'll get away with this, Grady. It's not thirty years ago. No matter what you do, there's evidence in every square inch of this room."

"You're right, Janie. Plenty of evidence. To show that Leroy, the infamous Haiku Killer, felt the need to take out both of the adorable Haiku Twins before taking his own life." He smiled, all resemblance to my brother replaced by the twisted sickness emanating from his every pore. "And here I am with a bump on my head because Leroy knocked me out while he killed my children in cold blood." He shook his head. "Real sicko."

"You have to at least tell us why," Jack said.

"Why what?"

"Why all of it?"

"No time for that. So sorry."

354

"But why the haikus?" I said, desperate to stall. "Why those victims? Have you always been like this?"

"I told you in the car, Janie, I'm not some puzzle you can assemble and label for the psychiatric journals. I am so much more than anyone will ever understand." He tilted his head. "But I do hate to send you to your graves frustrated—the way your mother went."

Without looking, I knew that Jack's reaction, like my own, was one of repulsion and horror.

"My victims," Grady said, "were all *people with power behaving badly*. My mother would have spit on their graves." He grinned. "I guess I made it easier for her, didn't I? Nothing beats power—nothing. Those men had it, they earned it, they existed in the upper echelons, mingling with the elite. But they all became sniveling, spineless wimps, mismanaging their gifts and begging a junior senator-to-be to save their sorry asses. I showed them what real power was." His expression grew animated and evil, filled with enough loathing to justify a dozen slain corpses. "I met with each of them. Very discreetly, of course. The professor with his pathetic liaisons, desperate for tenure but about to be taken down by the contrite, slutty daughter of a powerful businessman. The doctor who needed me to intervene because the judge presiding over his case was a friend of my father's. And the priest who wondered how I might be able to help him seal the records of a perverse coworker."

"But the haikus," I said. "Why the haikus?"

"Enough, Janie." He waved with his gun for me to move closer to my brother. "You came in together, you'll go out together. Ladies first, I think."

"Grady, hold up!" Jack said. "Abner Abel is on his way here. He left something behind earlier. You'll never get away with it."

"Really, John?" Grady said. "That's the best you've got? Thought I raised you better than that."

He pulled a handkerchief from his pocket, then turned and extended his hand toward Leroy's hip to confiscate the .38.

Bang!

A bullet ripped into Grady's chest. "What the hell?" he shouted as he fell to the floor. Blood seeped through his clean white shirt, but he looked more surprised than distraught as he stared down at his chest.

I glanced at the gun in my hand. It certainly hadn't gone off. And then it dawned on me. Despite the life-and-death circumstances swirling around the room, I couldn't help but be fascinated by what had just occurred.

"Cadaveric spasm," I whispered with awe and respect.

"Cat of what?" my brother said.

"Cadaveric spasm," I said, taking a slanted pleasure in Grady's attempts to stem his own bleeding with a throw pillow. "It's rare, but bodies can twitch after death, especially those that die tragically with muscles contracted. Leroy's hand was probably pretty tense."

"I still come out of this smelling like a rose," Grady panted, growing pale, but, as Leroy had observed, the insane could show remarkable resilience. He'd kept his pistol trained on Jack and me from the moment he hit the floor. He scooted on his butt toward Leroy's body, still determined to get Leroy's gun, still determined to kill us with it.

"All I smell," I said, "is a psycho's blood. You must be losing it at a rate of a pint a minute, Grady; a guy your size has only got about nine total."

"Then I'll have to make this quick."

"Must be fate," I said. "Even in death, the man who put you away the first time manages to take you out again."

He glared at me, its effect chilling. "I'm far from out."

In a flash, he grabbed Leroy's gun and raised it to my heart.

Jack and I launched into action at precisely the same moment, both going low to rush Grady. He'd only be able to get off one shot before the surviving twin tackled him, and each of us was willing to take a bullet for the other.

But before we took our first step, the sound of shattering glass and a rifle's report filled the air, disrupting Grady's aim but still allowing him to fire. His bullet slammed into my shoulder; it burned like hell and sent me airborne, back toward the center of the room, but I didn't mind. It gave me a great vantage point from which to see Abner Abel's load of buckshot come soaring in from the back deck and adjust all the mangled wiring in Grady's head, short-circuiting the sick bastard once and for all.

CHAPTER 55

Four hours postsurgery, my shoulder was in dire straits but apparently filled with so much potential that the docs said I'd be doing cartwheels in no time. The fact that I'd never performed a cartwheel did not deter them from insisting on its possibility.

Jack, who'd used his ample charms to get permission to stay by my side even in the restricted areas, had finally deemed me conscious enough to unleash his barrage of questions. We'd already covered the details of Sam's murder and were on to the haiku.

"Then who was the haiku for? Do you think he intended to kill Mom?"

"I don't think the haiku was written about her. I think he wanted a family, or at least the public illusion of one." I tried to shrug but my shoulder would have none of it. "Maybe it was for a fellow politician that bugged him, or maybe he was going to kill Leroy."

"Speaking of Leroy, I guess he didn't kill his sister. What did she die from?"

"Abdominal aortic aneurysm. Same thing that killed Leroy and

Betty's mother. I verified it with Sheriff Tucker to make sure I wasn't dealing with two crazies in the house. To tell you the truth, I was having a lot of trouble wrapping my head around who Grady might be."

"You were right all along," Jack said, laying his hand upon mine.

"I sure didn't want to believe it, but then I talked to Lenora Dabney, and Sheriff Tucker texted me back with the coroner's conclusion—all while you were next door making out with Annelise Abel."

Jack grimaced at the thought. "She would not let me go. Kept going on about all the good times in her cellar and how we had crushes on each other as teens but were too shy to acknowledge them."

"It's a scary place in Annelise's head. Which reminds me . . . Can you get something for me?"

"What's that?" he said.

"Can you gather every apology that's ever been uttered, written, sent, or imagined, and bundle it into a package? I need to hand-deliver it to Mr. Abel."

"If you throw in some gratitude, I'll deliver it with you."

"Maybe we can bring it to him at church on Sunday," I said. "Might do me some good."

Jack smiled. "We'll go together, but I do have a juicy tidbit for you."

"Do tell."

"When I was driving Jedediah and Mr. Abel home, Mr. Abel confessed something."

"I don't think I want to hear this."

"Oh, yes, you do. He told me how you were concerned about his connection to the Aberdeen Hotel and Mom and everything, and that he kind of blew up at you."

"I thought he was the third man for a while."

"Well, he confessed that he and the Aberdeen manager got buzzed on the house wine pretty often."

"But Mr. Abel doesn't drink."

"Apparently he drank quite a bit back in the day and even attended some AA meetings in Kingsley."

The strange pictures that Sam Kowalczyk had taken of Mr. Abel in that old Kingsley warehouse building suddenly made sense.

"He wanted me to tell you," my brother continued, "because he felt terrible. Apparently he drank some wine the day Mom got shot. That's why he didn't go home right away. Didn't want the missus to smell it on him."

"Speaking of wine, remember that story you told me years ago about Pyramid and Frisbee?"

Jack chuckled. "Pyramus and Thisbe. Those painkillers must be kicking in."

"Well, I don't think I want to return to Grandpa's house. It's forever changed, gone from an innocent childhood white to a stained, sinful red."

"I know what you mean."

"It'll never be warm again, filled with dreams and fantasies of a perfect mother. The magnolia tree's been toppled by Mickey Busker's deplorable actions. The living room has seen three dead bodies, and the walls will forever echo Leroy's sadness."

"All true, but remember something else about that story: Pyramus and Thisbe's tragedy started because of an unbreakable bond between two people, two people willing to do anything for each other, even die." He took my hand. "We have that strong a bond, Janie, and I'm sorry I ever strained it by putting distance between us. I promise you it will never happen again."

I squeezed his hand. "Can I take that promise to *the people*?"

He grinned.

"Jack, what are we going to do now? We're officially orphans. You've lost someone who was pretty important to you, and I've been through the emotional wringer on this one."

"We were never motherless or fatherless, anyway, Janie, no matter what anyone said. We were twins. We are twins. First and always."

"Grandpa's twins," I said, reaching out an arm to hug him. He grabbed me with both arms and his whole upper body and it felt right. It felt complete. I swallowed away a bevy of tears. When we finally let go of each other, Jack took a moment to gather himself. "Speaking of Grandpa, I don't think it's going to be a problem to sell the house right away. I've got some news."

I gasped. "Oh, God. No."

The door flung open, followed by the big, sturdy foot that had kicked it.

"Mr. Perkins!" shouted a nurse's fed-up but overjoyed voice. "I told you not to be wheeling yourself all over tarnation just yet!"

In rolled Grandpa Barton with full color on his cheeks and a grin wider than the Blue Ridge Mountains.

"Grandpa!" I shouted.

He pulled his wheelchair up to my bed. "Now, Janie, you know I love you, but my takin' a few days off in a restful coma does not give you permission to go shootin' up the house and stirrin' up all sorts of trouble, ya hear?"

"Yes, Grandpa."

"Next time you want to kill a sumbitch, you use that new .45 I bought you for your apartment. Better yet, call me and I'll take care of it."

"My bad, Grandpa. I'll do better next time."

Jack helped Grandpa up onto my bed, then excused himself to get some coffee.

"My little girl," Grandpa said. "I am so glad you're all right. They tell me you'll be up and at 'em in no time."

I took his hand in mine and felt at home. "Know the first thing I'm gonna do when I get out of here, Grandpa?"

"Bake me a cherry pie?"

"No." I smiled warmly. "I'm going to burn down that storage unit you've got. Right to the ground. Every square inch."

"And they said those painkillers might make you sweet and sappy for a few hours. Glad to see they were wrong."

"Hey," I said, "Jack says we might be selling the place."

"Too big for me anymore, and I'm ready for a change. There's a new retirement community I can't wait to sink my teeth into."

I pulled a dubious face. Pinochle and backgammon didn't sound like Grandpa's cup of tea. "Really?"

"Of course. Can you imagine the killing I'll make selling funeral insurance?"

We were still laughing when his nurse returned. "Let's get you back to your room, Mr. Perkins. I'm breaking the rules as it is."

Grandpa winked and I knew there'd be plenty of fat-chewing sessions over the next couple of weeks. "Tell me something before they wheel me away and treat me like an old man," he said. "Who is that dang handsome fella in the hall waitin' to see you?"

My eyes brightened. "Is it a seed-spitting slob with perfect skin, or a clean-cut guy with impeccable manners and breathtaking biceps?"

"That'd be the latter."

I smiled, making no effort to reel in my delight. "That, Grandpa, is my new boyfriend. At least I hope it is. His name is Alex. Alex Wexler."

Grandpa raised a skeptical yet friendly brow. "We'll see about that, young lady. We'll see about that."

And I knew Wexler was in for a grilling.

362

Five minutes later Wexler skulked into the room, his face a handsome shade of rosy pink. "Your grandfather's one tough old bird."

"I know. But he's a lovable old bird."

Wexler sat on the edge of my bed and leaned in close. When his lips touched mine, I felt life starting over, a new chapter being written, and I couldn't imagine a better opening line than a soft, honest kiss.

"Tell me something, Perkins," he said. "What kind of twisted world is it where I'm out saving Schwank's ass but almost lose you?"

"Nicholls texted me. Said you single-handedly got the perp."

"Of course I did. Now back to you, Perkins, where do I begin?"

"Well, Alex, you can start by calling me Janie again."

"I can do that . . . Janie."

I wrapped my good arm around his neck and pulled him under the blanket with me.

EPILOGUE

My brother's victory speech sounded sincere and heroic. He was once again the brother who'd teased me yet protected me, annoyed me yet loved me unconditionally. When he called me onstage to join him in front of the cameras, I stood proudly and embraced the endless flashes. For the first time, the Haiku Twins were being photographed and feted for something positive.

Jack put his arm around my shoulders and kept it there as he waved with his other hand. Reporters scrambled and shouted, quickly turning their attention from politics to juicier topics, like murder and revenge. But it was okay. We were eager to keep cleaning up the mess of the past thirty years, though we'd never be able to whitewash it. It was our history, and ours alone, even if it was colored a permanent red.

After the fifth question, my phone buzzed—a fresh crime scene, only two blocks away. I made my excuses and let the new attorney general shine where he rightly belonged.

When I arrived at the scene, Nicholls turned, spit a sunflower seed on the porch, and feigned a pout. "I'm gonna miss you, Jane Doe. I really am."

"Maybe I'll have you over sometimes and we can play quarters, Nicholls."

"Can I bring Sophie?"

I smacked him. "No way! You're an item?"

"She thinks I'm funny, flawed, and devilishly handsome. Told me she might even put an etching of me on her fireplace, whatever the hell that means."

"I'm happy for you, Nicholls, but be careful—and don't turn your back on her."

He smiled, up for any challenge his new lady friend might offer, then he gestured to the dilapidated bungalow behind us. "You sure you wanna leave all this behind? 'Cause you won't believe what I got inside for you."

"It's time," I said. "Besides, I'm loaded. Jack and I got all of Grady's money."

"Gross."

"Yeah, but I plan to do good with it. Already put a down payment on a shuttered building in town. Going to open an art studio with classes for the city kids. Maybe give them a positive way to express themselves."

"Paintbrushes instead of pistols?"

"Worth a shot."

"Come on," he said, "you've gotta see this corpse."

In the rear bedroom lay a male body, well over six feet tall, with broad shoulders and wavy brown hair down to his chin. He was sprawled faceup on a queen-size bed, dressed in four-inch heels, a poufy white gown, and silk gloves. He looked, in all honesty, like a gorgeous princess in need of electrolysis.

"Big-time coke dealer," Nicholls said. "I heard he was a tranny, but I never believed it."

Nicholls headed out when he heard more cars arriving, leaving me alone with the victim and my camera. Next to the bed, on a tall nightstand, sat a green frog figurine with bulging eyes and bright red lips, the perfect prince for the princess on the bed. In a flash, I could turn this guy's humiliating final chapter into a fairy tale worthy of my finest work.

But some people's stories ended in tragedy, and nothing conjured or imagined could change them, not even an altered image hidden away beneath a floor.

I let things lie and did my job.

ACKNOWLEDGMENTS

Thank you first and foremost to the readers for allowing me to visit with their imaginations. It is an honor and privilege I do not take lightly.

Thank you to my friend and fellow writer, Jack Matosian, for the inspiration and laughs.

Thank you to Kjersti Egerdahl and the entire team at Thomas & Mercer for their expertise, enthusiasm, and guidance. I'll always treasure the first email Kjersti sent me. Definitely frame-worthy.

Thank you to Tiffany Yates Martin, a talented and astute editor, whose every contribution made this book a stronger work.

I'd like to thank those people who helped me with police procedures, weaponry, forensics, crime scene photography, and aspects of law and religion. Please note that I take plenty of liberties, and my sources can only answer the questions I think to ask; any and all errors are mine.

Thank you to Sergeant Jack Kilcomons of the Chesterfield Police Department in Virginia, for his thorough, professional, and timely answers, and to his wife, Kim Kilcomons, for introducing us.

Thank you to Chesterfield County (Virginia) Senior Forensic Investigator Cory Chatham. His keen insights throughout the story—especially the ending—significantly improved this book.

Thank you to Kathy Simpson for her boundless enthusiasm and for keeping me straight on terminology and titles.

Thank you to MJM and Ellen Canepa for their perceptive editing, fervent feedback, and innovative ideas.

Thank you to the Bird for allowing me to tap her legal mind, which is sure to produce an outstanding legal thriller in the near future.

Thank you to my book-crazy parents, Dan and Pat, for their excellent advice; to Mimi and Danny for their unending support and for creating my early West Coast fan base; and to Spanish Award Winner Jack for his always-succinct and intelligent answers to my strange and random questions.

Last, but never least, thank you to my patient husband and children for their love and encouragement, and for fending mightily for themselves when I'm in the midst of an editing frenzy.

ABOUT THE AUTHOR

 Anne McAneny honed her writing skills as a screenwriter for many years before turning to novels. She lives in Virginia with her family, a spoiled puggle, and an overfed cat who showed up eight years ago. When Anne's not writing, she enjoys exercise balanced by ample chocolate and cake, a scale that often tips toward the latter. You can find her on Facebook by searching for "Books by Anne McAneny." She relishes hearing from readers, so feel free to say hello or leave a comment. Be warned . . . she usually responds.

Other books by this author:

Raveled (Amazon bestseller, over 150 five-star reviews): A fast-paced mystery thriller that sends a jaded daughter back to the town and the deadly night that ripped her young life apart.

Foreteller: A pulse-pounding mystery with a touch of the psychic that forces an archaeologist to dig through her own past in order to ensure a future.

Chunneling Through Forty (Amazon bestseller): The humorous and heartening story of a woman's tumultuous journey through forty.

Our Eyes Met Over Cantaloupe: The uproarious tale of a cupcake shop and a female reporter's exit from her half-baked state of existence.